THE BEGINNING OF WISDOM

THE BEGINNING OF WISDOM

BY
STEPHEN VINCENT BENÉT

NEW YORK
HENRY HOLT AND COMPANY
1921

PRINTED IN THE U. S. A. BY

The Quinn & Boden Company

BOOK MANUFACTURERS
RAHWAY   NEW JERSEY

TO

SHREVE COWLES BADGER
JOHN FRANKLIN CARTER, Jr.
EFFINGHAM COCK EVARTS

Fellow Epicureans and very kind companions

NOTE

THANKS are due to Danford Barney of "Parabalou," Norman Fitts of the "S4N" and Christopher Morley of "The Bowling Green" for permission to reprint poems previously published by them.

"The fear of the Lord is the beginning of Wisdom. . . ."—*The Bible*.

"Lord—'to put the fear of the ——— into,' to astonish, to cow, to terrify."—*Harkett's Slang Dictionary*.

". . . . . And coolly from the waste
Now slender beauty rises, strong and harsh,
And with it comes a salt, ironic taste,
A tang of evening floating on the marsh.

That beauty is not delicate nor weak
It can withstand all mockery and doubt,
It is the very words the mockers speak,
And only hardy fools can find it out."
                              —*Phelps Putnam*.

CONTENTS

BOOK I

PROLOGUE TO PHILIP

BOOK II

PARABALOU!

BOOK III

"FRANKIE AND JOHNNY
WERE LOVERS"

CONTENTS

BOOK I
PROLOGUE TO PHILIP

CONVERSATION—1892

THE only sound in the big front room is the faint growling of the bright coal fire as it chars to the ruddiness of a winter apple behind the three black bars of its grate. Outside the wind slashes at the windows, flinging handfuls of spatting rain to run down the panes like long tears. Clove-black and brittle-brown as tatters from old sails, the dead leaves of the eucalyptus hurry past in the wet of the gust, to be heaped into overflowing gutters along with shriveled gray pepperberries and torn flowers and much red sand. It is pleasant to look once through the window at that scurry of storm and broken cloud and then turn back to the quiet crickling of the coals. A month more now, and in the East it will be old cold Christmas, with the ground frosted over like a cake—but this is California and the rainy season, and the earth will sluice and steam for three months longer in a continual pouring of clear rain.

There is another sound in the room now—a sound no one could have noticed before, it is so small and monotonous—the sound of even breathing. It comes from the great oak bed by the wall and the chair rocked close to the grate. Hearing it makes the room seem stiller and warmer. The fire shifts suddenly, throwing a gay flare on the face of the drowser before it, and the procession of dull-blue peacocks that parade the

3

ivory chintz of the deep chairs and tall curtains. From the bed comes an indistinguishable sleepy sound that, finding itself nonsense, stops, and a little later begins again, this time enough waked-up to be in words.

"Nurse!" it says. "Oh, Nurse!"

The rumple of starched linen in the rocker moves infinitesimally and relapses without answering.

"Nurse!" repeats the voice from the bed, this time with a tickle of laughter in it. "Miss Hollis! Sorry to wake you!"

And now the linen hears and crackles. The figure in the chair rises, a tall strapping girl with a tumble of blond hair coming out from under her nurse's cap. She looks as vigorous and healthy as a young tree, but the pulled-down droop of the corners of her mouth shows that she recently has been very thoroughly tired. She stands now with her arms over her head, yawning magnificently, and then, suddenly realizing what she is doing, straightens and starts to look very professional. But the next minute her hands are at her eyes again, trying desperately to rub away the sleep.

The voice from the bed is contrite.

"I'm awfully sorry. I know I shouldn't have waked you. I've been counting peacocks and peacocks getting the cruelty to. Because if you were as sleepy as I was—"

"You should have waked me long ago, Mrs. Sellaby." The full dignity of an expert has been recovered. "I had no business to sleep like that. I don't know how I—" A yawn splits this in the middle, but she goes on determinedly, "I don't know what I—" Again the annihilating yawn. This time she gives up. "Oh, dear," she says frankly, "I *was* so tired."

"I was a pig. A perfect pig."

This from the bed, then, inconsequentially, "By the way, that clock's still stuck at nine-thirty—"

Miss Hollis consults a small bangle of a watch. "Good heavens, it's half-past four! and Mr. Sellaby will be coming in, and the doctor—"

She busies herself with bottles and trays and pillows, hiding what yawns will come behind four fingers. The girl in the bed lies flat back, looking at the ceiling. Her hair, which is the color of pine-smoke, is in thick, soft waves about her face.

It is a face with that delicate tense strength you may see in the hands of a great surgeon—the soul beneath it has been tempered steely, is as exquisitely balanced and direct as the long springing blade of an old rapier. And at present, in spite of the weight and heaviness of exhaustion upon it, so deep as to be almost visible and clinging like a netted veil, it is overwhelmed with peace, absorbed in peace. She has that look of calm strangeness with her that will make even her husband, when he sees her this time, forget her as anything but a visitor from brightness. Her face and her throat might have been bathed in starry water. She turns her head to the pillow again and her eyes grow merry.

"Philip?"

But Miss Hollis is slow.

"Mr. Sellaby? The carriage hasn't come back yet." The girl in bed smiles swiftly.

" No. Not Phil. Philip."

This time she is comprehended with an answering smile of vast though somewhat technical understanding.

" Miss Woods has him, I think. Shall I bring him in ? "

" Please."

Miss Hollis vanishes with a laundered rustle, treading hard on her sensible shoes. An antiseptic smell—the essence of the endless tiled corridors of a thousand expectant hospitals, permanently anesthetized into rubbery quiet—drifts thinly into the air. Lucia Sellaby's hand, absurdly weak and uncoördinated like the hand of a puppet with the wires gone wrong, fumbles slowly with a stopper and closes the exclamatory bottle. Then she smiles again, this time with the fervent pleasure of a child that has just successfully carried through a mild naughtiness undiscovered. Miss Hollis reappears, carrying some crude sort of a bundle with great care. The whipping sound of rain on glass is broken in upon by flacking hoofs and the ripple of tired wheels that tattle and slur into a stop.

" Here he is," says the nurse judiciously. She is much too well instructed to crow meaningless languages at the baby or dig pointed fingers into his fat. That will be left to uncles and aunts.

Philip is put beside his mother. He is the color of the shell of a boiled crab—a creature of compound wrinkles and ugliness with the face of a cathedral gargoyle. This ugliness will be geographically examined by all visiting relatives for perfect resemblances to other members of the family. Cousin George Vane will remark with a happy appreciation of his own wit that the kid's nose is just as lopsided as his dad's and Aunt Ethel Sellaby will eat liver-tablets as she looks at him and say, as she crunches with a noise like breaking teeth, that it is perfectly evident to any one the Vane temper has come out in him already. But so far he has been a good deal too young to be seen and a good deal too busy with existing to be quite sure that he is existing at all.

He makes crablike movements of discontent, though, even in the crook of his mother's arm. She looks at him, humming wordlessly. His eyes are shut—squeezed in like a puppy's—but one formless paw crawls, feeler-wise, to the swelling curve of her breast. Miss Hollis busies herself complacently with her slops and linen and scissors—she has all the composed self-consciousness of a popular actor acknowledging applause after an un-usually successful first night. Under the calm sky of her satisfaction Philip and Lucia hold close, belong to each other, are contented. Footsteps and a soft rapping at the door break in upon the dream.

Miss Hollis answers the rapping discreetly, parleys a little, then admits Phil Sellaby—Philip Sellaby, Sr., now, of course. Handsome as a show red setter, young as a colt, he has more or less the limitations of mind of both animals while lacking their uncanny earthy quali-ties of scent and instant intuition. The crooked nose is there and serves only to add tricky good-humor to looks otherwise too regular to be interesting—and the eyes are gleaming and empty as blue glass. At present the man is nervousness, exalted relief, profound grati-tude and ferocious pride by turns. He treats his son alternately as if he were porcelain and rubber, and his wife as though she were a combination of descended angel and new and very startling machine whose actions and curious potentialities he had never before suspected. She loves him but is beginning to comprehend him—he worships her and never will, any more than he will why the pastel shades become her or why a sonnet should have only fourteen lines. A very nice fellow on the whole—though a little too much the sort of a man at his best in the lounge of a men's club. His youth suits him extremely—he wears it like a flower in his buttonhole—if he could stay in the twenties forever, he would be completely successful, for age will harden and veneer without greatly ripening him. But he has been standing at the door long enough.

He starts to run to his wife, decides that isn't dignified, and walks. Miss Hollis departs elaborately and is heard playing with faucets in the bathroom. As soon as her skirt has vanished behind the door, he runs over and kneels beside the bed.

"Darling, darling, darling!" he says in a cracking voice. Lucia turns her head and shoulder so that their lips can meet. The kiss is long and speechless and without any pulse or banner of passion. The man has put off for once the gilded metal of his attitudes. He is suddenly able to remain silent—he kneels unconsciously, in the posture of a devotional figure beside a tomb. And her hand is gentle with him in a calm gesture—she will need that gesture later, too, for the other Philip, when he has got acclimated. Miss Hollis coughs before reëntering, and the embrace breaks up on the instant like a half-played theme in a concerto when the musician takes his hands from the keys. Phil Sellaby gets up, half-tripping, and finds that his trousers are dusty. And Philip mews, wishing food.

The kiss has been good for Lucia, who needs actual present love as much to live as a pine needs soil and water and cannot exist by fractions. And the fact that this son of his can actually utter passable sounds sways the father back into gay arrogance again. He rips open a lengthy striped box that he has brought with him and tossed anyhow on the floor. It is full of pale and scarlet roses, long-stemmed and silvery with rain. Philip mews again, this time more decidedly, and Lucia, after cocking a doubtful eye at Miss Hollis' back, winks at him rapidly and furtively to show that he is completely understood, and begins to tug at the little bows on her nightgown. But Phil has got out the roses—he holds them high up—petals of stained silk and ivory rock and flutter and drift to Lucia's pillow—she shivers with the serene mirth of a bell. Philip opens his button-eyes—he sees the ripple of color, the few small sparkling drops that shower like globes of mercury from the shaken flowers, and, seeing, laughs, laughs for the first whole time in his life with a loud wide toothless chuckle and a striking of fists and feet at the great wonder.

Clink—tink—clitter of silver, tankle of forks on
* peach-bloom plates,*
Delicate ivory crunchings titter through foam-
* white biscuits and oozing dates;*
Trill, spill, ripples of laughter, even the dangling
* bags play tunes.*
Mandarin-buttoned and dragon-slippered, the tea-
* steam walks by the macaroons!*

PHILIP has been put into a white suit and a bad
temper and sent marauding through the rustle of guests
as a sort of wandering ornament. He goes through his
motions sullenly and without style, feeling as if he had
been starched all over. For him the whole high-voiced
confusion splits itself up into hats and hands. Hats
like fruit-salad and hats like painted bird-cages, long
chilly hats that rest the eyes like shade after hard reading, little round swearing parrots of hats, as reekingly
alive as tropic sunlight. Hats of every shade from pis-
tachio to flamingo—mauve, apricot, sherry, bisque—they
spot and color the green cool of the garden like a sudden
new creation of great, gay artificial plants. And below
the hats are the hands—hands of all shapes and tints and
firmnesses—from the limp, perspiring palm of fifteen-
year-old Marjorie Kellaber that crumples like a wet
rubber glove as you take hold of it to the dry sweet tiny
fingers of old Mrs. Janet Whistley who offers you three

of them like an investiture of the Garter in an atmosphere of lace and mignonette. Hats and hands, nothing
but hats and hands, and not a chance for Philip to do
anything but hand around baskets of pink-iced cakes and
have people pat him with squat hands and lumpy hands
and tell him what a polite little gentleman. What a
polite little gentleman—what a *polite* little gentleman
—and Philip, with a company grin outside, inside runs
through Mac the stable-man's best barnyard vocabulary
with the ease, care and devotion that a Buddhist monk
expends on his prayer-wheel. Then he looks to catch
a wink from his mother, but she is fenced behind hats
and hands and a vaporous silver urn, she is pouring tea
for countless hats and hands; and Philip puts down his
basket where a fat hat will be sure to come and step into
it, and sneaks off through the side-garden to the peace
and food of the kitchen.

> *Swerve, wheel, succulent incense, wave like the
>   tails of Persian cats,*
> *(Low light strokes flower-soft dresses, sweet-pea
>   veilings and fur-sleek spats),*
> *Bright, bitter intrusions of lemon, prosperous
>   gurgles of clotting milk,*
> *Even the wind is combed and curdled in cloudy
>   powder and crinkling silk!*

The Striped Aunt is talking to the Lozenged Aunt
while they trot up and down the brick walk of the rose-
garden. Their promenade is proud but with something
lacking in it, like the evening review of two large and
prominent peacocks who have mislaid essential fractions
of their tails.

"And just how old is that splendid boy of Lucia's?" says Stripes.

"Little Philip?" Lozenges' voice has that quality of medical oversweet to be found in popular cough-tablets. "Nine in November."

"And, my dear, you didn't think he looked delicate?"

"No." Then Lozenges reconsiders. "Not precisely. But he has that excitable Vane look. It always makes one fear for the mind."

"Why, there's been no actual *insanity*, surely—"

"So far? No." Oh, sepulchral Lozenges! "But with precocious children, when they have that queer look, you never ought to be too sure. No child has any business to draw or read or write so much at that sweet little fellow's age. If *I* were Lucia—"

"Give him a good sound spanking every time he touches a book!" Spinster Stripes rubs out all literature with one obliterating thumb. "It isn't normal. It isn't right."

"It isn't the way a sensible mother would act. It isn't what Grandfather Sellaby ever believed in."

They trot faster, chanting their litany at each other.

"It isn't proper or wise."

"He ought to be packed off to boarding-school."

"It isn't fair to the boy."

"Too much affection is *so* dangerous."

"His father should take a firm hand."

"He isn't like other boys his age."

The antiphony drops, commences again, sweetly choral.

"If Phil Sellaby wasn't so flighty."

" If Lucia didn't have such curious ideas."

" If they gave him a box of tools."

" If he played more with other little boys."

" If his eyes hadn't turned brown, when they were blue at first."

" If he took more after his Uncle Ashbel."

But even the tongues of Lozenges and Stripes wag weary after much good breath is wasted. They are warm—they sit down on a garden-bench, and huddle their musty, feathery gowns about them. Stripes waves a soporific fan, driving little sharp dusty gusts at the face of Lozenges. She cools and they discuss the sinful habits of some servants and most dogs and all small children.

> Plop, pop, bubbles of chatter silverly burst into
>   brightening spray,
> Blood runs from the reputations—every one knows
>   what They will say—
> Toast blooms like a field of buttercups, spoons
>   batter empastried shams,
> Cloyed, sirupy, over the china troops the parade of
>   the dark, proud jams.

For a few breathless seconds Lucia Sellaby has escaped away from her party. She has made the escaping an adventure, as she is able to do with most things, and now sits hidden in the little wistaria-arbor with her brother, wrapped in all the hush and attitudes of conspiracy she can summon up and yet help laughing, which is hard. Shreve Vane resembles her greatly—his face, for instance, is a first-class copy from her original, first class, but hastily done. Their minds have the likenesses and differences of the right and left profiles of a single countenance. His is sturdier and must digest most thoroughly before it can assimilate—hers subtler, twice as unexpected, with an intuitive gift for sudden flashing comprehension of a whole from one seen particle. There are no unexplored regions for him—he has atlased himself out with the thorough patience of a scientific geographer, down to railways and deltas and exports and towns of less than five thousand inhabitants—while she thinks of her mind, if at all, in the terms of a medieval map, full of castles and sirens and unicorns with the four winds bursting their puffy cheeks at appropriate corners of the compass. She won't let him probe the honeycomb of an empty hornet's nest to tease her— there is too little time for that.

"Phil thinks Philip ought to go to boarding-school," she begins without any preliminaries.

"Now?" Shreve whistles more piercingly than he meant to. "Good Lord, the boy isn't even nine!"

"Phil went when he was ten." A quirk of mirth comes over her mouth. "He was quarterback on the team when he was twelve."

"You never went at all though." Shreve is accusing. "You howled like sin when Mother talked about sending you. And after all, Luke, it's you the boy's like— not Phil at all, except for his pretty looks."

The nickname goes back to a fervently religious ten-year-old who insisted on her direct connection with and spiritual descent from the Third Gospel. Lucia hesitates in front of the matter of pretty looks, like a kitten before a new ball of string. But that isn't really the

question after all, and she withdraws from it with a
minor sigh of relinquishment.

"I don't want him to go any time—ever!" she says
flatly.

"He's got to be sent sometime, Luke. It's only
common sense. I know how you hate the idea of it."
With unusual fervor, "He'll hate it too, the first year,
anyway. Lord, I remember how I did!"

"That's just it, and I don't want him to hate it. It
isn't—I wouldn't—I'm really not like most of these
nice women, Shreve. I don't want him done up in cot-
ton wool and pinned to a card like a specimen boy—I
don't even worry about whether he's got rubbers and a
raincoat on—sometimes. I'm proud of him, of course,
extensively so. I'm fearful for him, too, horribly so—
till I've stayed awake nights wondering if there were
another earthquake and he were out there on the sleep-
ing-porch—" She breaks off with a little gesture of
cold. Shreve covers her hand with his.

"Back in the eighties was the last shake for a hundred years," he says with the wilful faith of all good
Californians.

"I keep telling myself that, all the time. But it
isn't *him* that I worry over, generally. It's the rest
of him, his mind, what he thinks about. He'll be lonely
a good deal and without much help—that's because he's
my son, Shreve. He'll take things he can't do to heart,
because he's Phil's. Lonely and off from most people
and getting a hard sort of joy out of loneliness. And
when he has to adjust himself to people and living, it
will have to be done with preparations. It'll hurt him

as much as his being born did. If the preparations are wrong—if they aren't at least approximately kindly—he'll just be driven in on himself again and eat at himself for years. You see?" She spreads her hands palm-up, to be helped.

Shreve sees. Indeed in spite of the respectable age and the correct clothes and the sober bank account he has industriously acquired, he still sometimes, in painful moments, has that nightmare feeling that these possessions may on the instant vanish away and he be left a small and confused child in a world of uninterested strangers that is the hereditary prerogative of the shy. But the feeling is too deep to be made into talk, just now. All he says is:

"Don't worry about it, Luke. I'll bicker with Phil."

She is grateful; it is exactly what she has conspired for.

"I wish you would. He thinks a good deal of your advice."

"I'm afraid it will be no go later. Phil will want to send him some time, of course, which ought to be all right, Luke, after all—when he's thirteen or fourteen—"

She nods dubiously.

"Perhaps. That's another thing. It has to be a school out here. If we were East; if we could send him East, very well—that's something else that Phil is against, and I must say, I am too. I'd rather keep him."

"Till he's twenty?" This is chaff, not meant to sting as it does.

"*No*. I'm *not* sheltering him, Shreve. But I do know about it. I know how alike we are. You'd feel it—you do feel it—if you won't admit it—and—"

Shreve has no course open but retraction and he takes it whole-heartedly, more especially as certain glimpses of poignant memory have deserted and gone over to Lucia's flag.

"Yes, Luke, I do feel it, honestly. As for 'sheltering' him—people always talk rot. Phil's right, too, that's the dickens of it—the way he sees it. He'd be right nearly always—entirely so—but he isn't quite right now, about Philip. I'll talk to him."

This satisfies her and she remembers her party. They slide out of the arbor, crouching like plotters in a film and both now enjoying themselves tremendously. As they leave Shreve decides to try a simile.

"When we're young, Philip and you and I and the rest of us, we're people who need some kind of mental armor," he starts timidly. "If we haven't it—we climb up into our minds and stay there. Now Phil—"

She—he—mumble of dowagers—chatter from lit-
tle old men in stays,
Thick, soft, glutinous spooning of guava jelly and
gorged patés,
Slip, slop, mayonnaise sandwiches burble delight to
a careless thumb,
White spite winks a decanter, chuckling a tot of
obsequious rum!

Philip, smudging his nose against the pantry-window, sees a crammed belated carriage creak away down the drive. The garden-party has withered into a few, middle-aged, exhaustless talkers and two stranded wives nervously looking around bushes for their husbands. Philip settles back to his cache of salvaged edibles; three sardine sandwiches, the wreck of a guava-jelly messed into the remains of some chicken-in-aspic, and the sticky internals of the ice-cream freezer. He attacks with technique, voracity and dispatch; inserts a crushed macaroon in one of the sandwiches, and tries the combination dubiously. Strange blends of abnormal foods appeal to him, and the maids, Lizzie and the borrowed ones, are too busy stacking dishes and comparing scandals about prominent guests to pay much notice. Philip looks and is more like his father just now than he ever will be again—the resemblance is of the kind that drives aging ladies to gentle sentimental tears. Any thoughts he has are chiefly about food and Mrs. Whistley's lent black butler, who is quite the finest and most overpoweringly-mannered gentleman that has yet come into his ken. Philip has been trying to draw him all day on the sly, and has only succeeded once, a wild, amusing caricature of him at the door of Noah's Ark, ushering in with effusive cordiality a procession of silk-hatted rhinoceroses. Philip thinks of the latter beasts and grins profoundly, before spreading guava paste on a loose sardine.

Lucia may have worried about him unnecessarily. He seems in most respects as normal and inquisitive as a terrier. Every emotion he has goes instantly all through and over him as a current of electricity pours through a wire—and he is still at an age when the space between shutting eyes at night and opening them again in the morning flicks past like the second-hand of a watch about its dial, and most dreams, good or bad, come from indigestion. He doesn't know what it is to be bored, has a quantity of humorous vanity, considerable physical recklessness and is beginning to develop from much scattered and unchecked reading an ashamed fierce curiosity in regard to matters of sex. His flair for mockery, with pencil or words, is his chief unusual quality and he knows quite well, to his own last adjective, exactly how unusual it is.

Lizzie, their own maid, skims by with a couple of empty cake-baskets, eyeing him askance.

" It's a pig you are, Master Philip," she calls in her soft slippery Irish. " What with Lee wishful to save them little fishes for your mother's lunch, this Saturday ! "

" Aw, Lizzie, he won't give a darn ! " and " Have one ? " Philip adds with mischievous good-temper.

" Have one, is it? It's none of you and your fishes I'll have, with me work to be done and supper to get and the hair that will fly when your Aunt Agatha sees the place the wall-eyed horse of Colonel Marley's ate off the cockle-vine ! Now by the Holy Fly !—"

The invocation interests Philip.

" What's the Holy Fly ? "

" It's the fly that lit on the face of Our Lord and him hangin' on the Cross and the one he blessed and took into Heaven with him along of the two thieves. Now go along with your questions ! "

" But why did Our Lord take it to Heaven ? "

" Because it was the holy wish of Him." Lizzie

crosses herself, with some difficulty, owing to the cake-baskets.

"But why did he want it in *Heaven?*"

"Because he did, and that's all, and bad luck to you and who are you to know what he wished or did not wish? Putting jelly on good sound fish as if it was bread they were, and not letting a decent girl go on with her work!"

Philip wonders idly what the difference would be in not letting an indecent girl go on with her work. Indecent. That was the word he looked up in the dictionary, yesterday, only to find it: "Indecent a., obscene, lascivious." Obscene is a good word to try out, then, though he is quite in the dark as to its meaning.

"Lizzie," he says with decision, "why do you call yourself a decent girl? You're obscene."

The cake baskets are put down with a bang.

"Out of the pantry it is you go this minute, you black-hearted, small plague of a bad child! Calling a good girl out of her name with dirty words from your father's books that you should not have read!" She advances upon him with a dish-towel. He holds his ground.

"You're obscene!" he patters off hurriedly. "You're obscene—you're obscene—a-ah, Lizzie, you're obscene!"

The dish-towel flaps into his face. "Out ye go!" whacks Lizzie. "Out ye go—you and your fishes and your abseens—"

But the tempest settles back instantly into its teapot as Phil Sellaby, who has come running over the lawn unobserved, raps suddenly on the window-pane with his knuckles.

" Play tennis, Philip? " he calls, in a voice that sounds funnily small through the glass, and Philip, forgetting everything else, rushes out and upstairs to get his racket and play vehement handicap-singles that his father always wins—through a slow, long sleepy twilight of dulling gold.

SUCCESSION OF DAYS—1905

THE skinny minute-hand of the white-faced clock over Major Stelly's desk in the big assembly-room hitches slowly from numeral to numeral. Philip looks up at it again from the glare of naked electric-light that floods over his cramped little desk. Fifteen minutes till Recall from study-period and he is so sleepy already that his eyes feel as if they had been washed with sand. He turns to the back of the geography for relaxation— what other lessons he has had to prepare are done. Tangier—imports, machinery—exports, silks, gold-dust and cinnabar. Cinnabar. Golly, what a name! He whispers it roundly, tasting it over his tongue. Morocco —imports, machinery—exports, leather and sackcloth. Sackcloth and ashes are in the Bible, but I suppose it doesn't matter what kind of ashes. Siam—imports, machinery—exports—must be white elephants—white elephants—big—whi-te—e-le-phants—

Philip pulls up his head just as it is about to drop to the desk-lid and tries to shake the heavy drowse out of it by one quick toss as a swimmer shakes off water. It's no good. He is smothering under sleep, and he mustn't, he mustn't go to sleep. Major Stelly caught Fat Clark sleeping ten minutes ago and gave him an hour and a half on the beat. An hour and a half sentry-go with a Civil War musket six feet high.

Now he's sitting up there at his desk—a little gray

wrath of a retired army-officer—with the sour eyes of a
biting horse. Ten years of teaching at Kitchell Military
Academy have left him with the restraint of a hanging
judge and the ingenuity in small cruelties of a Jesuit
Inquisitor. The great, hushed legend of the school is
of "the time when Woozy Fisher knocked him out."
Philip catches his glance for a moment and looks
away quickly. The clock-hand jumps. Four minutes
gone.

Madagascar—imports, machinery. Don't they ever
buy anything but machinery? A picture of thousands
of brown, sleek natives cavorting with howls of joy
about the vast bulk of a McCormick reaper, forms fan-
tastically in Philip's mind. Too hot there to want
other things, probably. Too hot even to handle the
machinery. As hot as this room.

The air is breathless and weighty over Philip—the air
is smoky with heat and the smell of pine and spilt ink
and boys. Philip takes a long sucking breath and his
will surrenders suddenly, without any warning. He
looks stupidly at the flagellating, harsh light on Fat
Clark's open history on the next desk. He feels as if
he were being pleasantly suffocated under great pillows
and bolsters of sleepy warmth. And then he doesn't
feel or think at all.

Vague discomfort—swift pain—he can't breathe—
he can't breathe at all—he is choking. He opens his
mouth and eyes with a gasp—a sharp finger and thumb
are gripping down on his nose. Major Stelly swims
cloudily into vision as he forces up his thick, drugged
eyelids. Major Stelly's hand is pinching his nose. The

whole room chirrups and swirls with muffled laughter.
Major Stelly's voice coughs dryly above him.

"Three hours on the beat to-morrow, Sellaby. Report from me to the Sergeant of the Guard."

He lets go of Philip's nose and turns to look for the
laughter. It stops as if it were blown out like the
flame of a candle. Then the little tin-godly man is
satisfied and his footsteps crackle back to his desk again,
leaving Philip to tender examination of his nose.

Out of the cool night that drifts and whispers like
snow against the stuffy squares of hot windows, expected
and clear and sudden, comes the brief falling call of
a bugle. For an instant it fills the sterile air, drooping
wistfully, a blown flower of silver spray.

"'Tenshun!" coughs Major Stelly.   "Sergeants,
take command of your squads!"

"Pinky" Kitchell—Dr. Ward Erastus Kitchell,
B.A., M.A., Harvard, B.Litt. Oxon.—has visitors at
the Masters' Table in Dining Hall. The cooks out in
the greasy kitchen know about it, and send nice food,
thoughtfully cooked, to him and the gobbling loud parents from Oakland who are "taking a look around the
school."

"Oh, yes, indeed, I always make it a practice of
dropping in for pot-luck with the boys every few days
or so!" says Pinky, the faint reddish fur of his whiskers
showing up like the brush of a squirrel as he slices himself a delicate wafer of ham. "It keeps our Chinamen
up to the mark, I find."

There is a sudden chatter of laughter from one of the

boys' long mess-tables. It comes from the pair sitting
on either side of Philip, who has just discovered a third
of a pearly worm inside a half-eaten leaf of boiled
cabbage.

"They look like smart little chaps in their uniforms,"
remarks the male visiting parent with the air of an
expert newspaper strategist.

"Such a comfort to think of the good home influence
Dr. and Mrs. Kitchell must give them," tucks in his
female, her voice like tallow.

"Good wholesome discipline."

"A Christian Church in the village."

Pinky inserts a word.

"Our little shop for manual training—sloyd, they call
it—the boys were in class when we passed there, Mrs.
Vorgas. It is an interesting experiment, nothing like
it to teach practicality, as I often say to my wife.
They make—oh, boxes—and ironing-boards—chairs—
sideboards, no, no, possibly *not* sideboards," but his tone
if not his sentence includes gigantic specimens of every
type of period furniture. "That comes, of course, as
an extra, but—"

"And our William is so clever with tools already.
We should want him taught, of course—if we could ar-
range—" The word "terms" hangs disembodied, as
it were, in the air, a mere specter of a noun, a phantom.

"Now, Amanda." This voice is as male as a cheap
cigar. "You must remember our little agreement. We
were to make no decisions until we had seen Mercator
and St. Vitus'."

"Quite right, dear. Still," and this with a candied

smile, " Dr. Kitchell has convinced me so far that this is the place for William. Thoroughly. If the terms— that is the terms—eh—"

" Suppose we leave *them* till later." Pinky's haste is a bit anxious as well. " They are business, my dear lady, horrid *business*. Now I always say that taking visitors about our little academy is one of the chief pleasures—"

The brassy clamor of a bugle cuts him short. The boys rise—the whole wide Dining Hall is broken into stiff ranks of slate-and-black soldiers. They are marched out—expressionless, for they march well. Philip tramps past Pinky's table, rigid and healthy.

Inside his mind: " You beast, you pink beast! Sitting and wetting your lips with your tongue and smiling and lying and getting fathers and mothers who want to be nice and decent to send their kids to your dirty, rotten, beastly school! "

The long Alameda pitcher winds up like a tortured spring. Philip watches him with frantic supplications, his hands hot, his eyes burning. A man out—man on second—Kitchell's half of the tenth. His gaze flicks for a moment to the scoreboard—Visitors 1, Kitchell 1. Thud! The ball shoots deep into the catcher's glove. Two strikes on Billy Harbison already.

The pitcher rubs the ball on his trouser-leg, then turns and insolently motions the outfielders nearer. The slow, gold flow of settling evening is beginning to haze the tawny patch of ground between the bases. As the Alameda centerfielder moves in scoutily over the clipped green sheen of the outfield, he walks with a dragging

shadow. Billy Harbison strikes out with a back-break-
ing swing that nearly takes him off his feet. The
stands sigh back into dulled composure. Dicky Tresola
up!

Philip gapes at the batter, full of worship. He is
seventeen—pure Spaniard—the face and hands by
Murillo. He steps to the plate swinging two glossy
bats, agile as a pouncing cat, calm as stone. The Alameda pitcher spits in his glove—looks doubtfully back
at his fielders and decides to let them stay where they
are. Ball one!

Dicky hasn't taken the bat from his shoulder. A
pucker comes into the pitcher's forehead, he eyes his
enemy a long moment, winds up craftily—Ball two!
The next is a strike, and the next. Tresola doesn't move
his bat at either. A sudden irruption of fierce single
yells bursts from the stands and is silenced as quickly
as it spoke. The pitcher is smiling, saved—and careless. Ball three!

The catcher snaps it down to second, trying to catch
Bunny Ilsley off. There is a scramble of arms and legs
in the sallow dirt. Bunny is safe by yards and sits
on the bag to prove it. The ball floats slowly back to
the pitcher's box.

"He's up in the air!" howls Philip. "His arm's
full of glass! Yow! Dicky, hit it a mile!"

The pitcher delivers the ball with the solemn fatalistic motions of a man playing lugubriously good poker
against a loaded deck. There is a chiming crack from
Dicky's bat—a wild hopeless dive backwards by the centerfielder—and in a tumult of screaming cheers and

running and dust, the two runs scuttle across the plate while Philip pounds the breath and sense and hearing out of the round boy next to him.

Philip, galloping through the little roofed passage between Ashmead Hall and Pinky's house, bumps square into Butch Draper and Star Hawes. Butch catches him by the wrists.

"And what the hell do you mean by running into us, young Sellaby?" he queries satinly. He has a big loose body and a face the color of a side of beef, but his voice is astonishingly puerile.

"I didn't mean it. I never meant to run into you, Butch. Ah, Butch, let me go."

"Let me go. Shall we let him go, Star?"

Star, a little mean rat of a boy with a skin like dirty tobacco, spits through his teeth on Philip's shoes.

"Let's keep him, Butch. He was fresh to me yesterday, damn fresh."

He locks Philip's arm into his. Butch puts torsion upon one of the imprisoned wrists. Philip's eyes go desperately all about him. It is a quiet place. Nobody at all will hear.

"Ah, Butch," he whines, wrenched down on a knee, "let me go, Butch. For Christ's sake let me go!"

"Listen to the kid curse! 'Ah, Butch. For Christ's sake, Butch!'"

Star takes the other wrist and experiments with it. In that thick, choking moment Philip knows, as only a boy who lives always by present seconds can know it, despair, utterly bleak and sardonic and final. They have got him and they are going to hurt him all they want. That is all. There is to be no escape, any more than for a worm stuck on a fish-hook. If he could, he would see them struck by lightning now, with no slightest feeling but thanks and relief.

"Let's take him behind the backstop," says Butch, mouthily. "We can do some things to him there."

"All right. Get a move on, Sellaby!"

They shoulder him down the passage.

"If you yell," whispers Star. "If you just yell—"

Philip nods. He has a dumb, cold devil of rage and fear. They are almost out into the sun when Froggy Stillman, Philip's age and another of the fleeing persecuted, steps blithely and unseeingly in front of them. Butch hesitates—his grip relaxes—he wonders if this new quarry is worth pursuit. Philip sees his chance in a second and kicks Star square in the shin, so hard he feels the bone through his shoes, twists out under Butch's arm, and is running like wind over grass to Ashmead and safety. Behind him are squeals and curses but no chase. The weasels have got hold of a different rabbit. Stumbling up on the porch of Ashmead, sobbing for breath and fright, Philip looks back just once to find what has become of Star and Butch. They have twisted Froggy Stillman between them. They are taking him over behind the backstop.

> *Young rain comes trailing silver sleeves,*
> *And wind, her dog, barks after.*
> *She desolates the striving leaves*
> *With chill and tinkling laughter.*

Sleet and the pouring gust like ink!
—New buds and tempers harden—
But that's what colors the purple and pink
All over your Summer's garden!

PHILIP, suddenly roused a second ago, after a bone-breaking night, by the running of the wet paws of a chipmunk over his face, takes another look at his watch and decides with resignation that he is much too waked-up to try and go to sleep again. It is very early—the pines around the lake have not yet stopped talking-over dawn, and all things are to be seen or shrouded in a daze of umber half-lights. Day has not yet fully ascended into her bright sky; she tiptoes languidly from her warm bed of mountains, leaving shreds and tangles of saffron and Chinese-yellow behind her, like lost feathers scattered about a nest of the clouds. The lake is a pale jewel veiled in silk, the outlines of the hills are furry with distance. Philip looks at it all through half-shut eyes, wondering how he can ever draw or paint or phrase any second of it.

The formless, sack-of-potatoes heaps in the sleeping-bags at each side of him snore on without stirring. He gets up somehow without disturbing them, and walks over to the white ashes of the fire. There's enough wood left to start breakfast with, anyway. He wonders if it wouldn't be advisable to wake Phil and go out in the boat after trout. In his ears the faint persistence of the water rustles gently. No—not yet for a while—that lake needs some one to swim in it too badly.

He goes softly to the diminutive tent—parts the cur-

tains with all sorts of apologies ready. Everything safe
—not a sound from Lucia, who is curled into the heart
of her scarlet blankets like a mouse under a pile of
ruddy leaves. Sylvia is quiet, too—one long braid the
color of harvest-wheat trailing her shoulder, her mouth
childish, her face calm pallor. For a second that
frightens his mind, he wonders if they would both be
like that, dead. Then he turns away.

Stripped and a little shivery at the edge of a ripple-
less cove that four black cockades of pines screen from
the camping-place, he tests the edge of the bath before
him, blue as ground cobalt, with the sandy toes of one
inquisitive foot. It is as breathlessly cold as liquid air.
He scrambles up the side of a square brown headstone-
rock that leans with drowsy thirst at the long shimmering pool, deep-clear as the patch of sky between two
spring clouds. His muscles set for the shock—he dives
into freezing light, to come up into the sun naked and
gasping, every inch of him frosted over with silver air-
bubbles and all the blood in his body swinging clean and
vivid through his veins. He ducks back again into
turquoise underworlds—he floats through glooms of
translucence—he twists like a sparkling fish—then gets
dry by racing up and down the sleek, hard sand, a running, chanting water-monster that sun and wave between
them have just created and called immortal and made
shout.

Room 642 in the St. Francis is gray with evening.
Philip, who has been taken out of school for a dentist's
week-end and the theater with his mother and Sylvia,

tries his tongue over the new filling in a molar and hopes it won't fall out this time. Lucia has gone off shopping, leaving Philip with some new dollar-bills and the instructions to tea Sylvia and himself to any extent, when the former arrives at the hotel. So Philip, back early from the blowpipes and pecking drills of dentistry, has devoted the last half-hour or so to rehearsing his father's lordly indifference with waiters.

"The check, please?" he says to himself for the dozenth time. "Oh, yes—" then the hand goes carelessly to the pocket, as to an acknowledged United States Sub-treasury of wealth. But the telephone birrs sharply before he has completed the motion of extracting many hundred-dollar notes.

"Miss Present wishes to speak to Mrs. Sellaby," a detached voice says in his ear.

"Oh—Oh, yeah. Well, Mrs. Sellaby's out. This is Mr. Sellaby, Mr. *Philip* Sellaby, Jr. Please send Syl— send Miss Present up right away, please."

"Very well, sir." The voice is smoothly amused.

Philip wishes by all the tuxedoed-gods of books of etiquette that Lucia had not left him here alone. Still, Sylvia wasn't so bad at camp last summer—for a girl, and a girl-cousin at that.

But when Sylvia arrives, she is utterly startling. He is used to her in khaki bloomers, with her hair done up in one long corn-husk rope. Now she appears in pink ruffles that spread like rose-petals, she is dressed with the superfluous perfection of a doll in a Fifth Avenue toy-store, and her manners while verging on the

simpering, overwhelm him with a sense of their completeness.

"H'lo, Syl," he says bluffly, shooting his hand
at her. "Glad t' see you. What do you want for
tea?"

"How do you do, Cousin Philip." She takes his
hand high up in shaking it, making it feel much too
large and too carelessly cleaned. "It is very nice indeed of you to think of tea. But where is your mother?"

"Ah, she went out to do some shopping. She'll be
back soon." With an effort, "Shall we—shall we have
tea downstairs?"

"I'm not sure that Mother would like me to." This
is merely a prim pawn of conversational chess, played
to be taken, but Philip knows nothing of gambits and
hastily takes her at her word.

"All right," he says with extreme relief. "We'll
have it up here." He turns to the phone. "This is
room 642, Mr. Sellaby," he begins. "Will you—"

A precise little titter from Sylvia reddens him up to
his ears. "Haven't you forgotten to take the receiver
off, Cousin Philip?" she says in an edgy giggle.

Half-an-hour later, things are better. Sylvia has
spilled marmalade on her sleeve, said "darn!" and shat-
tered her pose of young propriety. Philip is emerging
out of his mist of hot embarrassment. His voice is full
of excitement and English muffin.

"Just wait till we get up there next year, Syl," he
rattles, jabbing the points home with a sticky fork.
"Father says we're going to Freel's Peak, *sure*. Gosh,
and it's a two-week pack-trip there and back and we'll

take three burros for the lot of us. Won't that be swell?" Sylvia nods frantically.

"Great!" she murmurs, examining the empty cream-jug. "I hope they let me come, Phil. But they think they want to ship me to a girls' camp. Girls' camp!" She forgets herself utterly and makes sounds as unrefined as they are expressive. "Can't you *see* it, Phil? A bunch of talky *girls?*"

Philip rises, nearly upsetting the tea-table. He is hearing of a deliberate atrocity.

"Oh, gee, you mustn't let them do that, Syl! Why, if they want to do that— Why, it's a crime, that's what it is, it's a dirty crime!"

He waves his arms with the clumsiness of great feeling.

"Say, Syl, if *I* can do anything about it—" he starts harshly. Her hand lies in front of him on the chair-arm, helpless, soft, a bit jammy. He takes hold of it without in the least knowing why. "If I *can,* you— you tell me," he ends weakly. The whole pulse of his heart seems to beat for a second in the hand over Sylvia's hand. She is trembling faintly, but in control of herself; this has almost happened before, several times, but not with people known like Phil. She looks up at him swiftly, being conscious of the fact that her eyes are beautifully full of tears. Their lips meet once, almost casually, gulls calling to each other across white spray, then settle to a very definite kiss with the swift determination of thirst. It only takes about thirty seconds till Sylvia cries.

Philip feels as if the room were falling to pieces about him like broken eggshells.

"Syl, Syl, I didn't—I never meant—I never will again—Oh, Syl, for God's sake stop crying!" he stutters, unconscious he is repeating one of the favorite lines of all emotional actors, he is so desperately scared and in earnest.

"What did you *do* it for then, you, you *boy?* What did you *do* it for? I didn't mean you to kiss me! I just wanted you to be nice!" through Sylvia's tears. She, too, doesn't know that she has picked up the cue in Philip's speech as neatly as a star in a demonstrative second act.

"I don't know! It's all your fault, you made me!" An outburst of furious sobs, "Oh, no, no, darn it, damn it, you didn't make me! *Quit crying!* I wanted to—I—"

Again the noise of the telephone. Philip shakes Sylvia violently, kisses her again, attempts to express rage, shame, sin, unutterable feeling and despair in one great flopping gesture that merely gives the impression that he is trying to dislocate his arms and rushes to answer it. It is Lucia this time, and a voice as pleasant and sane as brook-water.

"Is Sylvia there?"

"No, yes. Yes, mother, she's here."

"What's the matter, Philip?" A little laughter. "Have you two been fighting again? She's your guest, you know."

"Oh, yes—oh, yes, yes, yes," with extreme emotion.

"It must have been a fight. Never mind. I'll be right up. Have you children left me any tea?"

She rings off before he can answer. He turns back ferociously to Sylvia.

" Now for Pete's sake, Syl—" he begins.

But her weeping has been turned off like a tap. She is sitting up. She is rubbing her cheeks with her handkerchief.

" I am quite all right, thank you," she answers with icy repose. " Quite all right. Please speak to me as little as possible."

When Lucia finds them, Philip is as blasphemously and completely puzzled by the whole affair as Adam was after his first sharp taste of Eden greening. Sylvia gives her aunt-by-courtesy a little-girl kiss with entire composure, a small, correct and figgily supercilious Eve.

" Sellaby," says Major Stelly, bronchially, " I have decided to make you a sergeant."

" Yes, sir." Philip stands at the ideal Manual-of-Arms position of attention, stomach cramped into his back, hands flat at sides, chest out.

" Ah—I'll be frank with you, Sellaby. For quite a time—in fact, for the first year you were at Kitchell—Dr. Kitchell and myself were a bit anxious about you. You didn't seem to get on with the other boys."

" No, sir? " The query is surreptitiously acid.

" No, but lately—you've developed. You've been (tck!) forgetting all that nonsense—doing your drill smartly—like a soldier, like a soldier, sir. So now we have decided to give you this chance—"

Philip's posture holds stiff and correct, but his mind drifts off from the little coughy man in front of him. He sees himself as he was when he first came to Kitchell, a scared atom of an " only child," to be kicked around and chucked into corners like Froggy Stillman's books. Now he has improved—he has the age and the muscles and the bag of dirty stories that will keep him from being bullied at all, that may even permit him to bully some one else. A fierce cramped hatred runs through him at the bullies and his new chevrons and Major Stelly and the whole air of uniformed stupidity and disciplined nastiness that hangs over the school like gas above a marsh. Lord! If he could only get out of the place!

"And so, Sellaby, man to man, we believe in you," ends the Major. His hand goes out tentatively. Philip shakes it in silence, loathing the moist, froggy palm. Then he salutes and makes his about-face perfectly. Major Stelly believes him righteously overcome with emotion.

In his room alone that night, Philip writes letters.

DEAR FATHER:

Major Stelly told me to-day that I am to be made a sergeant at next promotions. This brings up a thing *(crossed-out)* a matter I have wished to write you about for a long time. Father, I have been at Kitchell two years and I hate it more than any other place in the world. *(Some erasures of false starts with initial I's.)* This may come as a surprise to you, but I mean it. As a favor, do not send me back after this year, which I can stick out all right. I think I have a right to ask this now, as my being promoted shows that I am not effeminate *(inked over)*, that I have been able to get some good out of the training, but not enough to warrant my staying longer. Father, the place is a dirty hell, that's all, and I—

But here the page is torn right across its face. The writer rips his pen through the last sentence, crumples the sheet into a rag, tries a fresh one.

DEAR FATHER:

The weather so far has been fine. I am trying out for track—the sprints—but am pretty rotten, I'm afraid. The coach says I should have come out earlier. We play Lick to-morrow in baseball and, believe me, I certainly hope we " Lick " *(careful quotation-marks)* them as we ought to. Tell Mother the cake was fine. I need some socks. I have lost my allowance two weeks running now for minor sins, nothing to worry about. *(Sketch of a small and very impudent devil, labeled " Sin, Minor, One.")* I am having a good time. Oh, yes, I meant to tell you, Major Stelly said to-day that they were to make me a sergeant next promotions. Love to dearest Mother and Aunt Agatha and every one. And now I must close. As ever, dear Father,

Your affectionate Son,
PHILIP.

Scraggling pasture and stony shelf,
Little to munch but thorns;
But the young ram swears with pride in himself
And tittups stones with his horns.

He waggles his scut at the wintry crowd
Of ravens, sneering and old.
And the young-god sun steps out of a cloud
And covers his horns with gold.

GRADUATION — continual dress-uniforms — polished swords—white gloves, soft as well-soaped skin, your thumb kept over the spot in one of them—the long echoing floor of Assembly Room waxed to velvety slipperiness for the Senior Dance—girls—Sylvia in faint blue and shrouded silver, the delicate eager throb of her feet retreating before yours—music, now nervously barbaric, now young and full of exquisite, useless tears, slow long spoonfuls of honey-on-ivory. " Pinky " Kitchell—" Handing on the Torch "—" now quit yourselves like men!"—all the throaty emotion of Graduation Sermon, as sham and evident as false hair on a dressing-table. Everything with a certain hurried unreality about it, like a movie run too fast over its screen.

A sense that something is ended, something definite, though nobody seems to know exactly what. A desperate sense that hereafter things will be different, ordered and consecutive, clear and purposeful and efficient, like the autobiographies of bank-presidents in twenty-cent magazines. Old hatreds, old violences, old ardors washed away in twenty-four hours by a tide of kindly, sentimental " good feeling "—hard, emotional handshakes with old enemies instantaneously reconciled because both of you are leaving " the old school." Major Stelly, " Sellaby, you are one of the boys we are proud of—" Parents, little and big, obtrusive and meek, full of secret comparisons of their own sons with other people's sons, and that not to the disadvantage of the former. It all ends—it is as suddenly gone as foam down a freshet—and Philip's neat, strapped trunks come home with the shards and rag-bag remnants of six years of life inside them, done up in labeled, brown-paper parcels, heaped away in a disorderly muddle of letters and reports and scrawled-over dance-cards and old copies of the *Kitchell Weekly Bayonet*. Life is closing in on Philip, overtaking him with the sprint of a crafty miler in the stretch. Well, *that's* over!

A month later—and Tahoe and a sense of expanding, delicious freedom, tangible as honey on pancakes, connected somehow with a new equality in his father's talk and not having to account either to him or a first sergeant for any long idle minute of the enchanted day. The happiest summer he has had, a summer as clear and glowing as light through a piece of unflawed amber. Money in the pockets of loose comfortable clothes and a whole great fifteen months to chuck away as he likes, like pennies to a crowd of small boys—for Lucia is a little anxious about his eyes, and he is not to enter Yale till the Fall after this.

THE PROUD HUNTSMEN

(Being a poem Philip wrote about this time)

Cruel and careless, clean and chill,
March slaps awake the sleepy mind,
And past this hill and t'other hill
There is our phœnix still to find!

The raw wind echoes with his shout,
His track is on the ragged sky;
And we've the hearts to hunt him out
And live like gods before we die!

His eyes are fiercer than a star,
His wings are brighter than the young,
And every word he cries afar
Is with a lark's ecstatic tongue.

Past crumbling cloud and crackling ray
And wrecks of worlds not yet begun,
We'll hound him down the golden day
And kill him in his nest of sun!

For what is Fear? A limping fool.
And what is Death? A windy sage,
Not all whose vacant breath can cool
The sunrise of our pilgrimage!

Within the hand of Youth, our chief,
Lies Life, the bright and steely toy,
He whirls it like a spinning leaf
And shouts with mockery and joy.

There will be banners on the hills!
There will be scarlet in the skies!
When we ride back from Heaven's rills,
Bowed with our kingly merchandise.

There will be thunder in the street
When we ride back to our own town!
—The men with crowns beneath their feet
—The men who brought the phœnix down.

1911

WINTER on the white, South California beaches. The shells of abalones, murky-purple, the white shells of sea-snails, so pure, so sculptured, they might have been cut for an altar-screen. Philip, riding surf with Phil, both so shakingly weak in laughter at their own half-drownings that they can hardly stay on their shooting, slippery planks in smooth water. Lucia untroubled as the sea or the sun, a second youth of the sea come upon her, combing her heavy hair as she sits on a sunny, beast-like rock, a strayed maternal immortal seeming to share in the vagrant peace and calm incertitude of the whole fluctuating world of green swells and dripping foam. Sylvia in a sun-bitten, short bathing-suit, the brown swimming child of sea-sound and a mermaid, as beautiful and sexless a thing as the flight of a gull over waves. And in the crystalline hours before night's large stars, when evening departs with the languid magnificence of an argosy and the sky seems made of clear colors and dreams and the single cries of birds, Philip, lying beside the brimstone sparks of a driftwood fire, drinks in with every breath of his body this saturating and exhaustless life. Yes, and curled so beneath a wrecked and flying twilight once, he half-sleeps and imagines an insolent vision.

. . . The neat door of a very modern office. Three names on the frosted glass in gold, " Clotho

Lachesis

Atropos "

and below in large capitals, " PRIVATE." Philip nevertheless turns the knob and goes in. The chamber within is tremendous, labyrinthine, cut up like some vast bagatelle-board into a criss-crossing series of small stone covered and open mazes with green plants growing oddly in some of them. From the mothy vagueness at the far end of the room—if indeed it has an end, for Philip can see no wall there—comes the slumbering dark sound of continuously falling water, water that chuckles and chokes over worn-out stones. Three women are seated at desk-chairs—their backs are to Philip and they do not turn as he enters—each one has the mouth of a maze before her and they are intent on some sort of game with little colored balls. At the side, a small, inhuman creature keeps score with figures that Philip cannot read.

One of the Fates will take a ball up in her palm— all the balls have some faint individuality of tint or pattern and are heaped in huge baskets beside the chairs —examine it and pass it to her sisters. They may mark it with tools that they have by them, blow upon it, rub it on their sleeves, in the end return it. Sometimes the Fate inserts it in her maze alone, sometimes with others; after each has been swallowed up, all the Fates listen and watch together unmovingly. Philip can hear the click and slither of the balls as they rush down the roofed passages, can see them spot the maze with color for an instant, collide with other rushing balls perhaps, then vanish again into the gaping rambles of the board. Some fall through sudden holes without a sound, there are others that circle and circle and do not get free. But the Fates watch steadily with eyes that never blink till a faint plopping sound, the sound of a light thing dropping into water, ends their fixity. Then they all start slightly, and the creature makes his tally, and the game begins all over again as before.

Philip does not like the quietude of the Fates. At first they seemed merely aunt-like, they and their faces gray as ice, but their unwearying absorption in the clueless game and the recurrent tiny splashes of the colored balls as they fall and are swept away by darkling water wears at his mind like the scraping of chalk on a blackboard. There is a continual icy fingering on his spine. He grows stiff with the terror of nightmare. The Fates continue their sport, the balls roll softly . . .

The Fate in the middle has passed a ball to the others. They have sent it back, one has scratched at it with a needle. Now the middle Fate holds it up, dubiously, poised between finger and thumb. It is veined with purple like a chintz, it is a pretty ball. Philip looks at the Fate and finds he cannot move. It is his ball she is holding.

Philip fights the air with his hands, he rushes forward.

"Stop!" he says through the fog of dream that weights him like mail. "Stop! Stop! Give me it! Give me back my ball!"

The calm Fate stirs and opens her thumb and finger.

The ball clicks into the maze, Philip can hear it slurring over little bridges, down polished shafts of marble, racing and gathering speed . . .

He is wakened by Sylvia kneeling beside, tickling his ear with a long feather of dry seaweed.

" Supper ! " bawls Phil from the porch. " Come and get it, Philip ! Come and get it ! "

BOOK II
PARABALOU!

SUMMER WITH PHILIP

(1912)

NIGHT

THE wrenched boughs of the eucalyptus trees shiver and creak, the wind floods over them like a storm of dark ruffled water. " Fff," says the wind, " Fff," " Fff."

Oaks are realities, thick, solid. Elms keep a tame sort of mystery, though their dryad has long gone out of them. These trees are fever trees—saplings of the soil of illusion and the waters of nightmare. It is they who stand out of the ground like black, crooked fingers, trembling with an unconquerable palsy under the hush and lapping of the gust.

Sigh and turn your mouth to the wind, deep dreamer, it is cool on your face that sleep has smoothed and left empty. You lie upon the knees of wise Night and she touches you with her hands of air. She is sightless but her eyes are meditations.

Sleep, for if you awoke you could not sleep again, you could not take your eyes from the sight of the countless myriads of stars that shine, overlaying all heaven stainlessly with their radiant and glowing dust.

49

MORNING

Not a cloud, not a sheep of a cloud in all the limitless pastures of the sky, not the white of the edge of a feather, not the white of a curl of wool.

It is the middle of the dry, hot season—the earth turns brown—the sky is a blue crystal. For three months now there will not be a cloud.

Saddle your horse, Philip, and come looking for your friends, the clouds. Ride your horse down the shelving road to the bay, through dust that is like thick, fine pollen. Drop the reins over his head and let him graze in the patchy shadow of a pepper-tree.

Strip and walk into the green forest of the water— swing and shout upon the broad backs of calm and monstrous waves that roll like sailors to the shore. There are your clouds, Philip, but they have been broken into foam and bubbles. It is a froth of forgotten clouds that covers the tops of the waves like snow.

Afternoon

The leaves of the tulip-tree are so thick and so many that the sun sinks through them slowly, like gold tissue crumbling in a gloom of emerald.

The buds of the tulip-tree are the color of pure cream, they are little pale slender urns that hang upon the dimness of the branches like flecks of wax inside a jadestone.

When your shadow stretches out, a thin long man, and the light comes creeping and has lost its blaze; when a puff from the bay is tiptoeing in the grass-blades and your lips taste at it and are salt.

Then it is time to sit chaired in the boughs of the tulip-tree and watch, through its haze and glimmer of green lights, the whole and perfect orb of afternoon drop into the gray, cupped palms of evening as soundlessly as a gold leaf drowning in a pool.

EVENING

Coffee on the big white quiet porch. Long roomy cane chairs and a chance to stretch. The first stars, few and intense, have come out with the moths that fly at twilight.

"Philip, what do you think?" but Philip is in the snail's peace of laziness and will not come out. The talk, brittle as porcelain, crackles about him like broken candy. It stops, it is tinkled into motion again by the empty, gay bell of laughter.

"Philip, what do you think?" That the sky is like sooty velvet. That the stars have begun to march in order. That it is time for another cigarette. It is good to be alive. It is good to be tired in the dusk, and drowsy, and feel the burn of the sun still on your face. It is good—

"Philip, what do you think?"
"Oh—nothing."

SNOW AND ELMS—"LIGHTS OUT, FRESHMEN!"

(1912-1913)

THE big blue scrapbook with the staring white "Y," large as a football-letter, glued on to the cover that Philip bought with such innocence and pride his third day at Yale and carefully left behind under a dead straw hat as a pitiful sop for his untipped janitor at the end of his freshman year, contained only two clippings at its fattest. One was the *News* account of the Freshman Rush and the other a thickly underlined Schedule of Courses. And Philip was not of the species that snapshots hangdog and consciously affectionate groups on the Senior Fence or treasures light-struck films of forgotten baseball games and the stone-ax jests of fraternity "running" to delight the hearts of Class Book editors and mortify the friends thus permanently satirized past all swearing. So to him the recollection of the rapid, rich four years was like rummaging a sea-chest stowed away in an old attic—everything higgledy-piggledy, anyhow and comfortable—ivory monkeys jostling worn brass sword-hilts, yellow love letters stuck away in a sprigged silk waistcoat, a white beaver hat full of rose-shells and elephant-chessmen and Chinese cash. And the attic smells of tar and old leather and honeysuckle—May morning drifts through the win-

53

dows—the air is as light and heady as white French wine—

So dancingly, so careless of order, the memories crowd on him—little square living colored pictures, diminished but burning-clear, take form and glow on the white blank screen of the mind.

A long, sickeningly lonely walk down the two imitation-Broadway blocks of Chapel Street above Church, out the decorous length of Whitney Avenue with its placid middle-aged parade of well-mannered houses and well-pruned elms till it strips into naked country beyond East Rock Road. Then back through the humming swarm of all Sheff and Academic and fifteen hundred strangers, his own age or near it, from every state in the Union and all as little concerned with him and his individual vagaries as June bees would be with a peripatetic ant . . . First classes in Lampson and Phelps, Al Osborn, a steep hill of uncomfortable chairs, the bone in his throat when he is called on to rise and recite. The Rush—the sweaty pink wrestlers fighting in torchlight—the weave and swing of the snake-dance—rowdy Sophomores, amused Juniors, cool Seniors, hatless and statuesque like wandering marble gods—all a mêlée of breaking song, processional lights and cheers. Early mornings of Battell Chapel and its dim irreligious light with the whole sleepy College congregated together —his own class in the gallery observing that strange new entity, itself, with drowsy surprise and wonderment —two familiar faces in five hundred—the hiss of the esses in the " Lord's Prayer " as it runs through the kneeling crowd like wind through corn—the indecorous

stampede toward the doors after the fleeing President
when the Seniors have bowed him out, that the *Record* irreverently caricatured as " The Passing of Arthur."

Then there were preliminary football games watched
from the cramped hard benches of Yale Field under
the cider-apple air and swept gold sunsets of October
and early November—the smash of the two caterpillar-
legged lines together like the impact of shocking pool-
balls on green, white-gridironed baize, with the little
live blue dolls always breaking through, always gain-
ing. Lonely backs crouching taut before a trick-play
with the single will and hard eyes looking ahead of
weathered knights in a tournament or seamen holding
on to a bucking wheel. Bob Sailer, Captain and All-
American half, the yellow egg of the ball cuddled up in
his arms like a baby, in a fox-footed thirty yard run
through the whole Amherst team—the wrenched fierce
face of a full-back, running back to his position after a
javelin-thrust through tackle—yelped signals, strangely
distinct in the clear breeze that came with the burnt-
sienna decline of evening, and the stilt-like black H's of
the goalposts flinging taller, dark shadow-capitals, on
the ending battle that tore the careful sod to dirt and
torn grass.

Of the Dean's Office Philip's knowledge as yet was
fortunately small. He had stood in a line for anywhere
from five minutes to an hour and a half there at various
times, to be finally pushed up in front of a desk where
a large man with the sleepy kindness of a tired brown
seal had once advised him into a cubbyhole of a room
in Pierson, with roommate attached, and on other occa-

sions informed him as to his scant remaining chapel-
cuts or the fact that so far he did not even seem to be
trying to pass Physics. From the deadly little chamber
on the opposite side of the hall he had sometimes heard,
as men hear thunder in sleep, the shouts and sudden
trumpetings of the Dean—and had once been sent himself into that dreadful presence, to find merely a healthy
old gentleman with the frosty hair, red face and gusty
manners of a hunting squire, who, the moment Philip
appeared shrinkingly within the door, began to rate him
for throwing water-bottles out of his window (an ingenuous Freshman pastime in which he had not happened to take part) and left him with the general feeling
of having been out in a cloudburst without an umbrella
and the vague impression that he would have to stand
up straighter when he talked and specialize in Advanced
Chemistry and Business Economics if he ever expected
to leave with an A.B. Let it here be said, however, to
the credit of Tyrranosaurus Superbus (as Dick Sheldon
bitterly rechristened him after being made to sweat his
way through Elementary Geology when he had wished
to specialize in the Metaphysical Poets) that his yearn-
ing for forcing square pegs into the roundest possible
holes did not apply to offenders of Philip's stripe alone,
as the five wretched shot-putters and wrestlers forced to
flunk three hours a week of the History of Music because he thought they needed broadening, attested in
their own inarticulate but sad-eyed way.

Of Professors Philip made no friends as yet, they were
desked abstractions, to be handled like high explosives
and given " Good Morning " respectfully when met on

the street. Two stood out, an affable and interesting 1911 man, enabled by means of a private fortune to accept the poverty's pence of a freshman-instructorship —he gave Philip much kindness and advice, tea and scones from the hands of a delightful wife, and the highest mark Philip ever received in College. The other, a great, burly, bearish man with the face of a Visigoth king and a sandy beard that never seemed quite intentional and yet could not deliberately be called a lapse on the part of his razor, Philip always remembered as one of the few, rare, lucently-forceful intellects that can vivisect the smallest nerve or joint of a subject without ever losing its place and importance in the general anatomical scheme.

In *his* classes men neither yawned, wrote surreptitious letters nor tried to bluff. He taught History—a pell-mell course from the Fall of the Roman Empire to 1815—and before this year was over he had left his own signature and the skeleton facts of the case on the logiest minds in his divisions, as a stamping-machine leaves motto and pawing buffalo on the blank of a nickel in the mint. He taught roaringly to bump sleepy intellects awake, he would break long pieces from the end of his pointer (the length of a tall man's crutch the first of the week, of a worn-down pencil at the last of it), he would smash his watch down on the desk and jar its wheels apart in the stress of the moment's question as to the " sig-nif-i-cance " of Charlemagne's imperial title or the effect of the Reformation on German trade. This was necessary vaudeville—under its cover he dug to the essential roots of things—

and he insisted so forcibly on the same straining vehe-
mence of intelligence from his men that by February
they were running to keep up with him in as healthy
an ardor of pursuit as if historical causes were cats and
they were terriers. Only once did Philip see him
genuinely out of temper. He cared little for dates as
a rule, but when he happened to want a particular one
he worried the class for it like a ferret. It was four
days before Christmas vacation—an eight o'clock after
one of the Freshmen Dances. He viewed the somnolent
ranks before him with the amiable grin of a fed cobra.

"And now," he repeated for the ninth time, "and
now, just *what* was the sig-nif-i-cance of 512 A. D. ?"
He paused, the name quivered and struck like an arrow
"Mis-ter *Post!*"

"Chubby" Post, an impudent cherub, cox of the second Freshman crew, was jarred into round-eyed imbecility.

"Washington at Valley Forge, sir," he said in a
stupefied whisper.

The professor rose to his full tower of height, took
his watch in his hand and threw it out of the window.

"This class is dismissed!" he roared. They departed on tiptoe, shivering. And after that even Chubby
came to him with at least a flunking knowledge of his
subject.

The Fall waned through a Princeton Game at Princeton where Philip saw the two teams gore at each other
like fighting elk for the brief four quarters and emerge
at a 6-6 tie; through a Harvard Game at New Haven
that was to be the first of three successive Sedans for

Yale and the numb, sick disappointment of the sardoni-
cally-drunken evening that followed it; through Thanks-
giving to the first pale flurry of snow that soon turned
to a sodden blanket of freezing slush and made walking
galoshed and aquatic for the next four months. Philip
viewed the first flowerlike settling of rustling crowds
of swift flakes on Campus and Green with poetical rap-
tures—the pallid glowing light that accompanied them
enchanted him—he was found in a chilblained daze on
the steps of Dwight Hall, trying to sketch the brick
Noah's Ark of Connecticut under its deluge of white
fluff and whispering scraps of frost. Then the cold
that he had never known got in between his bones and
he went around barking and sneezing with an open box
of cough-tablets in one coat-pocket and all his roommate's
clean handkerchiefs in the other. He shivered like
a Malay on a Polar Expedition on his way from one
classroom to the next, pared his board-bill down to a
shaving and spent the money on immense wood-fires.
That his roommate insisted on opening all the windows
at night, while he recognized the health of the measure,
was a deliberate insult to every muscle in his body. He
dreamed of California continually, of picking oranges
from the tree under a sun as dry as champagne *sec*.
And besides his adventures with every kind of " Kill-
Kold " and " Grippe-Buster " nostrum and gargle, two
things of considerable importance happened to him. He
heeled the *Lit.* and the *Record* and began to make friends.

The first two occupations came easily enough—he
had passed the Summer scribbling industriously and
so had a reserve of some thirty various pieces of verse

which he fed cautiously, three or four a month, through
the letter-slit in the door of the *Lit.* office—a secluded
damp little cave in the basement of Osborn. His first
attempt, a long bloody ballad he had stewed out of the
bones of William Morris, appeared in the October *Lit.*
and was much more enthusiastically reviewed than it
deserved. After that he began to be known as " the
Freshman pote " or " that queer bird who writes those
crazy things for the *Lit.*" A legend sprang up that
he cut Chapel every Sunday and composed great works
in a vinous stupor on top of a keg full of California
claret—and the fable helped to raise his social position.
There was always the fragile excitement of padding over
to the *Lit.* window on make-up nights and reading by
sputtering match-light the white face of the swinging
card that held the list of accepted young sprouts of
fancy. And the joy of talking to and being talked to
by Senior *Lit.* editors, great prehistoric creatures who
quoted Dante in the original and unpublished and unprintable Eugene Field in the vernacular and wore the
glittering gold triangle of Chi Delta Theta with the
casual unobservance cradled royalty pays to its hereditary shining toys of Garter or Golden Fleece.

As for the *Record,* it was then in the hands of
three happy-go-lucky Dekes, with a wit as merrily and
innocently indecent as a Papuan's, who, having neither
expected nor received the gifts of the elder gods on Tap
Day, had neither bitterness toward nor the restraints
of Senior Societies, spent most of the advertising profits
on beer parties with the heelers (to the gesticulating
dismay of a strongly Semitic business board) and gave

the *Record* a flavor of Canton ginger and *crème de cocoa* that tickled every section in College, except that of the prematurely devout. Philip slaved over careful oils and pen-and-inks at first—they were uniformly praised and left unused—then he discovered a knack for absurd cartoons and broad splashes of decoration that made his name creep steadily up the list of competitors. He devoted unregenerate hours his fellow *Lit.* competitors were spending on clottingly-purple essays on Lionel Johnson's Prose to the construction of light verse and flashy sketches calculated to annoy the discreet— and was given much free beer by his superiors and on the whole, had an outrageously good time.

The friendships formed were like most Freshmen friendships when the men concerned have not come down together from the same school, somewhat tentative and on the basis of chance meetings, happening to room close by or sit next to a man in class, rather than by deliberate affirmation and choice. Some were lucky and grew to close relationships, others straggled out like chance pencil-lines on a piece of paper, or recoiled and hurt like snapped rubber bands. There was first his roommate, Tom Whitter, steady, humorous, whimsical and poor, working his way through unaided, from a small Connecticut town. A small chap carelessly built, with the face and long nose of an alert, good-humored mouse; fate and the registrar had thrown them together, and the accident developed into firm liking on both sides. Tom was as kind as bread and as trustworthy as salt— in their two years of rooming together they exchanged ties and confidences and families, tried on each other's best clothes and new opinions, shared an equal wonderment as to the internals of Life's machine and what on earth they and their class would be doing in the next ten years. When they parted, Philip to room with Dick Sheldon, it was, on Philip's part at least, with a sense of somewhat shabby desertion. But the twenty-four months current had forced their friends and interests diametrically apart—indeed, they had come to the condition of so many roommates who hardly see each other at all, except before chapel in the morning and in bed at night. They kept up the friendship, however, because they were gentlemen, and with strain because they were young, and before the class graduated were honest if temperate comrades again. But Philip never thought of Tom later without a sense of undeserving gratitude and much taken for little given—he had not even been able to get him into his own Junior fraternity on account of the ferocious party wars in his particular delegation. " Good Lord, we couldn't get Jesus Christ by this crowd without four blackballs! " said Dick Sheldon acidly after an unusually bellicose session. And they cheered the remark but went on excluding Tom.

Billy Stack lived across the hall from Tom and Philip, blond and huge, his tongue had the German burr. To the strength and placid disposition of a Great Dane, he added a consuming love for hot chocolate, the movies and bowling. Philip partook of all three with him, even wrestled with him on occasion, much to the excruciation of his muscles, for Billy would get so interested explaining the theory of the " scissors " that Philip's stomach, the object used for forcible demonstration,

would be squashed into his spine like a muffin before
frantic kicks finally made Billy realize that anything
was the matter. Stacy Cooper, a dark-pompadoured
musician with sweet wit and the ironic mind; Paul
Stannifer, a grotesque like a resurrected dodo, who did
nothing but grind, play chess and read *The Christian
Science Monitor;* Hank Cummings, that useless
clothes-hanger; Tuck Carson, a stupid ex-Exeter beauty
gone to seed; Nick Wayne, another of the many putting
themselves through—he had been everything from bell-
boy to stoker on a Lake Steamer—faint hair, pink al-
bino eyes behind tortoise-shell rims, a ribald mouth—
they trundle like Jack-o'-lantern ghosts out of the
wraiths of that dim first year, mow, posture and are
past.

So the days crowded to weeks and the weeks trickled
off and ran away from Philip like bran out of a broken
sack, while he drifted the eddies of Pierson with the
great unorganized of his class. The young entry-poli-
ticians, the men from the bigger prep. schools, the fellows sure of athletic numerals—the grotty ones and the
snotty ones—were most of them collected in Wright.
Loose " crowds " were beginning to form already, the
wise ones were making out fraternity-lists, the uncanny
ones held hushed converse with the blinds pulled down
as to their own and others' chances for Senior Societies
two years away. Distinct cleavage between prep-school
and non prep-school exists only in Freshman year to
any extent—and then generally in the mind of the non
prep-school man. For a Yale class, like most real and
historic democracies, begins with a hereditary aristoc-

racy, grows tired of it and knocks out its underpinnings so that its members slide gently back into the general mass. So Philip by the nature of his case was delivered from premature politics and the Greek gift of early prominence that inflates certain unfortunates to the transitory blossom and limp rubbery ending of a night blooming cereus and leaves them in that tiny hurt minority that votes its first year its pleasantest.

Philip took long walks in the weeping month before Easter when he dared consider leaving off fur gloves. He splashed about in unbuttoned galoshes through streets and under skies that were glutted with gray heavy glistening rain. The sopping walk crosswise across the campus from

> " Osborn, that weird fantastic dream in stone,
> Crouched like a squatting toad with open lip,
> Or like a ferry-boat, banged, battered, blown,
> Bumping a beaten nose into its slip,"

past Connecticut, under the draggled, brown-sugar tower of Phelps with its four green-rusty turrets that clear night and a moon make shine like silver helms, was on uneven flags, glinting dead-leaf-color with the wet. On Philip's left was the brown New Library, a square tall block, flanked on the Art School side by the squat Chinese-parasol top of Chittenden Reading Room, on the right by the four fretted spires of the Old Library that rose so blackly satisfying against the colored dome of spring sunset. In May and early June the Library ivies talked; musical over and over with the soft continual curring and whistle of birds. Mushroom-shaped, mush-

room-colored Dwight Hall on the left again, on the right
the red high honeycomb line of Lawrence and Farnam,
slantingly ahead the gray hulk of Battell Chapel with
its chiming, gold-handed clock—Miller Gateway and
the great rocky mass of Durfee. All around the little
patch of soaking earth and its trees and its statues ran
the Fence, sacrosanct, covered with generations of ini-
tials. At the end of the path, Wright Hall, with its
paved and hollow court and its two prim lions. Young
melancholy in all its poignant satisfaction, Philip had
always from that three minute walk, when the ground
was covered with rotten snow or bare, and the elms sigh-
ing and leafless. But when Spring came—Connecticut
Spring as frail and intoxicatingly green-and-gold as the
limbs of a Puritan girl turned oread—or rich Autumn
wandered the round calm hills and brown fields, shaking multitudes of scarlet and tawny leaves from the
profusion of his wine-stained reeling cup—Philip found
such happiness as is not given twice. He tried to put
it down in rhymes often enough but knew each word
that came to him fainter than the thing. But the map
of the campus stayed in his mind—bitten there as an
etching is bitten into a plate. He could remember it
always, later, under every trick and pulsation of shade
or weather, and it always brought with it peace and
that sense of fed accomplishment that comes like sleep
after hours of annihilating toil.

Other snapshots were his to remember too—Book
and Snake tomb under April moonlight, serene as the
face of Pallas, the Greek temple of a dream—the statue
of Nathan Hale on the grass in front of Connecticut with

red wintry sun like a libation on bronze shoulders, bronze throat, bronze eyes—the clamor of Mory's at mealtime, only needing the brassy flutter of a horn or a call for grilled bones to make it a coaching inn like Mr. Weller's where all the characters of Dickens could be at home and drink ale out of toby-jugs. Philip had the romantic eye and the wandering mind. They are priceless exhausting burdens in a practical world.

One more picture—Philip alone in his room on an idling May afternoon. He starts to read, but the letters stay letters. Starts to draw, produces three witless caricatures in five minutes and scratches them out disgustedly. Looks at his watch, decides it is too early for the movies and marches aimlessly for a while between bed and desk. All day something intense, something nameless has been working and fretting at his spirit like brewer's yeast. He wants something, something tremendous and unnamed, something outside of himself and bright and entire and huge. The want has grown fiercely painful now, it has taken possession of him completely, but the thing desired is so great and so external it is as if he wished for the properties of the lens of a camera or an eye to be able to shrink the whole vast face of the moon into a little black-and-white pitted scene that vision and brain can understand. He sits down at the desk, takes paper and pencil, stares at the wall. It dissolves, so intently does he gaze at it— wreathing bodies and eggs of smoke appear, grow clearer —out of the nebulous rolling world in front of his thought appears a lit, hard, definite form, a woman walking. It is Isis, queen of blue Heaven and the two

Egypts; she is hooded in silver silk. Bells tinkle and
jar as she walks, a multitude of throaty small golden
bells. She stands before him motionless, the burning
gems of her eyes lift to his gaze, she begins to sing.
Behind her the Sphinx lies down like a lion asleep and
there rise against the sky the three stiff horns of the
Pyramids.

Philip drops his head on his left arm, his hand begins
to make shuddering progress across the paper. " Isis "
it writes and erases, then " Isis of the Sands," draws a
line under it, hesitates doubtfully, but lets it stand.

" Measureless sand . . . interminable sand . . . "

The pencil shakes and crawls, the hand moves spider-
wise, the letters form more carelessly . . . if he can only
grip and paint clear what he sees with his eyes . . . !

" . . . the Sphinx alone
Couched on her forepaws, like a sleepy hound
Under the weight of a caress of rock
And smiled her woman's and chimera's smile
Inexorably, drowned with the savage dark.

The black tide filled the heavens up and ceased.
A little tongueing flame ran on the sand . . . "

Isis is speaking now—she has loosed the first of her
veils and her voice sways and floats like a pennon of
clouded red. The words swing into lines, the lines
inch down the page, slow and cautious at first, with
many scratched out or written over, then swifter and
more swift, untroubled, an effortless dancing, a stream-
ing current. The daze of creation makes all Philip's
body hot while its passion lasts. After an amount of

indefinite time that has no division into minutes, the
tide crests and turns to its ebb, the writing runs down,
the shapes disintegrate, thin into wraiths, are nothing.
Philip wrestles them back before him with a rasping
effort of will, writes four quick lines in a strain like
the last spurt of a sprinter, relaxes utterly and throws
the pencil up to the ceiling. He then looks at his
watch, it is six o'clock and he has been writing five
hours without a break. He chuckles and shakes himself
all over like a dog coming out of water. After a while
he starts to re-read his poem.

Tom Whitter, coming in about seven, finds him typing
and cursing softly as he types.

" Hi, Tom! "

" Hi, Phil! Had dinner? "

" No."

" Why not, you silly idiot? Do you know what time
it is? "

" Sure," with conscious pride. " I've been writing."

" Well, you look pepped-out enough. Come over and
get a shredded or something."

" Wait a minute. I've got one more page to go. Oh,
just wait till I show you this, Tom! It's good—I know
it's good—I know it's damn good—damn good for me,
anyway—oh, Tommy, it's the best thing I've ever done
in my life! . . . "

Exit Freshman year in a worry of last exams. and
packing trunks. Philip went home for the summer,
found his family amusing, Sylvia inclined to be oppres-
sively cocky after a strenuously-popular first season and
five proposals, and his father's chop-strokes at tennis

still unfathomable. He loafed and experimented with water-colors and came back in the fall prepared to answer the inevitable " Good vacation, Phil? " from every renewed acquaintance with " Sure—wonderful! ", and take up his position as acknowledged minor demigod with the three hundred and fifty others of his class, minor demigods, too, now that Freshman year was passed.

SUN AND PEPPERS

(SUMMER OF 1913)

FAMILY—I

FATHER and I are alike when we leave a room. We take hold of the door-jamb and swing ourselves out by one hand. Our fingers are the same—we can both crack nuts with them—and we are alike in the way we laugh.

Father, when he is awake, looks young, but asleep the lines creep into his face like writing and he lies with his head bent over one arm like a tired cat resting on its paws. Father isn't so old, though. He wasn't much more than my age when I was born.

When the Druggist made up the prescriptions, he put more bad-temper and courage in Father's and more fool dreams and talk in mine. If he'd mixed us different entirely what a fine time we'd have had, but we're too much alike to get along. So we just sit still here and

look at each other as you look at your reflection in the
mirror when the mercury at the back has begun to run.

FAMILY—II

"Mrs. Sellaby is such a beautiful woman." Funny
to hear that hen's voice coming through the window and
know it is Mother the hen is talking about.

Yes, but you don't know how beautiful she is. Yes,
and how her hair when she coils it in the morning still
winds into thick, soft ropes, blue-black and fragrant like
a living thing. I yelled for her once when I was ten
and she came up and let my crying spoil her dress!

Slow patience and the infinite peace of a rich heart.
The laughter of a young, proud, stately girl and the
hands that are so strong and calm yet whiter than the
untouched blooms of the magnolia. How on earth
could you know how beautiful she is, my beautiful and
adored and darling Mother?

FAMILY—III

Aunt Agatha is a very old little silver lady. She
is so old that to pick a handful of sweet peas is a trouble
and an adventure. In summer she sits all day on the
upper porch where she can look down into the nests of
the young housekeeping birds and knit blue slippers.

Lee is a Chinaman, as full of good buttery things as
a yellow drop of oil. He never has a cross word or

makes bad pie-crust and the smile on his mouth is as
soft and immutable as the glow of his copper saucepans.
Lizzie, the maid, is Irish. She says she sees ghosts.

Prince is a curly dog with a sad priest-face and the
manners of a copybook gentleman. Fred Fish is a
mossed old carp that lives in a fountain and comes to
have his head scratched if he likes you. If he doesn't
—he splashes water.

Let's see—that must be all my family.

Books

"Your majesty shall shortly have your wish and
ride in triumph through Persepolis." Then Tambur-
laine speaks, slow at first, because he's handling the
words as if they were kings' crowns. Your breath
catches and everything in you tingles as you look at
the little black spiderings on the page.

"And ride in triumph through Persepolis." He draws
his three bloody companions and the armed and silent
armies of the world around him with one sweep of his
hairy arms. "Is it not brave to be a king, Techelles,
Usumcasane and Theridamas, is it not passing brave to
be a king, and ride—" It comes like a falling sword,
it colors your mind like scarlet.
"And ride in triumph through Persepolis!"

It would be worth while getting eaten up like a snail

by salt and the sun for that—even to be only Usum-casane.

NAME

What does it mean—this thing that people call you by? Philip Sellaby, philipsellaby—say it over a dozen times and it starts to sound like nonsense, maybe it is.

Walking along a road, hot days, if you aren't think-ing of much, you can often step clear out of your name. You can climb into somewhere different where your name and your eyes and your body aren't any more you, really, than the clothes you take off at night. And the you that is detached, that sits apart, can look down upon the other you and smile.

I think that's why you feel sorry, sometimes, for the other you—for that poor, stupid walking automaton of white bone and senseless gristle that other people have to label all the time with a couple of guttural noises so they can tell it apart from the other animals.

"THE JUNIOR FRATERNITIES ANNOUNCE THE ELECTION OF . . ."

(1913-1914)

WHEN Philip and Tom had exchanged the reforma-tory-walls of Pierson for the stuffy comfort of Durfee and discovered that all prints and pictures, however framed or hung, harmonized just as badly with the weak arsenic green of their present quarters as they had with the tomato-bisque plaster of their former ones, the five Junior Fraternities started calling on Sophomores.

At least it seemed that soon, though in reality a month had fled by and lost itself in October's scurry of sunset-colored leaves and Philip had had time to be elected to the Elizabethan Club. He drank his first self-conscious cup of tea there on the big leather lounge in front of the fire and felt hugely out of place as the gay toy-balloon of amusing talk was batted about from hand to hand under the wreathing smoke of churchwarden pipes by men he scarcely knew. But there was a comfortable informality about the Club—a balancing of ultra-violet æsthete against *News*ily solemn industrious apprentice amid general mild chaff at the expense of both—that made Philip enjoy his increasing excursions there in the same pleasant ratio that one enjoys the subsidence of a Virginia mint-julep into its ice. That a Club founded for avowedly artistic rather than Arty and Crafty purposes could exist in and have the healthy nicknaming respect of the most American of American colleges was enough to shock Philistine and poseur out of every one of their two senses. Philip cartooned it as he thought it would have been at Harvard —a classically anemic Boston salon, cold teaed to death under wax busts of Emerson and Bryant—at Princeton; the Mermaid Tavern under the Restoration with Rochester, crowned with a pint-pot, leading the revels. "But, Philip, my dear man, don't you *see* we're having a literary Renaissance right here and now?" asked Johnny Chipman, of the class ahead, with a shake of his tawny squirrel's brush of hair. "I guess we are." Philip said, "I guess we are. This place—and the people at the Press—and people actually come out of Yale Station reading the *Lit.*—counted five of 'em to-day myself in half an hour." Then gravely, "Awful responsibility to be a whole Renaissance, isn't it, John? Let's have some more mild fluid on it. Lemon or cream?"

Johnny Chipman was the principal reason why Philip got one of the last five hold-offs to A. D. when the fraternity elections finally came. The "calling" was a singular business—much heavy tramping up and down the entry stairs—appearance of a group of four or five tongue-tied or professionally affable strangers, each giving a mumbled name and a set firm handshake as he entered—ghastly spurts of forced talk of the "You fellows certainly live a long way up!" or "Pretty nice lot of pictures you've got here" order—an obviously relieved departure after two minutes of such uneasy badinage and long stares, with consultations sometimes cruelly audible, on the part of the calling committee as soon as their last man shut the door and a general sinking feeling on Philip's part that he had ruined his chances with *that* bunch forever and ever as he and Tom dashed for a hidden Pot-Pourri to find out, by looking up as much as they could recall of their visitors' grumbled appellations just what fraternity it was that had called.

"Hey, Phil, that guy's name was Keating, wasn't it?"

"Keator, I think."

"Well, there's a Keating in Zete and a Keator in Psi U. Remember any more of them?"

"Smith," doubtfully.

"Oh, Lord, there are four Smiths and they're all different places. Call 'em Zete—if they are that makes three calls from them. Could you see their pins?"

"Not a chance. Now who were the crowd that skinny fellow named Wilkes ran with?"

Tom flutters the leaves obediently, another committee knocks and instantly enters—a Campaign Committee this time by their funeral derbies and the grim fixed grin on their mouths. Tom and Philip are caught red-handed but the former's kangaroo leap to sit on the incriminating book brings a roar of laughter that saves the situation. And so it goes.

After three such evenings Psi U, which Chubby Post has nicknamed "The Holy Ice House," since it runs to the pious athlete, prominent Christian and impeccable parlor-snake and has more fanatic internecine feuds and a larger proportion of men in Senior Societies than any of the others, decides that Philip is a good deal too queer for even their carefully-preserved reputation for impersonal selection and they don't want the trouble of educating him up to Brooks, Frank's, and the Lawn Club Dances. Philip's Senior friends in Deke have done their best but the class has such a large number of pleasant liquorers and friendly muscular mammoths that it is like trying to gain for a singing-mouse the friendship and trust of a herd of respectable bull-elephants. Bete and Zete, Religion's Serious Call and the Sporting Life, the sacred and profane twins of College politics, trail on to the end but only to shake their heads.

Meanwhile Johnny Chipman, over whom the shadow of approaching Bones hangs even this early in the year, an amiable and portentous cloud, jams Philip into A. D. almost single-handed, because he is his friend and he believes in him. Philip recognizes effort and result, is secretly and immeasurably grateful. He had not expected to make a Junior Fraternity for another year at least. And his friendship for Johnny, that tricksy, sensitive, lovable New England Puck-Ariel, begun last winter in the *Lit.* office, has been one of those instantaneous affairs when two natures meet and combine with the sudden explosive certainty of oxygen and hydrogen in a chemical experiment. They are alike in many ways and are to have much the same paths in college— both " poets," both Chairmen of the *Lit.*—and the fellowship between them, between dreamy, snowy Vermont and dreamy, sunny California is only to age like Burgundy as the years go past.

Hold-off night, and the Sophomore dormitories tense and sweltering as air before a thunderstorm. The silent or nervously chattering fraternity men with their carnations, blossoms colored with fate, making bright spots up and down the entries and under the yellow lamplight by the Fence. The strain of the last ten minutes before seven, like the strain before the start of a crew-race that makes graduates drum on their knees with white-knuckled fingers. The breathless jokes between men who are " sure," the executioner's quiet of the doubtful. Clustered chairs and a dumb, small, anxious crowd in front of the room across the hall where Deke, Psi U and Zete are to fight it out over the modest and undecided body of the first-string quarterback. Then Battell Clock starts its clanging, casual chime—and Farnam and Durfee and Lawrence burst on the instant into a madhouse of shouts and cheers and running shapes. Philip waits in his room, no one has come for him, three minutes past, he is sweaty at the hands. Steps trample up—and past—a dark, straining figure bolts up the stairs outside his open door—there is a shriek, "Yeah! we got Bunny Vick!"—and two men with Zete carnations come rocketing down like a charge of horse, the dazed Vick between them, his hat crammed over his eyes.

Tom clears a dry throat, "You'll get it, fellah!" he says. "You'll get it!"

"Hope so. Listen—Deke's starting to go off, I think—"

He pokes his head out of the window. A broken, gasping snatch of song begins, breaks, rises to a roaring chant with the crash of rollicking feet beating out the tune.

"The *jolly* brothers of *D. K. E.* we march along—"

"Phil!" screams Tom in his ear.

He turns. A panting classmate rushes in followed by two pink-carnationed A. D. Juniors and jams a square of paper under his eyes.

"Will you accept a hold-off to Alpha Delta Phi if it is offered you?" is written on the paper.

Philip nods. "Yes," he says thickly.

His hand is shaken violently three times, nearly wrung off.

"You come with us Friday night," yells the classmate and he and the Juniors ramp away like the close of a waking dream.

The fraternities, singing loud, rock off the campus— Noise dies, against Philip's eyes night is cool and dark. Through the tatter of elm-leaves he can see three silver pricking points that must be stars . . .

Tom congratulates him gravely. Philip feels happy, enormously relieved and—let down, like a man after a strenuous ten minutes in the hot-room of a Turkish Bath.

"Come on and go to the movies, you old tin-pirate," he suggests, and they wander over the peace of the campus down Chapel Street to the Globe, to sit dopily through two hours of Bessie Barriscale and other people's breath.

The rest of the year according to Philip divided itself up into a quintuple friendship and three parties. Besides these and because of Skinny Singleton, in his own A. D. delegation, he discovered the extraordinary achievements of the *Dramat*.

Skinny Singleton, with his face like a white three-quarters moon and long humorous jaw—with the tall gesticulations and proud walk of a Gascon poet—with the fantastic visions and bitter-almonds wit, quaint speech and complete generosity of a troubadour-grandee. The light never went off all night in his room on the ground-floor of Durfee, and at any time from one to

four in the morning Philip could go over and be sure
of finding him there, drawing pictures for the *Record,*
designing scenery for the *Dramat,* writing wild short
stories for the *Lit.,* putting his own or other people's
roommates safely and drunkenly to bed. Together they
made the *Record,* ate ripe olives and drank May wine
at Mory's reciting impromptu odes the while; and forced
an unfortunate candidate for A. D. to appear cowering
and green-ribboned before the Dean, a copy of the
"Rules and Regulations of Yale College" in his hand,
and explain to that white-haired Majesty that he, the
candidate, had read the proffered little pamphlet with
such keen critical enjoyment that he must really ask its
official author to autograph a copy. That the jest nearly
brought about the excision of themselves from A. D.
and A. D. from Yale did not greatly perturb, in the
end, either Skinny or Philip.

They also devised a new and malicious pastime—
whenever bound for a silly adventure they would first
meet by careful appointment in some other man's room,
preferably that of a mutual foe or a total stranger,
which would lead to scenes like the following.

*(Bill Arbroath's room. Solid Bill, a prominent and
respected "soul saver" and four serious-minded
friends are doping out a Bones list in peace and quiet.)*
Bill (oracular): Stan Ballard, *sure.* That makes
eleven.
Bob Meredith (a chorus): Why not Keys?
Bill: Wouldn't take it on a glass dish—he's sore at
the crowd that are going. Who'll be twelfth?

Ted Van Sicklen: (Once voted, " the boy who had done most for his prep. school"—and he has never gotten over it.) " What about yourself, Bill? "

Bill (without a smile): " First substitute Ted. I'll never get it." *(He is probably the surest election in the class—and knows it. Murmurs of " Sure you will," " Wish I had your chance," and " Safe as a church.")*

Ted: " How about Sellaby? "

Bill (ponderous): Drinks. Too flighty. *(Knock at the door.)*

Bill: Come in! *(Enter Philip, jauntily.)*

Philip: Hello, Bill! Hello, Ted, Bob, Bunny, Stu!

All (rather sulkily): 'Lo, Phil!

Philip (stretching out on the most comfortable part of the windowseat): Skinny Singleton been around here?

Bill: He lives over in Durfee, doesn't he, Phil? Ground floor, entry next Chapel.

Philip (impassive): Sure. Said he'd meet me over here, though. *(This seems a little startling, but Philip is blandly casual.)*

Philip: Mind if I wait for him, Bill?

Bill (Christian to lion): Oh, no! *(A stiff silence.)*

Philip: Sorry to bust up the party. What were you people doing, anyway—packing Bones? *(Everybody in the room gives a slight, nervous jump. Bill looks as if he had just seen the family banshee.)*

Philip (his chance shot having hit between wind and water): Why, Bill! And a whole long year ahead of time, too!

Bill (bluff, but viciously embarrassed): Kid's trick, I know. We were just making out a list—

Philip (plaintive): A list? Bill! Was I on it, Bill?

Bill (worse): We were just, just—just coming to you—

Philip: Must have gone pretty far down on the list, Bill.

Bill (absolutely up in the air): Oh, I think, we all think, you've got a good chance, Phil, a peach of a—

Philip (nipping him off expertly): Thanks so much. *(Tableau. Bill speechless. The door slams open. Skinny, late by prearrangement, enters scoffing and careless.)*

Skinny: Hello, boys. Phil Sellaby here? *(seeing him.)* Am I late, Phil?

Philip: Only about twenty minutes. What were you doing—praying?

Skinny: Had an official appointment, Moon-face my pet, the Bursar wanted me to call on him. Coming along?

Philip (rising slowly): Sure. But what do you think I found these innocent people up to, Skinny?

Skinny: You don't mean they've had Louise here again? Or Peggy? or Olive? *(A flush settles pinkly on Bill and two of his child crusaders.)*

Philip: Oh, no—no—none of that mere viciousness.

Singleton: They were doping a Bones list for the class. Our children!

Skinny: We ought to take it away from them. *(The others gape angrily but are dumb.)*

Philip: We will. We'll come back for it. Where we going—the Bije?

Skinny: Poli's. There's a Diving Beauties Act. " Rabbit " Winston's seen it four times.

Philip: All right—on your way! *(Exeunt arm in arm. The martyrs relax and look at each other. A second later the door flies back again with a crash.)*

Philip: Anybody want to go to the movies? Bill? Teddy? Bob? Bill? Oh, Bill? *(The door slams shut before any answer can be given. Steps trip down the hall.)*

Bill (with a long breath, heartfelt): Je-sus Christ!

It was Reggy Evans' and John Castine's room in the first blind blackness of winter evening, when the college is trooping back through Yale Station after hasty dinner at Commons or the College Street " joints." Philip and John were talking in front of a three-stick fire. Having all Freshman year regarded each other from afar with no words but with perfect recognition and hate as probable rivals and certain enemies, they had now worked round to the surprising status of complete and intimate friends. Philip had heard of John as " one of those snotty St. Markers—acts like a personal pal of John the Baptist "; sat above his window in Wright on Tap Day and taken an instant dislike to everything about him from his pink face and tortoise shell glasses to the sad droop of his roommate's mouth. A little later in the year Seth Stevens, who roomed across the hall from John, had come up and solemnly congratulated the latter on his future Chairmanship

of the *Lit*. " Thanks awfully, Seth—but why? " John
answered, somewhat puzzled, " I'm six contributions behind Phil Sellaby in the comp., you know." " Why? "
Seth retorted. " That's why! My Lord, John, I've
just seen Sellaby! "

But Philip and John had made up the unspoken
quarrel over a bonus quart of Great Western champagne
in the *Record* office, and begun a diffident acquaintance-
ship that had strengthened rapidly. They supplemented
each other like cheese and crackers (" Yes," said John,
when the simile was propounded, " fire-crackers and rat-
trap cheese! ")—viewed the painfully indefinite whirl of
existence from much the same rather humorous, rather
arrogant intellectual critical angle—and knew each
other's virtues and faults like Renaissance swordsmen.
A word-and-a-half from either could make the other
complete the thought that never had to be wholly uttered, and fling back comprehensive understanding. " I
think, on the whole, Phil, we do each other good," was
John's verdict after five years of it; and the characteristically mild and difficultly spoken sentence went to roots
and memories in both that made back-slapping and
loose confidences seem meager.

Philip runs down the last typewritten page of a manuscript, tosses it back.

" Well—what do you think? " from John.

" I like it. I think it's clever as hell. As I get it,
it's all about a shy, hypocritical young man in a very
embarrassing situation—a part both of us ought to know
pretty well by heart."

" Think the *Dramat* would do it? "

" Don't know. Show it to Skinny—he'll be amused."

" I will. Fire's nice, isn't it? "

" Um. See any pictures in it, Editha, my child? "

" George Warren frying in hell." He pokes his foot
at a bulky, frizzling chip.

" Here, here, mustn't be so violent. He's a brother
of mine."

" Well, he isn't of mine anyway, thank the Lord! If
he ever does fry, I bet he hogs the biggest and most
prominent flame." He starts to hum, " Oh, I haven't
the *News* to go Deke, I haven't the car to go Zete—"
" Psi U and A. D. mean nothing to me—" Philip lends
a vacillating tenor to the air.

A voice from without. " *Oh,* John Castine! "

Neither moves. " That you, Dick? " John shouts in
return. " Come on in and bicker."

Dick Sheldon, temperamental as a débutante, easily
hurt and pleased as a child and demanding and getting
a child's unreasoning devotion from his intimates,
slumps in and flings himself heavily in the Morris-chair.

" Christ—I feel low! " is his greeting.

" What's matter, Dicky? "

" Oh, nothing—everything. Nothing *you* people
would understand." He sinks into a pose that suggests
Niobe. " Give me a cigarette." Rejecting John's proffered paper-package indignantly. " A *good* cigarette,
you Shylock. You've got some, Phil, I saw you take
them out of your pocket a minute ago." He selects
three with care, pockets two, lights the other and seems
revived. " Where's the sullen Evans, O angular Castine and frog-eyed Sellaby? "

"Going to wait for us up at Mory's." This is from Phil.

Dick is as pleased as an infant with something new and shiny.

"Oh, we're going to Mory's? We're going to have a party? A nice party and sing Christmas carols just as I said we would?"

"Are we?" John's accent is intentionally snarkish.

"Oh, God, I wasn't talking to you, Castine. Everybody knows what a grinning, stupid, rosy-faced Cheshire Cat you've made of yourself ever since you went Psi U and got a chance to suck around Stan Clark and Bill Arbroath all day long! Are we, Phil?"

"I guess so, Dick—as soon as the crowd's cleared out and Steve comes."

"Oh, if you don't want me. You weren't like this last year though, Sellaby, my footless friend. This god-damn Junior Fraternity system makes you all think you're little Sèvres gods on ebony tables. I'm not coming." And, purring over his soul-satisfying climax, Dick relapses into a grandiose fit of sulks.

Steve Brackett, plump and smiling, round as a beaver, with the cherub's bow mouth of a Love or a pleased small boy, appears, dressed as ever in the most impeccable clothes in college.

"Hello, Steve!" from Philip and John, and "Hello, you potty little fool, when are you going to get me into Deke?" from Dick, over his shoulder.

"Well, well, well," chuckles Steve in the deep cracked voice of a genial bittern. "When's the party going to start—and what have you people been doing?"

"Making nasty remarks to me." But that is Dick, and nobody pays attention.

"Half an hour or so, round man. Come in and play hearts—Reggy's tutoring, he'll meet us up at Mory's."

"All right. Just one minute while I light a cigar." He examines John's apparel with searching eyes. "My Lord, Castine, when are you going to get another tie? That's the same string tie your grandmother gave you when you first went to St. Mark's—and the Castine finances must have been scraping the bottom right then, because it looks as if it had been part of the family quilt or your great-grandfather's flowered shirt. If I *buy* you a decent tie, Castine, will you *wear* it? I can't lose my social position with Rosy the cleaner by going around much longer with people dressed like you."

"Let me pick it out and you pay for it." John is unruffled and, "If you buy him a tie you've got to buy me one too," from Dick, who is trying hard to combine injured dignity with avid interest in the conversation.

"You'll pick the most expensive one you can find, and it'll probably have magenta bolts-of-lightning all over it. Oh, all right, all right—I've been ruined all my life by my friends' riding gravy, but I'm going to get you dressed up so you look like a candidate for Keys, Castine, if I have to sell the eating-joint to do it. You'll be able to walk through the Biltmore lobby without having girls turn round and ask who that poor boy is who's collecting for the Salvation Army, when I get through with you. Hearts? Very well. I never won a game of hearts in my life."

The three of them play for ten minutes before Dick
consents to be included. John then succeeds in sticking him with most of the high hearts in the pack for
three hands running and he overturns the table and
throws the cards at the fire. There is a general scuffle
that only succeeds in breaking the one whole electric
light bulb in the room. They go out, Dick linking arms
between Steve and John.

"You people are so nice to me it makes me feel like
a bum," he announces inconsequentially as they march
up Elm Street. "What makes you all so darn nice,
anyway?"

"Just our natural sweet natures," John suggests,
to which Dick replies characteristically, trying to trip
him, "Great Bill Arbroath, Castine, you know blessed
well I wouldn't stand your God-damned snottiness from
anybody else but you!"

At Mory's they find Reggy Evans, vacantly studying
back numbers of the *Lit*. Everybody orders milk-
punches. They start to sing. Snow taps and feathers
on the frosty windows of that shut-in room full of warm
yellow lights and voices. "Frankie and Johnny" gives
place to "Jolly Boating Weather" and that to "Venite
Adoremus," in shaky Latin for the benefit of Bill, the
steward. More drinks wander in and are consumed. A
bland glow like the touch of summer sunlight flows in
upon and gentles the mind. The tunes rise and float
in the air like great radiant bubbles—voices carry them
easily now, a proud, bright load.

> "*Good King Wenceslas looked out*
> *On the feast of Stephen—*"

And even the cold hush of graying dark into which they are ushered when the doors of Mory's close and the whole sky seems to be collapsing from heaven in an infinite falling of minute and hurried flakes does not touch the released calm flame of their chanting comradeship. It is something whole as a golden orb, as a golden planet; something youthful and vividly careless, frail, poignant and without name. . . . They recite Ariel's lullaby to the Campus policeman; and so vocally home to the deep sleep of happy blasphemers.

There was also the Eton-Harrow banquet on prep-school Alumni Day with the College largely deserted by most conscientious or moneyed prep-school men. It began by John and Reggy discovering that they had both been to Eton with Lord Kitchener and Queen Victoria, and Skinny Singleton and Philip forming a Rugby contingent strong on "bloodys" and reading aloud to each other in the pause between drinks and drinks the more righteously British passages of "Tom Brown," while Dick, a bitter minority, defended the fame of "grand old Harrow" with amazing wit, vigor and profane invention. It ended in a solo Bacchante dance by Steve, which he insisted was called "Bouncing the Butterfly" . . . a Virginia reel joined by three over-loaded Sheff men and a local judge . . . the crowning of a scandalized waiter as Alfred Lord Tennyson, Queen of the May . . .

And then there was spring hold-off night, when Philip, for the first time in his life, got thoroughly drunk. He had been out with Skinny Singleton in the hour between

six and seven, discussing the Grand Style in Writing
over double Bronxes in the cool leather-lined cavern of
the Taft Bar and the discussion had reached the " What
I mean is gra-grand—grand, y' understand? " stage
when it was time for both to return to the rooms they
were guarding. Both watched the proceedings through
a jocund fog and adjourned to Mory's and as much as
they were able to poach of the various fraternity green-
cups. Steve has gone Deke, and they congratulate
him with reservations. Mory's is packed and turbulent
with the warring crowds and songs of three fraternities.
Philip drinks steadily and of anything that comes handy,
and begins to feel his mind expand like a blown-out paper snake—expand and at the same time grow uncannily,
unearthly clear.

Physically, he is seventeen yards tall, he could break
a varsity tackle between finger and thumb. A vast pity
—the pity of the broken-hearted ancient gods—falls on
him like a silver mist, for all this shuffling riot of
humanity that swarms about him. He treads like a
god on shoes covered with wings over the crystal wreck-
age and crumbling jeweled shards of disintegrated
worlds. Stafford Vane, king of Deke and his pet ab-
horrence, puts affectionate arms and a weeping face
on his shoulder. He is filled on the instant with immense and nameless pride. " Staff'd's not all right,
but *I'm* all right—*Staff'd's* not all right, BUT *I'm* all
right! " juggles through his head like the ring of the
Marseillaise. " *I'll* give you speech! " he shouts,
clambering a table. " Good speech. Fine speech. All
'bout how A. D. cleaned up on Deke! . . ."

Suddenly, he is out on the street, reclined on the steps of the Zete tomb . . .

That passes in a phantasmagoric flicker. He is ascending stairs, intolerable, unending stairs.

They are the stairs inside the U-Club. A boiling crowd of Zetes, Psi U's and Dekes greet him with affectionate whoops. Somebody gives him an open quart bottle of champagne. Somebody else pulls his chair out from under him. He gets up with a vague lust for indefinite blood but every one has started to march around the billiard table singing, " We'll drink, drink, drink, drink, drink, drink, drink to the Eta," and he joins the distorted procession with eyes that make every color screamingly bright and hands and feet that seem six miles off from his body. " 'S this is a merry-go-round? " he asks uncertainly. " Where's the horses? Where's brass rings? "

Somebody starts throwing pool-balls . . .

There is a great ocean of voices talking somewhere far outside of him. He listens, bends his will like a spring and reduces the voices into words.

One, faint as a gnat's, is shouting, " Hey, Steve! Hey, Billy! Come out here. There's a man outside your door that can't speak and doesn't know his own name! "

" 'S absurd! Name's Alg'non Swin Swinburne. Grea' poet! " murmurs Philip.

The last memory is that of being inserted, pajamaless into a bed.

" Put p'jamas over me," he explains. " On top. Useful. Warm. Ant'septic. D'corative."

Steve's face rises over him like a moon.

"So drunk," it says. "*So* drunk. And such a good time!"

GROWING PAINS—I

(SUMMER OF 1914)

SEA-VERSE

LIFE is a dream, yo ho, yo ho! Life is a dream, yo ho!

The boat slides through the blue, chucking water like a sled over slippery grass. The bright water sparks and dances under the kicking heels of the bright breeze.

The tan sail slats—we are nearly across Muchacha Straits. Sitting at the tiller with the whole live boat under my hand, I am as much a part of the sea as if I were a Triton.

When the rainy season starts there will be dish-water days enough to be gloomy in. But who cares now if we bump a rock or a mermaid? Who'd be sorry to drown in such jewels of reckless water? Who gives a damn, while Life is a dream, yo ho?

LAND-VERSE

Riding a loping horse, I chase the white snake into the West. The red, huge sun sees me coming and flings arrow after burning arrow.

The hoofs of my horse go trample on the white snake's hide, but still his coil laps miles and miles ahead of me and when I turn in the saddle and look back, he is suddenly crawling the other way, miles on lapping miles behind.

He is not to be caught, that serpent of a road, though I drum on his scales forever he keeps just as far aloof and away. If I caught him there'd be no more pride in riding. And my horse lopes and I ride and ride and ride.

ANTS

Near the tennis-court there is a city of ants. Four holes in the red earth and four little red dusty mounds. Underneath it must be as full of tunnels as Chinatown.

Three ants are grappling a eucalyptus-nut, dragging the mountainous thing along by their pen-scratch legs. It fell that time and one of them was hurt. He's got up again. What strong ants!

Ants scurry like business-men around the little mounds. They dive into the ground all of a sudden— hurrying to catch a train!

They seem to be having a wonderful time. I think I'll play God and knock down the city.

TOWN

Four cheap saloons to a corner and a church with a spire like a skewed top-hat. A scattering of baked brown little houses, as carelessly scrambled together as thrown dice, choke slowly in the dust of the white road. The New Palace Hotel has two stories but already the paint is scabbing from its walls.

Smell of acid, rosin and leather from the tannery. Smell of sour wine and dregs from the saloons. Smell of stuffy rep pew-cushions and cracked hymnals from the church, but nobody ever goes there, of course.

Old men warm chairs on the hotel porch, buzzing together like drowsy flies. They tell about the time San Esteban was the capital. And San Esteban sleeps in front of them like a mummy. It hasn't been alive for forty years.

Down on the broken wharves—there's where any soul it has is, maybe. A gray rat scuttling by weedy timbers scared of the quiet, little, and sick and old. A rat gray as ashes, hunched in the blinding sunlight, thinking about the time it used to sail round on ships.

HILLS

This is a country of hills—where earth has been left alone here, there is nothing anywhere at all but great brown rolling hills. Smooth wave after mountainous wave of ocean between one billow and the next billow of this tossing and eternal sea of land.

One hill is exactly like the next hill. There is no more difference between them than between two big turtles sleeping on a beach. And their backs are rounded and huge as the tortoise that holds up the weight of the world.

A blue patch of alfalfa in the short spring when the rains stop. An orange slash of poppies, with their perfume, acrid and dark, scattered like incense-grains on the coals of the censer of July. Scrub-oak, those sentinel trees wind hates and wrenches at. Here and there a lonely giant of a eucalyptus, stretching stripped long arms into the sky.

Color enough, you'd say—but it all fades into one among the hills, the color of drought and burning. He must have been young—not more than ten æons old—Whoever made them, to make so many and so alike and all at once.

GROWING PAINS—II

OF all that summer—and Philip took Steve Brackett home with him for a six weeks' dash through the Yosemite—it is a little figure of Sylvia alone that Philip brings back to New Haven inside his memory. It came thus, for instance, on a blazing morning in August.

" Game — set — match — tournament — oh, damn ! " Sylvia shakes hands over the net. " Wait till next time, Phil, and I'll try and show you up ! "

" You could do it all right if you could smash better." Philip is frankly pleased. Sylvia was ranked 14 in the state last year. " Those lobs of mine were dirty, that was all—and you got the second set on me as it was."

"I know, but I wanted to *beat* you!" She scuffles her sneakers half-angrily in the dirt. Philip looks down on her from an advantage of four inches and notes dispassionately that no matter how hot Syl gets, she never becomes either scarlet-faced or trickly, those two fatal stigmata of the average " athletic girl." They drop on a bench to cool off, each chewing the stalk of a eucalyptus leaf with ruminant calm and kicking idle heels in the dust. Philip looks at Sylvia and wonders if he is in love with her. He doesn't think so, quite, but is not too sure. He wants to kiss her very much, kiss her all over. The heady heat of noon envelops them languidly. Unconsciously they sway toward each other like tired animals, closer, almost touching now, p-e-r-h-a-p-s—

Then the queer pulsing moment, sudden and sleepy-sweet, as suddenly passes. Sylvia jumps up with a little shiver of her body and gets ten yards start on Philip as they race to the house.

Or again, Philip is reading his poetry to her under the tulip-tree. Her hair has discreetly come down—it is hot, and the coiled mass uncomfortable—and Philip, trying to find similes for her, thinks she looks half Alice-in-Wonderland little girl and half restless Atalanta with the hunt in her eyes. He pauses at the end of a sonnet, expecting appreciation.

"You know, Phil," she says suddenly instead, " I think a girl in society has a pretty rotten time these days, by and large."

" You don't seem to—from what I've seen of you."
He grunts peevishly. She is generally sympathetic.

" Oh, going around to parties and things—that's nice,
but I don't know. And all these boys—where does it
get you? "

" Gets you married, Syl." Philip is practical.

" I know, but I don't want to get married."

" How about your friend George Carpenter? "

" He's sweet, but I couldn't marry him—we'd start
breaking crockery in two weeks. I don't know anybody
I could marry that I'd want to."

" Hen Bristol? "

" And end up with three cocktails before tea every
day at the Palace? Not for this child. He'd like me
painted like a new Rolls-Royce."

" Oh, well, you'll find somebody. Prince of Wales,
Guynemer." Philip wants to get back to his sonnets.

" Phil, what makes you so suddenly sympathetic?
I'm going to sleep—you're a snob—you don't care for
anything in the world but your own rotten poetry."

She turns her shoulder, more little-girl than ever.
He goes on reading.

" JUNIOR YEAR WE TAKE OUR EASE—"

(1914-1915)

JUNIOR YEAR. Philip's pictures grow foggier and
fewer. Life rolled on, sleek, smooth and thoughtless,
like the life of a contented goldfish inside its bowl. A

sparkling life, a fertile life, a swift life, but a life more leveled plain without crests or dips than Philip had yet experienced. The war came, watched by Philip and most of his class with the fascinated interest of spectators before a burning house, but its cloud was as yet no bigger than one's personal convictions. Men took sides, ally or German, some from reason but more from the fun of taking sides, a fun comparable to that of backing the Cubs against the Giants. A handful left for ambulance service, two or three to join various armies— to the others no warning came at all that each casual step taken was on earthquake-ground.

Philip got together a book of poems, sent it to publishers and collected their printed rejection-slips to frame when he was famous. He worried through an abominable winter, smothered in snow, with a steady cold from Christmas to Easter that left him a legacy of persistent small coughs.

> "Oh, I'll be a lunger yet,
> I'll be a lunger yet!"

he would chant to Dick's amusement and his own bronchial disgust on January mornings as he came in from the icy mile-walk to and from the Physics Laboratory. He was repeating Freshman physics for the second time to the acute dismay of that worthy Department, for he could not pass the course and would not drop it, and so was hardly an encouraging influence on Freshmen getting their first taste of science.

Dick and he had spacious apartments in Fayerweather now, on the sunny side of the brick horseshoe of Berke-

ley Oval, and John and Reggy roomed across the hall.
Hence the four combined choice furniture, books and
best pictures and rehabilitated John's and Reggy's bare
chamber into an Official Reception Room or New Crystal
Palace (" to be frequented when the lighter diversions
of life are sought," explained Dick lucidly) while Dick's
and Philip's quarters are turned into a Library, Study,
Open Air Sleeping Porch (" complete ventilation
through all four walls ") and general den of iniquity.
But the people on the floor below usually spoke of it as
" Murderers' Row " and swore when the plaster-dust
started shaking down from their ceilings in the daily
scrimmages between Reggy and Dick. The two had
learned piquet together out of a tattered Hoyle and
played daily for vast sums which neither ever thought
of paying. " I don't mind your cheating at cards,
Reggy," Dick would say, after being piqued twice in
three deals, " but for God's sake don't cheat so like a
plumber! " and the fight would begin to the pianissimo
accompaniment of John's bitter wail that, after all, it
was *his* furniture they were breaking.

Winter and spring brought the five very close together. Friendship is as hard to define as the definite
article—it should be enough to say that these five were
unhesitating friends. Each gave as he could and as
much as he could to the mutual fellowship and the
clash of mind on mind. It was not an association that
found little watch charms and an elaborate club-ritual
necessary to ensure its permanence.

John's mocking mind, Reggy's perfect independence,
Steve's open-handed laughter (though he could be as

amusingly sour as a good crab-apple), the essential
mirth and affection that was Dick—Philip took from all
of these and felt nourished completely, as a piece of
grass is nourished by sun and rain. They had that feeling that together they could probably become lion-
tamers, great dramatists, or Mongol Emperors—that is
the enchanted inheritance of such a combination. As
for Philip and Dick, they only squabbled twice in two
years of rooming together and Philip learned to love
him as a brother, enjoy his flashing varying moods like
Shaw high comedy, and try and keep him from casually
insulting people too stupid to understand him, with the
patience and persistence of a favorite aunt. And of
these tasks the first two were much the simplest, for
Dick who had from his christening the rare qualities of
affection and heart of a jolly boy, could on occasion
make use of these qualities to the wild annoyance of
the young-old "unco guid." So the year paced past its
monthly mile-posts with the smooth devouring rush of a
speeding car.

Yet in many ways, besides the friendly, the nine
months were devoutly educational for Philip. His
courses were mainly voluntary—four of them under
first-class teachers—Billy Phelps, the most gracious
and attractive of all the literary traditions of Yale—
Stanley Cathcart, that acrid, eccentric genius with a
mind that had the illuminated solidity and continuous
fluctuating brilliance of a fire-opal—a professor of
paleontology who made the dinosaur as familiar a beast
as the camel and showed the solid crust of the earth
with its eternal hills flowing and melting like a wave

in the vast empty spaces of geologic time—an assistant professor of history with an eye for the purple and scarlet of kings and queens. Besides these Philip read continuously and haunted the library stacks, discovering a burrow in the section devoted to the Great Rolls of the Pipe where nothing else ever came but dust, and *Record* verse could be composed and such things as the Bible, Taylor's "Mediæval Mind" and the more risqué productions of Gyp consumed without ribald question or interference. His reading ranged through some desiccated Hegel to Gilbert Murray's translations of Euripides and back again through Wilfred Scawen Blunt and Paul Fort to the Catholic novels of Robert Hugh Benson and that astonishing sexual raree-show, "The Rainbow," by D. H. Lawrence. Much of what he read seemed unassimilated and indigestible at the time—but it worked inside his mind, eroded, built up, made deltas and straits and islands, pushed back the cloud from undiscovered continents. He felt growth, though exactly where or how he could not say—the sensation he recognized but neither its direction nor its cause. But there slowly evolved out of fog and the wreck of broken ideas and old prejudices a sort of informal synthesis of what he felt about Art (big A or small) and his own or any writer's or painter's place in the service of it. And this synthesis was infinitely aided by the casual long talks about everything for the moral surrender involved in "necking" to the benefits of an absolute despotism as a system of government that came between the five companions—an interchange in which each benefited tremendously by having his own most cherished delu-

sions and towers of ivory logically and swiftly abolished
by combined attack. In other words, Philip was bursting out of his mental clothes all year, like an eight-year-
old boy who has been compressed into six-year-old
trousers. To parallel him with the molting snake,
June saw two cast skins crumpled and left behind. One
was labeled " L'Art pour l'Art " and the other " Inspiration is Perspiration " and the both of them he now
regarded with immense distaste.

He wrote little—that spring had run suddenly dry.
As for painting, he had not tried to paint in oils for a
year. In spite of which occurrences he existed and was
very happy, though he had to fight torturing doubts now
and then as to whether either craft would ever return
to him. He felt that both would in their own impera-
tive time—that this year was preparation—lying fal-
low. But the feeling was so strong and reasonless it
almost amounted to a personal superstition, and he
laughed at both fear and confidence in ordinary moods.

In the social and hospitable life of New Haven he
took mild part. He went to the various dances, and
discovered the insolent pleasure of walking back across
the Campus from the Taft or the Lawn Club in full
dress and broad daylight, just as startled Freshmen
were trooping across to Chapel and honest working men
arriving late to their jobs. And for calls and so forth,
he and John worked out a nefarious system, which
entailed rather cautious planning but brought perfect
results. Over as large a tea as possible at the Elizabethan Club, they would lay their plots of a Sunday
afternoon.

"We really ought to call on the Stoddards," John would declare—the two had a rule of hunting in couples. "They gave us a very nice dinner three weeks ago, you know, and we haven't been there since."

"All right, Stoddards first," from Philip, his mouth full of toast. "Do they tea you well?"

"Fair-ly." John was dubious. "Wafers and saltines —they used to run as far as lettuce sandwiches, but I've seen them when they went down to the crackers you get out of a barrel." His face brightens. "But they have those marvelous Persian cigarettes. Must be fruity with opium at the least, smoke two and you're off in a sort of Oriental haze for the rest of the day."

"Better take them as soon as possible then—we needn't stay long. I've got to call at the Verraynes'."

"Don't know the Verraynes."

"Come along anyway—they'll like you and they have crumpets and English jam."

"All right, but God knows it'll be a surprise for them. I got introduced to Mr. Verrayne once by mistake for my brother and he's cut me dead on the street ever since. Don't know what he has against Henry, but I wish he wouldn't take it out on me! Still— crumpets you said? It's worth trying."

"Good scout. We can't get away from there before half-past five, though. Question is—can we rush a call on the Fleetings in after the other two?"

"Doubt it. They'll think we're making a bid to stay to supper."

"So we will be—what of it?"

"Well, it isn't too damn Machiavellian, that's all."

"Well, we're only innocent Juniors—don't know what time they feed. Besides, they're tight with their suppers. I stayed there till half-past six once, looking starveder and starveder all the time, and all I got was an invitation to subscribe to the Suffering Armenians. We might look in."

"Well, if we have time."

"I'll fix it. The old signals—when I cough three times in succession you start working up to that nice little good-by speech we doped out together."

"C'est bien. I'll remember. Come on. 'For Duty, Duty, must be done—'"

"The rule applies—"

"To every one. And painful though the duty be—"

And the two tea-pirates depart, knowing there will be no need to pay for supper that Sunday evening.

Yet in spite of such harmless buccaneering, there were houses where they went by choice and where the food, if there happened to be food, was merely a pleasant accessory—houses like the Argiers' and the Vawtreys', the de Sessas' and the Harry Winchelseas'. Nights at the Winchelseas' with Dick stay in the recollection like the bouquet of century port, nights where the random, skeptic talk ran nosing like a foxhound through the arts and the ages, white nights, nights hoarded like a sheaf of silver arrows . . . Other nights, too, a night at the brass-band glitter of Savin Rock, where they rode and rode on the roller-coaster and introduced themselves to its proprietor as Russian ambassadors when he came to see if they had gone suddenly insane . . . A night on the desolate beaches beyond Momaguin, after three rum-sours apiece, when they watched the pearl, pale evening lie like milk upon the water, lit a fire and cooked burnt chops under a warm vast cave of darkness pollened with stars . . . Clear nights, nights ardent and unforgettable, nights, soft with lilac, dyed white and ruddy with wine . . .

Externally and internally as well, Junior Year was, for Philip, extremely successful. He was elected Chairman of the *Lit.* and Art Editor of the *Record.* John Castine held the Chairmanship of the latter and both he and Skinny Singleton were on Philip's *Lit.* Board— an interlocking directorate all three viewed with some amusement. On Tap Day Philip promptly went to Wolf's Head with Reggy, Steve and John—thus breaking a tradition as old as the *Lit.* itself, that its chairman went to Skull and Bones or nowhere—and for once in his life felt completely content with one of his own decisions. Keys he had never considered, and Keys had repaid the compliment. The Tap Day was uneventful, and as Philip was lucky enough to be tapped in the first five minutes he had no chance at all to feel the shivering white tenseness that comes toward a quarter of six and the end of the lists. Two things in the day's proceedings he never forgot—the smack of Sam Austin's hand between his shoulders and the cheers of the class as each man left the Campus. Skinny Singleton went Keys, twelfth man, Bill Arbroath and Bob Meredith Bones. Then came the initiations. And over what Philip said or did or had done to him when he finally passed through the spike-topped *chevaux-de-frise* that guards the mysterious building on Prospect and Trumbull Streets, a veil of perfect secrecy will be drawn.

END OF A CYCLE

(SUMMER OF 1915)

EXTRACT OF LETTER FROM PHILIP SELLABY, SAN ESTEBAN, CALIFORNIA, TO JOHN CASTINE, WESTBORO, MASS.

BUT I still don't get what we're going to do when we leave College, John. Pimping, you suggest—but they probably have a Union now and make you Do It Efficiently according to the latest uplift books and the Taylor System. I write poems and paint pretty pictures—at least I used to and I suppose I will again— you are all around clever at various things—but, Isaac, where's the percentage in it all? I'll be damned if I'll starve. I'll be blessed if I live on my father: (a) I don't want to, (b) He wouldn't let me if I did; and you don't seem to have developed a very healthy private income yet either. All the pure push in painting or poetry appear either to have had large personal fortunes, died in the gutter, or sponged on their friends and relatives. I've just been reading Stevenson's letters, and I must say they ain't too brutally encouraging— " a circle of hell unknown to Dante—that of the penniless and dying author "—and R. L. S. was six or seven years older than either of us then.

Also, I suppose the Marriage Question arises some-time and Bringing Tender Little Lives to Roost on the Cold, Cold World. Any lives I thus en-couraged any time in the near future would have to Scratch Dirt or Pass Out, as I see it. Ah, what the hell, kid; is Fate going to put us away in the first round as easily as all that? Not a chance! But how not?

Added to this, I can't do a lick of work—my tennis is as soft as a spoiled peach—and I am holding my breath to keep from falling in love with that Sylvia Persent I've told you so often about. Good Lord, she's a lovely, companionable person! *(Three lines of words x-ed over by the typewriter.)*

Don't you wish you knew what *that* was?

My vacant ideas on Art. You have to give your life, lungs, liver, lights and everything else to it. You can't "write down" or "paint down" without taking the fine edge off your mind—that is, if you keep on doing it. The grand manner forever, and the flat of your palm and the sole of your foot to the too-clever, the George Moores and the just pretty writers. A small income, a violent mind, marriage or its substitute (the latter helpful but can be dispensed with) are what is needed. Selah.

My best to Steve—how is the fat little boy? Why can't you both come out here for the start of September and drive back in my uncle's car if I can borrow it? This is serious—let me know right away if you can.

Must quit. My best to you and Steve, something

else to P—, T— and A— and kick T— under the ear
if you see him. Write me.

As ever,

PHILIP.

P. S. Summer here—miraculous. No cough—everything lovely. I send some vagrant bits of spotty prose—
all I've done in two months except lie flat on the grass
under a pomegranate tree and thumb my nose at the
Presbyterian gods. On the crest, really, John, on the
crest!

(Enclosed in the Letter)

CITY DANCE

The eight nigger musicians make a curdled sound
with horns and drums and glass. The tortuous music
is impatient—it frets like a spoiled child that knows
too much, for every one to go out and dance to it. *"Got
to dance—got to dance—got to dance"*—that's the hurry
it puts into your feet.

Margaret's in black with jade earrings. May I cut
in? Don't have to talk to her, thank God. You can
get drunk dancing with her though.

What does she think about, anyway? Has she any
mind or insides or thoughts, that mask-on-a-husk of a
person opposite that I don't know and never will know,
except that she's warm and our bodies like each other.
Would anything last of her if she died now, or would

she just stay dry and rattling like the shelled pod of a pea? If I asked her, she'd think I was drunk or crazy.

"Waaah!" goes the peevish saxophone. "*Got to dance with somebody else—Got to dance—*"

COUNTRY DANCE

Girls in bunchy white with hair-ribbons and powder over their sunburn. Boys in blue serge suits with the pockets cut like cheese-rinds—faces shiny with soap and rubbing, and their hair slicked back with tonic. Purple and yellow paper festooned all over Odd Fellows Hall.

They waltz around sweatily awhile to the tunes people whistled five years ago. They spill pink lemonade on the floor, and the smart boys cut up rancidly, and the girls giggle and slap them.

Then they start the "Portuguese Jig" and the bare, scrubbed boards rock and shiver. The fiddle sings honey out of its strings, and the boards are the deck of a ship somehow—of a galleon tossing wild in blue water— and it reels like a house in an earthquake to the shaking dance of glimmery sea-girls with coral and clear pearl-shells for their side-combs and burnt sailors with bright guineas at their ears.

THE THOUGHT

Dawn, wan Dawn, naked silver girl with a young child's breasts, blow the yellow scent of the trumpet-

honeysuckle over Philip's mouth as he turns in his
sleep; dust upon his lips the stinging fertile pollen,
borne by the bee gone drunken to his hive!

Day, radiant Day, flame-footed runner, beat upon the
heart that sobs beneath your treading, heat and troubling
dreams of a dumb, stark rapture, mist and aching
hunger that moans and cries aloud!

Night, black Archer, take an arrow from your quiver,
poison it with sweetness that his parched mouth thirsts
for; ring the starry clang of the loosed, belling bowstring; run him through and through with a barbed
and golden thought.

THE WISH

When the fog of sleep rolled thick with spume, and a
vacant mist hung low between sleeping and waking, I
looked in the face of a dream and shuddered and was
afraid.

Dreams melt in a single instant, they grow tiny like
a dead man's voice and pass—but this dream had white
hands and would not vanish. I held her. There was
the perfume of her in her hair.

It is not meant to dream so. It is not right to think
and bleed for a visioned mouth whose kissing is like
grapes. It is not just that air and earth and water
should be hurt flame and sand and a starved wind ghost-

ing, because of what I have seen in the deep eyes of a
dream.

The Fever

Sometimes the thing is only fantastic—the street parade of a circus, reeling through the mind in color and
noise and dust. Clowns and healthy animals laughing
and happy and bawdy. Best to take it that way and
not worry any more than dogs.

And then, wanderingly, quick breathless perfection
—careless humming pride as if there were wings on
your arms—Beauty stooping suddenly and yours, yours,
like the face of a star seen close.

But, in brief and mourning eve-lights I have seen it,
too, and then been sick with horror. I have seen it like
the smoke of burnt flesh cloud and cover every planet
in the heavens. I have seen it brood and furl all the
universe in the black dead pinions of a bat.

BOOK III

"FRANKIE AND JOHNNY
WERE LOVERS"

SUNG IN A SUMMER GARDEN

Bitter December broke the ground!
The plow, ho! the plow, ho!
He clove it in two with a clanging sound.
Oxen tug at the plow!
It crackled like steel at his horses' stir,
He beat the snowstorm out of his fur,
The least of his wear was miniver.
Plow you stubbornly now!

February the monk sowed fair!
The seed, ho! the seed, ho!
He pattered his beads at the agued air.
Wrinkled imps in the seed.
The frosty sky was a caldron cold,
He flung the crooked seeds in the mold,
And the earth was fat and the earth took hold.
Sow, you drinkers of mead!

Gallantly April stooped to the bud!
The bloom, ho! the bloom, ho!
Crocus and thorn were mixed in his blood.
Wind and rain on the bloom.
He gave it a couple of careless bees
To dust its pollen like gold on their knees,
While its petals swung in a silken breeze.
Swarm, black bees of the coombe!

August hot comes harvesting home!
The pipe, ho! the pipe, ho!

Crunching his teeth through a honeycomb.
Satyr, sound on your pipe!
What shall he have for a throat like chips?
Berry-black sweet that the wine-cask drips
—And your wise, cool lips on my thirsty lips.
Pluck, for the fruit is ripe!

Looking back on it, Philip thought he could not have devised if he had tried a more worn and mechanical beginning for something that was to smash through his carefully constructed Yale self and scheme of existence as a bullet goes through a plaster duck in a shooting gallery. For want of anything better to do he had gone to the movies with Ken Gavin one Monday night in October, a night warm as milk with the last sweetness of Indian Summer. The jumping grasshopper-figures on the screen were flashing through the sloppy motions of that stupidest of our new conventions, a " sure-fire " comedy—everybody was throwing custard and losing their trousers and saying, " You tell 'em, pieface "—Philip wondered idly at the yahoo insolence of the producer who could water such near-beer humor through five long reels and the steadfast idiocy of the theater owner who would run it, for even a sledge-hammer on the head of the First Murderer in the piece failed to rouse the audience to any sign of appreciation beyond the staccato mastication of gum, except for three small boys in the very front seats who shrieked with unabated delight at each new sore kick from behind. The film was just starting to mix in Philip's mind with Coventry Patmore's Odes and a picture of Io he wanted to do, as well as an Arab sheik who appeared out of nothing with the urbanity of a leopard and began to talk about Sylvia, when a high, whinnying giggle from a skirted bundle next to Ken woke him out of his doze. He scowled at them reprovingly, annoyed to be brought back to the frantic comedy and the cabbagey scent of the Polack family behind him. Playing " footie " with the jitney *demi-vierges* of New Haven was a Freshman sport he had always drawn away from with supercilious distaste. He turned blinkingly resolute eyes at the sad uproar on the screen, but the giggles went on and were followed by little squeals—" the mating call of Woolworth's to the Vice Crusader," Dick had called them, and the two heads drew closer and closer in hushing talk. Scraps of it drifted over Philip's way, " Say, you're cer'n'ly a speedy guy on first acquaintance! " " You Yale birds all act alike to us poor little unprotected girls! " " Now, Lizzie, be calm, be calm! " " No, I *won't*, but who's your friend with the icy eye, a prof. or a female detective? "

Philip's mind idled back to his only experience of real " necking "—a party with three, half-a-candlepower minor lights of a number two road company at a beach whose chief reason for existence was the cheap liquor and cheaper dancing at its hotel. He had left after perspiringly embracing a fattish girl with blond sausage curls in a secluded corner, and spent fifteen minutes in the entry-washroom brushing his teeth with four different tooth pastes to get the feel of her damp ripe mouth away from him. That had been enough—the whole process was so mixed up with Jockey Club scent and the smell of bad gin that he was no longer even amused at

the prideful accounts of a few expurgated Casanovas of
his acquaintance of their dealings with " some girl, that
little Peggy, some wild girl! " The film tagged to its
end, and an educational one began with a weary parade
of hunted-looking Japanese divers. Philip and Ken
stumbled out into the cool air.

" Going back to the room? " asks Ken. Philip yawns.

" Guess so. Nothing much else to do—getting a cut
in my eight o'clock."

" Think I'll sneak up and get the car and take that
kid we were next to out for a run. I like that baby, you
know, she's got a mean eye. Want to come? "

" Uh—uh—"

" Say, she's got a friend that's pretty snappy—little
brunette. Come on along, we can have a time—trickle
out somewhere and dance. I know where they've got
the heck of a good coon orchestra."

" But look here, Ken—I—"

Philip wishes devoutly he could have remembered to
plead a test in the morning. Moral scruples are so
viciously hard to avow.

" Oh, I know you aren't one of the little Don Juans of
the class, Phil, but if this lady can shake a hoof that's
as wicked as her line, she's there. All you've got to do
is dance with her friend. But it's the dickens going out
alone, much more fun in a party. Come ahead, I'll
blow you to it and it won't hurt you. Think what inspiration you'll get—whole epics and epics. And the
Stutz is running as sweet as ice-cream right now."

" Oh, all right—but I don't have to talk to these silly
wenches, do I? "

"Rats, no. Spout them some verse if you feel inclined to, or act like a prehistoric man. That's the best stunt—this strong, silent but, oh, so gentle stuff gets away like a bat out of a fire. Are you set?"

"If we make it Dutch."

"Well, if you insist. It won't hurt us much—she didn't look too expensive. Want to come up while I tune the car?"

"Absolument—you're on."

Philip thinks it incumbent on him to assume a knowing, rather satanic sort of sprightliness, as much like his idea of a prominent turfman as possible. His heart is stuttering a little but Ken takes the whole affair as so much a matter of course that he soon calms down.

"Treat these little sardines just like infants, and they'll behave," he says as the car slides out of the garage. Philip nods.

They find the two girls waiting for them outside a drug-store, pick them up, Ken's discovery in front beside him, and the "little brunette" in the back seat with Philip, and the car purrs off again like a cat over a cream-saucer.

"Oh, say," Ken flings back over his shoulder, "I forgot introductions. Ladies, pardon me!"—snickerings and "Gee, you're a funny sketch!" from his red-haired friend.

"Not so funny as you are, sister, by two shades of Irish Peroxide. Miss Jenny Argyle, Mr. Bill Arbroath. Miss—"

"Stillman, Milly Stillman," supplies Miss Argyle.

"Mr. Bill Arbroath." Philip gasps a second, but

hands are taken and dropped. "Glad t'meet you!" say both girls dutifully. "There now—everybody happy!" Ken concludes and turns back to his wheel.

"Say, there was a yellow-haired fella with a dinky mustache I met and *he* said his name was Bill Arbroath, too," Miss Argyle murmurs doubtfully.

"You ought to be careful of these Divinity School fakers," Ken declares demurely. "That which reposes behind you is the only original Bill." The sport of giving the surname of a prominent Christian as alias in such amourettes as these is then comparatively young. It is to have somewhat sultry consequences a few classes later when the then President of Dwight Hall, the College Y. M. C. A., is to be brought up before the Dean for unbecoming conduct, to discover to his innocent rage that seven different girls have handed in his name as that of the only man they are absolutely sure they went on a party with.

The car runs out of the glare of New Haven and soft stars leap at once to their places in the mild calm sky. "Gee, I love ridin'," the girl beside Philip says in a fluttering whisper and Philip turns, numbly shy, to give her an answer and so is able to take a good look at her for the first time.

Miss Argyle, her friend whose petulant slaps and noises are now forcing Ken to drive rather wildly than well, is as normal and obvious as a piece of cheap candy —her red hair has just escaped being brick and her mouth will lose its present tight sauciness as the weak droop in it comes out with the years. Her clothes are as shoddy and gay as poor French pastry, she wears

high white glacé kid shoes and her voice and laugh are
a succession of high flats. The Stillman girl is as
different as country strawberries are from soda-fountain
strawberry syrup. Black hair, black as a blackbird's
feather; black eyes, black and sootily warm as the glow
of a flame on black onyx; mouth like a child's kissing
a poppy; through her skimpy, chic, silly dress each line
of body and limb so clean and effortless Philip's fingers
itch to sculpture her in the light fantastic stuff of an
evening cloud. She cannot be more than seventeen,
she has all the pride and witchcraft of first youth still
upon her—youth even flamboyantly wasteful in its giving when it has so inexhaustibly much still to spend.
Philip stares at her, his breath taken deep into his
throat. A little fateful hammer that titters and pulses
begins to tap like sticks on a drum inside his brain.

"*What* did your friend say your name was?" he
realizes that he is saying, and that his voice is as clat-
tering and stupid as the knocking together of two pieces
of dry wood.

"Stillman. Milly Stillman." Her voice has the little
creamy slur that belongs to soft Irish.

"Do you like me, Milly Stillman?" The question
is idiotic but he asks it as fiercely as if he were playing
inquisitor at the Last Judgment.

"Sure I like you. You look like a handsome, nice
fella," and she laughs, untroubledly, three delicate high
notes like water falling into a silver basin.

"All you Yale boys are nice—but some of you get
rough! Oh, my! Oh, dear!" She shakes her head with
the sideways quickness of a kitten, then turns rather

grave. "You aren't one of the rough lads, Mr. Bill Arbroath?" she says.

Philip blushes absurdly.

"Not very," he says and she is whole-heartedly amused.

"Well, you're a queer fella with your curly hair and your slippy talk. I like queer fellas." A hand, of which she seems quite unconscious wanders out and rests beside him. He tries to pluck up courage to take hold of it and finally does so, touching it as if it were a bomb or a biting lizard. Then his fingers close over it hungrily. A sensation of fluid strength, of sparkling lightness and ease, flows into him like a ripple.

"Oo—oo—I love to ride," and she stretches her free paw up at the stars that have not yet had time to glitter and be hard, that flow and are large all over the sky with the soft flaring radiance of burning wax. They are rushing at forty miles an hour past tall trees made of shadows and the white ghost-spire of a phantom church.

"I love to ride and I love to dance. Do you love to dance, Bill? I'm going to call you Bill, because you're a friend of mine. I'd rather dance than eat—and I'd rather eat than sleep—and I'd rather sleep than talk—except to people like you, Bill, who aren't mean about what a girl says to them when they take her out. Can you dance, Bill, 'cause if you can't you're going to be taught!"

"Yeah—rottenly—but with you—I'd be crazy to— you're so sweet—" The disjointed words tumble over each other.

"You're a kidder, Bill—and you don't kid well, but

I like you—and don't break my wrist with your hand, Bill, it's parta me and I've gotten sorta fond of it—"

"Oh, *Lord,* I'm sorry!" He releases his grasp abruptly. She wrinkles her nose.

"I didn't mean to tell you it *burnt* you, Bill—"

He notices her hands enchantedly; they are as restless as little waves; they talk, reason, swear, worry, expostulate, rejoice, drop beaten. Slender, thin, strong and hurried, they are possessed with that flush of nervous and palpitating life one feels under the hot feathers of a bird. . . .

"Last stop, people—everybody out!" yelps Ken, extricating himself from Miss Argyle. From the square wide-porched hotel that the four turn toward, arms linked, bleats a snatch of brassy jazz, blatant and fast.

"I want to dance,
I want to dance,
I want to dance with the big white Mo-on!"

hums Milly, snapping her fingers, a thousand long, "os" in the last word. She whirls Philip around and one-steps across the grass with him under the waving starlight.

The rest of that elfin evening went past like water under a bridge. Throughout it Philip seemed floating in a lily-pad pool of lucid music, with Milly like a breathing cloud always within his arms. She said little, a piece of slang now and then made quaint by her voice, but she sank herself in her dancing as a swimmer does in a wave or a poet in his verse, and her feet seemed only to tiptoe the floor she trod like a moth. Philip had always danced as he played bridge, fairly enough but without the fanatic absorption of the master. Now he realized that dancing might be a complete occupation and religion—why dervishes danced devotedly and the reason for the fever of dancing that attacked a mad year in the Middle Ages when all Italy seemed bitten by the tarantula, the dancing insect, and whole cities danced till the weak fell dead in the streets. He knew, he was part of the sun-dance of light over water, the death-dance of leaves and autumn dust, the swan's minuet of thistledown and singing wind. And "Milly—Milly—Milly" went the blood through his heart and "Milly—Milly—Milly" went the catch through his mind, a tune beaten out by delicate dancers, stepping lightly in the white glass house of the soul.

About one o'clock Philip and Milly were resting out on a porch—Philip holding both her hands since one didn't seem to be enough, when Ken and Miss Argyle appeared, draggled as wet crows and a little peevish.

"For Pete's sake, where you people *been?*" said Ken. "We looked all over the beach for you and thought you must have ditched us and started to walk back, so we took the car and went down the road a couple of miles and couldn't find you."

"We been dancing—just dancing, dancing!" lilted Milly with a sparrow's toss of her head.

Driving home over shadow-checkered roads, through scattery villages huddled up in sleep, Night's blanket pulled over their ears, Milly suddenly grew quiet and in the end fell asleep on Philip's shoulder with the uncon-cern of a child in the boughs of a safe tree. Philip felt the life come back into his feet—they began to burn and hurt. He put his arm about her body and held her so, relaxed and warm, her heart beating, without kissing her, without thought. For the second time in his life he felt eternal. The stars above them looked down with cold eyes of light—and within him he felt a life like theirs without end or beginning move and order him with the muscles of a giant. He was whole, not one fragment of his body that was not strung to the pitch of a concert-violin, yet the utter life that possessed him as fire possesses the substance of a leaf, was as passionless as a ray of the moon on ice—bodiless silver, light magnificence, cool and clean. Miss Argyle in the front seat wriggled, said, " Ah, cut it, cut it ! " The car jerked round a corner and made more speed.

Milly was waked when they finally nosed out her house, far in the suburbs on a side-street that cut across Chapel. " Won't your folks mind ? " asked Miss Argyle in a terrified whisper. " God knows it's a quarter past two ! "

Milly rubbed her eyes open again with the back of her hand. " Not a chance—I've got a latch-key—father thinks I'm asleep—"

The shabby street was silent in a tired and shining doze. Philip took her to her door—she put her mouth up to be kissed like a good little school-girl.

" Thanks, Bill, it was an awful grand party." She yawned, winked her eyes.

" When'll I see you next, Milly, Milly ? "

" When you like, Bill dear. Not to-morrow. Next day at the drug store, maybe. You could take me to

the movies if you wanted to, Bill, and we could talk.
You're the nicest fella I ever went with, I think." They
drew closer into the stuffy gloom of the doorway. She
shook her shoulders. " Good *night,* I'm tired—and
father wants his breakfast so awful early."

He looked at her mouth and wanted her forever and
ever. So he turned her face between his hands and deliberately, as if taking part in a ritual, kissed her frailly
on the round of her cheek. She sighed. " That was
lovely, Bill," she said sleepily. Then the key clicked
into the lock and she was gone. Philip slept that night
as if he had been drugged with the perfume of a garden
of tiny flowers.

So began for both of them a loving which, as it progressed, gave Philip more and more the sensation of
being the only person awake in a world of perambulating
dreams. The College and what part he took in it—
even his Senior Society affairs which always held for
him immense comfort in gaiety and friendship—grew
steadily more unreal, more like the stage " set " for a
musical comedy, seen by daylight in an empty theater.
The exterior doings of existence dropped gradually away
from him—it was a quiet, steady, humorous automaton
that got up, washed its face, attended meetings of the
Lit. board, said " Hello " to every one it recognized on
the Campus, went to bed. His essence and conscious
part was entirely circumscribed by Milly and could no
more put on being away from her than a thought half-
known in the mind can without words. And the automaton served him well, developing powers of dissimu-
lation that would have admitted it to an unreformed

Society of Jesuits and attributes of secrecy that would have done credit to a modern safe. In spite of which, as young male friends have the noses of hunting-leopards in smelling out a love-affair, his fever was not quite as cleverly hidden as he might have wished. But it was supposed in general, and especially by Reggy and Steve who held a three hours' conclave on it in his room in Connecticut, that he was frantically *épris* of "that girl out in California" and that she had turned him down—a theory to which the scanty letters he ever got from Sylvia lent much color. Ken of course spread the story of the first party, but here Philip for the first time in his life found tangible advantage in a good moral reputation, for his class was amused for a week and then promptly forgot. He never went out with Ken again, and though he and Milly often ran into Jenny Argyle, she decided for some reason or other to hold her tongue. Indeed she put on a grandmotherly attitude toward them that cheered Philip as much as it irritated Milly—she regarded them as two playful youngsters wholly lacking in her own business seriousness and cash-purpose and tossed them informative scraps now and then from a past and present as extended as it was gaudy.

Moreover, such cases as Philip's and Milly's were the extreme exception. Whatever may be said by mild ministers on the danger of mothers sending their sons to college, there is no doubt that both precocious marriage and immature vice find a fifty times flaccider power of resistance in the honest young working man or the sheltered boy at home. Of Philip's class of three hundred and fifty, about two-thirds would have been willing to go on a "petting-party" with girls like Milly, ten or twelve—and certainly not more—might have proceeded to extremes had they found her attractively lacking in virtue, only one or two would have ever thought of falling in love with her. But Philip, for good fortune or bad, was the thirteenth currant-bun in the baker's dozen. Sensitive, worshiping beauty, humor and friendliness as a Parsee worships the sun, he found all three in Milly and so clung to her from the moment he met her with the stubborn simplicity of an unruly child with a knife.

And here had better be given what facts about Milly Philip ever was able to know. Her father, a broken-down painless-dentist, with a constant penetrating fragrance of yesterday's whiskey about him from his tallowy hair to the shoes cut open over his corns, had married in the hey-day of his existence a pretty housemaid three years over from Ireland. At that time he figured as a mild minor buck in bowling-clubs and the back rooms of more home-like saloons, wore plaid waistcoats and a solid gold tooth on his watch-chain and could color a meerschaum pipe better than anybody in the neighboring five blocks. But the wife had died of typhoid when Milly was six years old, Dr. Stillman had become interested in Old Crow and absorbed it with the regularity of a medical prescription, his more respectable trade had flounced away, the scrubby doctor's mustache that was the glory of his youth had been shaved off, and he had edged farther and farther outside his old prosperous neighborhood by a series of de-

creasingly successful moves. Now, sunk to a battered
half-house in a street that trailed off into frank slums
three blocks away, the dirty brass plate with " Ulysses
G. Stillman—Dental Surgeon," was the one dingy remnant of bourgeois gentility left to him. He still had
patients and made enough to keep himself and Milly—
but for amusements the latter had to take what she
could get, and being pretty and slangy and wanting a
good time she got drawn in with a small ring of her
school-friends who were taken out in cars, danced amor-
ously with, and kissed as frequently as possible by the
more daring or sophomoric of the College. It was a
juggler's life, a continual tricky balancing between giving enough so as to be taken out on another party and
not giving too much, with the inevitable " fall " and
its consequences—though in the latter case the male
wild-oat in question was rather more likely to be an
old friend from one of the cartridge factories or one
of the smart lads whose only business seems to be with
street-corners than even the most callous of Sheff. ath-
letes.

Milly liked the adventure of it, discounted the dangers,
and walked through such little flames as she encoun-
tered unseeing as a Minor Prophet, kept straight by a
natural cleanness she had from her mother, as innate
and unconscious as the sap that runs through a tree.
She had never fallen in love till she met Philip and
had accepted the random kisses that came her way with
some gusto but more philosophic indifference as the
necessary price for dancing with able partners. For
the only passion she had was for good dancing, and

that was almost austere in the lonely seriousness with which she pursued it. Her father, when wholly sober which was infrequent, loved her devotedly, but in general felt only the faded responsibility for her that he did for what vague remains of good furniture were still left them; if both were there to be looked at during breakfast, lunch and dinner, that ended his concern.

From October to April Philip and Milly met every day and evening that they could. Philip's Senior Society nights were exempt as was Sunday evening at first when her father stayed at home and went to sleep in his chair over rye and the Sunday papers. Mornings were almost always impossible and afternoons much cut into by classes. But three or four nights a week, as soon as she had washed the supper dishes and Dr. Stillman had returned to his three drinks an hour at McCabe's, she and Philip would trot out and explore the world.

Occasionally they dared one of the beaches, Savin Rock, or even the Taft Grill for dancing, but there Philip was pretty sure to meet some one he knew and he could not try too often. So they hunted out strange dance-halls where the admission was "25c. for gentleman, lady free" and a shirt-sleeved orchestra played discords to hugging couples. Twice Philip had all he could do to avoid fights with townies, in spite of the fact that he had disguised himself as well as possible in a waist-belted suit and bright green socks, and when he was finally able to purchase the wreck of a second-hand car after a correspondence with his father that was worthy of Talleyrand, they went out of New Haven

altogether and sought minor and often very disreputable
road-houses not likely to be frequented by students or
Milly's friends. Once indeed they were caught in a
raid—a moving-picture affair of blue policemen with
clubs and cowering waiters—and hid playing tit-tat-toe
in the kitchen for an hour-and-a-half to come out and
find the spiky-goateed proprietor concealed under a rug
in their car. They had driven a quarter of a mile down
the road before he arose like a ghost on Resurrection Day
and as Milly said made her heart go on like a cuckoo-
clock. He offered them anything in the house they
wanted from lobster Newburg to Santa Cruz rum, and
they thanked him politely, took his card and never went
back.

And then there was the adventure of the Bolivian
millionaire, very drunk, very affable, who sat down
at their table one night and started matters by ordering
three quarts of sparkling Burgundy. Milly sipped a
glass and refused to take any more as it felt like safety-
pins coming undone inside her head, so he sent it around
to the Hungarian orchestra and before the evening was
over the latter were playing an improvised Bolivian
National Anthem that rocked the glasses off the table
and the Bolivian was saying, " I have no chilsren. You
will come down to Bolivia and be my chilsren and I will
have you eat off gold." They declined the invitation and
the Bolivian was just wrapping his waistcoat around
his head to perform the dance of the mule-skinners of
Bolivia when the lights were turned off and they slipped
away in the dark, pursued by his plaintive Spanish
cries.

Most remarkable of all was the impromptu Christmas party on the first day of vacation, when Philip, coming early after lunch, found Milly and Jenny Argyle in the midst of improvising costumes for a masquerade-social to be given by the Little Sisters of St. Micah under the auspices of a most respectable church. Jenny concocted out of curtain-rings, glass beads and her warmest petticoat a cannibal-chief costume for Philip that he said looked like a Sandwich Islander's bad dream, Milly was a pink Pierrette and Jenny reserved for herself the bare knees of a Highland milk-maid— " At least I don't know if it's a milk-maid or an ad for oatmeal I've made of myself but it shows off my legs like a streak and they're the best part of me." They supped lightly from delicatessen food, Philip nearly scaring a baby into fits as he stalked to the corner grocery with a raincoat over his costume. Then Philip decided that as it was Christmas they must be waits—the car was luckily outside—and by Christmas songs and what Philip claimed were revivals of the morris-dances, they collected three dollars and forty-eight cents to restore the Temple at Jerusalem from a row of families as fatly respectable as their houses in the wilds beyond Park Street and west. A self-important bystander demanded a license for begging and they referred him to the Little Sisters of St. Micah, Jenny tripped him into a snow-drift as he started after them and they were gone while he was still making choking appeals to the police through a mouth full of snow. It all ended in Philip and Milly winning the prize for fancy dancing, awarded by a Little Sister as prim as a lemon drop who kept pointing with a bitter gesture to Jenny's knees, and then promptly starting an unauthorized Virginia reel that broke the whole party up into a howling, laughing cavalcade that casually brushed the presiding minister into the middle of a bowl of ice cream. The three criminals escaped, weak with mirth, built a roaring fire in the kitchen stove and told ghost stories till three in the morning.

So, in New Haven and out, they diverted themselves extremely and both acquired a nodding acquaintance with more of the amusingly vicious than most—and remained entirely untouched in the process. For they would spend these evenings in general, except for such occasional frolics as the above, entirely in dancing, both saying little or nothing but happy with the bliss of infants to be so in each other's arms. When the road-house or dance-hall closed, they would return, drink milk and eat sandwiches mousily at Milly's, and part some time in the small hours with one light kiss. Philip's habit of going to sleep anywhere and everywhere in the afternoons became the standing joke of his roommates. And this state of things continued till the short winter melted up entirely in April.

You see Philip and Milly were sure, completely, of themselves and each other and the hunger in them was kept in abeyance by being often, if so delicately, fed. And as both were incurable romantics, so neither ever looked beyond the present instant. They grew closer and closer yet in mind and emotion, yet with a passion that was curiously comradely. And then the three aunt-like fates that Philip had seen once in a dream scrutinized the loose golden cord that bound them together, shook their heads, and pulled the fetter taut with a jerk.

A dozen small accidents from a bad cold to an unexpected squabble over the election of the next *Record* Board had kept Philip from seeing Milly, except once for an unsatisfactory snatch of ten minutes, for very nearly a week. When he crunched through the light fluffy snow to her door on a brilliantly cold evening late in March, she answered his ring but he saw she was not dressed for going out.

"What's the matter, Milly dear?" he looked closer— her eyes had had tears in them. "Do you feel badly? You said we could go out to that Green Kettle place and dance."

"I don't know, Philip. I've been blue as the sky all day—just thinking and wondering like I used to when I was in grammar-school. Come on in—I've made a fire for us." She led the way to a small, crampedly-furnished back-parlor where a handful of coal burnt and sissed in a choked little grate. The room was as warm as breath and dark as a pocket.

His eyes were still dazzled by the abrupt gloom when Milly put her hands behind his neck and their lips met in a long fantastic kiss. He did not know how long he stood there, obliterated in her as if he were drinking wine, but when the embrace broke into two shaken and separate persons again he was trembling as if he had fallen on fiery ice. The heat of that single moment had changed them both, body and heart and wish, as the hotness of a spurting flame brings out

writing in invisible ink on blank paper. It was a cos-
tume-party world they had inhabited so long—a world
as sparkling as a bubble with all the foamy colors a
child gives to its games. They had lived through a porcelain fairy-tale—swung and danced in a kind and
airy vision. And the sky had been silk to look at and
the earth silk to touch as they wandered through a
country of unrealities like two sun-motes in the hollow
of a silk cocoon. This was finished. The wind that blew
over them now out of deep life was a fertile wind, but
it left them naked as scarecrows or the truth. They
were to have youth again and the darkness of complete
rapture, stiff pride, despair, and the knowledge of good
and evil, but never again first innocence.

They sat before the fire all evening, talking at random. When they kissed the kisses were long and had
hurt in them and stinging joy.

"Milly, oh dear, oh sweet!" said Philip, who had
to make phrases. "Do you know, Milly, it's just as if
we were drowning now? Going down and down in
sleepy, sucking black water."

Milly shuddered and twisted his hand she had between
hers.

"I never felt funny like this about any one, Phil,"
she says simply. "Not even about you before. I feel
grand and loving you always and a little wicked."

"Wicked?"

"I don't think you're wanted to love anybody with all
of you. With all of you from your hair to the bottoms
of your feet. They can't want you to, it makes you
so crying happy."

"I love you as much and as much more. I'll love you till I'm nothing but dirt the wind blows or water under the sea. I could die now, Milly, I love you so and it's so wonderful to kiss you."

Milly stretched five slender fingers at the fire. "I wish I was as beautiful as queens," she said gravely. Then presently, "Kiss me now, on my eyes when I shut them. Oh, Philip, but I like your mouth and your curly hands!"

"I like the soft of your throat and the smell of your hair. I could kiss your hair forever and ever, Milly!"

"Never tell Them that," she says, rapping gently on the floor, and her wide eyes darken as sea darkens under the shadow of an eagle as she stares with a stupefied happiness that is almost terror at the picture-making blaze and Whatever may be looking at them from beyond it.

"If you're talking about God, he might as well hear it as not. I don't care if he hears—I don't care if anybody hears. Your hair smells like violets and I could kiss it forever."

"It would get in your mouth at the end," says the practical Milly.

After this they were swept along by events and each other like the scud of a summer storm. Their love-making grew intenser and narrower, they could hardly bear the pressure of themselves on themselves without the other. Occasionally they returned to mere light-heartedness—they went on picnics as the weather grew warmer, sometimes taking Jenny Argyle along as a pretense of a chaperone and then they carried on with the laughter and pretty bustle of young deer. Once, also, when Milly's father was away they raided and rough-housed his grim airless " dental-parlor," doing all the things that people have ever wanted to do with a free hand at the distorted tools of dentistry, even to boring woodpecker holes in the wall with the electric drill. But such gaiety came only by snatches, for the most part they were broodingly expectant like men waiting si-lent before a window for a flash of lightning to awake and tear the sky. Philip asked her four times to marry him and she refused in each case absolutely flatly and would give no reason except " I would shame you and make you sorry before your people, Phil. I am not the girl you should want." He consulted Jenny Argyle on the subject and she argued with Milly with the exas-perated patience of a court interpreter with a stubborn female witness. But to everything she said Milly would docilely agree and say all that was very true but she was entirely decided not to marry Phil.

Philip cut classes wildly and went on probation for the first time in his whole four years. His marks went down like mercury in a thermometer during a cold snap, and the fact that he might yet flunk out of college be-came ghastly clear. His sleep was a phantasmagoria of reeling dreams and while he ate obediently of what-ever tasteless material was placed before him, he had a look that made John say he was undoubtedly a case of demoniac possession and Steve remark that that was what came from ruining your liver by not always eat-ing over at his joint. As for Milly she began to find nerves all over herself that she had never suspected and prayed to have some one or something tell her what to do as she had not since, when at seven, as a consequence of a gory lecture on " The Cross and Its Martyrs in the Dark Continent," she had passionately besought her Maker for two months thereafter not, as he loved her, to make her go and be a martyr. The consequence of which was that the two quarreled fiercely from excess of affection and made up after exhausting scenes. And in the end the patience was worked out by naked Chance with the most clear and ironic simplicity possible.

It was a Monday night around the first of May, a night of opening buds and winds full of white rain and white flowers. The solemn sky held soberly the vast pale round of the moon, curved and wide as the flying wing of a white owl. Philip had meant to get out to Milly's before nine but Steve had insisted on his coming up to Mory's for talk and a cheese sandwich and it was half-past ten before he even got started for a street-car. And the car, after being waited for through long minutes, proved a creeping thing, devoutly attached to each uneven inch of its rails. Philip had no watch but when he finally swung off at the right corner he knew himself absurdly late and half-resolved to take the next car back. But the night was as sweet as first love, a spangled night to walk through, and he thought he might at least discover if there were a light in Milly's window before he turned home.

The light burned but was faint through a drawn blind. He did not dare to ring or knock but stood wavering on the doormat, wondering what on earth to do now. Finally he turned the knob of the door and pushed softly. It was unlocked and opened instantly with a startling creak.

There was a thump of bare feet on the floor above, then Milly's voice, drowsily low, from the head of the stairs. "That you, Jenny darling? Shut the door."

Philip obeyed—it closed with another denouncing whine. Then in the voice of an asthmatic conspirator, "It's me, Milly dear. Philip."

Silence, heavy and thick as restless oil sucked over and drowned his words. He paused with one hand on the banister.

Milly's voice came again, tensely changed but drowsier, weighted with sleep.

"Philip—I thought it was Jenny Argyle—she was coming to stay with me—Father's gone over to Aunt Kitty's in Bridgeport for two days. I—I guess Jenny isn't coming now—it's so late."

Philip felt his heart thud inside him as if it were being beaten by a multitude of tiny waves. His voice sank lower, tuned to her voice's drowsiness, grew dark with its slumber.

"Can I come up?" he said, and the last word echoed.

A heavy stupor of silence fell between them, it seemed for ages.

Then "Yes" floated down from the indistinctness above, like the whisper of a Chinese bell rubbed once with the hand.

He ascended with the slow, unseeing tread of a somnambulist. She was waiting for him, she was dressed in loose white and her hair was down below her waist.

He kissed her on the mouth and felt his whole body give in her clasp as if it were made of sand.

"Oh, Phil, Phil, Phil, I knew this would happen sometime—" she said as he gripped her hand and they went into the room.

Breathe low, woodwinds, softly, softly, rustling
the forest of star-clear notes,
Hardly a whisper, horns enchanted, out of your
husky golden throats,
Let the assent of the weeping viols build up the
chord to a chime like rain
*Here in a summer place, here in a green place,
the ancient passion is danced again!*

Hearts unschooled by the anguished rapture,
clouds that have never borne sun or moon,
Light shall envelop you, fire possess you, treading
the night to a light-foot tune,
Colors of blood and lions and jasper, honey-comb
sweet and a radiant pain,
*Here in a hidden place, here in a wild place, the
ancient passion is danced again!*

Little as winds in a marsh at evening, slender
and bright as a vine-crowned glass,
Over the tempest-blown pool of midnight the kiss-
ing-mouthed hours gesture and pass.
Fragrance trembles from wet wood-violets, perfume breathless from a poppied stain,
*Here in a stilly place, here in a young place, the
ancient passion is danced again!*

Sunlight, yellow with morning, came in through the window in a slanting flood and the sound of a robin followed it. Also, from the foot of the stairs a girl's voice, quacking and high.

" Mill-y ! "

Pause. Jenny Argyle pets an escaped rusty curl back into place with a hand full of glassy rings.

" Mill-y ! "

Milly, drifting like a radiant silver bubble in the black whirlpool of drenching sleep, stirs a little. Her fingers close tighter on Philip's fingers.

" Mil-lee ! "

Nothing but flecks of early light on the purple flowers of the stair-carpet. Nothing but the scuffle and running of a little gust of wind that has got caught between floor and ceiling and is fussing like a bird to get out.

" Happy days, she must be kin to the Seven Sleepers —and they had to get up *some*-time ! "

Jenny ascends the stairs quietly, full of that glow of pitying virtue that is the delighted possession of all those who wake up others. She pushes open the door of Milly's room, her mouth round for an arousing screech.

" Well—I'll—be—" and what she has to say goes off into an utter whisper.

They are sleeping with the abstracted smiles of the happy dead and the saturated peace of babies after a bottle. They are very pretty to look at, rippled over as they are by the dark soft stream of Milly's hair.

Jenny stands there with her breast going pitter for two minutes at least. Then a smile, not at all like theirs, comes upon her gradually and perks her coarse desiring mouth into something sardonic and wise with the wisdom of the burnt—and yet something that is most infinitely kind.

"The kids," she says to herself in an awed sort of rustle. "The poor little, nice, crazy kids!" and she closes the door with profound care and tiptoes back down the stairs again, to take the last three in a little dancing jump. By the door she pauses once more and shakes her hat.

"Oh, gee, I'm sorry—honest to God, I'm sorry!" she repeats like a meek satirical litany, but her eyes are sparks as she says it. She crams her striped toque down over her head.

"Ah, Peter, you ain't young more than once," she delivers as her final decision, chuckles lightly and bounces off down the street.

> "Phil, are you glad?"
> "Oh, Milly, I can't be!"
> "Are you glad for yourself?"
> "Yes, but—"
> "Well, I'm glad for myself."

Philip never could hear robins squabbling over a worm or smell elm-leaves on a hot spring morning without crushed pain and a fighting ecstasy at the strings of his heart. He remembered Milly's bare arms, as cream-smooth for hands to touch as calla-lilies, and the busy cleverness of her fingers when she knotted up her hair, wise eyes bright as a sparrow's peering at the swimming phantom in the mirror's pallor. Milly sitting cross-legged in the bowl of a chair, her small feet

playing and curling like leaves in autumn. Milly flat
in front of a fire with a book in both hands and the
cherry flush of the flame against her seeking face.
Milly burlesquing something he had done with the mocking of a lovely imp—Milly's long slumber in the dawn-
light, her breast rising and falling, certain and even
sweet—Milly's eyes as she turned them to him from the
pillow, deep nights, courageous and beaten and heavy
with love.

They were married on Saturday in New York before an unhealthy old Justice of the Peace, who spent
most of the ceremony telling them the exact amount of
his fee and looked suspiciously sure that he was getting
counterfeit money when Philip overpaid him. They
spent a night and a day of bizarre honeymooning at the
Hotel Lafayette and in Greenwich Village, then Philip
had to get back to his classes and furious printed com-
munications from the Dean's Office. What Dr. Stillman thought of his daughter's absence was hidden in a
whiskeyfied haze—she flatly told him she was going
down for the week-end with Jenny Argyle and left him
worriedly mixing up a silver filling that kept on being
added to unconsciously after her announcement, till
it was large enough to stop the back-tooth of a lion.
Jenny Argyle was the only person by necessity told
the whole story—Philip knew there would be explo-
sions enough from Phil when he finally got the news
and at that time an undergraduate could not marry and
stay in College. After Philip received his degree in
June—and Milly insisted on his working for it with a
persistence of which he had not believed her capable,

and most of his text-books in the end gravitated out to her room where she could keep a defiant watch on him—there would be time enough to think of what to do next. And so started a most rich and curious month and a popular report that Phil Sellaby had gone completely off his nut because nobody ever saw him except in chapel and at recitations. The College waited for homicidal mania with pleased expectancy.

Only one scene outside of Milly stuck in Philip's mind at all of those four weeks. It was Tap Day, a late Tap Day and on a breathless and honey-heavy May afternoon.

. . . Philip found himself walking on the Campus from the gap in the fence in front of Durfee. Battell clock had just beaten out a quarter of six. There was a crowd on the Campus, a pallid, strained, waiting crowd. He walked around it once completely, peering for Jack Elbridge, the man he was sent out to tap, his face rigid as chalk, his hands pulsing. He noticed, with the meticulous clarity of a man under torture, that not one of the crowd spoke to another in outright voices and that most were glaring steadily at the ground. Three lines of John Castine's flashed into his mind:

> " I have heard a hundred half-lights murmur their
>   little fears,
> The Dwight Hall Vice, the Dull but Nice, the
>   One Who Orders Beers,
> I have seen that poor dumb pleading look, as in
>   prebutchered steers—"

and he nearly snickered and broke his stiff-collared dignity into bits. Then a wave of sheer funk went over him—Jack Elbridge didn't seem to be on the Campus at all—could Keys or Bones have taken him off while he, Philip, was mooning over irreverent rhymes? Desperately he started to circle the crowd again like a sheep-dog around a flock of stubborn lambs. Thank God, there he was, with a sick grin on his face, too, and his hands jumping as he made play with a lighted cigarette—he had evidently given up all hope and was listening to such thorny Job's comfort as sincere and loving friends can always give. Philip made straight for the center of the crowd—it fell away before him like the Red Sea before the chariots of the Israelites—bored in behind the wholly unconscious figure, quite sure that he was coming for some one else, took a long breath and smote it on the back like a piston.

" Go to your room! "

" Yeah! " and all the strained hot nervousness of the whole crowd came out of their throats in a bursting yell. Jack Elbridge trotted on through them to Berkeley Oval and Philip stalked responsibly behind him, internally smiling all over his soul.

But as soon as he remembered Milly his nerves strung up again, for she had managed to contract the first of a summer cold, from him, too, he imagined, as the little hack of a cough of his Junior year had returned with the first slushy weather and still hung irritatedly upon him.

The rest of the month was pure Milly and in it he learned more and faster than he had been able to do through the whole of his expensive education. She was not, to put it mildly, an intellectual, but her mind was

singularly fresh and apprehensive and she responded
to books and other manners with the sensitive quickness of a compass-needle to iron. Besides this, she was
intensely companionable and her intuitions matched
and equaled all the logic he had been proudly able to
dig out of books. Sometimes he would wonder, when
they parted, how much of himself he was now and how
much of her, the two separate natures had so mingled
in both like the pollen of neighboring flowers. He
adored her, and loved her and never was tired of her—
and the month became a sunny sonata, no less rapturous
because all of its grace-notes came from a single crying
theme. Even the gadfly of writing and painting buzzed
and left him—for once he was too full with Life to have
any wish to record it. He scattered the days about with
the carelessness of a deity, he and Milly held the bright
spinning globe of the world, tiny, flattened down at the
poles, patched over with sandy continents and silver
seas, in the hollow goblet of their four hands . . .

Then the causeless insult came. One night near the
last day of May he noticed that Milly's eyes were drooping and heavy and her hands dry and hot as he took them
up. She coughed once or twice and he asked her to
see a doctor, for each cough seemed to knife through
her body.

She died of acute double pneumonia eight days later.
Philip spent the next two weeks utterly without feeling. At times he was even dully comfortable, it was
as if the touch of a surgical instrument had excised
certain centers out of his brain. He could move and
walk about and even think, but for anything that he

did he could find no reason, he did it merely because the voices of people told him to and must be obeyed even if one walked like a man under cocaine through interminable streets that were not worth opening eyes to see. As for Milly, the name throbbed somewhere inside him and would not let him rest, but everything else had gone out like the flame of a match. Philip was as patient as a lost dog these weeks, and as gentle, as if all life he had had been taken away from him like the air under the glass of a vacuum-pump.

Dr. Stillman knew that they had been married, and John and Reggy and Steve and Dick, so Milly had been buried with her wedding-ring on her finger. Philip had shut his eyes at the beginning of the barbarous funeral-service and kept them shut to the end, imprisoning a blind and horrible revolt that tore him with a wild desire to take Milly in her coffin away from all these nightmare people and keep her beside him till he broke his heart and died. Phil and Lucia had not been informed—and they were not coming on for his problematical graduation. Dr. Stillman seemed vaguely conscious of great loss, and kept looking around the room as if expecting Milly to come in. At nights he would go to the foot of the stairs and call up them, " Milly ! " listen eagerly and go back to his whiskey on shuffling feet. John took charge of what arrangements had to be made—and was pointed out as Milly's ruinous lover by all the little boys and old gossips along the block.

Philip took no examination and did not graduate. John and Steve spread the report of a sudden nervous breakdown to the Dean and around the class. Most of the truth leaked out, in the parti-colored costumes truth wears when passed from mouth to mouth, but the four friends managed to stop some of the worst of the lies. Finally, on the afternoon of Baccalaureate Sunday, Philip was alone with John in John's and Reggy's room —they had all been as gentle as mothers with him, all the four. Philip lifted his head from the book in front of him and the unceasing pictures that were always before his eyes.

"I think I'll go up to Montreal and enlist in the Royal Flying Corps," he said tiredly. "You remember Fat Carhart, 1915, he did it this winter. He said they shipped you across in a couple of months."

John looked at him. "Seriously?"

"Seriously. Best thing in the world to do."

"Mind if I come along with you, old fel'?"

Philip gaped at him vacantly.

"Don't be a damn fool, Castine! Why on earth should you?"

"Best thing in the world to do." John quoted with a diffident grin. "Got to get into things somehow. Talked it over with Steve—he says no go on the ambulance stuff. Wants us all to be English officers in whipcord uniforms. He'd come in a second. How about it?"

Philip rose and shook the lean nervous hand up and down.

"Oh, Castine, you blasted old fool!" he said and burst out of the room with his eyes full of tears.

Some saving iota of common-sense inspired the five

of them to take a preliminary physical examination the next morning. After it was over the doctor called Philip into the room where he kept his scales and his articulated skeleton.

"Mr. Sellaby," he said, smoothing his chin, "I am sorry to have to tell you that you have most of the primary symptoms of tuberculosis . . . Now a year in Arizona or Colorado . . . "

The arms of the doctor's chair came suddenly at Philip and he fainted for the first and only time in his life.

That night he was lying in his bed, staring up at the ceiling with dry and prickly eyes. Two currents of emotional thought fought over him, sweeping through him in the waves of chills-and-fever. Under one he felt a sullen thick delight that the business of limping about in a world of echoes and shadows would, if he merely paid no attention to it, be so soon and so definitely over. And with this came the remembrance of Milly, like the asking note of a bugle blown from the earth, a deathly perfume that hunted him and clung to him so that the only desire he had was to fall and annihilate himself in its piercing fragrance of wet violets and let whatever mechanics of being still kept him alive collapse back into their proper dust. The other wave was just blind vicious fear of death—fear that approached a madhouse vision in its intensity—and when it had taken him up in its teeth and torn him and left him quivering it was followed by a whisper from his rocking will that he still had a task to sweat at and carry through. He was not quite utterly like other people, the icy whisper said, for better or worse he had charred into his mind the triple-forked flame of the artist-maker. By that signature he had been since his birth ordered up into a battle that had no cowards. "And there's no dis-charge in the war," went through his head again and again like the squawk of a cheap phonograph by a sickbed. "There's no dis-charge in the war-r." Then the fear would come or the scorching longing to be quit and strive over him with the grips of exhausted wrestlers, until it seemed that his trouble would end automatically with a slurring break of something inside his brain.

He lay there, and the night grew, and as the stars tramped higher the dark became a little cool. From Wolseley, all the way across two streets and the Campus on chance ebbs of wind came the faint drums and mosquito-voiced fiddles of the Senior Promenade.

Once he got up and looked through every drawer in Dick's desk for the little .22 pistol he kept in it, nobody knew why. But Dick had anticipated him and the thing was hidden.

After his excursion he went back and lay down again under the incessant iron fingers of his riddle. At times his head seemed clogged and stupid with blood that subsided and left him wrapped in a sheet of vacant cold. And forward-back, forward-back, with the tick and recurrence of a clock swayed his two desires. At last they beat him down between them into what seemed to be a doze. At least he called it so when he thought of it connectedly, and yet he heard each quarter of that hour strike in turn and its proper order.

The scent that was Milly, the scent of the flowers he

had wanted to put on her grave, grew bitingly strong. It passed over him like a tide made up of a multitude of blossoms. It ended, and was followed by an instant of terrible peace.

Then he opened his eyes, or seemed to, and saw Milly walking toward him in her white nightgown with her hair down her back in two braids. But about her and beating from her was a light like the light upon a sword. He called to her, and his own voice rang in his ears like the voice of a ghost. She did not answer, but smiled with a mocking mouth that made him afraid.

Then she came and stood beside him and took one of his hands in hers and her touch was not cold or secret but vivid and alive. She took her hand away and laid it over his eyes. And at the contact, so warm, so delicate and hushing, he broke into a passion of tears.

He woke and found the pillow wet under his face and remembered what he had seen in a single acute and stabbing breath. Then he wept again as he had not thought it possible to weep and live. But when the fit was over it left him weak as a wave and quiet as starlight, and he put his head on his left arm and went instantly to sleep.

About noon, when the dancers heavily arose:

" By the way, Dick, got a straight razor? "

A startled voice from the other room: " Ye-es. Why? "

" Oh, nothing. You can leave it around again, that's all."

Dick, comprehensively, " Thank God! "

Philip went up with John to Westboro' for two weeks and there, with Milly in his dream before him any time he shut his eyes, composed a long explanatory letter to Lucia and Phil. He told everything without reserve. Lucia telegraphed him as soon as Phil showed her the letter, the sort of telegram he knew she would be the only person in the universe understanding enough to send. Phil's reply, a curious document, came later. Among other things it said that as Philip should go West to a dry climate for his health, Phil had got him a position as time-keeper with the Rusty Mountain Copper Company at Frickett, Arizona; "my specialist declares the climate ideal and the work is light though occupying," the sentence ran. Philip was expected in Frickett on the 20th of July. Letters from the company would follow. "Your aff. father, PHILIP SELLABY."

"Well, write me, Phil!" said John as they parted in the Grand Central. "I'll wire you as soon as I find out about the R. F. C."

"Fine. Write me. I'll need it."

"All I can. I wish I was going with you."

"Wish you were. So long. Don't take any wooden money."

And at breakfast next morning in the diner, Philip found the train plunging south and west through unfamiliar country, and New Haven, and the last four years, and Milly, out of sight behind the careless sunrise, like a ship, hull-down, gone over the edge of the world.

BOOK IV
COLD MOUNTAINS
(1916-1917)

PHIL and Lucia met him at Frickett and stayed there with him for a week. When they left Philip found himself enriched by the memory of Lucia's presence, an absurdly warm, and expensive sweater, six pairs of the best wool socks, a hot-water bag, which he threw down a cañon, and a quantity of intense good advice from Phil on the "Pull yourself together and be a man!" order that acted upon him as mustard would on a burn. Casual life—the casualness even of his own fairly considerable success in investing inherited money—had shaken youth's audacious elasticity out of Phil, he had grown a little hard, a little crumbling, like the rubber on the butt of an old pencil. Philip was still in the stage of grief in which loss, though borne, is as everywhere as light and shadow, and the combination of Phil's hearty appetite and bracing words of consolation made him mentally seasick with a nausea of grotesque fancies. Moreover, he could never have Lucia to himself, Phil was constantly coming around the corner or into the room with a strong cigar and a quotation from Shakespeare or the Bible, his voice soothingly low, his eye alert as a dentist's. Philip was not relieved when they went—for that took away Lucia's healingness—but he said good-by with equanimity and spent the rest of the evening grilling himself in his bunk of a room with the feeling that he was a very ungrateful son.

What he thought of Frickett he put into letters to John Castine; his epistles home were dutiful but deodorized and hence of a good deal less value. " Ah, John," he began, " and what was the first thing I saw as I marched up and down the windy platform of Frickett Junction, provoking the clerk in the pink shirt and baby-blue sleeve garters and a face that looked as if it had been badly whittled out of yellow pine to dry gasps of laughter at my childish attempts to walk on one of the rails? (The train service between Frickett and its spawn is every hour and a half and I had arrived at the wrong half.) It was—hold your breath, my Kipling subaltern!—a Cowboy, a real Cowboy with feather-bed chaps and a Mex. saddle and a yellow-eyed cayuse. I rubbed my eyes—I gathered my satiric soul in my hands —' Avaunt Douglas Fairbanks, O Bill Hart, O Diamond Dick, the Daredevil of Demon Gulch, I know you too well,' I cried, or would have if my lungs hadn't been full of alkali dust. ' Go back to the movies, you five-reel mammoth feature and leave me to Frickett Junction and coughs and peace!', but it didn't evaporate—it stayed—while I watched it it rolled a punk cigarette with one hand. I felt like Annie Oakley—this is the bad, bad six-shooter West, John, though indeed it's almost effete East from the place where I belong. You will hear of me next branding bullocks with the Lazy Lit. Triangle or eloping on a calico pony with Mamie, the Dance Hall Queen . . . "

" You ask about Frickett and the country around it— the only simile I can think of is the more horizontal

part of the Bump the Bumps at Coney Island, much the
same configuration and exactly the same dirty red or
light-beer-colored ground. The only tennis-court in the
place—at one of the young Sons of the Mine's grand-
pianoed, mission-furnitured, Long Island bungalows—
slants up hill about twenty degrees and if you paste a
ball over one of the backstops it rolls down two hundred feet into a gully. They have had to build the base-
ball-park at Frickett Junction, five miles down, on
the only piece of comparatively flat ground in three
counties, and that piece is due to an earthquake or some
such natural jest and was never intended by the Designing Architect. . . . The town is a sand-pitted half-
mile of frame shacks and tents, nothing over two stories,
but a pressed-brick bank and a graft post-office whose
imitation marble pillars glitter at the eternal sun like
a set of false teeth. Take San Esteban, where I come
from—you've seen it—pull it out like an accordion,
abolish most of the churches and one or two of the
saloons, and throw it down like a necklace of brown
wooden beads in a cup between a lot of tall, cold mountains—and there is Frickett, Arizona. The married
miners' section is small and pretty decent—rows and
rows of unpainted, sun-cracked, one or one-and-a-half-
story doll houses all turned out by the lot and as like as
checkers but clean and with perambulators and dusty
geraniums on the short front porches; also miners' feet
in the evening in blue and white socks, a continual in-
cense to the lares of the American home. The majority of the single miners live in boarding houses, tough
or tame according to districts, though some, as in West-

ern novels, camp out in tents. I'm in one of the tamer
boarding-houses occupied mostly by foremen and other
non-coms and lesser lights of the Co.

"Up past the mine, approachable on foot, is Red
Light Town, bustling at all times and lit at night by a
venomous shine of unshaded electrics. Farther up, oh, a
good deal farther up, and you go by a different road so as
not to be solicited by battered Cleopatras in kimonos, lies
Valhalla, the abode of the gods, cool bungalows mainly,
but a very few nice imitation Spanish ranchos with
open courts and red-tiled roofs. These hold the élite
—the lusciously-wealthy offspring of the Rusty Mountain Co., who wear tucks or bare shoulders for dinner—
the Young Harvard superintendents and managers—a
few rich casuals, lungers like myself, who are well and
fat as seals out here but can only go back East under sentence of death, and to whom, consequently, everything
from Chicago to Boston is as dear ' as to cadets in Hin-
dostan, the fading remnant of their liver.' They are
as strangely assorted as things sold at a church-bazaar,
and most of them quite amusing and companionable
with the spontaneous free-masonry of the confirmed
T. B. One admirable silvery antique of a doctor, who
can recite pages out of Boswell's ' Life of Johnson ' and
thinks Pope the greatest poet that ever contributed to
the paper-shortage, and is always in a stew about the
unnatural healthiness of Frickett—he was a gynæcologi-
cal expert before he came here and most of the rare
births roundabout are accomplished with the ease and
celerity known to rabbits. There is also an Assyrian-
nosed friendly Jew, who made a fortune in the N. Y.

theater and got T. B. along with it; and his tales of various stars and asteroids are purple in the extreme. But he is a generous cuss, has the only stock of French cognac in town and a period victrola with God knows how many good records in it. So I go up to the doc for an old-fashioned whiskey cocktail and medical advice and wild arguments on Pope vs. Shelley; and to Sam Cohen for liqueur brandy and Chopin and more Chopin till the room starts to sail away like a genteel balloon into a sky full of gold-colored fluffiness and I forget I ever had lungs or lights that were used for anything but breathing . . ."

" . . . Every time I draw a pay-check, and that's as frequently as they'll let me, I'm astonished honestly and heartily at the lax munificence of Big and Bloated Corporations. Why, they're giving me ninety-eight dollars and some odd cents each month—and, as wages more or less run with the price of copper, if copper only goes up enough, they will shortly hand me out yet more. I don't see how in God's name I can be worth that much real money to anybody outside my family during the obligatory years. Then I go down town and pay a quarter for a shave and ten cents for a New York paper and notice that my board costs nearly as much as if I were eating at Mory's. *(These are 1917 prices— S. V. B.)* and feel like the down-trod wage-slave that it is not so awful much after all. However, I can live on it with comfort though without particular enjoyment or gust—the latter ceased when you know.

" Considering the work I do, yes, it is gratuitously

liberal. I told you I was surveying and you say you picture me wandering saw-toothed hills with a ball and chain and a vague, inefficient smile. You are clair-voyantly correct. I think I have climbed every hill within ten miles of Frickett—I am beginning to know the lot of them like my pajamas. Also, as I am a sort of a general errand-boy and handy-man, I have dug post holes, paid off men, checked ore cars, twice gone down into the mines with a crew, but the last was ac-cidental for I am a delicate plant and must be kept out in the open air and well-fertilized. Also excavating mysterious diggings in earth's bowels and helping erect barbed-wire fences are my specialties.

" I never knew anything about the eight, ten or twelve-hour day before or the effect of hard work, not games, but work that actually takes all the pith and sense out of you. Now I claim to be an authority on it all. I know the lead, stupid, somnolent effort that gets nothing done in the last twenty minutes before knocking off at noon—the virtuous brightness and speed of early morn-ing—the death-in-weariness attack that comes just in front of the final whistle. Also the bed at 8:30 P. M., because you are too drunk-tired to hold your eyes open, and the cheated feeling at six the next morning when you've just shut off the alarm-clock that yesterday you didn't do one damn thing but work, and sleep went by so fast and hard you knew nothing about it. Now my muscles are hardening, and my hands—I am a Piece of the Cuticle of the Calloused Proletariat. I eat with the zest of a cougar, I brown like toast. And, John, even at nights, I am too damn sleepy to read! . . . "

" . . . Your letters are infrequent and so are mine
—and it is unavoidable, for such is the blasting effect
of continuous hard labor on the finer sensibilities. However, I have good news for little Philip—the Doc says
that while there's evidently something old and fruity
the matter with my internals, it's the queerest case of
threatened T. B. he ever diagnosed and sometimes he's
tempted to think it's something else entirely. Long life
to his stethoscope—I only hope he doesn't saddle me
with leprosy or botts instead. Sellaby the Muscular
Muse of Molokai, the title is tripping enough, but I'd
just as soon shirk the fact.

" By a course of judicious silences and a little pyro-
technic cursing in your own best manner, I have managed to get quite chummy with some of the miners. The
Harvard lads and the Gods of the Mountain in general
(except for the Doc and Sam Cohen) hold aloof and
don't seem to be haled into bliss by my winning smile.
So with them I cultivate the Higher Interior Snottiness.
But the work-gangs are good boys—everything from
sour Scotch to indeterminate Hunky and the Irish to
fizz up the mixture in their usual ways. Some of them
belong to the I. W. W. and its headquarters, over a
pool parlor and run as ' The Frickett Mutual Benefit
Association,' has the only good modern library and most
of the interesting talk in town. While there I, for the
most part, preserve a discreet and absorbent silence—
except once when I got into a mixup with an old line
Marxist on Fabian methods as opposed to sabotage and
was routed by more quotations than you ever saw on
an English exam., much to the stealthy amusement of

those listening in. I started inventing authorities myself but he spotted me at once and took down names and
titles, sober as church, till I finally brought up Vin-
cente Aneurism, the terrorist who strangled the King of
Bavaria by substituting pieces of fried white rubber
hose for H. M. H.'s favorite evening dish of noodles,
and then he laughed like a defective air-brake—he was
Scotch—and came over and put his paw on my shoulder
and said: ' Lad, lad, but ye have the preecious gift of
the gran' lee!' So for that night, at least, I got
away . . . "

" . . . You ask me about my interior circumstances
and feelings, since my exteriors seem both to please and
to amuse you. It is a question that could only be put
by a perfect fool or one of you four—you will realize
that I am not being uncomplimentary. Well, they get
along, that is all there is to be said. Certain things in
me—a bright casualness, complete confidence in the universe and in myself; carelessness of soul; possessed rapture of mind, as I had, as you have, if I judge rightly,
now, in flying—these are finished. Their places have
been taken in a measure by fear, in a measure by revolt,
in a measure by irony. I have ceased being stunned or
dazed—the body is a human mechanism and reacts.
That it should react is the sick disgust of the idealist
and the sentimentalist, but react it does, and that, too,
is weight to be carried. I can carry it better from the
fact that I have utterly lost resilience—I walk like a
man with broken arches, but at least I walk firm, feet
on the ground. I have even been, for hours at a time

out here, endurably if vegetably happy. But even such cow-happiness as that I find that I hoard with the sedulous patience and concealments of a conspirator—I am afraid about it and that something will take it away from me. Also at times I rebel—about as effectively as an ant alone in the middle of a stove. This realized, for the unbearable sensation of bound powerlessness that follows—no, not bound for no one is enough concerned with you even to bind you, there is no crack open for escape and even if there were the above would still stare at that hopeless attempt with the same bright enormous indifference with which it regards your crippled gyrations now—for this pinioning of spirit and mind, like a chicken sent to the butcher's, there is no cure at all but irony, that ineffable clear attar of scorn and pain. Irony suffereth long and is kind, is not puffed up. Blessed are the ironists for none of them want to inherit the earth. Irony believeth nothing, endureth all things. Oh, all ye works of a persistent Irony, bless ye that Irony, praise It and magnify It forever. And so on with the rest of the Litany and Beatitudes.

" This is not a complaint and it is not as a complaint that you will take it—it is a medical statement of facts in reply to your query. All that is implied in it I know you will recognize without need for re-reading—our moods are too kin for you ever to fail me in a major matter. As for work of another kind from the one that gives you a healthy sweat, I don't know when I'll be fit for it, not now certainly, never perhaps. I have certain talents, as we both have had to admit, and I have played with them and made toy-trains of them as we

both know. If I am ever let really use them again, I
shall not be particularly surprised—but I shall be
thankful. It is all on the clay knees of the Ironic
Spirit.

" Your talk about Oxford and the shaved lawns and
the flying men dining in Hall makes me spiritually
homesick or greensick or both. Lord Lucifer, will we
ever get drunk on English ale in a tavern together?
Yes, by Baal, and take cockshies at dons and intellectual
poets with pewter tankards and write hedge-verse under
a hedge with the tinkers who remember about George
Borrow. I tried the red-eye native to Frickett with a
new acquaintance the other evening—the hairiest man
I ever saw, a chest like a yak's or a doormat. Result,
passed out cold at 10 P. M. in a minor dive quoting
the ' Shropshire Lad,' woke up 2 A. M. and walked
home to Mrs. Grady's with a head that seemed full of
lighted pinwheels through a freezing bath of blue night.
Got up 6 A. M. as usual and worked ten hours, feeling
like a burnt out wick the while and ready to put my
lunch most of the time. Man I was helper to, Mac
Gregory, the Marxist Scotchman, very sympathetic, let
me sleep an hour at noon, and kept telling me of his
wild young days in Edinbro' and a party he and some
friends had with milk and eggs and three cans of
shellac . . . "

" You to be at Oxford—you score, blast your tortoise-
shell grin, you score! Oh, go pipeclay your silly wings!
I bet you look like a Cockney T. G. in your baggy, beery,
bloody English uniform! Think of me as an inefficient

specter among a host of efficient specters on a copper-colored mountain . . . "

" . . . My I. W. W. friends get more interesting and informative all the time. They split into three classes—the sweets, the sours, and the half-and-halfs. The sweets are the Utopians, the theorists, all varieties from my modernized Highland cateran of a Scotch Marxist to an animal of a Polish Jew, the ' bright,' greasy kind, who is Secretary of the local branch here and has all the latest direct-action, gory-revolution palaver at the ends of his long, scrimy finger-nails. Some are just unbearable wind-bags, all constant arguers, most as stodgily, solidly Socialists and Anarchists as other people are Republicans or Quakers or Benevolent Indians. They propound large theories of indiscriminate massacre but take it out in talk—they are as ready to squabble and fire off long set speeches and bicker till they fall asleep in their seats over the pettiest details of the plumbing of Arcadia as ever a congress of Ph.D.'s is over a disputed spelling in a worthless Elizabethan play—they duel about the pure commune as opposed to the soviet with the acid strife of close relatives over a rich uncle's will. I like to listen to them—they are in general so heavily respectable and so set in their ideas and the Semites so convinced that they are dangerously advanced.

" The sours, on the other hand, are the real hard-boiled boys, the men with grievances eating them up, the fighting core and *élan* of the I. W. W. Some are mere filibusters and frondeurs but most, at one time or an-

other, have suffered very definite injustice and are ready
to come back at Those on Top with dynamite or anything else that's handy.   They are the Faubourg St.
Antoine of the country and mostly recruited from the
two-fisted, brass-knuckled class of floating skilled or
semi-skilled workers, structural iron men, miners, rivet-
ers, and all such other Dekes of the laboring world.   The
Masses, I think, had a story about one of them.   Hop-
fields worker gets pinched and beat up as I. W. W.
They find his red membership card.   ' Will you quit
the I. W. W.? '   ' No.'   ' We'll tear up this card.'
' Go ahead—I can get another one from headquarters.'
' We'll tear up that! '   ' Tear and be damned—you'll
never tear what's on it out of my *heart!* '   Rather bom-
bastic and over-fluent for a genuine sour but—it gets
the spirit quite admirably.   The sours believe in the
approaching class-war and the ultimate victory of ' the
One Big Union,' as Peter the Hermit did in his Cru-
sade.   They make up about 15 per cent.—even in the
I. W. W. which is the Jacobin Club of the present labor
movement.   The sweets come possibly to 15 per cent.
The rest, the loitering majority, is half-and-half, the
dough of the bread where the sweets are crust and the
sours yeast.   They are just like the rank-and-file good
sheep of any party, they take the kicks, believe in the
platform, subscribe the funds and in general come when
called.   Pardon this long digression on superficial data
—it's all getting important here, especially as the sours
are increasing their percentage and more of the half-
and-half are turning sour, for which both special conditions at Frickett and the wide labor ferment all over

the country are responsible. The sours are the cream of the lot to talk to . . . I am having a desultory nibble at all brands of socialism . . . "

" . . . I took a walk the other evening up past Prostitutes' Row, in which you might be interested. No, it was not for purposes your offensive mind will instantly leap to, you with your R. F. C. commission and half a dozen assorted Countesses and bar-maids to serve your immoral ends. But the spectacle was indeed a curious one and worth recording.

" I sauntered slowly up the road away from Frickett as lonely and eerily sad as a coyote in full moonlight except that I did not express myself in howls. There were other men ahead, two boisterous, one furtive, so I stopped and sat down on a stone till they had gone out of sight. The night was lazy and warm as a sleeping dog and the mountains in front of me stood up like a scene cut out of black paper against the liquid welling billow of white-silver behind them where the moon had not yet risen but only trickled through in spurts and crevices of dripping light like quicksilver running over black cloth. I regarded the moon with an eye as cold as hers, an eye full of irony. Then I proceeded, the friends of Venus having passed out of vision, walked five minutes, turned a corner and came out into a glowing street.

" It was raw with lights and lined on either side by houses about the size and shape of box-cars. Occasionally there was a larger hut or middle-sized tent, preliminary dance-halls I surmise, for from them proceeded

music, shrieking and thin, and the thump of feet.
Sometimes the box-cars were diversified by names—
'Josy,' 'Mexique' and 'Little Evelyn'—one had
'Idlewild,' ah, there was a spiritual soul!—but in general they were without name or number. In many the
blind of the front-window was drawn and yellow. In
others, one viewed inhabitants before a mirror, refresh-
ing the paint no doubt. In other still the inhabitants
walked the porch in kimonos or rocked, and with them
all, as with Pater's Mona Lisa, the eyelids were a little
weary. They called at me, they displayed charms and
moved about. 'Come up and see me, dearie!' 'I'm
Rosie, I'm an awful nice friend to you boys.' 'Won't
you come in, honey?' 'Say, sweetness, what's your
hurry?' and all such banter. I promenaded the street
imperturbably, a chill goblin in a forest of cawing goblins. At its end I smoked a cigarette and looked at the
mounting huge cheese of the moon.

"Once I saw a man come out of 'Idlewild,' a man in
a white Panama hat. He looked as ridiculously out of
place as he would have at a formal wedding or in hell.
He had all the satisfied sleekness of a cat as he made off
down the road. I examined him for pad-feet and a
waving tail. If I didn't sleep so wearily hard at night
that hat of his would mix unfortunately with my
dreams.

"When I had looked enough at the moon, I went back,
tasting my mouth and finding it bitter. This time the
cries that pursued me were more insistent, even a little
strained. I was spoiling trade apparently by my demure
behavior. A mulatto, purplish with powder, even rose

from her rocker and followed me a couple of steps down
her stairs. I went down the shelving road again, that
was full of the moon, smoking bad cigarettes—no good
ones, they are thirty cents a package here—and my mind
was salt the while with such pitiful irony as I have
seldom known . . . ”

“. . . Had a tummy-ache the other day, too much
canned corn, I guess, and in the day off thus made necessary managed to write a poem which I enclose for what
it is worth. Not Plato but Pluto is the inspiration of
the gastric-stricken bard.

QUITS

Pale riders of the stumbling road
With the eyes of beaten men,
Who are you, that the youth in me
Should ache like wounds again?

Are you dumb devils made of air
Or pictures out of the mind?
For both of you look like Despair
And you are not humankind.

The first one lifted up a head
No thunders could have bowed.
His voice was foolish as the wind
And gladder than the cloud.

The drench of that satiric rain
Ran on his face like tears.
“ I am the thing you were,” he said,
“ When you had twenty years.

"I am your golden corpse, my friend,
A corpse that you have seen.
Never again you'll make me live
Nor ever kill me clean."

The next was hot and galloping,
A skull within a cloak.
His fingers were like clicking bones,
He coughed before he spoke.

"To see What Was, my empty boy,
Has sacked you like a town!
And dare you look at me, at me,
And stare What Will Be down?

"I am the shadow at your soul,
The nightmare that you see.
When all your fires are silly ash
Men will remember me.

"Drink to the poison you must be!"
And, shrieking out like birds,
The two swept back along the track
While I fought long for words.

"Though broken up like Folly's speech
And vainer than her boasts,
I have one shield I shall not yield
For any troop of ghosts!

"A bloody taste is in my mouth,
A black sardonic smart.
Sweet is the wine of honest men,
But this wine's from my heart.

"The mind that has such gall to drain
No torments can dismay.
And there is bitter peace for him
Who drinks his heart away.

" Pass on like foam before the wave,
Lost specters of a youth!
For though that draught grows old with pain,
Its least bleak drop is Truth."

They dimmed like water in the sun,
They faded with a cry.
And left me like an angry tree
That surges at the sky.

I tossed my hat above the boughs
And spat and swaggered South.
The black heart's blood within my lips,
The verses on my mouth.

" . . . Wilson's last note to Germany is over all the
papers—I suppose America will be in it in a month now
at most, in spite of the ideas of my wiciouser colleagues
in the I. W. W. on the subject. Well, in five more years,
if the war drags out that long, I may even pilot a Spad
myself, who knows? Then watch out, you Daredevil of
the Clouds, you Yale Face! . . . "

So Philip got through the winter and the spring
and a multitude of puzzled consultations with his doctor. The day after America declared war he tried to
enlist and was rejected with what he complained of as
almost indecent haste. April passed and May—it was
very nearly a year since Milly had died. He kept her
feasts still and always and carefully, and pain would
come in a recurrent stroke, squeezing down over his
heart like a hand, but in him, as in a city that has been
rocked to its foundations by earthquake, the major shock

was past, and a noise of building began. He began to put out tentacles in a dozen different directions—toward the miners and the I. W. W. till he dreamed himself, with the blasting facility of the writing temperament, as everything from a lesser John Leitsch to an American Danton. Toward his work in the Rusty Mountain Company and vague visions of becoming a bearded, patriarchal copper king, a cross between Abraham and Andrew Carnegie. Toward a Wellsian intellectual aristocracy—it was about this time he read " The Research Magnificent "—a samurai order of science ruling the world from aeroplanes with the lucent unintelligence of a chemical law. Toward a Whitmanesque submergence in " The People," largely connected with heartier hand-shakes and fewer baths. Toward the Secret Service and a death like Nathan Hale's with Cambronne's repartee at Waterloo spat out at a carefully-posed panorama of stout German generals—toward anything and everything, and, in most cases, toward something wildly impossible—but at least they were stirrings toward action and connected thought and you cannot remain a shadow among shadows if you are troubled by such noisy and active dreams. It is true that often he felt extraordinarily empty, and empty in the sense of a used paper drinking-cup rather than that of a goblet waiting for wine.

And from art and anything connected with the making of it he was inhibited by a restraint almost physical in its strength. He was sick of himself and putting himself with ink on paper or with paint on canvas; and as himself is the only person the jejune artist knows with any degree of certainty, it followed that canvas and paper were, where he was concerned, to stay blank. And if he couldn't write with his arterial blood he wouldn't write with anything else and make tushery or costume-romance. And so much is probably too much about his moods—the progress of a mental or physical convales-cent is a genuine saga enough but apt to be a stupid one as well, if minutely recorded, unless the convalescent in question is one of those two fascinating people, myself—or you.

Philip got as hard as a brickbat and astonishingly healthy, except for rare spasms that left him weak and rancid with nerves; so healthy in fact that his doctor in-sisted on calling in various specialists. He was given a raise by the Company, and the raise was not wholly due to the skying price of copper. They were losing men and he was spoken of in weary conferences between divisional superintendents as a " steady young chap with a chance."

The I. W. W. and Sam Cohen took fewer of his off hours, the " doc " and an elegant young Princeton pro-consul with a Farmington wife, boisterous year-old baby, and something mysterious the matter with his pancreas, more. " I'm afraid I'm gradually being made a respect-able citizen, John," he wrote, " and, O Lord, as the story goes, how I do dread it! But it's good to have some-body to talk football and the New York deb. gossip with and have them give you tea out of luster china and real marmalade full of orange-strings with fat pieces of toast. Also whiskey that isn't alcohol plus caramel and pure spirits of wildfire. But why should I tell these things to you when you are buying Pol Roger at some absurd number of depreciated francs a case? "

Meanwhile the mines began to grow sultry and restless, little clumps of men gathered in the street after the knock-off whistle, there was much loud talking in saloons, and the words that went through the mass of the miners like a fuse through a bunch of fire-crackers were " Six a day or quit," " Two men on a machine," " Strike." The grievances were real enough—most other mines in the state worked two men on a machine, a proceeding that made for safety on the men's part and expense on that of the company; six dollars a day with war-prices bought no more than three-and-a-half two years before. On the other hand the American Army private was getting thirty dollars a month. But neither worker or employer had perspective—both saw the immediate thing and nothing beyond it, the miner the extra nickel on the price of a can of beans, the boss the extra dollars spread like grit over his payroll to cut his war-profits. It must be remembered that the country at large was still in the " Business as Usual " period of the second month after the declaration of war. And through the bungalows of Valhalla was trotted a rustling Red bogey-man and " it's all these dirty foreigners— they aren't Americans—and that damn I. W. W. crowd." And between the sunburnt rows of shacks that made up Frickett went the word by grapevine telegraph, " The big stiffs are going to get a bunch of gunmen up from the city and freeze us out." So the pot seethed and simmered and began to boil over—and there appeared to stir it one of those " strong " men in authority who seem born for the purpose of making colossal mistakes.

Philip was down at I. W. W. headquarters two nights before the strike vote was taken. It was sweltering June and the tin roof over the " Frickett Mutual Benefit Association " radiated heat like the lid of a steaming kettle, but the three long rooms like bath-houses put end to end were packed and sweaty with men. Philip had come with Mac Gregory and saw a few known faces in the jam; Sour Scattergood, the philosophical anarchist who had once taken part in a riot led by William Morris and still carried two white welts from his cheek to his jaw from an affray with the Liverpool police; Izzy Wicez, the Polish secretary, dirty and scented, nuzzling about the crowd like a cur-dog picking up scraps; Bud Egan, a kicking colt of a twenty-year-old, the best rough and tumble fighter in town; Honest Louis, the steady, peaceable Swiss who read the Appeal to Reason as if it were a direct revelation from the Creator and settled the various little disputes that were brought to him to judge with the even-handed justice of Justinian; twenty or thirty of the keenest and most intelligent men in their gangs; a sprinkling of fire-eaters and troublemakers; a host of the vast indifferent. The crowd had the heaving restlessness of oily water, they talked little and mostly about big-league baseball, the war, the prices. " The fules, the silly bits of fules, they dinna ken what they're here for," grunted Gregory.

" Well, what are they here for, Mac? "

" A parcel of nonsense. The strike commeettee's in session yon "—he waved his stubby hand at the front room—" but what gude can they do the commeettee by crackin' wi' other fules like themsel'? All they need is some word to tell their wives, the fushless people!"

"Will the strike come off, do you think?"

"I dinna ken. It's a cuddy's trick, strikin' the noo."

Bud Egan wormed over toward them.

"Mac, Phil," but his eyes were wary as he glanced at the latter.

"Think they'll put it across to-night, Mac?" he asked lippingly.

"I dinna ken, lad. I dinna ken." But he cracked knotty fingers, calloused and scarred from the handles of tools, against each other and his eyes were bright blinks of gray.

"Aye, but I'd like fine to be in a strike, a real strike, just the one more time." His mouth set rigid as the lips of a vise. "A real strike wi' heads broken in the streets." He repeated, "A real strike. Mon!"

"I haf seen too many strikes bust into half," came a deep boom over his shoulder, Honest Louis, "they are no good. The Company bring up their scaps and the bulls they lift up their clups, and that is all. And then your name is on the black-list and the next time you get a job and you strip your clothes for them to look at your sveet pretty self—the doctor peeks through his four eyes at you and says, 'Bum heart! No good! Ged oudt!' And you—proot!" He exhaled a balloon of blue tobacco smoke. Mac chuckled creakingly—the physical examination required by the companies and its use to disqualify undesirables was an open joke at the time.

"Say, I'd like to see them try that business on me!"

lipped Bud Egan. " Say, I'd like to see any wise guy
tell me I'm sick ! "

" They'll tell you you're sick enough any time, Bud,
and prove it, if you don't act sweet and nice to every
stinking scissors-bill of a foreman that's too good to
eat lunch with his own gang," put in Sour Scattergood
and " Sour, Sour, my vriendt, you are not the lad that
should tell the boy to be sveet," from Honest Louis.
" When we have the One Big Union, Sour, ve will make
you eat six kinds of sveet pie a day," and the four went
off into a discussion of the crimes of the A. F. of L., the
bosses, and Gompers. " He iss a jellyfish, that Sam, a
jellyfish with glasses," while Philip scrouged back
against the wall and looked around him. Everywhere
was the same queasy whisper of question and answer,
the same talk, drifting and purposeless as seaweed, the
same uneasy milling to and fro like cattle before a
thunder-storm.

A starchy voice burst out of a group across from him,
shrill as a tin whistle. " The war? To hell with the
war ! The bosses get fat on it and the poor boobs who
enlist get a ' Gates Ajar '—that's all ! Oh, America's the
hell of a fine country for the guy with a million iron
men but it's the hell of a punk country—" A leather-
faced miner was talking to a friend who kept chewing
a wedge of tobacco over and over like a cow with a
familiar cud. " And Joe he writes me from camp and
says he's been made a corporal. Pretty fine, Buck? "
" Sure." " Well, I write and tell him what the hell
does that mean and how high is a corporal, for it just
seems like it was a minute ago when me and Molly put

the little sneezer into his first pair of long britches, eh,
Buck?" "Sure." "An' he sends me a postcard back
and says a corporal ranks a K.P. but is way down below
a shavetail like the wheels is under a tin lizzie. Why,
Molly and me thought we'd split when we got that postcard, wouldn't you, Buck?" "Sure." Mutual wheez-
ings of mirth and expectoration. A saloonkeeper in a
flopping white vest went nosing from one bunch of
talk to the next like a little, mild, worried rat. "Say,
boys, now don't you go and strike on us—you'll do us
all dirt if you strike. Why, I was just going to get a
nice big plate-glass mirror up from Phœnix to put over
the bar in my place, and now if you boys go and strike
on us, it'll go and bust business wide open and I won't
be able to get a *thing,* not a *thing.* My God, why did I
ever locate in a mining town, anyhow? I've done a
lot of nice things for you boys, you know—"

But such high spots of chatter were infrequent. Most
of the random constituents of the Irish stew of humanity
just stared about, whittled at the window-sills, smoked
steadily or spat inaccurately toward the three tin cus-
pidors. The minutes perspired away, Philip dripped
and leaned against the wall. The reëntrance of Izzy
Wicez, full of unpleasant importance, shut off the vague
growling hum of the talk completely. Izzy flapped his
arms like wings for perfect silence—he mounted on top
of a bookcase.

"Men," he yelled in a high whine—and the room
grew suddenly electric and thick and tense—"men—I
have an announcement to make to you. For the strike
committee." Mac Gregory was knocking one fist against

the other fist, Sour Scattergood had the beatific eyes of a saint before a judgment, Honest Louis looked puzzled and hot and scared.

" The strike committee has not yet been able to decide anything. They will meet here to-morrow at the same time. Thank you." He jumped down, disinflated, and an explosion of laughter followed his words. All tension evaporated instantly like a bubble stuck through with a straw. The crowd started to dribble away, a few humorous and indecent comments on Izzy spotting the general disgusted noise of talk and feet.

" Ah, Christ," said Bud Egan peevishly, " that's the way it always is. Wouldn't you know it? "

" No strike," murmured Honest Louis inside his throat. " No strike—that is gudt. Now I can buy the express-wagon for my kid." He smiled immensely. Sour Scattergood fell into the unprintable and Mac Gregory relapsed to dialect. Philip felt as relieved as if he had been hauled up again to firm earth after swinging on fraying ropes in a bosun's chair slung over the edge of a precipice.

Nevertheless, eight days later, the miners struck.

Philip heard talk about trouble, saw straws of trouble floating and dipping in the soup of every-day conversation, but trouble, in any capitalized or carnivorous form, materialized not at all. He had been sent on a week's trip, half-survey, half-inspection, to an undeveloped property of the Company's some fifty miles up state as aide to the Princeton proconsul. Smoking beside a camp-fire with the intense night stars above them crowd-

ing the plushy sky for place, all the concerns of Frickett
and the universe in general seemed as far removed and
unimportant as a dance of midges in June. When he
got back, two-thirds of the miners were out, the streets
filled with them as if every day were Sunday. There
was no real disorder, only a few loose threats from
boys or drunks. His boarding-house was largely ten-
anted by foremen and shift-bosses, loudly confident of
the strike's collapse inside a month. There was picket-
ing at the mouths of the mine and mine offices, and
guards around the mine-properties, but both bosses
and workers were disciplined except now and then in
epithet.

The whole town had the atmosphere of a poker game
with two pat-hands trying to bluff each other out.

Once, going over to the mine-office for his pay, Philip
passed Mac Gregory on picket. A sour and friendly
grin came over the man's face.

"Come on over and join the party, laddie!" he yelled
companionably; and Philip, "Sorry, Mac, but you guys
are holding up the war." All the sympathies of his
mind were with the Company as long as they played
fair—the fact at issue now was to beat Germany, that
effort the strike retarded and so must be broken as soon
as possible. On the other hand, his feelings and emo-
tions ranged completely beside the men—what fair wages
and decent living and working conditions they had, had
been, in general, battered out of unwilling companies by
force and the one weapon of the strike. Also an uneasy
thought kept humming inside his head wondering if it
were wholly worth while to abolish injustice abroad, if

while doing so, injustice was set steadier in the saddle at home.

"These loudmouths who talk about the damn ignorant laborers are gradually dyeing me carmine," he wrote John. "Their only solution for the labor-problem is a machine gun—oh, when will anybody show up Amurricanism? Amurricanism is subscribing $10,000 to the Liberty Loan and ditching the Government out of $50,-000 on streaky contracts. It is marching in Preparedness parades and saying you can't look out for employees who enlist. It is calling 'Spy' and 'Traitor' and 'Bolshevik' like a bad little boy on a street-corner and then breaking food-regulations in private like a bad little boy stealing candy. All Amurricans wear the Amurrican flag on their collars and have tricolor ice-cream on the Fourth of July. They want blank *lettres-de-cachet* and clean cells in a mammoth Bastille for all

"Socialists (every kind from Charles Edward Russell to Bill Heywood),

"Writers (except of cheerful, patriotic stories about Pershing's Sammies),

"Furriners,

"Suffragists (damn hens!)

"Cripples,

"Opponents of the President,

"Admirers of the President,

"Personal Enemies,

"People Who Can't Support Selves or Family on What They're Paid,

"Free Speakers,

" Art (except piecrust movies and smutty magazines)',
" Interesting People.

" Some day you and I will write a history of the Amurricans. It will begin with the Congress that badgered
and baited Washington, go down through ' To the
Victors Belong the Spoils! ', the Carpet-baggers and
the Wavers of the Bloody Shirt, past the Pure Brass
and Bad Canned Meat or Hanna Epoch and end up
with Anthony Comstock and the Committee on Public
Information. And, oh dear, it will make the ' Innocents Abroad ' seem as humorless as the book of Jeremiah. Not that I don't dislike the milk-shake Nihilist
and the poison-ivy professional walking delegate of the
type that ruled when the Unions tyrannized San Francisco just as much. I do. But the latter are fewer,
right now at least, and the Amurrican ramps about unassuaged."

The draft came and Philip registered for it. The
specialists summoned by his doctor and paid by Phil
had arrived, looked respectable through *pince-nez* and
delivered an opinion. The tuberculosis diagnosis was,
though tempting, false. The trouble was peculiar, connected with the canals of the ear and a once-infected
tooth. Philip thought they had the attitude of Probation Officers with a wayward but attractive girl as
they spoke tenderly of the canals of his ears. He must
have an operation. He must be drained— " The whole
thing makes me sound like a piece of marsh they want
to reclaim for cultivation," is the tag-end of a letter.
He would certainly not be fit for military service for
two years, probably not for five, and the operation had

best be postponed a month or two that the system might
be still further built up.

When they had left the room with the stateliness of
departing penguins, Philip executed three steps of a
double-shuffle and started chanting the chorus of
" Christopher Colombo " before he remembered where
he was. He had not recognized how binding and leaden
the sentence of permanent disablement had been upon
him, until now it was suddenly lifted at a touch. It
was like walking after walking in armor—like waking
out of the racing disquiet of fever and looking at the
sun on the wall and feeling cool and knowing you were
going to get well.

" If they only hadn't looked so blessed important I'd
have bought them all the liquor there was in town ! " he
confided to his Princeton friend. The other shook hands
ceremoniously.

" Which is the cue for—? "

" Well, really, I think you owe me one. You don't
get cured of T. B. every twenty-four hours."

" It would have about the same effect on my
Scotch, Phil, if you did," sighed Princeton. " Now
where on earth does Louise think she keeps the ice-
pick? "

" By the way," said Princeton, later in the evening,
" I think they're going to pull off a trick play in a
couple of days that will bust this strike into little
pieces."

" So? What's the idea? "

" Well, I really don't know very much about it—some
stunt of that film-hero sheriff of ours. What I do know

is confidential. You won't spread it to the scarlet comrades? "

" Not unless it's anything important."

" Maybe so, maybe not. Except that the Company and a lot of the substantial people in town are getting pretty sick of the present mess. It's holding up our government shipments, you know. And everybody's scared out of their shoes if you go and say ' Boo! I. W. W. ! ' to 'em."

" I know that, good Lord, the strike's been peaceable enough so far."

" Well, it's going to stay peaceable. The sheriff's up on his ear and the thing's to be settled, one way or t'other, before the end of the week."

" Federal troops? "

" Nothing as drastic as that. Phil, has anybody in the Company ever called you for being so thick with the hard-boileder of the miners? "

" No," stiffly; " didn't know I was so important to the Company."

" Now don't go off your head. But I've heard some ungodly things and stopped them as well as I could—from hearing that you were one of the big guns in the National I. W. W. to having told me confidentially that you and Bennet Starbox were planning to wreck the mines with TNT."

" Well, I don't even belong to the I. W. W.—for one thing I don't agree with them about the war. And Bennet Starbox is the best lawyer in town and doesn't know me by sight. But, good Lord, how screamingly silly! "

"It is, but you know how people get. Look here,
I've got a job I want done up Cripple Cañon this week—
will you go up and do it?"

"And have all the poor fools you've been talking
about say that I fled from whatever vague wrath you're
prophesying to come? Not for this child."

"It isn't that—it'll show where you stand, that's all."

"On the fence?"

"No—with us."

"But suppose I'm not with you?" The little red
devil of argument is cakewalking around in Philip's
head.

"You're bound to be. Look here—there may be
trouble—there may not be. If there is, are you going
to act like a simp or not?"

"Like a simp, Peter, whatever happens."

Peter laughs in spite of himself.   .

"Oh, damn it all! I can talk myself dry but I suppose you will."

In a black early morning Philip is stirred into half-
aliveness by many feet going past under his window.
The feet do not have the casual clop and shuffle of a
crowd, they crackle like a marching column, thudding
by in ranks and under orders. He wonders what the
dickens has happened—an accident at the mine?—
blinks at the radium figures of his wrist-watch and sees
it is only a quarter past four. When he wakes again,
with a sudden leap from dream to complete consciousness, it is six and the room is dripping with a pale
pearly wash of even light.

He dresses and goes down to breakfast, marveling at the corpse-like quiet of the house. Something curious must be doing, the air is as thick and fateful as air before a wind-storm. On the long table is a clutter of dirty dishes that no one has taken away and the pink toothpick-glass has turned turtle and scattered its little wood nastinesses around like spillikins. He calls.

"Oh, Mrs. Grady!"

There is a scurry from the kitchen like the noise of a frightened cat. A head with a knob of streaky gray hair—fluffy and wild as if it had been pulled out of the middle of an old mattress—pokes cautiously through the door.

"For the love of the Holy Virgin, who's that?"

"Only me, Mrs. Grady, Mr. Sellaby. What's up? Why has everybody gone out?"

The head takes courage and, emerging, shows itself stuck on to a figure like that of a badly-stuffed rag doll, wearing a dirty blue silk sacque, the cast-off of some wealthier doll, over an apron spotty with kitchen accidents.

"Praise be, Mr. Sellaby, but I thought all the time it was one of thim murderin' wobblies! They're cleanin' thim out of town, the bize are—the sheriff, God bless his eyes, has put it all in the pa-aper!"

"Cleaning who out?"

"The rids, sirr, the rids. They've got a thousan' speci-al deppyties with guns, and a thousand from the Citizens' Protectible Le-ag with more guns, and they're roundin' thim up by the Post-Office and shootin' thim down by lashins and lots and I wouldn't go out in the

street if I was you! Grady's with the Protectible Le-ag
and they've give him a gun and a club and if he doesn't
come back with a bomb put through his stomach I'm
not the honest woman I've been for these thirrty years.
But read it, darlin'," and she thrusts into Philip's hand
a newspaper screaming with headlines that are, by some
unconscious satire, a most vivid red.

Philip glances at the third extra the *Frickett Banner* has published in fifteen years. "Keep Off the
Streets To-day, Women and Children! ! !" roars the
opening sentence. Then, in a double-ruled box down
the front of the page, "Proclamation! !"

"All loyal Americans . . . by the authority vested
in me as Sheriff of Frickett County . . . to arrest on
charges of vagrancy, treason and being disturbers of
the peace of Frickett County, all those strange men
who have congregated here from other parts and sections
of the country for the purpose of harassing and intimi-
dating all men who desire to pursue their daily toil . . .
rights as Americans . . . we can no longer stand or
tolerate such conditions . . . This is no labor trouble
. . . etc., etc." At the end a flaring signature, Thomas
D. Vanguard, Sheriff of Frickett County. The
"strong" man has known his hour and run head down
into his folly.

At first Philip is inclined to laugh—some of the
statements are so pompously ridiculous. As if everybody didn't know that it has been one of the most or-
derly strikes in the history of copper! As if any one
were expected to believe this fairy-tale of a multitude
of blood-lusting Bolsheviks springing up from behind

every clump of sagebrush for the one purpose of disturbing the peace of Frickett County! Then he looks
at Mrs. Grady and sees that her face is gray. "It's
lucky we are at all, not to have all our throats cut by
thim wobblies while we slep'," she says, her hands
trembling over her apron. But the thing is prepos-
terous! But—

A little slow flame of anger begins to fume and heat
in Philip's mind. Whatever the rights or wrongs of
the strike itself, this business has nothing to do with
either. It is not American, it is not even Amurrican,
it is blatant exercise of fist-law by bull-minded stupidi-
ties in power.

"Can you give me a sandwich and a cup of coffee,
Mrs. Grady?" he says. "I think I'll go out for a while
and see the fun."

About this time Sour Scattergood, the philosophical
anarchist, his sock feet propped on the rungs of a
chair, his back to the wall, is reading with great approval a paper-covered volume of Robert G. Ingersoll's
speeches, nodding his lean, scarred head, like the head
of a tired cab-horse to the ten-cent-store-jewelry glitter and flow of the prose. A neat black revolver lies
on the pillow of the bed beside him, uglily out of place.

There is a turmoil outside that shakes the rickety
stairs. Hands rattle the door-knob, pound on the flimsy
door.

"Scattergood! Oh, you Scattergood!" shouts a suety
voice.

Scattergood lays his book on the bed, marking the

page. "What's up?" he says pleasantly. He is answered by the yell of a dozen throats.

"Come out here, Scattergood, we're going to ship you out of town! Come out, you damn Red! Take your medicine!"

Scattergood removes his spectacles and puts them on the bed beside the book.

"Got a search warrant?" he asks in a high voice, "or a warrant for my arrest?"

"Don't need one for guys like you! We've got the goods on you! Come on out—there are a bunch of us here with guns!"

Scattergood's hand fists over the neat black revolver.

"Go to hell," he remarks distinctly.

A shout comes back like the belling of dogs who have treed a coon. A panel of the door splits in under a pistol butt. Scattergood shifts his chair a trifle, takes scrupulous aim and fires.

The spat of the sound like the pop of a big hot chestnut splitting open is followed by an instant of utter silence and the wet voice of a man saying, "Christ! I got it!" Then the Citizens' Protective League breaks down the door.

Ten minutes later the room is full of the vacant, gold-dusty peace of a summer morning. There are spots and streakings of blood, already darkening, like the stains on a butcher's block where the Citizens have carried their dead man down the stairs. Scattergood's spectacles and book lie on his bed—a gust of air ruffles the pages of the "Speeches of Robert G. Ingersoll." Scattergood's feet protrude without curiosity from his door into the hallway, an air of extreme detachment in their gray socks. A fly hums in through a window and flirts busily down to inspect him.

Philip gets out into the street about seven despite the religious protestations of Mrs. Grady. He looks up it and down it—and in both directions it is perfectly empty like the street of one of those shells of towns that a boom has made, deserted and left lying like an eviscerated tin can in the sun and the sand. He walks two blocks up toward the drugstore and is startled at the loud solitary sound of his own feet. Suddenly five men, armed with rifles, slide out of a saloon and cross the street toward him at a dog-trot.

"Here, stranger, what's your business?"

Philip produces his identification-pass to the mine-offices.

"Got anybody who knows who you are?"

Philip names the Princeton proconsul.

"Guess you're all right—sorry we haven't an extra gun, you could come along with us. You can get a gun and a badge over at the sheriff's office if you want one."

Philip smiles. "Thanks."

"No trouble." They are very polite. "Sorry to stop you but that's our job."

"Sure."

They trot back to their ambush. Philip notices that they have the hot serious eyes and clipped speech of little boys playing a game. The meeting gives him a thrill of pure adventure, it is such ridiculously good melodrama. Going past the drugstore a long "Ssss" hisses into his ear like a sigh of escaping steam. He turns, the proprietor, a fat keg of a man, who rejoices in celluloid collars and tie-clips, is beckoning him frantically.

"Better come inside for a spell," he whispers as a leading villain might say "Hist!" "They have just went and killed three men in the house next door. I heard the shots as plain. And then there was groans!" The fact that murders and groans were nothing but a disturbance caused by a near-sighted girl falling down the back-stairs and believing them a trap laid by the I.W.W., for her special benefit, has not reached him yet to spoil the taste of his fantasy.

Philip hesitates. "Think I'll go up to the Post-Office."

"You'll get shot sure! They're shooting 'em down in rows up there!"

Philip nods. "I guess they won't shoot me," he says and turns the corner.

The Post-Office, a pillared architectural blight in the center of town, is the point on which the five armed posses of special deputies and Leaguers have been ordered to converge with their prisoners. As Philip approaches it, he notices that some forty or fifty uneasy miner-pickets are still undisturbedly guarding the mouth of the mine. Suddenly and in a dramatic flash, like a scene seen out of a Pullman window at night, a small compact gang of armed Citizens swarms out under the false Greek portico of the Post-Office itself and is on the miners like ants on a piece of apple. There is a babble of talk from the latter, and some ironic cursing and shouting, then they are marched down in front of the Post-Office and the Citizens stand guarding them in careless postures. One prisoner asks permission to get a drink of water from the office cooler and emerges, wiping his mouth. Most of them sit down or sprawl in the scanty shade—two start playing stick-knife and get as absorbed as if they were ten years old. The Citizens are extremely casual, a couple of them bring out chairs and make themselves comfortable in the road. A sentinel crosses over to Philip.

"What's your business, Bill?"

Again the identification-pass and the name of Peter Lascelles. The sentinel offers tobacco, which is declined.

"Guess we'll clear 'em all out of here by noon to-day," he remarks as he goes back to his post.

Philip starts to turn back toward Mrs. Grady's, half his anger taken away by the obvious good humor with which the affair is being conducted on both sides. As he does so, though, the end of the street is black with the head of a singular procession. Posse One has done its job and returned on schedule—there must be three hundred Citizens in hollow column swinging rifles or flourishing pistols as they saunter along. In the center of the human sandwich like the pips inside the cut half of a pear is an indiscriminate mass of miners and loafers with a sprinkling of white-shirted business men. One woman of thirty-five is near the middle of the column and she carries her head up as proudly as if it were set on a pike. In the front rank, between two overalled miners, walks the immaculate Bennet Starbox,

who has openly told his friends that he thought the
strikers had cause to strike.

So Philip, for the first time, saw the bitterest force
for disintegration in America, the mob. They came at
a measured pace, they were under commands, they carried arms, but the mind and will of every Citizen there
was sunk into the mind and will of the weakest and
silliest and most bullying and brawling in their ranks.
The parade came closer and closer, as strange a prodigy
on the everyday street as a dragon, a beast with the
brains of a hen and the body of an elephant, a beast
that had the brutality and force of a tiger and the
jackal cowardice of a street-cur snapping at men's
ankles. Philip looked at it and felt physically sick.
The marching halted, the prisoners were herded together.

A loud red-faced man came by Philip, patting his
rifle as some uncles pat children's heads. " Pretty good
stuff! " he sang to himself. " Pretty good stuff! Run
all these dirty Reds out of town and give 'em a coat
of tar and feathers, that's the ticket! Pretty good stuff
—hey, brother? " and he jerked Philip playfully in
the ribs with the butt of his weapon. The hearty gesture
set all the dry fierce rage Philip had kept in for two
hours crackling like burning brushwood.

" You big stiff! " he shouted passionately, " you big
fat stiff! I think it's the dirtiest thing I ever saw! "

His voice fell heavily off into astonished silence as
a body falls into a pool. He stood there with hands
twitching and a tingle of hot blaspheming mirth ran
all over him.

" Get in with the rest of those wobblies, you lousy Red ! " said the red-faced man, recovering from his O-mouthed amazement, and this time he poked Philip in the stomach with the barrel of his rifle.

Philip once tried to assemble and write out the events of the next three days in an hour-to-hour diary. He only got about half-way through the task and then tired of it, but this is about the way it would have run.

8 A. M. Still lined up in front of the P. O. What a mixed-pickle lot of people, all swept out struggling together in this general patriotic " house-cleaning," with about as much in common with each other as the original population of the Ark ! One of those pale grubs of boys that run pool-rooms and spit through their teeth is whimpering, " I'll get these stinkers yet, by Christ— by Christ, I'll get the dirty stinkers yet ! " A miner, a six-foot statue in dusty bronze, argues mildly with him. " It ain't *right,* buddy, and the Gov'ment'll stop it. Why, I've lived and done my job here in Frickett twelve whole years ! " A Greek, who owns a scrap of a grocery down-town, rolls liquid eyes and seventeen-jointed curses at the C. P. L. sentinel. " I leave a store—a boys run off wit' a stuff—a woman an' a keeds they have nothing to eat an' a die ! " Bud Egan is telling anybody who will listen, " Well, after this I packs a gun when I goes to work. I packs a gun in my pants and any squeeze that butts into me gets somepin' outa it." Truly, a sort of Ishmael's parliament of lost dogs and under dogs !

8:30 A. M. Good Lord, are they going to deport all the miners in Frickett? There must be nearly two thousand of us now. That roast-beef-faced fool who petted me with the gun is talking about Amurrica. I'll bet a crayon-portrait of Washington that he's draft age and one of Jefferson full of whiskers thrown in that he'll claim exemption.

9:30 A. M. Five miles of slogging through rusty dust, the whole straggling curio-collection of us, to the ball park at Frickett Junction. Accompanied by boisterous wit of the " Better look out, we may be going to wash you! " type. Chivied into the ball park while guards about as heavily armed as British battle-cruisers parade grandly up and down with an eye to their own picturesqueness. As one of them is round as a squab and another perishing skinny, they are not too impressive against the skyline. Attempted singing of the " Star Spangled Banner " by Citizens and Special Deputies, quite successful at first and we join in. We are instantly told to keep our mouths shut, patriotic airs are not for the likes of us. The band gets three bars ahead of the crowd and sticks there like a fly in cold syrup and the second verse, which our wardens carol as if it were solely composed of " tya-tah-ta-ta-ta-*ta*," completes the rout. Three would-be martyr I. W. W.'s strike up the *Internationale* in a reedy pipe. We hear it carefully to the end in complete silence, most of us taking it for a praiseworthy attempt at comic vocalism. " Now give us an honest-t'-God *funny* one."

10:30 A. M. More suspects keep being shoved in all the time, just why I don't know. I suspect the Deputies of rolling poker-dice as to whether a man is deportable or not—they could have done the job in just as superbly intelligent a fashion by picking every other man with brown eyes. We are not allowed in the grandstand— the Citizens fill the grandstand—but on the lower rows of the bleachers we may rest. We revolve up and down, to and fro, like batter being beaten around in a dish. Most of us have the dazedest, most lost expression I have ever seen on faces. The handful of strike-leaders and agitators are sore clean through—they get together and argue like a baseball team that has led every inning up to the ninth and then watches the umpire throw the game to their opponents because he likes the pretty color of their uniforms. But the crowd, on the whole, isn't sore—it's just stupefied, as if water had started to run up hill.

Honest Louis comes up with a grin like a gargoyle. "Well, Phil Sellaby, and why *zum Hölle* are you here?"

"Well, Louis, and why are you here yourself?"

"Some one push a long gun under my nose and say, 'You, Louis, take a walk.' So I walk with him. But I do not admir his soc-ial circul!" and he wags a thumb at the guards.

"Same here. Where's Mac?"

"Swearing his oatmeal-soul from off him with the strike committee. He will be here in *ein Bisschen*. He says he will come and shelter little Louis from the naughty big boys with the guns."

Mac arrives, gray granite with cursing, but he snorts amusedly as we greet each other again all round.

11:30 A. M. At last we know what's going to happen to us! We are to be shipped to Liberty, N. M. (ominous name!)—and not, I imagine, in Pullman cars. " And, thank God, the State of Arizona is rid of you! " ends some bawling Citizen orator. (Cheers.) The State of Arizona is rid of us by dumping us on the State of New Mexico. Will New Mexico pass the buck, too, and us along with it, I wonder? If she does we ought to see a good deal of the country.

12:30 P. M. A sennet. Alarums. Excursions. Exit the dangerous Reds—2,000 of them in 24 cattle and box-cars without food, though many luxurious cars have actually a whole bucket or so of drinking-water. As an exhibition of the Mailed Fist—there are probably few parallels in American History. Well, it is something to know that you are going to be a historical parallel, even if you and 86 other humans—I counted 'em ten minutes ago with some difficulty—are jammed into a slatted cattle-car meant for and recently inhabited by a dozen cows.

It is hot enough in this car to fry eggs on the floor, if we had any to fry, and there are enough assorted stenches from the 87 sweaters to set a chemical laboratory analyzing for ten years. It is funny; just as on a shipwrecked raft or a pre-Napoleonic Europe, in this little, stinking, rolling community of ours the strong man takes control; this time it is Mac, and under his guidance we have already adopted one desert-island rule. There is not room for all or two-thirds of all to sit. So the weaker, selected by Public Opinion (and very fairly, some men trying to beg off) sit at cramped ease, the strong stand and feel self-sacrificing. Alas, I am one of the strong!

1:30 P. M. Long bicker with Louis about democracy —both bending and straining tortuously to ease our cases of floorwalker's feet. He doesn't believe in it— don't know as I blame him—logical solid position; master and man. Master gets cream, man skim-milk and leavings. Every one wants to be a master. Advantage of America is, better chance to rise to master-class quicker than in other countries. Masters may be decent or otherwise; either way under present form of government it is they who have the power. Vote means nothing but money in the pocket on election day. One Big Union would solve things but probably won't come. Fatalistic p. of v. mixed in, too. *Che sera, sera.*

My pos.—Mob spirit greatest danger in America. Can convince one man by reason, deal square, mob brings every man down to lowest common denominator or worst man in it. Difference bet. army and mob. Democracy *will* work, does work where people know each other. Athens. The free cities. New England town meeting. But there is a spiritual force in it.

Louis won't admit. Pure machine.

All I know is, any time I ever see a mob again I'll feel just as I did when I was a kid and saw my first snake. Felt so to-day. Funny.

All the same I'm right about democracy.

2:30 P. M. Water getting low, even with rationing. A great fuss and business of Fords full of armed C.P.L.'s patrolling road beside train. Train moves with the celerity of a caterpillar about to go into a co-

coon. Sang "Over There," much to annoyance of
guards. They told us to stop and we told them to go
and play marbles. As their only resort was indiscriminate slaughter, their bluff was called.

3:30 P. M. Water about through. Am beginning to
realize exactly what hunger with no food in sight may
do to you. What a well-fed life I have spent! Four of
the men have lunch-boxes but we need a new miracle of
the loaves and fishes to do any particular good. For
what are seven ham sandwiches among so many?

4:30 P. M. Heat, never knew heat that soaked into
you so—makes you feel as if you were wrapped in a
thick wool blanket, mouth and eyes, too. Wish I were
a dog in somebody's front yard under one of those
whirling lawn sprayers. Told this to Mac, he clicked
and chuckled. "Lad, lad, I was but just thinkin' the
noo' how gran' and cool the job I had once in the New
York Morgue was. But it's little we care for braws
while we have them wi' us."

5:30 P. M. Talk with one of the small shopkeepers
—lived in Frickett four years, wife, two kids, nice little
Jew. "They come into my store. They say, 'What you
think about this strike?' They look like miners to me
so I say, 'Fine, fine'; all for business, don't you see
that is good business. They say, 'Come along with us,
we run you out of town!' And my wife? And Becky
and Sammy?" He looks about him with the gaze of
an intelligent pet cat that got into the pound by mistake
and has a general idea that there is chloroform and
death in the air.

6:30 P. M. Dinner time without the dinner, thus

carrying on, in me at least, the actions of breakfast time and lunch time. Most of us settled into a lumpish doze. One man, a big fellow and looking as hard as nails, is suddenly violently carsick. I hope it isn't contagious, that's all. He apologizes prodigally between convulsions, rolling at us the terrified eyes of a nauseated horse.

7:30 P. M. Cool, thank God.

8:30 P. M. Cold, my Lord! A desert and biting cold that you only get in Arizona and New Mexico. The temperature drops like a bucket down a well ten minutes after sunset.

9:30 P. M. Night, fallen all over the car and the country like chilly soot. A few red sparks where people smoke—I can't really, on as vacant a tummy as mine, besides they may set fire to the car and griddle us all like pancakes. There are only a couple of armed flivvers left on the road—now and then they buzz up like fireflies and yell spiteful remarks. Guards on the roof, of course, guards on the engine and in a few of the cars. I shouldn't mind if we went under a very low bridge.

10:00 P. M. Arrived Liberty, N. M. Parked out in the yards. Some food shoved in by anonymous benefactors—I get segment of hot dog and one WHOLE tamale. And water, greasy, but water. Whee—God bless our home! Whole affair absurdly like picnic. Satisfied crunchings as of lions at meal time from all over car. Honest Louis, " Oh, girlies, don't you feed or annoy the wild Red animals! " Howls like leopard and switches imaginary tail, much to every one's amusement. A session of dirty stories sets in. I'm going to sleep.

12 M. Wake up to find somebody's boots around my throat. We're on the move again. More sleep—too much trouble to poke person belonging to boots, though they are no rose-garden.

NEXT DAY

3:00 A. M. Stopped again, outside jerkwater depot and usual flea-and-sand-bitten desert town, of forty houses size and shape of condemned horse-cars. Sign on station " Cholo—" then cut off by end of car. Cholo —what? Irritates me unmentionably not to be able to see the rest of that fool sign.

3:15 A. M. Mac, Honest Louis and self being nearest door, find the same is not locked and so crawl out to investigate. Promptly shot at from roof, merely as warning, I imagine, for shots hit dust about forty feet ahead. A dozen or so stabs of red fire. Strident voice, " Get back into that car, you bastards! " We obey, meek, chastened.

5:00 A. M. Wildest collection of dreams imaginable —probably due to boots as most of them concern death by strangulation. One, however, disconnected and very perfect—Io of the old Greek fable walking through field of most marvelous and impossible flowers, hollyhocks like towers of silks and scent, she, silver as a new dime and naked as the harvest moon. Superb idea for poem— —must remember it somehow.

6:00 A. M. Dawn—first a red crack in the East like

a break in a piece of gray-purple china. Widens—pours
over the desert and the town like scarlet dye—the hot
round ball of the sun, hard with heat, pops up spectacu-
larly, a fire-balloon, leaving the sand and the houses
breathless with day as it floats higher.

7:30 A. M. This car is not a pretty spectacle. In
it 87 men have been shut since twelve noon yesterday,
smoking, spitting, eating, sleeping, performing natural
functions.

8:30 A. M. Oh, the blasted American sense of humor
—it is bigger than love or hope or fear or fate or death
or patent-medicines! In this box-car pilgrimage an
equal number of any other race would have gone mad
or murdered. These people merely flop around and
smile and swap cut-plug and yarns and lies. And a
bunch of them have wives and families in Frickett,
three-fourths have been deported for no cause and all
without vestige of law, any one may be in jail or at
the end of a patriotic lyncher's rope to-morrow for all
they know. They have a courage and a silence that
could shut up the Sphinx and a disreputable mirth that
would make Peter the Apostle fall off the jasper walls.

9:30 A. M. Hunger, thirst and fatigue come, I see,
to have definite colors in body and mind, the last a sort
of gelatinous dirty-tapioca gray. Hunger is crimson as
a grenadier's coat and sits around in your stomach like
a cat, pushing out and retracting his needling little
claws. Thirst figures as burning blue, the blue of the
sky we see through the slats of the cars, and industriously sandpapers your throat till swallowing makes
it raw.

10:30 A. M. till 12:00 Midnight. Thirst; hunger; natural functions. Exhaustion and the laughter of exhaustion. What a caricature, what a carrot-doll, what a ridiculous atomy of a wishbone-puppet is any man in the broad fat palm of a comic and cosmic Irony like this. Here we are, all eighty-seven of us, scuttering over that palm like so many enlarged fleas. Suppose it shut—what is flea-eternity?—a juicy inexhaustible arm to discover and bite? "Plays such fantastic tricks before high heaven as makes the angels weep."

Grit in the mouth. Ideas about Democracy. Not a democracy of the full belly. Not a democracy of words and Fourth of July orations. But a real democracy. An arisen spirit. A wind-blown fire. A salty laughter. And God's face and God's body made out of the million dirty faces and dirty bodies of an infinite number of tired, dirty, comradely men.

I believe this train of box-cars is one of the few real democracies in America and the universe at large. They ought to send us all over the country—and very possibly they will—as a rolling exhibit A of how the trick can be done.

All the same I wish they'd deported us at the very beginning of the week. There would then be a chance that some of us would have on clean shirts.

Irony, delicate, bitter food of the clear-eyed, careless and melancholy solution for all base frets, wave of foam and brine where the mind may drown eternally and lie like a drowned man on the floor of the indifferent sand, loose hands playing with coral and shells and men's white thigh bones; be with me now, be with me and cover me—for without you I am going to be just as emetically sick as a dog.

Power of brain over matter. The qualm passes. Nothing left but my old pals, hunger and thirst, doing business at the same undistinguished stand. And both of them are getting merely gnawing and dull like safety-razor blades one has shaved with once too often.

Coolness. Night again like a salve on the body. Sleep and vicious dreams of immense meals of steak and great tubs of all the icily-clinking drinks in the world. Democracy—we're all little crumbs of Democracy—a loaf of Democracy in 24 slices of box-cars, baked crusty and toothsome and sweet in the stinging sun. Take. Eat. For this is the body of Democracy. . . .

Even if all these visions of gorges and wakings to find them lies went on for weeks, I'd be glad I'm here and not in Frickett or sitting up on top of one of these cars with a C.P.L. badge and the heart of a fool and a shiny loaded gun.

NEXT DAY

The Regular Army, by all the satires, has gone and adopted us! And the President has sent an inquisitive little telegram to the Governor of the State and to Thomas D. Vanguard, Sheriff of Frickett County, asking reasons for the sudden exercise of unconstitutional powers on American citizens. Why, we must even occupy a column on the front page of the New York papers! And we have a special escort of U. S. Cavalry just like a foreign ambassador, and two carloads of army food are due to arrive some time in the near future, and we're even going to set up a pretty little camp for ourselves half way between Liberty, New Mexico, and the Mexican border—

The procession from the train out of Liberty to our camp site was most extraordinary. Two thousand rather more than less filthy, shambling ragamuffins, gaunt in the eyes and shaky in the knees with two days of little food and less water, reeling down a sandy road with jingling guardian-angel squads of regulars fore and aft, sun-mahoganied, fit and humorous, the whole Rogue's March yelling " John Brown's Body " at the top of its lungs. It was like a turnout of all the broken toys in a giant baby's nursery—a general review of every dilapidated human patch or tatter from the general ragbag of the world. I got so weak laughing I could hardly stand up and Honest Louis and Mac had to take me between them to get me along at all. Then the three big water tanks where our camp was to be and two thousand stone-naked men trying to bathe at the same time in one of them—a sight to make a convention of Boston intellectuals fall over dead by battalions. And the food—the big rations of food—canned beef, canned tomatoes and bread—they wouldn't give us seconds on it, afraid that some of us would expand too much and so pass away, but firsts were enough, Lord knows! My emptiness embraced that food like a rich uncle returned from the oil fields.

Then we pitched camp—again under the instructions of the regulars—and a more comfortable and neater camp never existed—it's as tidy as a New England kitchen and as clean as the deck of a yacht. And the night—and the red eyes of the cooking fires in the evening—and talking to Mac and Louis under a sky like a black satin dress covered with tiny bangles—me smoking one of the few good cigarettes of the last year, bummed from a sergeant who once upon a time belonged to A. D. If we got the inferno of democracy yesterday and the day before, these are the sports and pleasures of it.

NEXT DAY

Work all day, putting in shower-baths and occasional tent-floors, stringing telephone wire from Liberty and other general fixings. Everybody anxious to lend a hand. Only discord—Izzy Wicez, the Polish I. W. W. secretary. He shirked work and was warned three times and went on shirking. So we ducked him in the water tank with the hearty approval of the Regulars, and he spouted water, and after that was a good Indian. This is the simple life, all right, and the satisfying one, led rather in the hunting spirit of the well-greaved Achæans. And the talk goes from Napoleon to General Booth and back again by way of Christ and Judge Gary and Luther Burbank.

The draft comes off this week. Must get hold of a list as soon as possible.

End of Philip's Diary

Philip found that his draft-number was sixth in the order of call, stayed in the camp another week till it was reasonable to suppose that he should be summoned for physical examination, and then went back to Frickett, not without material doubts as to whether his second exit from thence would be on foot, on a rail, or prone with his hands folded across his chest. He might, quite possibly, have had the examination transferred, but the thought simply didn't happen to occur to him and besides he felt rather pleased with his own foolhardiness.

He parted from Louis and Mac with love and no ceremony. The last ten days had twisted the three close together. "When you make your pile, keep a piece of it for leetle Louis," the fat Swiss grinned, "and withoudt you this camp vill be less fun than a twelve-hour shift and no time off." "Good luck, lad!" said Mac, bruising his fingers. "Keep your chest warm these nights and I'll write you how this dogfight comes out— though, bucko lad, but I'm no great hand with a pencil!" Then the two fell into an exchange of sorrowful curses that lasted until both sank hopelessly asleep.

Philip slipped out of camp an hour before dawn, past the sleepy back of a guard who was thinking of a Mexican girl in Phœnix, and got into Liberty in time to catch the early train. His clothes were crumpled but clean enough—he had had a chance to wash them—and the station-agent sold him a ticket like any one else. The train was slow and he arrived in Frickett about two in the afternoon. He walked up from the station to Mrs. Grady's nervously alert, with a boyish feeling that

if he didn't look over his shoulder continually something behind him would hit him in the back. But, even
discounting his active imagination, the town had a
hangdog look. It had come out of its brief intoxica-
tion cold-sober and still ached with the bursting head
of the following morning. Moreover, its ears were ring-
ing with the sarcastic comments of other towns' newspapers and the mushroom tales of what utterly foolish
things it, in its sudden drunkenness, had done. If
Philip had marched up the center of the street with a
Red flag in his hand, he might have been hesitatingly
asked what he was advertising, but that would have been
all.

He did succeed, however, in scaring Mrs. Grady very
nearly out of her feeble wits when he walked in and
demanded his mail. After she had sat down on the
dining-room floor and fanned herself with her apron
and given a confidential account of all her sensations
to her favorite saint, she finally produced the expected
notice from the draft-board which she had just been
about to forward wildly to Philip, care of President
Wilson. "Not knowin' your permanint address, Mr.
Sellaby, and I hope you'll pardon the liberty, but they
said he was takin' care of all you lads that was shipped
away."

The notice ordered him to report for examination the
next morning, so he lay *perdu* till a little before the
knock-off whistle and then called up Peter Lascelles.
The latter, after one gulp of astounded surprise issued
an invitation to dinner and to stay the night, as he
thought it would be safer. " Sorry—we'll have to more

or less hide you during the evening—Louise is giving a dinner-party—but I'm damned if I'm going to have your blood on my head, and they might get peevish with you at Mrs. G's."

So Philip made himself as inconspicuous as possible —the Lascelles' house was fortunately far back from the road—entered without being observed, and was given dinner upstairs by Peter himself from the wreck of Louise's party. He felt quite like a Secret Service man 'in the heart of Berlin and was enormously gratified when Peter, entering with a fragmentary job lot of vegetables, solemnly drew down the blind, saying, " You mustn't be seen here, you know, if it's avoidable. And there's always the chance—"

Peter also found that he had neither money beyond eight dollars and thirty-two cents nor any idea at all of what he was going to do if he were rejected for the draft. He lent him a hundred dollars and advised him to go home and consult the San Francisco specialist recommended by his doctor about his lungs. Philip took both cash and advice with open arms. He could neither go back to Camp Democracy nor stay in Frickett. If he didn't have tuberculosis, there was no need for him to stay in Arizona at all. Once his classification in the draft was definitely settled there would probably be some sort of war-work that he could do. He went down-town to the draft board and was rejected for all military service, his own doctor officiating at the obsequies, inside of half an hour. The officials, the doctor, knew fully both who he was and the fact that he had been deported, and ignored both facts with a bland positiveness that made Philip feel as if he had suddenly become invisible. One man even asked him, with no hint of sarcasm, if he didn't find Arizona climate the best medicine in the world for lung-trouble. He shook hands with his doctor and got from him a letter of introduction to his San Francisco colleague, said good-by to Sam Cohen and Mrs. Grady, had a final cocktail with Peter and Louise Lascelles, and left for Frickett Junction and California on the one-thirty train.

"But what did you *acquire* out of your excursioning around in a box-car, you silly Bolshevik?" asked Peter, as he set down his glass.

"Fleas," Louise suggested primly, "and then? Go on."

Philip flushed a little.

"Oh, democracy in general," he said haltingly. "And a particular comprehension of wide life and a little death and all hell-on-wheels!"

BOOK V

AMATEUR THEATRICALS

(1917-1918)

Adam was my grandfather,
A tall spoiled child;
A red clay tower
In Eden green and mild.
He ripped the Sinful Pippin
From its sanctimonious limb,
Adam was my grandfather
And I take after him.

Noah was my uncle,
And he got dead drunk.
There were planets in his liquor-can
And lizards in his bunk.
He fell into the Bottomless
Past Hell's most shrinking star,
Old Aunt Fate has often said
How much alike we are.

Lilith she's my sweetheart
Till my heartstrings break,
Most of her is honey-pale
And all of her is snake.
Sweet as secret thievery,
I kiss her all I can,
While Somebody Above remarks,
"That's not a nice young man!"

Bacchus was my brother,
Nimrod is my friend.
All of them have talked to me
On how such courses end.
But when His Worship takes me up
How can I fare but well?
For who in gaudy Hell will care?
—And I shall be in Hell.

PHILIP hadn't realized how hard it would be to explain matters to Phil. Talking together in the cool of the library that had always seemed to Philip the ideal den for a leather bear, it was so buff-colored and dim and secluded, both voices sedulously low and pleasant but with something made out of conflict sawing and snarling under the tones and ready to bay out with the sudden scream of a whistle if the genteel voices were raised just a little, little bit higher—Philip knew he hadn't realized by the tenth of a decimal fraction just how very hard it would be.

He had dropped off at San Esteban that afternoon without warning or telegram, wanting to surprise Lucia, tasting lingeringly in anticipation all through the blowsy day in a daycoach that seemed full of spilled box-lunches and babies with prickly heat, the tingling pleasantness of that surprise. He discovered that Lucia was at San Francisco—kept there over the week-end by an important meeting of the Red Cross. Lizzie, the maid they had had ever since he could remember, opened the door for him and gave him the information with the well-bred civility due to a visiting minister. When he had expected and braced himself against a middle-aged Irish rush for his neck, this left him chilly and stiff. She relented after a little, even bullied him with some of her old fervor over the question of clean clothes, but her voice had a sorrowing affection in it the while that puzzled him; it was the stern pity of a Calvinist nursemaid for a charge that has contracted measles in some imbecile escapade outside of bounds. The water in the tub ran tepid when Philip tried to take a cold bath.

Phil would not be back until after supper, and supper alone might as well have been composed of baked Apples of Sodom. It was served by Lizzie in dejection, to an accompaniment of civil but mournful sighs.

As he burnt his tongue on the bitter little demitasse that concluded it, Lizzie, with the pained face and suppliant eyes of an invalid martyr who has just been reprieved against her will, came in and laid a pile of assorted journals beside his chair.

"Ye might like to look at the papers, Mr. Philip," she said grimly. "Ye're in 'em!"

Then she vanished like a ghost at cockcrow before he had time to ask her any questions.

He began to turn over the papers idly. They were in order, he saw—all the news of San Francisco and the Coast for the last three weeks. He glanced in the sports in one—at the society column—it seemed good to read about all the petty details of City affairs again, it gave him as keen a flavor of home as the sight of a pepper-tree—it revived his wilted feelings like a judicious cocktail. Mrs. Jimmy Traintor had just given another of her big dances. The *Chronicle* clamored for a reform administration and war with Japan. The Seals were leading the league.

Then his eyes wandered down into the account of the Frickett deportations and he jumped as if somebody had left a red-hot horseshoe in his chair.

He read them over, every one of them, down to the *Stinging Lizard,* that vicious little journal of backstairs tittle-tattle that apes so successfully the blackmailer's bad manners of its Eastern contemporaries.

He read them with burning care. In what New York newspapers he had seen his name appeared only once and then so blithely misspelled as to be unrecognizable. But somehow, somewhere and for those unaccountable "news" reasons that impel a Press to pick one man out of a hundred and hold him up for a week between finger and thumb in large type, squirming with imperishable notoriety, the San Francisco journalists had nosed him and tracked him down. He had almost as much space in their columns as a good second-class murder. There were pictures—and not of him alone, but of Lucia and Phil and Shreve and relatives he had never even seen.

It all came from Lucia's father having been Governor and the fact that his uncle Ashbel was once President of the Bohemian Club, he realized with vivid anger. And Phil had a fatal facility for getting on committees. He, Philip, was the "Son of Prominent S. F. Broker Deported as Red," in the *Blade,* the "Young Yale Bolshevik Agitator," in the *Clarion,* the tawdry slacker and cheap revolutionary pointed at by the slimy tail of the *Stinging Lizard.* He had even, it appeared, given the *Argus* a lengthy interview exalting free-love . . . there was a hint that he had been expelled from college for bomb-making after a thorough horse-whipping by a justly incensed student body . . . there were sneers at parlor anarchists with influential relations and young wealthy fribbles who found themselves too proud to fight . . .

In fact for four days the local dailies and weeklies had played St. Sebastian with the stuffed dummy they had created out of straw and nonsense and given his

name. They had feathered the dummy all over with
poisoned arrows. And then what political influence
Phil had frantically been able to bring to bear had done
its work. They had left him riddled through and tied
to his stake and barked off after fresher scents and
saints. There were even a few "apologies" enigmati-
cally worded in the obscurer sections of the more respectable . . .

Philip dropped the papers on the floor and was torn
between blinding rage and blinding laughter. It is unfortunate that Phil should have chosen this particular
moment to walk loudly into the room. It is still more
unfortunate that his opening remark should have been
"Not very pleasant reading, are they, son?"

Phil had always had a turn for the heavy sarcastic
father. He used it with devastating effect in the three
hours' talk that followed. He sat down on every reason
and explanation Philip offered with the mountainous
decision of a stout comedian subsiding upon a silk hat.
At first Philip, though prickling internally with all the
numberless small annoyances of the day, had been logical, calm, concise. When he finished he was shouting.
Gradually and inexorably his father became to him a
figure entirely monstrous; a placid figure with vinegar
on its tongue to whom nothing could be explained, for
it would not listen, to whom nothing could be shown, for
it would not see. A stupid, deaf, dumb, gigantic figure;
a hateful figure; a padded, well-dressed, respectable figure that repeated forever and ever in the brawling automatic voice of a conductor calling off stations, "I would
not mind your disgracing yourself, my son, but you have

disgraced the family." When this figure repeated this for the tenth time with the blind stare of a bribed judge charging a jury, Philip said, " To hell—to hell— to *hell* with the family ! " and, as the figure pursed up its mouth in the amazed wrath of an insulted wax god, stamped out of the room.

The voice of the figure pursued him, thin and scratchy like a worn out phonograph record.

" When you can come here in the uniform of your country, sir, your father will enjoy your cleverness a good deal more ! "

The stagy coarseness of the sentence struck Philip in the face like a piece of dirt.

" *Can't* you understand even *now* that I've *tried* to get into the army and they've thrown me out ? " he flung back in a last despairing effort.

" You seem to have been healthy enough to stand the physical hardships of being deported as a Nihilist," came the spaced, iced words of the figure.

" Oh, Christ ! " said Philip and went out of the front door.

When he was gone the figure rose from its chair, shaking a little still with the dyspeptic wrath it had not quite wholly controlled and tapped a cigarette on the smooth hairlessness of its palm. It had been " giving the young man a straight talking to." It smiled, its face was hot with virtue and indigestion. It sank back into a chair and felt like the elder Brutus. It had spared neither rod nor child—and every one of the star-spangled conventionalities had been scrupulously observed.

Philip walked till the sun came up over the marshes and his head had ceased to seethe and devise the most crushing repartees that had never been uttered. When he passed through the next small town, he saw that he was a third of the way to San Francisco and he kept on, the exhilaration of his wrath still strong in him like brandy. About seven o'clock in the morning, however, his feet began to weigh as if they were made of stone, and he realized that he had had no sleep all night. He approached a suitable barn and was bayed at by a toothy black dog. He longed for another town and a hotel, but the road seemed as suddenly townless as if it ran over the sea. Finally, hungry and sweltering, he came to a rotten, deserted wharf with a cabin on it which looked as if any puff of wind that had made up its own mind could blow it to bits of wood. He entered—it stank of fish long dead but it had a sort of mortuary coolness to it and a bench where he could stretch out. A rowboat as crazy as the cabin was tethered to a ring in a pile—but to this he paid no attention.

When he woke, after an uneasy dream of something formless stooping over him, it was to hear the concussion of hurried oars on water. He ran out into a world blazing with noon—a red-haired man in overalls had the rowboat and was pulling with bitter vigor across the strait. He shouted, and the man bent to his oars with the stubborn energy of a man fleeing plague. The boat dwindled. Philip laughed and went back to get his coat.

His mood was less humorous when, after combining two skipped meals in an enormous platter of ham and

eggs at " The Railway Hotel—La Vaca," he came to pay
for his refreshment and discovered that his wallet and
all his money except for ten dollars kept in a watch
pocket had disappeared. He took the road again, inventing vast rhymed curses on red-haired men and men
who went about in rowboats, and all Judas-topped
thieves who sneaked upon wharves and robbed poor
travelers. He had meant to take a train for San Francisco, instead he walked and thanked Heaven for good
shoes and the leathering experiences of Arizona.

The day's inventions included a panful of sour milk
thrown at him by the nervous wife of a truck-farmer
whom he came suddenly upon from behind and asked
for a drink of water. A fresh peach pie presented without money or price by a spectacled grandma who vaguely
assumed him on some important military mission in
disguise. A sleep in a barn—a stray spark from a cigarette—five minutes of agonized trampling at a small
but nasty fire—an artistic raking of hay over the burnt
patch on the floor when the fire was finally out—and
some heart-felt thanks to his boots and the Ironic Spirit.
Early rising and an uneasy departure under the accusa-
tory yaps of a fat, round puppy.

The sky, flower-blue at first, then heating to a color
like the blue of melting blue glass. The road curved
into runes, snaky or straight. White dust and a
droughty smell wherever he turned. Wayside adventures—two stolid lovers whose Ford he cranked and set
going again—a verminous tramp with the face of a
nasty girl who followed him with horrible companion-
ableness for two hot miles and finally desisted only

under threat of a punch in the eye—the cool vacant porch and aisle of a village church with an old man praying devoutly in a pew, and two boys dumbly fighting as to whose turn it was next to swing on the bell-rope —country getting fenced and housed and tennis-courted and suburban. He could have got into Oakland that night if he had wished, but preferred to sleep deep under an alfalfa stack instead.

He arrived at San Francisco about ten the next morning, called up Lucia at Red Cross Headquarters and found she had gone back to San Esteban the previous night. He went down to a Y. M. C. A. and wrote her a long, difficult, explaining letter. Seeing a sign " Enlist in the Marines," he gave a bored recruiting sergeant and alert doctor the trouble of rejecting him. His ten dollars had now shrunk to five and in the last two days he had walked over forty miles. He felt as if life had come to a full stop—as if the spirit that ruled and wrote him had run out of commas and put the largest and blackest period possible after both Arizona and San Esteban and all their appurtenances. He drifted about the streets all day like a scrap of torn newspaper, and toward evening swung into an alley just off the Barbary Coast where two negroes and a Mexican were shooting crap.

He entered the game without ceremony—he was dirty and lounging enough by now to attract no comments— and lost two dollars out of his five in three passes. The dice came round to him at last, he rolled and rubbed them in his palm, they were warm, he felt a ripple of perfect confidence wash through him.

"Shoot two bucks," he said casually. It was covered. He rattled the clicketing cubes on the sidewalk.

"Little Phœbe!" he chanted. "My own lil', lil' Phœbe! Come on, you Phœb'!"

Little Phœbe obliged in two rolls after a spectacular instant in which she almost transformed herself into a goblin seven.

"Lets 'em ride! I looks at 'em and I lets 'em ride!" The pips showed five and three.

"Ada from Decatur! A five and a three. A six and a two. A mess of fours. Roll, you thighbones, roll!" The lady from Decatur hesitated, was coy.

"Ada! Ada! Hot dice, white dice, dice full o' grease, come and eight for Philip, two fours apiece!"

The bones surrendered to lyric rhyme, they laid down two fours with the shy subservience of a well-trained waiter. One of the negroes rolled profound and sorrow- ful eyes. The Mexican swore like a spitting cat in Spanish.

"Lets 'em ride!" said Philip largely and was covered, though with more of courageous despair than hope. He made his point again in a single throw.

"White boy, you is hot to-night—you is hot as Mam- my's stove!" gulped the other negro.

"Shoot the wad!" Philip answered, adding three dollars from his pocket to the sixteen already on the ground. The first negro dug a hand like a black ham into the loose of his trousers.

"I covers it all!" he growled, and slapped down a crushed plaster of bills. Philip rattled the dice again— he felt as if he were made of springs—he knew the galloping thrill of riding Luck and Chance like a couple of barebacked horses.

"Big Dick!" he moaned to the bones that clattered like spilt teeth. "Come, Big Dick!"

"Sebben!" grunted the negro. "Oh, you sebben! Sebben years in jail and sebben great angels of the Lawd! *Let him sebben!*"

"Big Dick, you know your baby!" whined Philip, and Big Dick did.

Half an hour later Philip had eighty-five dollars in his pocket and eight on the sidewalk. The Mexican, completely cleaned out, confined himself to looking on, and the negroes were praying to voodoo gods.

"He sevens!" chanted Philip. "He sevens!" The big buck instantly sevened on his second pass and gave a bellow like a charging ram.

"You's a h'ant, white boy! You's a h'ant!" he roared. "It ain't nach-ul to treat nice clean dice like that!"

Philip picked up the money and took the dice. His first throw was a natural. The negro made a sudden dive for his shoe.

"You hold his fists and feet while I carve him, Sam!" he shrieked. "He's put witch-grease on my bones an' I'm gwine tuh slice him like a ham!"

Sam gripped Philip's feet with long apish arms as he tried to rise. His friend wrenched a beaming steel thing out of his sock.

"Hold him!" he panted. "You hold him still and I'll lesson him to voodoo my bones!"

Philip jerked one foot away and kicked Sam violently

on the chin. The other negro, plunging to the attack, fell whack over the Mexican's outstretched leg, his razor chinking on the stones, his head butting into Sam's belly. A great " Whoosh! " went out of Sam like the noise of a burst paper bag and Philip was running up the crook of a dirty lane with the Mexican behind him.

At first Philip freely suspected the latter of good intentions, even slowed his stride to allow him to catch up. Then he saw that the negro's razor shimmered and glinted in one tight brown fist like a splinter from an evil moon. Philip sprinted—the Mexican sprinted and closed in—Philip's feet seemed to stick in the earth at every stride. The Mexican was running him down like a greyhound, he felt in his neck already where the slicing edge would settle like a wasp. The alley turned corkscrew fashion and came out on the greasy cobbles of the waterfront. Philip turned with it as it turned and rushed at the Mexican, with a blink of his eyes as he ran in under the dirty sheen of the blade. He shook the man like a sack, he shook the razor out of his scratching fingers and sent him spinning into a wall. And a street-car, a heavenly street-car, grated drowsily past the crimps' boarding houses and bawdy saloons, clanging a mournful bell. Philip ran for it like a hunted cat; a sidewalk tough stepped out to trip him, spat, and decided it was not worth while. He swung on the running-board of the car and scrambled inside to the peevish surprise of a sleepy Chief Petty Officer and three neat poor women. He took the air into his lungs again and felt it sweeter than any air he had ever known.

He glanced back once before the car swerved round

a corner. The Mexican, a diminished and violent figure, was standing in the middle of the street, looking sadly down at a glistening thing in his hand.

"Hey, Bill!" yelped the conductor angrily. "Come back here and pay your fare—don'tcha see this here's a pay-as-you-enter car?"

To describe the devious route which finally landed Philip at Los Angeles would be like giving the separate biography of each dot that stands for a house in the map of a city to scale. There were high spots—at one time he nearly got himself inducted into the Refrigerated Meat Division of the Quartermaster Corps, and was saved or lost by the fact that the ex-shoe-clerk second lieutenant in charge had a vicious prejudice against college men. He spent three weeks in the hop fields, eating and working and sleeping in a cloud of yeasty, savory dust, got the back of his neck sunburnt anew to the point of peeling agony and made new friends with the workers who ranged from shipping-clerks out for vacation money to whole families gone gypsying from grandfather to grandchild, and living eight in a tent with every kindness and vice and species of vermin that flesh is heir to.

His funds had given out in the interval and he tried tramping with a little butterball of a contented hobo whose monicker, Dago Slim II, was, he proudly informed Philip, "right under the washstand in pencil in every depot toilet on the old S. P." This ended when, after nearly losing a leg in an inexpert attempt to hop the blind baggage of an east-bound fast freight, he and Dago Slim II were arrested on a charge of chicken-stealing the moment they set foot in a little town near Sacramento. Cindery as he was, with a rust of dried blood reddening his hair, Philip managed to get an interview with the town marshal, found him a graduate of Leland Stanford, disclosed his own affiliations with Yale, and, by means of immense important hints as to an undisclosable connection with the Department of Justice in investigating I. W. W. activities in the labor camps, got himself and his companion off after a good night's sleep in a speckless airy cell. " 'Tis an illuminating experience to be in jail, John," Philip wrote. " There's nothing like it—every young man should try it once, just to find out why monkeys rattle and bite at their cage bars."

After the hop-fields incident was over, he made south through Stockton and Fresno, and in the latter city was whistling his way along a side street when a beautifully dressed old gentleman with the white floating whiskers of a mountain goat suddenly stopped him with the remark, " Young man, I am God."

" How interesting," said Philip. " Very glad to meet Your Reverence in Fresno."

The old gentleman looked sorrowful.

" I do not mind you youngsters being flippant," he said ponderously, " but I think you should treat your Maker with more respect." And Philip suddenly saw that his eyes were as bright and empty as pieces of washed glass.

They wandered down the street very amicably, and God was just confiding to Philip his personal reminiscences of Isaiah, "A rough, headstrong fellow, my young friend, and do you know, I'm afraid a little *Jewish* in his point of view——" when an unfriendly person in blue took God away. Philip wished that things had been the other way round, for God seemed to be unhappy with his keeper and Philip had never before gone about with so amusing a deity. "Still, I guess the asylum's the safest place for him through the war," he mused. "Whenever either side gets hold of him they make him give bright lively little patriotic speeches till it's a wonder the poor old man doesn't have to retire for good and all with a nervous breakdown." Then he felt a little sickish in his interior, for he remembered the vacant gray clarity of the old man's eyes.

He wrote about all these things to Lucia, but got no answers from her as he was always too much on the move. San Esteban he might never go back to; if he did it must be in uniform for his own satire's sake, if for nothing else, and that seemed as impossible as wings. He arrived at Los Angeles in the warm last of September. As his stock of money was dwindling again like hot wax, he spent the night at a Salvation Army shelter, singing "Sometimes I Grow Homesick for Heaven," and "Sinner, There Are Flies on You and Me But There Are No Flies on Jesus" with profound enjoyment, and sleeping clean again with a puppy-like pleasure quite as boyish and unprofane.

Next morning he saw a burglary take place in broad early daylight while a policeman kept back the crowd and a thin black box on stilts clicked the whole proceeding away into its internals. So he knew that he had come to Movie Paradise, and, like every other unemployed person or thing in the city, started haunting the studios for a job.

It was in a "society" film that he finally got his chance. The well-barbered, two-stomached director was talking matters over with an assistant inside the low wooden fence that shut off the sacred inner offices from the long waiting room where a lugubrious crowd of "extras" ranging from "good motherly types" to mere floating constituents of a lyncher's mob or a German army, turned wistful animal eyes from the stiff wooden benches.

"Look here!" the director was saying, "this is an élite scene, see? Biltmore stuff—Rolls-Royce stuff—country house on Long Island with ten butlers and a private ticker stuff. It's a dance—a Newport dance at a place like Vincent Astor's. It's so swell that not one of the crowd even bolts for the champagne when it comes, they sip it, they just sip it and feel ennuied. It'll knock every nine-o'clock town in the country for a gool if we do it right! And what happens? We get a lot of extras and we dress 'em all up like plush horses, fit to kill. And we start to take. And the whole foul bunch acks like waiters—that's what they ack like, cheap waiters—they ack like the Mike McGraw Tenpin Club and Social Circle's Annual Fishbake. My God, I can put all *my* brains into the picture and I can stuff it full of jack, and I can work a star till she'll let me tell her the right way to powder her nose and

put on her corsets—but I can't make ladies and gentlemen out of a hundred two-case-a-day hams in fifteen
minutes; no, not in fifteen *years!* For God's sake, Billy,
get me crooks, get me bums, get me bananas, get me all
the sweepings of town, but get out of here and don't
come back till you've got me a block of extras that'll
ack *refined!"*

Billy, slick hair parted in the middle, slick clothes
seamed at the waist, slick shoes the color of fresh blood,
tripped over to the fence.

" Any of you people ever been to college? " he bawled
in a voice like a klaxon.

Philip, a clean youth with a prominent fraternity
pin, a gummy-lipped boy in a check cap, two sport-
sweatered girls and a gray-haired woman arose.

" Gosh! " said Billy disgustedly.

He ran over them with his finger.

" You, Mrs. Boocock, chaperone. You'll do. You
girls—what school? "

" U. of C." Both giggled at once like twins.

" You? " He looked at the gummy-lipped boy with
disapproval.

" St. Agatha's. Freshm'n," the boy said mouthily.

" Ah right. Got a dress suit? "

" Nah."

" Six bits is all you rate then."

The gummy-lipped boy muttered deeply but nodded
his head.

" You? " The clean youth confessed to Lehigh. He
turned to Philip.

" Princeton," the latter said sweetly. He was not

intensively proud of the other college samples so far displayed.

"Ah right—you report about ten—get your cards. Any of you that's got dress suits or dresses get two, the rest one and a half."

He looked at the clown's brigade as it filed away.

"Pretty punk," he remarked very clearly, "but I think I may be able to dig up some real ones."

Philip found himself conducting a class in ballroom etiquette before the picture was finally taken. The director swore like a mule driver at the end of a first rehearsal.

"You're better than that other bunch of yaps, but, Great Henry, you certainly ack like a wagon load of bad carrots," he ended, exhausted. "Here, you Princeton man!" He singled out Philip with a wag of his thumb. "Take that pink young woman with the spit curls and show this lot of vegetables how to dance."

Philip seized on the partner suggested, a wide-eyed snickerer, and succeeded in putting her through the paces of a decorous fox-trot to the squeals of a tired piano and greasy saxophone.

"That's better," yapped the director. "That's the stuff. But it ain't quite, quite—" and he circled his pudgy arms in the air.

"If the music wasn't so utterly vile it would be a good deal easier to dance to it," Philip offered, with his voice as distinct as possible.

The director turned on him as if he were going to knock him down with his megaphone. Instead, "Yeah," he admitted suddenly. " Yeah—you're dead right. But what's the use of wastin' good music on boobs like this lot? "

" It's your business." Philip made the concession. " But if you want to have these boobs dance like anything but a bunch of sick rag dolls you'll have to give them the best jazz band in town—they need it ! "

The director turned suddenly to his familiar.

" Billy," he said, " you call up the Sandringham and find out how much they'll take for their orchestra for one afternoon. Make it fast."

" Now, Princeton, my lad," he finished, flipping back to Philip, " you show these baby birds how every little thing ought to go. Half of 'em, that is; I'll go and take the other half myself."

A mad three hours followed. The ballroom, needless to say, was a studio interior, a glass-roofed slice of two-thirds of a plaster palace. The guests were in full evening dress in the glare of high noon, their faces ghastly with screaming paints that would make beautifully natural complexions on the deceptive screen. The star was an overstrung regular actress with the temper and temperament of an ash cat. And more and more as the paunchy sweating director wrought and molded the inchoate mess of sloppy humanity in front of him did Philip admire his friendly courage and Buddha-like patience. He never swore while actually working; he was as gentle as a nun and as firm as a nurse with a cranky child. And gradually with interminable pains, the soup of extras took on some semblance of gentility and manners.

Philip copied his stubbornness in persistence as well as he might. He taught girls from unheard-of small colleges that cheek-to-cheek dancing is not practised in the middle of the floor at the most exclusive functions and that it is not necessary to hug your partner like a teddybear to give an impression of ease and gay social abandon. He showed pompadoured males that one may cut in on a girl without slapping her previous possessor on the back like a drunken sailor and that while a gentle lizardly wavering of the shoulders may be respectable, the python clutch went out with large white kid gloves. From the handkerchief carried protruding from the corsage like a favor to the handkerchief used prominently in the stag line, from the skirt that shouted aloud the presence of knees rather than informally suggesting them to the turned-down collar worn with a dress-suit, he issued a series of " don'ts " as numerous as the general orders of a chief-of-staff. He reduced three young women to teary faces by making them go back and put on corsets and unclocked stockings, and got a challenge to come out and fight like a man from the gummy-lipped boy when he told the latter to dance more like a vertebrate and less like a rubber frog. But he succeeded, he succeeded inordinately. And it was only when the Sandringham orchestra had arrived in taxis and tuned up, and the director waved to him to take the star and dance her for the first thirty feet of film till the great Stanwood Fane (carelessly posed so as to fight her acutely for every inch of footage) should cut in that he realized how extreme his success had been.

" It looks very nearly human now," Philip observed

in one of the pauses after the director had yelled " Stop Camera! " to attend to a minor detail.

" Human? My God, it even looks *decent*—Oh, Auntie, won't this lay them out in the sticks? It will. It will," the great man mumbled through his cigarette. Then he looked up at Philip sharply.

" Smoke? " he said. " Have one. You come around to-morrow. I want to talk to you. I always play my hunches, and I've got a hunch right now you got a future."

Philip realized as he inserted two fingers into the paper package that once more he had the gaudy raw ball of Luck at his feet.

They were running over " Serpents of Sin " in the projection-room before Elgar Hay, the director, Billy, his devil, Philip, and some others. The ball scene flashed on. Philip with a queer jump of his mind saw himself, a black-and-white enlarged automaton dancing and bowing and smiling with the rest of the dumb flat giants that flicked over the screen like shadows across a wall.

Elgar Hay saw the *döppel-ganger* too, and reverted to bucolics.

" Fresno raisins! " he simmered, chewing softly. " Hey, Princeton, where did you get that face? "

" Grew. What's the matter with it? "

" Oh, nothin'. Nothin' at all. Only it screens—that's all—it screens like a blessed Greek temple."

" I always took good photographs," said Philip, immodestly.

"You can't ack," went on Hay. "A baby could see you can't ack. But you know .it, and there's things you can do where you won't have to ack a little bit. The public's gettin' restless at all this hick stuff," he mused. "I had a kick on my last cow-fed picture the other day. Two months ago it'd a turned them away from the doors in droves. They're just like school kids, you never can tell what they'll want." He sat comatose till the reel was over, his eyes blank and cogitating. Then, "Oh, Sam," he asked gently, "Sam. Will you just run that dance-set once more?"

"Sure," came a voice from a nest built into the roof. Hay watched this time, in eager silence, paying special attention to the dancing shadow of Philip. When it was quite over.

"Billy!" he said, and his voice had the sharpness of reveille.

"Yep."

"Got any young college man scenarios? Doug. Fairbanks stuff without the circus stunts—you know?"

Billy took a little black notebook out of his vest.

"Guess so. Randy Spiker can dish up somepin'. Want it quick? A week?"

"Quicker than that. I'm going to play something across the board. Nothing flighty or wild—clean comedy with a bunch of heart throbs. Two days. Look here. This is it."

He outlined the story in jerks. As "The Way of a Man" is still running two years later, in patched, punctured, spotty reels in the theaters whose admission tickets are only six cents with amusement tax, and its

effect on any audience from cutaways to mackinaws is as
certain as that of water on dried apples—it seems
hardly necessary to put under the microscope here the
jellyish protoplasm of a production that has made a continent laugh and cry in the ways it wanted to. But Hay
was as insistent as a tackhammer in driving his main
point home.

"This guy *isn't* any hero," he repeated and repeated,
"not a piece of a hero at all. He's just human. Just
them. He goes to college but he doesn't win any football
games or lead any promenades. The other guy does that.
When he gets into the war he's just a second looey like
the rest of his crowd. The other guy's the big cheese.
And then—" He smiled like a little boy with a jam-pot.
"I got a trick that'll take them all away in hearses!"
he confided, and in three slangy sentences sketched out
the two-minute scene just before the end of the fourth
reel that draws tears as surely as rubbing the eyes with
an onion.

Even Billy, who made it his business never in any
event to be either surprised or respectful looked at the
swag little deity with something approaching awe.

"You got it," he said, and made notes with furious
zeal.

"You take hold of these snakes here yourself, you
and Mike, and cut Fane wherever you've got an idea
he may not notice it. I'm going where I can think.
I'll see Spiker in my office in an hour—get hold of him.
As for you"—he turned to Philip—"you come along.
Don't say anything, for God's sake, just sit around and
let me look at you while I'm thinking."

"Say!" Billy called as the two stumbled out of the pocket of dark. "Who's going to take the footage in this new one?"

Hays stabbed Philip in the kidneys with his forefinger.

"This guy, if I can use him," he said, and they departed.

Hay was right—Philip could not act. He had no voice, in the first place, and a stage and an audience would have reduced him to as pallid a stupor of fright as a fall into a nest of serpents. If his class in college had balloted for the handsomest man in it, he would not even have been able to command his own vote. But the camera, that tricky magician that reduces heavenly color to a smear of gray and regular good looks to the smouched pale insipidity of the face of a paper doll, played Whistler with his crooked, laughing nose, gray eyes and faunish ears. It gave him the distinction of a white peacock and the subtle uneven grin of a merry satyr. It lent vagabond leanness to the legs he had never dared put into knickerbockers and accentuated each scoffing point of his gaunt, long-fingered hands. Philip recognized himself on the screen, but that was all; when he looked into a mirror the contrast was too pitiful for words. And Hay played up every angle of his new incarnation with the remorselessness of a man trying to sell a fool a horse.

"You'll be gettin' a hundred and fifty mash notes a week, Pete, when we get through with your lovely face in this bunch of close-ups!" he simmered enthusiastically while Philip writhed. "All you got to do is walk around

and look natural—look natural and yearn right into
the box's eye!" Philip mocked him, obeyed and yearned,
and the stubby god swore with extreme delight.

It was just that, just looking natural or over-natural,
and the whole movie-world was such a phantasm of
unreality that Philip went through his paces in it with
zest and a fiery irony of mirth. To hold a romantic
posture two minutes longer than any human thing with
a sense of shame could bear to do, so that it registered
properly—to go sliding through every motion of life
too fast or too slow—to sob great glycerine tears over
the shoulder of a fluffy girl with a face painted in
streaks like a Congo medicine man's—to be drawing an
absurdly luxurious salary that seemed to go up in
jumps each week—all this was too creamy a jape to mar
by carelessness.

He had taken the name of Peter Sands for display
purposes—Peter for Peter Lascelles and Sands for
Arizona—and it seemed to him as the weeks blew by
like leaves that Peter grew more and more of an inde-
pendent personality that took most of the labor and
play of standing in front of the camera off Philip's
shoulders. "I've sold my soul to a jocular devil,"
Philip thought, "but at least he's giving me the world
and the flesh along with it."

Hay had turned up trumps as usual, he had a habit
in life of cutting aces from the middle of the pack.
The public was wearying of the simple, blue-jeans
hero, they were sick to agony of the mustached, white-
gardeniaed hero, the six-shooting, trailing-spurred hero
had ridden his loping pinto out of their affections as

the war came closer and closer like a falling shell. Philip was one of the first of the normal heroes—the hero a fraction better than normal—who did all the things the soda-fountain clerk had always wanted to do and yet showed such flashes of consoling imbecility the while that the soda-fountain clerk felt nobly sure that he could do those very things himself if he were only once given a fair chance. And to this conception Philip added a swart mirth and sardonic gallanting of his own that caught the taste of the shop-girl and unoccupied woman like a new kind of candy. And "The Way of a Man," moreover, was the first "war-picture" that had dealt less with elaborate blank-cartridge carnage and more with the average sensations of the average case.

Because of the dervish energy of Hay, the film was ready for release the end of December. Philip liked and admired the squat sorcerer better all the time, especially when he realized how greatly he differed from the typical idea of the typical director. For one thing, he smoked cigarettes instead of cigars; cigars, he confided frankly to Philip, always made him violently sick. He had gone through the rocket-rise of the rest of the business; the son of a prune-rancher, he had gone to agricultural college for two years, seen the first spotty beginnings of the films in the college "Opera House," and instantly given up prunes forever to follow his star. He had the American capacity of squeezing the last atom of work out of his subordinates; and while nervous as a bride while a picture was actually in the making, was extremely un-American in his lack of worry as to its after monetary success or failure. Despite this he had made his million in ten years, and 1917 saw him swimming like a goldfish in a golden flood. The greater part of his success he ascribed in secret to a small nude celluloid doll with a pink ribbon around its navel that he carried in the vest pocket over his heart, never showed to any one, and never let out of his touch for a second. He had picked it up in the road the day he got his first job in the movies, known it as Fortune, and cherished it ever after with the proud superstition with which a serpent in a Russian fairy tale guards the duck's egg that contains its death.

Hay had talent in many directions and genius in one, that of flooding a picture with all the light it would bear. He told Philip once quite solemnly and unprofanely that he thought the command, " Let there be light! " was the biggest and most sensible idea in the whole Bible and that the Old Testament could very well have shut up shop and let it go at that. Also there was to be found in him, besides the vast personal egoism of a dreamy girl, an instinct as certain as it was un-schooled for clean sweeping line and the large calms of beauty. He had no feeling whatever for words and the subtitles he thought of were Victorian grotesques, but he could make a field and an apple tree letting fall its blossoms appear on the wavering silver sheet like a snatch of red Adam's mournful dream.

Besides him, as Philip rose swiftly in the social scale and found that curt nods from sixteen-year-old stars changed to long *tête-à-têtes* on the screen-hoggishness of their leading men, he began to get some general conception of the whole arabesque and painted world into which he had stumbled. The clue to it all was artificiality and easy money from studios that were steel and stucco copies of Renaissance châteaus to febrile, sex-precocious little girls, who drew salaries in the thousands and lived in the conjugal intimacy of a bedroom-farce when they should have been getting ready to put their hair up and bid hidden, weeping farewells to their favorite dolls. It was a world that revolved like the spinning wheel of stiff horses in a merry-go-round to a syncopation of all the jazziest musical-comedy tunes. It was a world in which temperament abounded like an overdose of paprika on fish—a world where every one seemed to revel in pink-and-purple striped limousines, cellars full of expensive cordials and permanent cases of actor's head. Not that its inhabitants did not work and work hard—when they worked it was with the hypnotic energy of slaves on a sinking galley, when they played it was with the spectacular abandon of hasheesh-eaters. Of course there were quiet ones and saving ones, gentle ones and honest ones, but the loud ones were so in the forefront and so dizzied Philip with their colors and their clamor that it felt as if he were being shaken up inside a kaleidoscope and he had no time to take his eyes from the fizzing pinwheels of tints and spitting lights in front of him to seek the meek ones out. Into the swim he went, head over heels, like a dive into a paint pot.

There was Char-ruls Springset, for instance, that hill of flesh, and his partner "Hurry-up" Selleck, thin as a pin. Together they fell down trick stairs and broke wax bottles over each other's heads to the infatuated

roars of the country at large. Both pursued each new
comic effect with the deadly intentness of adders, each
was viciously jealous of the other, and they battled for
the center of the screen like two Chicago *nouveaux-riches*
for a select dinner-invitation. Both carried large in-
surance policies against any diminution or addition of
bulk respectively, both weighed four times a day with the
religious lugubriousness of middle-aged women, both
pursued the same lights of love—and the Decameron
of the amours of Ribs and Lath, as they were irreverently called, would have fitted out a year's amusement
for Marguerite de Valois.

There was little Daisy Dilley, the acknowledged first
attraction of the pictures, the "Everybody's Home-
Town Girl," to whom stout manicured Middle Western
clubwomen made pilgrimages of gush from their
"burgs" and "villes." In spite of astonishing wealth
following equally astonishing poverty and a rapid succession of four husbands and three divorces, little Daisy
had retained the candor, the simplicity and the reti-
cence of a hardy garden. Philip thought of pinks and
phlox when he saw her—of a privet-hedged lawn and a
white pool and cool brick paths. There were vampires
of the screen with good-natured husbands and bobbing
little girls in private—there were *ingénues* with the open
faces of pansies and a vocabulary in which a Parisian
Apache would have felt at home. There were any number of overdressed young men, and most of them used
scent, either in private, where it was a vice, or in public,
where it became a disease. There was a Harvard man
who had played the lead in two Hasty Pudding shows,

a Serritt of Boston, where the Serritts marry Cabots, and a youth with the breeding of a greyhound and a scarred and valuable mind. He was keeping up the house on Beacon Street and the summer cottage at " Sconset" with his salary and was regarded by his family as delivered over bound hand and foot to a bourgeois Evil One. Above all there was youth—hardly a star was over thirty, and the feminine element averaged under twenty-three—youth turned footloose and free into a gigantic nursery crammed with every sort of luxurious and dangerous toy.

Philip, when "The Way of a Man" had started its triumphant tour, slid easily into the conventions of stardom. He acquired a valet, a suite at the Grantmore and a red Stutz, he joined unemotionally in liquor-parties that reminded him of the less expensive orgies of prep-school boys bent on proving themselves hardened in sin, he attended dances from the respectable, which were amazing, to the otherwise, which were very dull. He wasted a good deal of money and put a good deal into Liberty bonds. He took pure pleasure in informing Phil of his present status and received no answer.

The letters he got from Lucia hurt like medicine. She regarded the quarrel as a silly and unworthy incident to be forgotten as soon as possible, but she blamed both Phil and Philip equally for it; and justice, in Philip's present state of soreness, was just what he shied at constantly. She wanted him to come home at once and make up, but Philip had too fatally good a memory of all that Phil had said to return as a civilian prodigal son. She came down to Los Angeles for a week,

Philip was tired, she was insistent, they misunderstood
each other and it took all her courage to prevent things
happening that would have pained them both beyond
remedy. Then she gave up the attempt and went back
to San Esteban, leaving them both rather sick and
strained at heart.

Meanwhile the war fell over the world like rain and
every now and then the pressure and noise of it would
come tearing at Philip's ears like a saw over steel. This
did not conduce to healthy sleep, but Los Angeles streets
held daily every uniform from a Roman centurion's to
that of one of Napoleon's Old Guard, so that when real
soldiers passed in swinging lines of drab they seemed
but one more eddy of the play-acting, false-fronted
cosmos into which he had slipped, that was all. Then
in January, when he was deep in his second picture—
a straight war film this was to be—three things happened: he met Sylvia again, the Pancha Verschoyle affair began to give trouble, and he got a long letter from
Dick Sheldon.

Pancha Verschoyle was almost middle-aged, according
to the movies—she admitted to twenty-five among best
friends. She had started on the cheaper burlesque
wheel with an individual song-and-dance act opening
and closing in one and consisting chiefly of skin-tights
and dubious patter. From this she had been rescued by
Elgar Hay, who saw in her salacious blonde vivacity the
makings of an original eccentric comedian. But she
would not have taken advice or directing from a cherub,
and when he dropped her after three weeks of squabbles
and tears she went over to Incando Films, his principal

rival, and played secondary villainess parts with weasel-like agility and success. From this she had risen to "vamping", reformed when the sinuous destroyer of souls began to lose vogue, and was now, as a leading innocent in bread-and-butter dramas dealing with the misadventures of young wives, on the highroad to success and her own company.

Philip had made her acquaintance in the rôle of unsuccessful life-saver. Incando Films had been doing a shipwreck picture in Catalina Bay. A big scene was the rescue of Pancha and her pajamas from the billows and a subsequent towing of her by the hero to the beach of a desert island. The director had asked Pancha before shooting the set if she wanted an experienced swimmer to double for her in the parts that required actual submergence—the wreck and everything about it was to be as realistic as possible. Pancha had once taken a course of swimming lessons in the shallow end of an indoor pool and, having the heart of a gamecock, answered carelessly that she guessed she could do the job all right herself. Philip, at the time, with Daisy Dilley, her sister and her present husband, had chartered a glass-bottomed boat and was floating about admiring the strange sea-gardens. The sight of a film being taken drew them instantly to the location.

When Pancha, shivering in her thin silk trousers, stood by the rail of the sinking barge, whose side had been camouflaged to the appearance of a section of a liner, she wished from the bottom of her soul that her previous hours of aquatics had been put to more practical use than that of flirting with her instructor. But she had a defiant courage and when told to jump, she jumped. She sank like a diving-bell immediately and came up to splash wildly at the water and shriek and choke and sputter in the fear of death.

This was splendid—the director, a stickler for minute telling details, thought he had never seen better acting. "'At's the stuff!" he grunted to the cameraman. "'At's the stuff. That girl has her nerve along with her all right!"

"I'm drowning, you damn fool!" Pancha tried to scream, but the waters went over her and she sank for the second time.

"Ned!" said Daisy Dilley, "she's really drowning!"

Ned gaped. "It's all in the picture," he said uncertainly. "Darn good, too."

"It isn't—she's *scared*—I saw her eyes—if you won't go after her, Ned, I'm going to!" and she started to undo her shoes.

"I'll go," said Philip instantly. He chuckled at the thought of what would happen if Daisy Dilley were wrong. Incando Films would think it a deliberate trick on Hay's part to wreck one of their famous realistic scenes. He stepped gingerly over the side.

"She's *drowning,* you fools, she's drowning!" called Daisy Dilley. The whole wreck halted undecidedly. Heads bobbed up out of the water and looked about. The cameraman kept on grinding. A "body" floating on the waves trod water abruptly and lost its expression of bloated *rigor mortis*.

"By God!" said a voice uncertainly. "I believe she is!"

Pancha's next sensation was caused by some one kneeling on her stomach and kneading her arms up and down in an attempt to pump her out.

"You blasted idiots," she said feebly, "I could have drowned all day there for all the attention you paid to me. Oh, Lord!" and the pumping process was assisted.

Philip had not arrived quite in time, she had been hauled up from her third sinking by the long arms of a bashful supe. But she heard about his dash to the rescue and the sacrifice of a new pair of white flannel trousers later and asked him to tea in her overgrown bungalow at Hollywood. He came, and before the hour was over she had decided that she wanted him to play with for a while and set herself about the business of getting him with as little bashfulness as she would have shown in going shopping for hats.

Now Pancha, née Hilda Swenson, for that was what she had been christened, though she had the morals of a raccoon, had been able to pet her body for the last three years as a raccoon pets and washes its fur. She knew it was as beautiful as she could make it—she even gave her shoulders little love-bites now and then when she stood bare before her mirror—and she had the inborn faculty of making men unobtrusively aware of it and dowagers admit its effectiveness. At times, when she was particularly pleased with herself, her skin had the liquid brilliance of light through sheer silk, her flesh would seem to glow of itself like a lamp with all the abundant youth and original sin that possessed it lover-wise. Moreover, she had a flip tongue, a heartless valor, and the simplicity of a modern débutante in asking for what she wanted.

It showed no particular perspicacity in Philip that he knew very well what she wanted of him after the third time he had attended one of her teas for two that were served in a cushiony room full of soft glooms and candles and the scent of violet powder. But it amused him to play Joseph from the country when she was so obviously eager for the rôle of Potiphar's wife, and the illegal Potiphar in question was none other than Stanwood Fane, who had the conceit and the stupidity of an ostrich and whom Philip found it very pleasing indeed to annoy. His irony kept him from more and whenever Milly wandered into his dreams he would wake with a thick feeling in his throat in the morning and resolve to insult Pancha permanently when next he saw her. The resolve was not kept, for Philip, with his money that flowed in so effortlessly and all the other monogrammed silk-underwear appurtenances of a star, was getting soft and full and flabby in body and thought. Going out to Pancha's, playing with Pancha, was like sinking back into the cushions of a sofa, and he was at a loose end now and had lost all hardy desire for the starvation and tricks of wandering. His body had kept him out of a man's or a poet's part in the war that had eaten up his friends—now he would let his body go along as it would and, like a tired horse, choose the pleasantest paths and the softest footing.

He could never put on the misfit private's uniform he wore in " Hearts of Valor " without Puckish disgust at himself and everything about him—and because of this, probably, Elgar Hay swore frequently that the new picture would make him a millionaire all over again, for Philip threw into his acting all the impetus of his starved scorn and stubborn dreams. In the picture, while the camera was actually clicking, he found some sort of release, he could take himself seriously, believe for a moment that the fire-pots and smoke-bombs and artificial trenches had actually some coherent relation to that long line of holes in the earth and dying men that ran from Switzerland to the sea. When the camera stopped he felt the bleak hurt of a child snatched suddenly out of the middle of an intoxicating game and put back again into dresses. " There are three classes of beings in the world now," he wrote to Lucia, " men, women and physically unfit. I belong to the third half-sex and we bear about the same relation to normal humanity that eunuchs do." But because of his fever for work " Hearts of Valor " was sure of a finish in record time. Elgar Hay had already mapped out another one—a spy-play this time with a Kaiser and a studio Berlin.

The climax came, as Philip's did, all at once and with the decision of a pool ball knocking down a row of toy bricks. He often wore his uniform after working hours —it was a private's for one thing and annoyed other stars who went about as elaborate French aviators or British majors. Besides, when he wore it in the street, he could imagine for instants that he was part of the mass of healthy people and not a buffoon as separate from the run of his kind as a diseased animal is from sound animals. Occasionally it would give him unbear-

able twinges and make him feel like a soiled mas-
querader in stolen clothes, but he saluted with a punc-
tiliousness that would have aroused unholy laughter in
a real buck private, and even such senseless acts gave
him an unreasonable relief from his own thoughts.
Both attitudes of mind were indubitably quite foolish,
but it might be remembered that Philip was not even
yet very old.

He ran into Sylvia one day in the lobby of the Grantmore, when the picture had kept him late and he had
come in to dinner with Hay and a friend without having
time to alter his protective coloration. She had a can-
teen-worker's uniform on and was frankly and extremely
glad to see him. She came at him with both hands outstretched.

"Why, Philip, how perfectly great!" she said and
then, "And when did you get into this man's army,
old fellow?"

His voice stuck in his throat as he shook hands with
her. He was utterly, stabbingly miserable—he would
have given everything he had for the wit to lie.

"Sorry, Syl," he told her, and his voice was stupid
with bitterness, "but you see I'm not in yours or this
or any man's army. I'm a movie-actor, Syl, and these
are my working clothes."

She stood looking at him as if he had slapped her in
the face.

"Phil!" she said and "I don't understand!" in a
queer little cry.

Philip heard a noise in his ears like the sound of
ice breaking up in a river. His face must have looked

inhuman for "Are you sick?" she said and put a hand on his arm. He smiled with movements of his mouth.

"Oh, no, I'm perfectly healthy. Just slacking."

If she had either believed him or laughed at him he might have kept her there for hours and told her the whole of it. He felt a torrent of speech behind his lips—it beat at them, praying to get out. But—

"You *aren't!*" she said fiercely. "You aren't. You couldn't get in. Oh, I'm sorry, I'm sorry!"

It seemed to him that her pity at the instant was more than he could endure. It burned through him as if she were pointing at a crippled hand.

"So am I," he said stiffly. "When are you going across?"

They talked for ten minutes about meaningless things and parted with indefinite promises to write each other. She was sailing from New York in three weeks, "If I'm lucky." When Philip joined Hay and a man in a green suit in the dining-room, he discovered that he was sweating as if he had been marching with a pack under the sun. He drank all three teacup-cocktails in successive gulps—a proceeding that was put down to the eccentric rudenesses of genius.

"Hay," he said, as the benevolent Manhattans began to fume over and blur the bad quarter of an hour, "when we clean up this damn film I'm going off to Wake Island for a rest. It's only got a population of six, I hear, and they never even heard of a war. I'm through."

"Well," Hay remarked imperturbably, "we only got the big battle stuff to shoot."

A week later the film had been completed. Philip,
dog tired, had come back to his rooms at the Grantmore
for a bath and dinner before the riotous celebration
that Hay had arranged at the studio for a select few.
While he was eating, in the comfortable undress of
underwear, the food that had been sent up to him, he
noticed that his secretary had put some mail on his
dressing-table. The secretary was a recent purchase, a
middle-aged woman ex-school-teacher who took to the
movies as she would have taken to drugs, shamefacedly
but under the influence of a force too strong for her,
and absorbed a comfortable salary in an efficient way.
Philip picked the letters up—one had a B. E. F. post-
mark and was censored. He laid it aside and opened
another, mauve-colored with scent that stuck to the
fingers.

It had no preliminaries and read:

> " Why don't you come out and see me about ten
> to-night, Phil? I want to talk to you. I have
> settled with Stan for good.
>
> " P."

Philip chucked this into the wastebasket, rescued it,
reread it and then carefully tore it up. He had no idea
of playing Antony to Pancha's Cleopatra now that
Cæsar had been given his *congé*.

The others were unimportant, " mash-notes " chiefly,
selected by his conscientious secretary with an arid
humor. The only other one unopened was the foreign
one and that Philip finally settled to read. The

first sentence made the room seem to rock around him.

"DEAR PHIL:

"I suppose you saw John's death in the casualty lists, but I know you'd want any details we could write—"

John! He had written to John three days ago.

"Supercilious as ever . . . there are no words . . . we had gotten closer than most brothers get . . ." His eye skipped down the page.

"The last action was so characteristic of him. John was one of the best pilots in the group and had twice been recommended for the Flying Cross. Always doing things on his own in that snotty, superior, crazy way he had. Well, he and an English kid from Cambridge, Fluffy Rockett, went out together that morning on a patrol. They got separated a little—Fluffy was new at the job—and were attacked by a whole squadron, some of Richthofen's old Flying Circus, I think, for Fluffy said they just seemed to fall right out of the sky. Both beat it back to the field, but something must have happened to John's engine, or perhaps he was hit, for Fluffy looked back once and saw two German planes square on top of him, loosing off machine guns, and then saw him go into a tail spin. He almost straightened out once but the Germans kept forcing him down and in the end he crashed behind their lines. Fluffy couldn't do anything, he had three Huns on his own back and just got away by bull-luck. The Huns dropped a letter over later saying they'd buried him and giving his name

and rank. I know how hard this will hit you, Phil—
it has made all of us as sick as we could be—and you
and John were pretty nearly best friends. I only wish
you were here with us to get a crack at the Boche who
got him—"

Philip read the rest of the letter with great care and
twitching eyes. There was only one other sentence in it
that did not slide off his mind like a waterdrop from
polished wood. " Steve is in hospital of course, after
his scrap, but sends his best with the rest of us."

There is a complete grief and humiliation of the
spirit that has no resource at all but a certain whimsy
of laughter. In the next half hour as he dressed in his
uniform again—Hay's party was to be in costume—
Philip laughed rather more than was good for him.

As he started his car to drive it to the studio a sort
of swinging dizziness took hold of him and he felt as a
man just dismissed from a hospital feels who has not
yet had time to adjust himself to the loss of a leg or
an arm. He had thought himself an adept in irony, but
when he had mixed for a few minutes in the squawking
confusion of men and women and drinks and confetti,
he knew that he had never realized in his life what cheap
and scathing irony certain seconds can hold. The whole
business of toasts and speeches and yelling laughter was
like an aimless walk through a second-rate part of hell.
He wanted with a stifling passion dark and silence and
a chance to think about John. Since he could not have
these he sucked at the sour irony before him and managed to drink a good deal with no more result than if he
had poured the cocktails into his shoes. About ten-

thirty he managed to look at his watch—it was while he was sitting out in an alcove with Bessie Arbiter, and she was asking him, with a loose, unhappy smile if he thought her husband would notice anything if she drank a couple more stingers. " Oh, Peter, I need them bad! " He remembered Pancha's rather large invitation, said he'd talk it over with George Arbiter, man to man, and so got rid of Bessie, and escaped.

" John's dead," kept running through his head. " John's dead and I'm alive—isn't it funny? Sounds like a nursery rhyme or a piece of Mother Goose. John's dead. If things were the other way there'd be some sense in it—but there isn't any sense in anything. John's dead. I'm alive and John is dead."

He swung the nose of the car around towards Hollywood. Since the path that had courage and John in it had fallen out of existence, he would make what speed he could along the perverse one and run down a steep place into the sea with the rest of the snouted animals.

Pancha's bungalow had a high porch with vines and a discreet light still burning over the door. He rang, wasted a moment, rang again impatiently. It was really highly unladylike of the devil not to meet you half way when you had once decided to go to her. He swore, rattled the knob and walked in. Pancha's undressed voice came far-off through the sudden pungent dusk of the rooms.

" Who's that? "

" Peter Sands. I got your note but didn't have time to phone you."

The voice became suddenly alive with a note that was

as eager and clear as the scent of a bag of musk.

"Oh, Peter—I'm sorry, but I've went and gone to bed. You can come and call a little if you want to, though. I won't get up and let you in—it wouldn't be nice."

"Couldn't stand life another minute without seeing you, Pancha. Where on earth do you keep your room, anyhow? I'm as blind as an owl in sunlight here."

She laughed pussily.

"Straight ahead of you from the door, Pete dear. Look out and don't kill yourself on my pet furniture, it's scattered all over the place."

Philip took two steps, barked his shins and heard her laugh again. He had a picture of a great white shameless cat, purring and licking itself in the middle of a silken bed. He rubbed his shins and began to tack across the room with the straining eyes of a deaf man in the middle of a street. He got through it without further accident —there were three more and the last of all was Pancha's.

"Ah, Pancha, open your door!" he said in the voice of a querulous husband.

Another laugh, sleepy and gurgling, came out to him like the warmth of a stroking hand. His eyes were more used to the gloom now, he stepped forward confidently, in the right direction, he thought. Then a ghastly reminiscence of Milly went like ether over his limbs, drugging his heart.

He stopped as if he had stumbled and stood a moment hardly knowing how to breathe. The whole world seemed for that instant to turn round inside his head. He suddenly knew both what he was and what he was doing. He saw himself all over, inside and out, and the sight shook him as if he had stood in front of his own corpse. Another picture of the white cat in the room to which he was going came to him, only this time the thing was heavy with sleeping and its paws lay over his face.

"Peter!" came that hot mewing voice again through curtains and dead fragrance. "Peter Sands!"

He stood there, stupid and shaking. Pancha's laugh trickled over his body and left it strengthless. He moved forward again with the gesture of a man about to step wilfully into bitter filth. The odors of the shut, woman-ish rooms, languid and fleshy, climbed up to his mouth like a wave. And then, ripping them aside as a hand tears down a curtain, came a clean unearthly scent, en-gulfing his soul, the scent of wet white violets.

Philip shuddered as it pierced him and gave a great cackling cry.

Then he turned and ran back through the dim rooms with the desperate haste of a boy hunted down by witches. He got a jar from the end of a table that seemed almost to crack open his knee, but he dodged as if from the blow of an airy club, fell, got up again, and burst out of the door. He heard a shuffling in the perfumed staleness behind him and dropped clumsily over the porch rail square on to a pile of ornamental rocks. When he scrambled up he felt sure that he had broken a leg, for he could not put his left foot to the ground without fainting pain, but he managed to start his car and drive away before the disgusted Pancha knew what had happened, except for the destruction of an ex-pensive bowlful of highly unseasonable flowers.

The scent of violets was frail with Philip all the way, a fading wraith of clear fragrance, and he talked to it at times almost as if he had Milly there beside him.

When they found out about Philip's injury next morning, the latter was kept in bed and treated with the exclusive care of a rich woman's sick Chow. Hay got the finest surgeon in Los Angeles on the telephone, and bribed him with an unheard-of price for instant attention.

The surgeon arrived, and found out in five seconds that Philip's only trouble was a badly sprained ankle. He was a tall man, white-haired and scornful, with a face that, when he saw Philip's " Hearts of Valor " uniform on top of a wardrobe trunk, looked as if it had been cut out of frosty steel.

" What was the use, please, of bothering me with a case like this? " he said curtly as he took his bag to go. " I have work to do—we're training men at the hospital—and no business to waste time on healthy exempted film stars."

" Mr. Sands is physically unfit for service," said Hay.

" Unfit? He's as fit as any man I ever saw, or will be very shortly. What's the matter with him? "

Hay produced Philip's draft-card and showed it, to the other's annoyance. The surgeon was instantly interested and set down his bag.

" Do you mind my examining your heart and lungs? " he said briskly, taking assent for granted. He punched the tubes of a stethoscope into his ears and applied it to Philip's chest.

"Say *ah!*" he commanded fiercely. "Now, possibly, you may give me some sort of chance to earn my ridiculous fee."

When the usual process and some special frills were over, the surgeon looked at Philip with sleety eyes.

"If you have any real desire to get into your country's service," he said, "I can perform an operation that will leave you fit inside of two months. It will be an expensive operation and very possibly a painful one. I shall ask you to decide about it at once, too, Mr. Sands, as my time, while not as valuable as yours, has some value nevertheless."

"You can make me *fit?*" asked Philip amazedly.

"Yes. The trouble is not organic. Any resemblance to tuberculosis is entirely superficial. You have led a very healthy life for the last year or so and, to tell you the truth, the organ has healed as much as it could of itself. Well?"

Philip grinned.

"Just as soon as you're ready for me, sir, I'm ready for you."

And a week later, in spite of Hay's anxieties and expostulations, Philip, prone, was rolled on a rubber-wheeled table into a white room full of antiseptic figures and glittering steel.

"Breathe in deeply!" said a voice in his ear. His hands were folded in a prayerful attitude, a cone pressed down over his face. He strangled and coughed and began to breathe choking sweet, and then fell out of his body entirely into a pit full of stinging blackness.

BOOK VI

THE TINSEL HEAVEN—A DREAM
(1918)

OUTSIDE HEAVEN

HE woke to a sensation of faintness and great cold. He was lying on his back in the middle of a limitless white billowy plain and the three gray Fates were sitting on their heels beside him. He looked toward them, saw their eyes, and covered his own.

"About time you got up!" said Atropos, in a voice like the sucking of wind through the skull of a horse.

Philip rose with a scrambling movement, but his eyes were still under his hand.

"What do you want?" His tongue was thick and he spoke huskily. "And am I in Hell?" Then he added incongruously, "Please!"

The Fates laughed together.

"Not yet," remarked Clotho unpleasantly and Lachesis scraped one finger over the other and added, "Only outside Heaven." All three looked at him with a harsh expectancy.

"Are you ready to play?" said Atropos.

"Play what?" requested Philip, in the tone of a self-conscious youth about to be lured unwillingly into a game of Post-office.

"The game everybody plays when they come here." The three stained voices rustled together like silks. "The game you've been playing since you were born. The game we like."

Philip looked around him despairingly, but everywhere was the same wide empty brightness, the same lone pale expanse, like an endless feather in the wing of a great white bird.

"I'll play," he said, and squatted down in front of them like a tailor.

"We thought you would," giggled Clotho.

The small deadly thing that belonged to the Three took dice out of its mouth and flung them down.

Philip hesitated. "I haven't any money!" he yammered, "or any clothes, either, for that matter," he added, observing himself completely for the first time.

"You have yourself," answered the Severer. "The stakes are lower than those we are accustomed to playing for, but one must make exceptions for youth, eh, sisters?" and the others nodded their heads like palsied women.

"Your dice," said the Spinner peevishly and dropped a pair of burnished things into the shaky cup of his hand.

Philip took them. They seemed quite ordinary dice, except for the fact that the pips were wet and came off red on his fingers.

"On the first cast, your body; on the second, your soul; on the third, your mind," pronounced Lachesis, "for those happen to be the rules of our little game."

Philip rattled the dice about and they chattered in his hands as his own teeth were chattering in his head. All the dice-talk he had ever known had gone out of him and he could remember nothing but scraps of infantile prayers.

" Now I lay me—" he whispered as he rolled them, and the hairs of his head stood up.

The dice showed ace and ace.

" Snake eyes ! " said the Spinner of Threads. " I'm afraid that that was a foregone conclusion."

She rose stiffly, as if she walked on crutches, and the Twister sat down in her place. As they shuffled and changed seats Philip felt depart from him all the pride of the flesh, all the pulsing ardors of the body, all the leaping heat and delight of blood and bones. He became wavering and thin as the steam of a kettle and had no more substance now than a fistful of air, for the creature of the Fates had sprung on him and stripped his body off his back as a cook strips the green pod from a pea. It lay there at his feet, a baggy huddle, and the face was turned up at him like the face of a horrible doll.

He plucked up the dice again in a ague of inhuman terror, and this time as he cast he had no words left to say.

The dice showed deuce and deuce.

" That's a hard point, Philip ! " grinned Lachesis and Philip snatched at the dice and shook them and threw them away from him with all the force of his soul, but they seemed to halt in the air and fell gently as snowflakes and quite of their own accord. Philip did not even need to look at them, for as they settled down and were still, a thing like a brilliant bird flew out of his mouth, and with it went love and peace and the seven wise virtues.

Atropos, the Severer, hunched over to face him for

the last decision. She petted the bones all over her dry palm and the look in her eyes was subtle and mocking and assured. But Philip looked at her and knew that his mocking was greater than her mocking, and he burnt like a driftwood fire with hate of her and thrusting rebel hardiness, for with the loss of body and soul all fear had passed.

"Step on that slut, you dice!" he cried as she cast, and the words echoed violently up to the vault of Heaven.

The dice showed three and three.

"Jimmy Hicks!" murmured Atropos cautiously. "Jimmy Hicks! We are now Jimmy Hicksing, Philip! We are starting out to build ourselves a big, brick house!"

"You'll never live in that house," Philip bawled with all the lean rage of his mind. "It's a three-way point but she sevens! She sevens till the snakes run out of her shoes!"

The dice chuckered over the cloud, lay down, were as plain to understand as print. Atropos stared at what they said with dumb unbelief.

"Read 'em and weep!" yelled Philip. "Read 'em and weep!"

He gathered up the saving seven and turned on the Twister. "Soul!" he shouted and clattered the cubes at her feet like shot. "How's that for a natural?" Clotho made snarling assent.

"Body!" he said, and the chills-and-fever countenance of the Spinner dusked like cooling iron as she saw her own pet spaniel of Luck turn and bark against her.

Philip stood up in his body again and knew that he was trembling all over. The creature clawed at the useless dice and popped them back into his mouth.

" Want to shoot a real game? " inquired impudent Philip. The Fates wagged their heads in dissent. " A little later perhaps," mouthed Atropos, and somehow Philip wished he had chosen a more clever taunt. He stared at his hands a moment, there were little scarlet flecks on them that melted away as he stared. . . .

" The proper gate is two turns right and then straight to the left," said Clotho stiffly. " Till we meet for another session! *Au Revoir!* "

INSIDE HEAVEN

PHILIP wandered all over Heaven in one afternoon and discovered that it was a good deal like the deserted stage of his old toy-theater. It also greatly resembled a dullish house-party, for there was much too much company and nothing at all to do.

In the first place, he had never imagined that it was made of tinsel.

They had taken him past the gigantic Gate of St. John, so huge that it expanded rosily above him like the open mouth of a whale before a swimming minnow.

" This gate is composed entirely of sardine stone and measures precisely 10,189 cubits at its longest dimension," said the conducting angel in a voice like a golden megaphone.

Philip touched the tremendous wall with appropriate

reverence, and his finger went through it, for it was glued together out of colored paper.

"Why—" he began.

The angel silenced him hurriedly.

"Or rather *was* composed entirely of sardine stone," he explained. "But modern improvements, of course— a cheaper and quite perfect substitute—produced in bulk and serves every purpose—"

He seemed rather embarrassed, for an angel.

"Oh," said Philip, "I see."

Another curious fact to be astonished at was that the various cherubs and seraphs, though multitudinously winged, had given up their white, trailing, Biblical robes. They wore a very comfortable shiny costume that greatly resembled a celestial Palm-Beach suit.

"In the interests of economy," said the immortal guide, "and of course the changed fashions—Heaven must be a progressive institution—"

Philip noticed that among the souls of the Redeemed —they wore a simple but distinguishing stripe across the left sleeve—while many had rapt faces and faces consuming with light, there were others who seemed ill at ease, even a little discontented.

"Late arrivals," the angel explained, "the last two centuries or so—and yet, you know, we've absolutely done all that we could for them."

He spoke as a vintner might speak of a lot of uncommonly scanty or stubborn vines.

Philip grew to hate him viciously within the first half-hour of their companionship, he was such a muscularly Christian angel and believed with such thorough heartiness in the Church Efficient.

"By the way," said Philip, anxiously, "hate, you know—that still exists, even here? With the rest of the passions?"

"We have to deal with the souls of human beings," said the angel, dryly.

They passed by a gilt paper parapet and found a soul sobbing there as if it would break in two. The angel approached it with elaborate affection and there was some talk and manly words and pattings on the shoulder, but when they went away, the soul was sobbing worse than ever.

"Her sister is in Hell," the angel boomed smugly. "At least we are not quite sure that there is a Hell, but if there should be I am afraid there is no doubt whatever that her sister is in it. The saved sister wishes to rejoin the damned one wherever she may be, but that of course is not permitted."

"And the saved one cannot forget, and there isn't any Lethe here, either?" said Philip.

The angel seemed shocked. "Oh, dear, no!" he said with a flutter of pinions. "Of course I know that some of the old Fathers once adhered to that doctrine, but really it is quite a Pagan idea."

Philip felt all the hot angry essences in his soul stir up like broth from the bottom of a pot. He doubled his fists—but there is no way of killing angels.

They came upon a fat silly soul with a harp, who sat on a glittering pavement and chanted melodiously and constantly, "Heaven is sweet and I am saved! Heaven is sweet and I am saved! How sweet, how sweet, how exceeding sweet is Heaven!"

The angel paused with some pride. "One of our best examples," he said respectably. "Some eternal day you may reach such a peace as his!"

Philip shivered and looked into the mind of the silly soul (for a number of powers had been given him), and he saw that that mind was like the body of a eunuch, so he smiled at the soul because it was utterly happy, and felt full of pain and blasphemy as they pursued their journey.

Then they came to a noise in front of a tinsel mansion and found it was St. Bathylis and St. Beaugarde and that the two old ladies were calling each other names.

"Where is my second-best halo, you wretch, you shameless?" asked St. Bathylis with a strong West Saxon accent. "Didn't I lend it to you for the Feast of the Frisian martyrs with my own hands, and don't you tell me now that you never saw it at all?"

"Ach! Ach!" said St. Beaugarde, and she scraped her forefinger tauntingly. "What a fuss the poor body makes about a halo I never borrowed and anyway it was scratched and didn't fit! Ach, make some more halos on your griddle there and don't bother a better saint than yourself with your nasty face!"

Now St. Bathylis was fried on a griddle for the greater glory of God, and this remark incensed her. She pulled St. Beaugarde by the hair and the two began striking at each other like feeble dogs.

The angel separated them, and they wept and said

that there was no justice in Heaven and that they would complain to his superiors. But the angel was firm though tolerant, and both saints went away like children, wiping their eyes with their hands.

"Heaven seems more and more like an old people's home all the time," thought Philip, and the angel perceived the insolent comparison and his plumes grew iridescent with wrath.

So they proceeded through Heaven all afternoon and in many places they found little knots of the Redeemed playing knucklebones or checkers on the synthetic emerald squares of the sidewalks and the elder ones were talking over the good old times of Heaven. "For Heaven is not what it was," said a Coptic Saint who had never washed on earth except once when he had been ducked in a pond by the ungodly, and a hunting parson agreed, lamenting Earth and his foxes. A minor seraph made nervous mention of the great days before the War.

"All my flock are here and I preach to them till we grow weary," mourned a soul with a Massachusetts twang and a nose like Jonathan Edwards, "but they sleep with a profounder ease than they were used to on cushionless pews and there is no spice left in things when I cannot shake them to pieces with the dread of Hell."

"There is no Hell," said the angel.

"There should be," said Philip, looking at him sourly.

Then the conversation switched to Infant Damnation and Philip tugged at his Norfolk belt and somehow got him away.

"Do people ever come back from here?" asked Philip,

stopping suddenly in the middle of a courtyard that
shone as if it had been made of white porcelain. It was
cardboard, though, for he dinted it with his heel. The
angel, having no body, seemed piously surprised at this
demonstration of strength.

" Come back? " he repeated, a trifle puzzled.

" Send messages," said Philip irritatedly. " Mediums
—tipping tables—ouijas—all that sort of thing. And
if they do—why in His name don't they ever talk co-
herently and sensibly for more than five minutes at a
time? "

The angel flickered with the tints of a lunar rainbow
at the utterance of the Name of the Divine.

" That is managed by a Bureau of Mortal Information," he answered. " Propaganda, I suppose you would
call it. St. Praxed is in charge and the material is syn-
dicated to the various mediums. By the way, have you
seen our latest arresting message, ' All the Comforts of
Home in Heaven or Astral Cigarettes for the Saved'?
He has some first-class advertising men to prepare the
copy."

" And this is Heaven, apparently," said Philip
biliously.

The angel seemed to grow taller and his face was
illuminated by a radiance startlingly unlike the reflection of light on tinsel.

" How do you know that this is Heaven? " he whispered gently. " It may only be the vacant shadow of a
thought in your own mind."

" You mean—" said Philip, surprised.

" I mean that nothing may exist at all," said the

angel, "and all things are only appearances and simulacra. Space is an illusion of time and time is a figment expressing space—Heaven and Earth and I may exist because you have thought them and in five minutes you may make them over again with a new thought."

"How do I know though that I am not the embodied specter of one of your thoughts instead?" Philip asked.

"I think chiefly of pleasant things," said the angel, nastily. Then he added, "And, then, of course, we may both be thoughts."

"Who thinks us?" queried Philip.

"Heaven is no place for philosophizing," replied the angel. "Besides, can you take a piece of curtain string and a bent pin and fish from the battlements of Heaven to hook the Cosmic Irony out of its sleepy waters under the world?"

"Give me a couple of worms," said Philip, "and I will try."

"You should never have come here at all," snapped the angel, sharply. "You are entirely too young for a place of everlasting peace. And then, you know, all things may be real after all."

"I think I see your point," answered Philip slowly, "but my head is going round and round."

"I am glad I have neither head nor body," smiled the angel.

"You would never know what to do with the first if you had it," said Philip neatly, and they left the courtyard and tramped off to look for a truly contented soul.

They found one, it was the soul of a cobbler who had

been blind from birth and had never even seen his own awl and threads. Now he saw, and he went around Heaven whistling. Philip looked at him for a few seconds of Eternity and then went away because he was both awed and abashed.

" You see there are some points about Heaven after all," said the angel mockingly, and Philip stopped in front of a shimmering pasteboard tower and beat against it with his hands till the tower rocked.

" I cannot understand," he howled furiously. " There is no sense or order in anything and yet there is such joy and sorrow here that it tears me apart. Take me away and show me the reasons of things, for in Heaven as well as in Earth there is nothing that I can understand."

" Well, what did you expect to find here? " asked the angel.

" I don't know," Philip cried. " Oh, I don't know at all. But there must be one or two reasons at least for things as they are, or I will go mad and run around naked through all this tinsel."

" That would neither create any disturbance nor help your present unfortunate state of mind," said the angel, reflectively. " As a matter of fact, when you ask for reasons, you ask to be taken to God. It is not a course I should have advised, but he who appeals to Cæsar, to Cæsar let him go."

" That remark seems sacrilegious, for an angel," said Philip through his teeth.

" I am an angel," announced that creature proudly, " and hence, being composed of infinite religion, it is evident that I could not be sacrilegious if I tried."

"I hate intellectual arrogance," muttered Philip.

"But, as I have told you, I possess no intellect," went on the angel smoothly, "so how—"

"Oh, take me to God, for Heaven's sake!" said Philip, "or anywhere else that is out of your moral presence!"

So Philip was taken before the Face of the Almighty. He had expected—he was a reader of modern novels— to find a business-like God in spectacles in the middle of strange experiments in a perfectly-equipped chemical laboratory. But again, the prophecies of things were oddly changed.

God was middle-aged and sat on His proper Throne, surrounded by the vocal Beasts of the Apocalypse, full of songs and eyes. But the Audience-Chamber was lit by a kind of heavenly electricity and there were comfortable, modern chairs with cushions for the older prophets, for Heaven had changed since Creation and the steam-engine. They had even presented the Recording Angel with a card-index system and each soul was cross-referenced at least six times with a different colored card each time. This annoyed the Recording Angel, who was set in his ways, and he was thinking of taking his first vacation since Genesis.

There was some delay before Philip could put his questions, for a prominent Archbishop had just written a pastoral letter on the extravagance of the poor that had been brought up to the Throne with the testy comments of St. Peter. In fact, "Bosh!" in a stubby handwriting was scrawled right across an elegant plea for misunderstood millionaires. This pause Philip employed in the contemplation of God. There was nothing in God that was strange or alien or efficient—he was the God whom Philip had always visioned vaguely as a strong, kind and terrible man, when in the brittle days before he went out to boarding-school he had said his prayers on his knees beside his bed. Philip looked at the lion face, at the august face, at the face that shone like snow under winter sun, and all the irony of his mind went out like a candle, and his knees shook and his body bowed down to the floor.

The discussion of the Archbishop was finished. Philip approached the mountainous knees, feeling very small and like a fly in that shining amplitude. All the beasts sang louder and turned upon him multitudes of blazing eyes.

God lifted his hand over Philip like a forky cloud. " Well, my son—? " said the voice of God.

" I want reasons," said Philip meekly.

" Reasons? " said God, but the voice was thick, and middle-aged.

Philip lifted his eyes very slowly and a black horror of soul came upon him.

" I think I met you in Fresno," he said uncertainly, for he had looked into the eyes of God and they were as bright and empty as pieces of washed glass.

" You may have," said God and he hid a smile with his hand.

But Philip had been overtaken by fury.

" This is a sham! " he cried violently till the star-speckled roof was full of echoes and the prophets twisted their beards. "This is a sham and Heaven is made of tinsel and there is no God, or if there is he is mad, and I will break this sham into bits as a man breaks matches. Heaven is false and Earth is a spent dream—there is no order in anything and nobody who will give me any reasons!"

"You are young," said God, rather tiredly.

"I will have reasons!" shouted Philip, this time almost pitifully. "I will have reasons or I will not stay in Heaven."

"You may do as you like, my son," said God, and Philip saw that there was more than emptiness in his eyes.

"Good-by!" said Philip desperately, and he ran across to the glistening wall of the chamber and tore a hole like a door in its tinsel with his hands. Two seraphs tried to stop him, but God lifted a finger.

"Let him go!" said God in a voice like summer thunder, and they stood in their tracks. "He has been tormented enough."

And Philip stepped out through the fluttering tinsel into Space.

PAST HEAVEN

THERE was an endless drop like the smooth rush of a descending roller-coaster through reeling darkness and star-milk, head over heels. He grew giddy with falling, he saw his body glow and brighten appallingly as he fell and wondered, in the shuttle of icy wind that hissed over him like pouring water, just when he would burst into flame, and if he were fated to tumble incandescently forever through black bottomless skies like the spinning tail of a meteorite. But his body grew airier and airier as the light in it increased, effulgence burst from his feet and hands, he shined exceedingly and knew that he was becoming a star. All substance, all form and thought and density, flickered out of him, his speed decreased, he began to sway like a tiny pendulum on the clock-face of night. The end of the journey came with a soft jar that sent ecstasy through him, a detached hard pulse of ecstasy, for now he was nothing but a sparkling center of irradiate light. He swung low over the moons of a whirling planet like a flying owl, and his journey slackened and ceased. It seemed that for uncounted ages he hung in the soft dark web of the sky, and, being a star, he shone, and rejoiced with the strength of an angel and the innocence of a flower in the pure ferocious vigor that rayed from his heart.

After æons he was aware of another star in his heavens. It shone below him, a brilliant stud of white, and its light was greater than his light.

After æons more the cold palpitating essence of Philip, the star, was full of bright agony with the intensity of its wish. It desired to drink and be one with the rebel star below it as one drop of water drinks and is one with another and then to live alone in the skies and be full of light.

Philip, the star, awoke and strained at the threading impalpable bonds that shackled it to the sky. It broke these bonds with a wrench like the parting of body and soul and crawled down the heavens like a shimmering beetle to leap upon the other star. It flared with colors of unbearable pain and its light grew crippled and violent, but it kept its course. Over the gleaming anguish of that march the years fled by and were gone like ripples of water.

The other star was now very close, and at times it seemed as if it held the face of a girl that Philip had never known, and once the stone eyes of the Severer looked out of it, but as Philip's star halted and shuddered and plunged at it with a sparkling sound, it suddenly shone all over and its countenance was massive and leonine, the tremendous face of God. And Philip's star trembled all over like a bush stricken to pieces with fire, and its being was lost in God and its arrogant light consumed like a piece of tinder and was utterly quenched. . . .

. . . Again, Philip was being tortured on a bed-like rack by a number of large rats with human faces. The pain went through him like a continuous driving in of small blunted nails and he mocked the rats with every witty obscenity he could think of. He made rhymes about them and laughed till he hurt his sides, and it seemed as if Pain were only a key that turned in a lock and released fantastic pleasures, a swaying red palanquin in which he was jolted toward something rendingly lovely and quite unimagined. A girl appeared suddenly beside him and looked at him with dark, steady eyes. She was neither Milly nor Sylvia nor any other human, but she had an austere likeness to every beautiful thing he had ever seen. He had looked at her face in dreams, he thought, the calm face of a silver statue, but the cloud of his body and senses had kept him from remembering her when he waked. She was the single image behind the possessed eyes of all good madmen and artists, the sea-lily growing wild in copper marshes, the vagrant saint, the swift counselor, the proud, secret and speechless friend. She carried two cups of yew-wood and she put the first of them silently at his lips. He was thirsty as sand but he turned his head away writhing when he tasted what was in the cup.

"It is salt," he said difficultly. "I cannot drink it."

"Drink!" she said. "It is your fortune, for it is naked scorn."

He turned to it again, and drank like a child at the breast. The draught ran through him like the brine of the cold bottom of the sea. The rats went on with their work and the cords were tightened.

He lay there, and after the desolation of the cup had passed, the rats could not have harmed his body if they had sawed it apart. But his thought fought unceasingly with their delusions and was wounded.

She pressed the angry edge of the second cup against his mouth.

"Drink!" she said. "It is your strength, for it is mockery and complete defiance, a black juice of thorns."

"I cannot," he told her childishly. "It is sour and thick as curds."

Yet he drank, and the liquor in the bowl was bitter as ashes and made his flesh creep and sweat as if he had seen a ghost. But the rats made a noise with their

yellow teeth and ran away, for their delusions fell dead
around them like winter flies when Philip's thought,
washed clear with that gall, had seen them. He lay
still on the rack, and he was bound, but the bonds meant
nothing.

Then the girl stooped over him and kissed him lightly
on the eyes.

"I am your soul," she said laughingly, "and now let
us go away from here, for you have much to do and
many things to make me."

And the ropes fell off from Philip like leashes of
wind and he arose and took a stringless harp that stood
in the corner and made such insolent music on it that
the heavens trembled about him like a house of cards.

Once more the great solemn Face hung over him like
a tilted sky.

"Well, my son?" said the voice that was summer
thunder.

Philip and his companion had been running a race
down the ring-finger of the Hand. Now they stopped,
and the girl smoothed her dusky hair back out of her
eyes.

"I don't know that I want any reasons," said Philip
vainly. "We are only thoughts, my Lord, and you are
as I, and no thought can destroy another thought
through all the eternities."

"You are beginning to see, a little," said the tones
of earthquake.

"As for reasons," said Philip, "I will do what comes
to my hand and abide the issue. For I have scorn again

and defiance again and my own soul again. Reasons?"
He paused a moment thoughtfully. "The thing is to
live," he said in the end, "and that is hard enough at
any time, including the present. And now if you'd
like to hear something that I've just composed on the
subject—"

He settled himself in a recitative posture. His soul
lay down by his knees.

But the Face began to diminish as he spoke, and the
cosmos rocked, fell apart, was a turmoil of shifting
planets. . . .

He was suddenly conscious of a violent ache in his
throat. The Face became human and small, the lips
spoke, a sick sweet and loathsome smell of anesthetic
was all about him.

"He's coming out of it nicely," said the far-off voice
of the doctor, bending over his bed.

BOOK VII
TERRA FIRMA
(1918-1919)

IT took Philip two months to get out of the hospital and another one to get into the army. Meanwhile he discovered with mild amusement that Hay's Yankee shrewdness—the kind one associates with nasals in the speech and codfish and east wind—meant to hold him to the cancelation clause in his contract, so that after Philip had paid his hospital bills and the gorgeous forfeit to Hay, he left the pictures with as little actual cash in pocket as he had when he entered them, though he still possessed some thousands of dollars in Liberty Bonds. Hay, whose generosities and greeds were cryptic and alike in their suddenness, offered to take the latter off his hands at par and Philip assented for as much as was needful to cover the convalescent's vacation that followed his operation. The frosty surgeon arranged matters with a local Draft Board—Philip's classification was changed to A1—and by a little ingenuity he managed to get himself inducted into the Field Artillery where his status as a Yale man, when Yale was the only college to possess an F.A.R.O.T.C., might count for something. He departed for camp about the middle of June with a contented spirit and a document full of American eagles, Whereases and Greetings. Two weeks of the vacation had been spent with Lucia—Phil was off making patriotic speeches most of the time, but there had been several cheerlessly amicable meetings between father and son in which both took great pains

281

to behave well before Lucia and the servants and neither
said what he thought. The day before Philip left
Los Angeles he got a formal congratulatory letter from
his father, between whose lines could be read much
heavy self-satisfaction. Philip tore it up, answered it
with one word " Thanks " and put San Esteban behind
him.

The most glamorous parts of being drafted were the
heroic pictures of death or the D.S.C. that would run
through his mind to the jeers of the ribald parts of
him, going down in the train. When he actually got
to camp he found it rather like a gigantic, rigid outdoor
boarding-school with reformatory manners, run by and
for men, whose members were chosen by lot and whose
vacations depended largely on the luck of the draw. It
was a grown-up Kitchell fairly run, with a tenseness
of purpose in every small second of the day that made
college seem like a lotus-eater's island. There was the
first week, when dazed Italians wandered desolately
about trying to buy a yard of picket line or find the
officer who kept the key of the parade-ground—when
calisthenics created unheard-of muscles only to make
them sore as stubbed toes—when an appetite was no
longer well-mannered or even civilized but a ravening
physical emptiness that had to be stuffed into quiescence
as a mattress is stuffed full of hair—when Philip had
his first experience of peeling a washboiler full of scald-
ing hot potatoes on K.P. Philip jumped like a startled
aunt at any and every bugle call and spent most of his
spare time, it seemed to him, in saluting second-lieu-
tenants, policing barracks, or buttoning the thousands

of errant buttons on his uniform. He took care of those buttons like a mother with a croupy child, yet one of them was always sure to be flapping from some unsuspected place whenever he came under the disciplined, burning eyes of his superiors. He and all the new men, poor goblins, wished fervently for eyes wherever they had buttons and for automatic recording gramophones instead of ears, for they were always doing the wrong thing in a desperate hurry or waiting dazedly for further orders until it was too late to do the right thing at all. The city ones recovered the power of heavy sleep, when the night hours were like solid blocks of ebony laid firmly and softly on each other, edge to edge, till dawn and the whinnying bugle broke them apart. And they all discovered such an interest in eating that for some the problem of extra pie became as intense a concern as was the salvation of his soul to a Spanish saint.

But even when the first ten days were up, they began to walk and talk differently, pick up doughboy slang, roll their own and fit steadily into the machine. They were broader, they stood up straighter, they tanned in every color from brick to burnt olive—there developed a certain team pride in the piece, in the squad, in the battery, in the brigade. The making of a battery of artillery out of a disconnected job-lot of raw men and half-cooked officers is as interesting and arduous a process as birth by Cæsarian section and the labor-pains are distributed down to the cooks. When July was passing into August and dust lay like heavy talcum on the throat in hot route marches and fools emptied their canteens the first half-hour, Philip took stock of his new possessions and decided that they were satisfactory.

Item—Officers.

Captain Lisbee, the lucky best of the First Plattsburg experiment, just, tireless and always ready to learn, du Guesclin three years out of Harvard with a Florence Nightingale hatred of messiness, dirt and careless subordinates, as well as much of Florence's hard, humorous sincerity. His men exasperated him in secret with their human lack of instantaneous comprehension of new situations and their human anxiousness to be led, but he took care of them as if they were orphans he had to bring up. They laughed at his broad flat " a " 's and continual baths, but he could have taken them all across a plain as hot as a frying-pan into direct machine-gun fire.

Lieutenant Hastings, capable, conscientious, colorless, cool. An ex-West Pointer, and a little supercilious toward the New Army with the bored tolerance of the undistinguished professional toward the able amateur. Followed and obeyed with accuracy but without enthusiasm.

Lieutenant Whittle, a young somber idealist of a San Francisco millionaire. The least apt of the lot at handling men but with a patience that redeemed most of his actual mistakes. Tolerated rather than liked or hated, and nicknamed " Little Jeff " for the bustling, loose-jointed way in which he busily ran about.

Lieutenant Stannard, Philip's direct superior who tried to hide a weak mouth with a nail-brush mustache,

and shifty eyes by turning them up at the sky when he
talked to you.   Very cordially detested as a temper-
ridden Achilles of the "duty before decency" stripe.
Large gory threats were whispered in the company room
or after Taps of what would happen to him if the battery ever went into action.   The British private, after
four years of war, had transferred what venom he had
against the ruling Powers to Staff Officers or safe,
plump Generals at Headquarters, but the American private, being new at the game, took it all out on his own
immediate non-coms and lieutenants in the old demo-
cratic way.

Item—Men.

These ranged from the University of Texas first-
sergeant with hair and manners to officers as slick and
smooth as a wet rubber raincoat to a middle-aged hired-
man from a peach-ranch with hands like roots who had
trustingly brought two flannel nightshirts to camp and
so acquired a nickname that stuck to him like a piece
of flypaper.   They were a mixeder lot than the Frickett
miners, drawn from every class and many of the trades
in the Republic, but the backbone of the battery was the
ranchworkers and the city clerks—it split about fifty-
fifty between them—and the pallid stamina of the latter
matched the former's uncoördinated strength at everything that did not call for muscles in bulk alone.   There
was, or tried to be, the battery bully, 'Lige Denan, who,
after swelling about for two weeks with mouth on one
side of his face in the approved hard-boiled fashion,
got into a dispute in mess line with a large cow-like

being from San Diego and that evening found himself being as thoroughly and scientifically beaten as if each of his opponent's hands was a living hammer before he could gasp out " 'Nuff ! " and discover that the San Diegan was the proprietor of " Professor Monte's Boxing and Athletic Academy."

There was the battery funny-man, a scrawny little mole-face who had grown like a barnacle on the San Francisco water-front. He had the quacky voice of a tin duck and knew all the underground folk-ballads of the United States from " Down on the Lehigh Valley " to " My Girl's a Lulu." His wit was gnomish and as American as ice-cream soda, and he got laughs fat vaudeville comedians would have given their false noses for when the battery broke ranks at the end of a greasy day of unsparing heat and sweat. He composed the litany of " C " Battery, roared out whenever possible at all times of ease and stress.

Micky (*interlocutor*) : Well, fellas, and who's Uncle Sam's pure-hearted little Sunday-school boys?

Chorus (*enormously sardonic*) : Us, *God* damn it !

Micky (*pained*) : Dear, dear, and what did Uncle Sam's pure-hearted little Sunday-school boys do all day?

Chorus (*a roar*) : Shovel !

Micky (*with a wicked drawl*) : And what, oh, what, did Uncle Sam's pure-hearted little boys spend all day shoveling?

But here we had better leave him.

There was also the battery butt, a tow-headed Swede

with blue gollywog eyes. He was so eager to follow instructions—so pathetically anxious to do as he should—
so utterly certain of never by any possibility being in
the right place at the right time. His feet were not
unduly large but he spent most of his waking hours in
falling over them—it was a legend that he had once
stumbled and fallen flat on his face on encountering a
stray dropped safety-pin in the middle of the company
street. He was always on K.P. for misdemeanors and
there led the terrified existence of a persecuted puppy
under the voice and hand of the blustering cook who
hated "hynephated Amurricans" with crusading zeal.
Ole was constantly putting salt in the pies instead of
sugar and mixing raw potatoes with cooked apples,
"they ban look so moo-ooch alike." He was shown a
dozen times how to make coffee but persisted in regard-
ing dried beans as a necessary ingredient till the whole
mess threatened to boil both him and the cook in their
own pots. There was the battery dog-robber, a plump,
plausible oily lump of a Greek who licked non-commissioned boots and greased non-commissioned palms and
applied for a three-day pass every fortnight with a new
unpronounceable relative sick each time. There were
the sergeants and corporals themselves, those you could
work and those you couldn't, those who stood on their
position and their warrants like pouter-pigeons on a
roof, and those that were "pretty good scouts," the
serene and the bluffers, the loud, the silly, the quiet,
the effective, the dogs in office, the infinitely various
children of men.

Philip had dreaded his identification with Peter

Sands the actor, but it proved not to be as inevitable as he had supposed. He had restrained Hay almost by a use of physical force from playing up the fact of his enlistment in the various picture-magazines, and his film presentment was enough unlike him to ensure comparative security. He had the sense to keep rather silent his first few weeks without being unnecessarily aloof and when " ridden " on the resemblance turned the jokes aside with a few necessary lies. Besides, the battery was incurious, it ranged through so many occupations as it was that the discovery of Philip's would have caused no disturbance—but the discovery never happened to take place till the very end of things. Once indeed he heartily enjoyed an hour or so of cursing Peter and his kind as slackers, superiors and parasites in general.

There was Philip's particular buddie, in so far as he had one, an ex-taxi-driver with long nervous nicotined fingers and spectral eyes. He had been a power in third-rate gang politics in Oakland and had regarded being drafted as a personal insult, but now, after two months in the army, he was physically healthy for the first tired days of his life. He had been in love with a Chinese girl and she had been sold over his head to a bigger boss—he still carried a notch in his ear from a tong-man's hatchet. He told Philip all about it in a slumbering whisper through breathless nights when sleep did not come at once.

" So I get into Sing Loo's place by the window," he droned. " There's a hell of a big room and it stinks with joss-sticks like a Chink New Year's Eve. There

ain't no lights at all and I'm scared—am I scared?—
say, I wouldn't a been any more scared if they'd got
me in the chair and was just gettin' ready to throw down
the switch. But I know she's in the little room behind
and I crawls over to it on the floor—belly down. Once,
say, it was funny—" He laughed under his breath.
" Once I put my left hand up to my head and think,
' Say, where in God's name did I spill a lot of hot glue
all over my nut? ' It was blood, a course, and I was a
boob not to know it, but I didn't.

" She was in the other room all right and Sing Loo
was with her. They was both hittin' the hop with their
eyes shut—I could see from her pinched nose and the
look of her cheeks she'd been doin' it regular since they
took her away. I played my flash right over their mugs
but neither of them even winked. And I could see
another thing when I turned the flash on her. She was
going to have a kid, and it wasn't my kid either, for
they'd kept her where I couldn't find her for pretty
near a year.

" Well, buddie, what could I do? I couldn't take
her through the window, hopped like she was. I couldn't
shoot up Sing Loo, they'd cut her up when they found
him. What would you a done, guy? "

" I don't know," said Philip, truthfully.

" Well, I did somepin else. I just couldn't stand Sing
Loo any more when I looked at him, he was lyin' there
sweatin' all over himself and openin' and shuttin' his
mouth like a big yellow frog. He'd had her for a year
and she was doped now and it was his kid that was
comin'. I held his mouth just like that when he opened

it next and I made him swaller his tongue. He didn't
know it, he was too full of happy-juice, he just made
a lot of funny noises and pretty soon he died. I didn't
do anything to her, not even leave a letter, she was
different, she wasn't the cute little kid she used to be,
and you never can tell with Chinks. They was a couple
of spots of blood on the floor and I wiped 'em up with
my sleeve. Then I went back."

He sighed.

" All the papes said he kicked out with heart-disease.
They gave him the swellest funeral you ever saw, fire-
crackers till it sounded as if hell was poppin' all over
Chinatown and a big silver joss and a p-rade and lots
of punk. I guess they must a thought he swallered his
tongue accidental, and anyway they didn't want to put
the bulls wise to the hop-joint he'd been running on the
side and they'd never gotten their piece out of. Anyhow
they didn't bother me."

He rolled over uneasily, squeaking the springs of his
cot.

" She and the kid both died when it came," he said
softly. " Too muchee hop. And then I started sniffin'
the white stuff."

But the tale of how he took to heroin, became a
" snow-bird " and finally broke the habit, in so far as
it can be broken, after a two years' horrible wrestle
by sheer violence of will, was another saga, true or
false, but one that Philip didn't happen to hear that
night.

As a final flourish, the middle of a chance letter of
Philip's to Dick does as well as any.

"They are as various a bunch as the letters you find in alphabet soup. A plumber, a sign painter, four chauffeurs, many farmers or farmers' sons or hired men. A couple of stenographers, a broken down Yale reprobate who gives me no peace, a barber, three bartenders, the last of whom kept a bawdy-house on the side. But his wife has taken over his job now that he is in the army and manages it, he tells me, quite effectively—another case of a woman releasing a man for war-service. . . ."

Item—Horses.

Philip had always thought himself a fair enough rider, even though he had ridden little or not at all for the last year and a half. He was therefore free of the unholy awe that assailed the more cityish of his fellow recruits at the first encounter with creatures whom they regarded with much the same dread as geography lions. But the beasts that had been shipped to "C" Battery were savages, technically broken because a buster had ridden them once but wild as headhunters and hating all men like Amazons. Philip was kicked once and bitten twice in the first quarter-hour of riding drill and after that lost all reverence and respect for that noble animal, the horse.

Feeding them, harnessing them up, were as adventurous experiences as riding surf in a sieve. "You sneak up on the brute from his rear when he isn't looking," Philip explained later, at length. "You take fair aim and kick his rump over to the other side of the stall. You then slide in with your buckets, keeping both eyes at once on teeth and feet or you'll know it. You deposit the feed, he tries to bite you and you whang him in the jaw. In grooming him, always be ready to kick him in the stomach on small provocation or you will be slain. I tried gentling and soothing mine for a few downtrodden days, but it was no more use than reading the Gettysburg Address to a painted cannibal. I clucked like a hen at him in the most approved English 'ostler way and patted his pink nose and he very nearly had my thumb off before I could jerk it away. Moreover, it's no use to treat him like a gentleman for as soon as one horse gets to know you and only kicks you now and then as a matter of principle, he gets switched to another stall or some rank sergeant gets hold of him and you have the whole thing to go over again with a fresh new devil unleashed whose previous valet never came nearer a horse than the wooden ones in the merry-go-round before he got in the army.

"And watering the things, my aunt! It isn't a column, it isn't a march, it's a charge, a dead run away of the whole blame barebacked battery till they hit the river like a bursting shell and the horses try to slip and roll over on you so that you'll drown. The sight is stupendous in the pink early emptiness of dawn, hundreds of horses gone loco and running like stags with all the officers and non-coms in sight cursing their lungs out because we can't hold them in, and we sticking on anywhere from the ears to the end of the tail, a bunch of scared, khaki-colored centaurs (if you can imagine such things) with the horse part always ready to bust off and break away. One thing—it does teach you to ride—at the end of it most of us could have straddled a primeval moose with equanimity.

"My pick of them all was The Goat, he used to eat sections of his harness when I wasn't looking and then get, oh, so sick! till he wore the stable-sergeant away. Once I'll swear he had two brass buckles off his head-stall for dessert—when I kicked him next I could hear them jingling around in him like sleigh-bells. He was a sweet thing with a face like Torquemada, long yellow ivories and a rocking-chair canter. I gave him two cakes of chocolate the day we were mustered out and he bit me friendlily on the cheek—pure affection, it wouldn't have hurt an egg."

Item—Guns.

No wonder that guns used to be baptized at the foundry like children and have polysyllabic names and elegant Latin mottoes scrolled into their backs—for Philip soon discovered that each gun in "C" Battery had the individuality of a demigod, though all were as mathematically alike as human ingenuity could make sure of. "Benny" came first, so named because of the coughing gorilla-like bark he made when he spoke and an obscure racial jest connected with Jews. Two-Gun, sulky as a sow, and picking up all kinds of dirt with astonishing ease. Three, "Greasy Ann" that waddled along with her limber like a washerwoman. Four, "Little Joe," since her crew were all frantic crap-shooters. Philip belonged to Benny, and he got to know the sleek steel animal as a bridge-shark knows the cards in his opponent's hands. From the soft chock of the breech-block that smacked home like a closing metal mouth to the dot of a flag from the signal pit showing that Benny had plumped square on his target again and the burnt chemical whiff of smokeless powder in his nose and on top of his tongue, Philip acquainted himself with every trick and idiosyncrasy of the play.

The guns were still virgins, of course, for they had not killed as yet. When they had, good gunners would regard them with odd worship as a combination of wife, god and favorite horse. Now, after two months of it, with the battery shaking into shape, the unmarried, the young and the heedless thought of them and the whole business of the army secretly as huge fabulous playthings in a keen and dangerous game, though publicly all cursed out the entire system from the first sergeant's liver to a lack of milk in the Java with the heartiness of soul and epithet that has been the peculiar possession of privates since the Tenth Legion's disreputable jests on Cæsar's bald head. Only the married, the men over thirty and the few sensitive souls to whom the perspiring publicity of barracks and showers was like an enforced hair-shirt looked ahead and saw France and action and death dropping toward them as softly and surely as a falling parachute with the drilled march-past of each rapid twenty-four hours. Man always mercifully believes himself and his chief friends immortal until definitely proved otherwise—if he did not all Earth would be a congress of shivering children in scientific hot-houses by now.

But this is a digression from the guns. Philip, Brick Bennett, a man named Lewis and an inarticulate farmer boy, Simp Stevens, were out on the baking range one day trying to find what shade there was under Benny's belly and wheels in a pause of the firing.

"Got a hump, Sellaby?" said Bennett, lazily reclined. He was indefatigable at bumming cigarettes and generally got them, for he had a wide pleasant smile. The habit had once settled upon him the nickname of "Fag Hound" but that had led a tenuous existence and died, for no other appellation could stand against the ones due his hair, which was brighter than a strawberry. Philip produced a twisted package, shook it hopefully and divided the last crushed occupant with some exactness. Brick sent up a little blue puff toward the speechless heavens—Lieutenant Hastings was wisely lenient in little things.

"Fat Wilson says his cousin who's clerk at H. Q. says that Little Jeff was talking to the Old Man and he says that we may get outa here in three more weeks."

Everybody took up the latest rumor at once.

"Th-th-that's all right," stammered Stevens eagerly, "b-b-but I was on g-guard the other night and I heard one of the 'A' Battery Looeys jawing with the Cap a-and he said we might get shifted any day now, but it would be to Texas a-a-and—"

"Simp, Simp, you're too full of goldfish—they've gone to your block." Brick cut him off disrespectfully.

"Why in the name of the Old Man's shirt-tail should they want to ship us to Texas? We wasn't drafted to fight sandfleas or greasers—we're a brigade of mo-bile light artillery. Now *I* think, your uncle Henry thinks, we're going to be seasick in less time than it'd take to grease a goose. They been doubling up forced marches on us till I musta lost ten pounds in two days."

This produced a laugh, for Brick was as skinny and strong as a horse's leg.

"Any time we don't spend half the day out here and get fried in the sun like eggs, I'm a Swede," put in Philip diffidently. "There must be some reason for it— the little boys with the new brass bars don't love to come out here and sweat so much."

"You're right, my son, you're right and you've said a faceful." Brick grew pontifical. "In three weeks we'll be down at Jackson. In three more weeks we'll be going across. In a month after that we'll be honest-Injun Sammies"—he lent the word an accent of indescribable scorn—"and Benny here will be getting all hot in the throat and the bunch of us will hafta look around and pick up pieces of Simp." He grinned annoyingly.

"Yey w-w-w-w-won't!" sputtered Stevens. "You— you—you—" He opened and shut his mouth, started again, "You—you—you—" By this time the whole gun crew was choking and snickering. "You—you'll be dead first, you Brick!" he ended triumphantly, leaving the latter in convulsions.

"Oh, turn off the alarm-clock," he gasped. "Turn off the alarm-clock, darling, wifie's awake!"

"H-h-hell!" gulped his butt disgustedly. "H-h-hell!"

"Calm down, Simp boy," advised Lewis, a taciturn, efficient cog. "You ain't going to spit at the Germans, you know, you're going to shoot them."

"I wonder if it scares you as sick as they say it does when the other guy's shells start coming over," said Philip casually.

"Sure," answered Brick. "We'll all be scareder than pups."

"The geeks on the other side'll be just as scared." This was Lewis.

"M-m-maybe they will, but h-how the heck will we know it?"

"Use your 'magination, Simp, if you've got one."

"Oh, we may be scared but I guess we'll keep on shooting," said Brick lightly.

"Sure—we got to. And anyway we ain't got such a rotten job as the doughboys."

"D-do you know, I wouldn't mind that so much, B-Brick, i-it's getting bumped by somebody you can't see that's the bum idea."

A slight nervous tension, the tension of the untried, twitched over the sitting or sprawling figures.

"If you're dead, you're dead," announced Brick didactically. "That's all. What's the difference how you get put away?"

"L-lots. Y-you don't believe in im-immortality, Brick?"

He rose and stretched his arms. "Immortality—hell!" he said, but "I dunno," he added at once, with puzzlement. "The priest, God bless his fat soul for he's been a decent man to me, used to talk a lot about what would happen to me when I died. But look here —here I am"—he hit himself on the chest—"Brick Bennett. If somebody comes along and blows a hole in me, where am I? Up the flue? I'm alive now—you can't show me I'll be living then—any part of me I give a damn about. That's why I'm going to keep alive as long as I can and Lord help the man who tries to stop me."

"The Bible says," said Lewis, who was a Methodist.

"I know what it says, but it said it about a lot of sheenies, didn't it? Well, I'm not a sheeny. I'm Irish. It's a g-r-r-rand race!" He waved his long arms and laughed.

"So God help the little French girls and the connyac too when I get amongst them, for I'm going to keep alive as long as I can."

"You're a materialist, Brick," said Philip.

"Sure I am—it's a nice long word. And what do you think—you went to a college once?"

Philip remembered the tinsel heaven.

"It's too darn hard to explain," he said gingerly, "but I think I go on, even after somebody fills me full of lead pills. I think we all go on. Even you, Brick."

"That's lovely of you. How about the Simp?"

"Oh, nothing could ever bust him. But the thing, the force that's working with us is caught on its own fishnet. It can't get loose from us now if it wanted to, it's made us too subtle and too amusing to cook in anybody's hell or put away on ice in anybody's heaven. We go on and we get changed as we go on. Maybe we come back here in body after body."

"That's all bunk," said Lewis decisively. "You got Heaven and God and the Bible and Hell and Christ.

You act right and God will take care of you. You don't
and you better look out."

"Th-that's so," said the Simp. "Th-that's so. I'm
re-religious myself."

"I like Sellaby's idea a whole lot better," said Brick,
stirring up dust. "All the same if I ever do come back,
by swipes, I hope I'm a millionaire!"

"You—you'll be a white wing, th-that's what you'll
be!" snapped Stevens, angrily.

"Now, Simp, what rude, rude words!" He scuffled
dust at the stutterer's face.

"Listen," said Lewis. "Two mornings ago when I
was on sick-call, the Doc was spreading it with that
fat 'A' Battery Major. And he said—"

A sharp coughing order split the calm like a stick
ruffling lazy water. The lolling shapes snapped up into
their places. There was nothing in the world but wind-
less skies, brown earth, sunburnt toy-soldier rows of
stiff men and squatting guns, and heat.

Item—Snapshots.

The " Y " reading and writing room. "Write to
Your Mother!" "Write to Your Mother!" Everywhere are signs, signs full of exclamation-points, signs
sedulously affectionate, signs about keeping pure, signs
jovially Christian, taking Christ by the arm, signs of a
piece with the professional heartiness of the sparrow-
shaped secretary who bobs about like a bird in a red-
triangled uniform and *will* call sergeants " dear boys."
The long tables are crowded with heads, torsos, and
writing hands, the air is misty because there are so many

men in the room; some scribble fluently on both sides
of the cheap flagged paper and when no one is looking
put sentimental crosses below the signature and "Pvt.
1st Class"; others have tongues in the corner of their
mouths, trying to help the unwieldy letters form out
of a pen held like a fork in an ink-smeared fist. Piers
Plowman and a certain rich man elbow each other, writing much the same kind of letter to their families and
their girls. The letters are crude, jerky, affectionate,
cheap, full of harsh wit, jocose, unmentionable, homesick and very alive. Everybody is absorbed in pencil-
and-paper—this is one of the rare free half-hours of
the day to be spent as lingeringly as liquid out of a
dropper. But the secretary gets up on a chair and
struts.

"All together, boys!" he shouts, and the scores of
heads jerk uneasily and come back out of their separate
dreams. "All together now, we want to sing some of
the grand old hymns!"

He is the only person in camp who wants to sing the
grand old hymns, his sheep here want to write, to put
some faint symbol and semblance of their new strange
muscular days on the " Y " paper that fills the pen with
tiny hairs, to give these days a little eternity in cum-
brous sentences, to have their people read through the
paper and see them, soldiers, in unfamiliar earth-colored
clothes, broad hats, big shoes. But a few feeble obedient
voices, the voices of those who will always be led, join
the syrupy booming baritone at the second verse of the
grand old hymn. Others chime in reluctantly, after a
while there is too much noise for any one to write—the

room tramps with an affirmation of the worthlessness
of man in the eyes of God—the secretary is quite exalted.
But when the singing ends and the half-hour is over,
many letters are stuck away unfinished.

"Write your mother?" says Brick loudly as he and
Philip go out. "How the blazes am I going to write my
ma with that man always hanging around like a fly in
me ear?"

The secretary goes to bed full of apostolic satisfaction. The " Y " has not yet learned, will not learn in
the main, the one great art, that of leaving people alone.
And the usual American, or human being, is never content with looking gift-horses in the mouth, he wants
to pull down the creature's lips and count all its
teeth. . . .

A night on guard on the post down by the river.
Black water slides under low swinging branches tangled
together like a game of cat's cradle—comes out into
broad gleaming flats in the pale light of one o'clock—
rushes back under intricate designs of lacing boughs
where it is patterned like a black-and-silver rug by the
shine of the moon.

All things are as quiet as the breath of a sweet sleeper.
The only sounds in Philip's ears are the riffle of the
water and his own crunching steps, heel and toe. He
walks his post rather slowly, sleep burning at his eyelids the first half-hour. Then his mind goes out beyond
sleep, he feels calm and relaxed and smooth through
every tired inch of him, so large and complete is the
dazzling colorless silence of the sky. It takes him into

itself like a bath of fragrant water and leaves him swingingly refreshed.

He might be Adam just wakened under the apple-tree or the last Esquimaux watching the stars fall out of the sky, he is so alone. There are other sentries but the beats are long and leave little chance for stolen talk or cigarettes. He is completely by himself and achingly happy. The hours pass like dark falling feathers, he walks in a glittering trance with the rustle and sight of water in his ears and eyes.

All the same when his relief comes in and he yawns away in a most unmilitary manner, he knows that he couldn't have stood it a second longer without falling asleep as he stood, like a tired horse. . . .

Route-march, jingle and squeak of the harness, slur of the wheels through dust, clacket and pad of horse-hoofs, grunt of the limbers complaining like fat old men, the strong noise of human voices trying to sing.

> " Oh, it's hi—hi—hee in the Field Artilleree.
> Shout out your numbers loud and strong!—
>   One! Two!"

" A " Battery slaps the numerals out of its ten-score throats with the crash of the elephant's salute to royalty. " B " Battery starts vocalizing on its own account. " The artillery, the artillery, with the dirt behind their ears," it bellows.

> " The artillery, the artillery, that laps up all the
>   beers,
>   The cavalry, the infantry,

And the God damn engineers!
They couldn't lick the artillery in a hundred thou-
    sand years.

"C" Battery is not to be silenced, it calls on its
chantey-man for the large, almighty song that has drifted
home on odd currents from the A.E.F.

"Hey, Micky! Oh, Micky, you mick! Give 'em
Hinky Dinky, Micky! You tell 'em, kid! Let's go!"

Micky raises his fluting treble, pure as fresh cream.

"A Mademoiselle from Gay Paree!" he lilts.

"*Par*-lay voo!" from the chorus, full throated, making the horses put back their ears.

"A Mademoiselle from Gay Paree!"

"*Par*-lay voo!"

"A Mademoiselle from Gay Paree—"

The notes soar, liquid and floating; the chorus chops
them off like an ax.

"Th-there's going to be more truth than potry for
you in that tune, B-Buck," mutters Stevens, trying to
recover his breath. The song goes on.

Past a wall of Lombardy poplars like green feather-
dusters on end, past an orange-grove picked out with a
few late, red-golden bubbles of fruit, over a bridge that
sharpens all noise, back to dust that muffles it like felt.
Sweat and the smell of leather and dust and horses,
dark stains on the horses' backs, the dust stirred to
blobby, schemeless designs as if a beast with a thousand
stumpy legs and wheels were passing.

"The General got the Cross of War!
Par-lay voo!

The General got the Cross of War!
Par-lay voo!
The General got the Cross of War!
But nobody knows what he got it for!
Hinky, dinky par-lay voo!"

The identical little boy with the flag that there is on
every road, frantically waving, giving vent to an ecstatic,
piping " Yeah! " as the battery clinks and chumbles
along. The hard ease of sitting on the caisson—the
heat, direct and intense but dry and clear, heat that
would brown this paper to the color of pale toast but is
not the sunstroke kind—a long, thirsty drink of some
colored stuff mostly fizz and foam in everybody's mind
if they ever get back to camp. The horse of an officer
whickers, blowing out nostrils, at the sight of a mare in
a fenced field who runs over to the bars with the sweeping grace of a canoe and stretches a long roan neck wistfully at the harnessed, obedient parade of possible husbands. Ribald comments flicker down the column.

" Oh, Farmer, have you a daughter fair?
Par-lay voo!
Oh, Farmer, have you a daughter fair?
Par-lay voo! "

Fat Wilson wipes his dripping face. " Must be going
to fight the Japs this trip! " he wheezes. " Seems 's if
we're half-way to the Pacific already! " Drab-uni-
formed, khaki with dust, grinning and singing and
talking, the horses straining, the guns jolting, the
wheels squealing, they simmer down the road and are
out of sight, a thousand or so young men, hard as nails,

burnt Indian-color, most of them happy, all sure that
they are riding to the wars. . . .

The third day out of the trip across continent in the
troop-train. At one end of the car a crap-game with a
sentry on the lookout for officers, and Brick Bennett
with a pile of bills in front of him like a heap of green
leaves. At the other a stud-poker tournament where
Philip is losing a month's pay. In the center, Lewis,
the Methodist, and a shy youth from Agricultural College coming very nearly to blows about God and the
Single Tax. . . .

More of that trip—the hysterical young woman on the
station-platform who kissed every soldier she could
reach, nor that to their distaste for she was soft with the
dark, ripe prettiness of a plum. When they pulled out
of the station her hair had come down and was stream-
ing to her waist and she shrieked after them in a high,
knifing voice, " Give 'em hell, you boys, give 'em hell ! "
Philip thought of the Valkyrie at first and of vultures
later. He saw her afterwards in dreams, she had pinions
and flapped and screamed over a new skull. . . .

The husky tension of the last week or so at the new
camp. They had their overseas outfits, " go to hell hats "
and all, and most had spent last leaves with families
before leaving the coast. Men made or altered wills,
there was a sudden run in the stores on little leather
pocket photograph-cases. Half the brigade had never
been on the sea in their lives—and the muttered conversation of bunkies after taps turned on mal-de-mer

and all the manifold perils of the great deep. The last days were both sober and flushed. "They're fighting mad to get a crack at the Boche!" said a colonel, preeningly. Well, they were, three-quarters of the time. The brigade as a whole had the pride and wonder and doubts of a Kentucky thoroughbred before the feel of her first real race track under new shoes.

The great vivid instrument quivered, hesitated, reflected, joked at its qualms, swore to give a bitterly good account of itself and fulfil the stubborn purpose for which it was made. The last six months had been teaching a giant baby how to walk, now the child was on its feet, about to take the first firm step towards the dark cloud, the dark pool which lay ahead, the dark semblance, the dark ignorance, which with a few steps more it must wholly enter, to live in, suffer in, come back from, or be consumed.

This was all in steamy Carolina at the idle, maple-leaf-colored height of a southern fall. So, like every other body of troops between Maine and Oregon—if you believe in what you are told—the brigade was just on the point of sailing when the Armistice fell into the middle of it like a grenade.

They rejoiced officially and cursed in private. There is no doubt that the vast majority of them were stunningly disappointed, and those who were secretly glad proclaimed their discomfiture in the most blaspheming tones. They had been tempered, drilled and exercised for anything from five months to a year, tuned up till the whole brigade ran together like the engine of a millionaire's limousine—and then, at the end of it all, marched square into an anticlimax to the sound of an ironic bugle. "Ah, hell, it was such a nice war while it lasted!" said Brick disconsolately. Relief did not come till later—they had never seen action at all. "Papa, what did you do in the Great War?" growled the stable sergeant, an old regular. "I curried up a lot of wall-eyed plugs, me son, while me buddies went out and got plugged at Chatto-Teary! If the little geezer ever asks me questions like that, I'll push in his face!"

The days until the brigade was finally demobilized were the most staringly dull that Philip had ever spent. The whole business and end of existence had lost its salt. What was the use of drilling or marching or obeying orders if you weren't going to fight? The hours passed in mechanical duties, slackly done, in a fever of gambling, in long parliaments as to what they were going to do when they got out. It was the exception who was able to say flatly that he was going to take up his old job where he had left it—most had been wrenched violently from the life in which they had grown up, traveled out into larger air, seen men and cities, grown restless as crows and hungry for something undefined. The city boys imagined themselves farmers till they talked to the boys from farms who looked back on their monotony and crampedness with vast distaste and wanted to get to the city where something was doing all the time. "I hear it's pretty easy to be an electrician if you take some courses," said a bootblack, pleadingly. A cigar-store clerk was going to study dentistry. A farm hand had bandit visions of driving a taxi. A dozen asked Philip for advice on getting into the movies—for his secret was more or less out. As for Philip himself, a plan began to form in his mind.

When they reached Los Angeles on the government's transportation, red-chevroned and taking immense delight in ostentatiously ignoring officers and M. P.'s, Philip, Brick Bennett, Simp Stevens and Philip's buddie, the ex-taxi-driver and dope-fiend, had a historic dinner in celebration at the Grantmore. It was an affair of as many courses as a Middle Western city's banquet to a mayor who has just been whitewashed by the Grand Jury, and when the first half-inch of ash had been knocked from cigars, Philip, who had been able to get hold of Elgar Hay by much hurried telephoning, adjourned them to a private room and produced two quarts of five-star Haig and Haig. Next morning they parted, Stevens back to raise alfalfa, Brick for " the best damn garridge in Mendocino County," Moke Wickering on the Oakland train. Then Philip loafed through a whole large day, spending most of his ready cash on a Turkish bath and unfamiliar civilian clothes, the trousers of which, especially, flapped so loosely about his ankles that he felt nervous and undressed. He went out to dinner with Hay that night and they talked till two.

In the first place, Philip didn't want to go back into the films at all. If he did, he wanted a free hand and entire supervision of everything in his pictures from the original script to the titles and final cutting. He realized that this was something to which Hay could not possibly accede, and he did not greatly care. The films, as they were made at present, it seemed to him, bore in general the same ingenuous and illegitimate relation to the arts that advertising copy did to literature. Besides, he had other work to do, and he could not waste time.

The two parted with respect and entire incomprehension.

" You aren't going to ditch me now and ack for Incando, are you, Pete?" Hay asked doubtfully as they shook hands.

"Incando? Rats!" said Philip. "No, I'm not going anywhere in the films at all. I'm going off where I can get by myself and write some poetry."

Hay stared at his retreating back.

"Poetry?" he said. "Poetry? Well—I'll—be—*burnt!*"

So next morning Philip found himself, like most of the just demobilized army, out of a job.

He had the impulse to rush back to San Esteban, but again both pride and sense interfered. Phil had never written him a line since his stiff acknowledgment of the fact of Philip's enlistment, and while Lucia said much of "Your father's pride in you," Philip looked dubiously at the picture of himself turning up at his father's door, quite penniless except for a few bonds which Phil would undoubtedly regard as treasonably unpatriotic of him to sell. He felt that the rôle would be less that of the prodigal son than the fatted calf, a burnt-offering to Phil's bad temper. Besides, he knew in himself for the first true time since college, knocking like a hammer, the driving impulse to make glistening shapes and angry stars with words. And for this he wanted three things, seclusion, loneliness, and some physical work for his body part of the time.

He sold a hundred-dollar bond—his army pay had gone in learning not to draw to a pair and a kicker—and spent a week in employment agencies discovering that the words " Just discharged from the army," or even " from the A.E.F." were not always lucky-pieces to bring instant offers of occupation to their fortunate possessor. " The longer the pay-roll, the shorter the memory," thought Philip unjustly, for the large corporations as a class were as fair and unfair as the small employers. It gave him a sardonic twist now and then to see or read of gold-striped men selling newspapers or begging or trying to stumble their way through some of the giant creepers of red tape that hedged the various bureaus of vocational training. He made a note on a scrap of old newspaper that fitted the case. " In the Middle Ages, the ingratitude of princes was proverbial. We have progressed—and royalty's place and business in that as in other things has been most efficiently taken over by enlightened democracies."

He got a job driving a team and held it for a week, but it left him at the end of the day too tired to think or write, so he quit it without remorse as soon as he had drawn his pay. He parted from the horses however with apples and some sentimental regret—one of them had a wicked sidewise slash of the head in biting that reminded him of the Goat. He tried being an elevator boy in the employ of a concern that had loudly announced its policy of " A Job for Every One of Our

Heroes," and then proceeded to sweat and underpay
the said heroes as early and often as they could. Theo-
retically, the comparative solitude and silence of an
elevator cage during certain hours of the day would
have made it an ideal if migratory hermitage for the
composition of verses on Greek divinities. But the
continual up and down motion of the hot little cell,
rising and falling like an excited mechanical monkey
on a long smooth stick, produced queer rebellions in
Philip's stomach and after a couple of days of queasi-
ness and nights of indigestible visions, he found that
the only metrical thoughts that came to him were in
the mood of Brooke's " Channel Passage " and so simply
failed to turn up for duty at all one morning. And,
meanwhile, he was losing weight and healthiness, for
the thing that he wanted to write, that he must write
for his own soul's and irony's sake as a mastery of and
answer to the last four years, kept fretting and gnawing
at his brain as a mouse gnaws sugar. And yet, when he
had perfect leisure for the poem and sat down with a
flat white sheet of paper before him, not an atom of it
came, except in scattered words.

" Io lay sleeping, a white sheaf of lilies."
                " And the milky skies
Were one pale thunder with the wrath of Zeus."
" The gadfly, in his voice of withered leaves."

Inconsequential tatters and fragments, scales from
something deep and living in the brain, they teased and
buzzed at him all day long like mosquitoes. And behind them he saw the lucid vast orb of his poem, yellow

and whole as a cask or an August moon if he ever could touch it and make words of it and see it shine.

He could have had office work, no doubt, but he was too canny. "Writing on the side," if the writing was to be anything better than salable soufflé, after eight hours a day of the mental prickly-heat of desk work struck him as rather like trying to run a hundred yards in eleven seconds after a morning spent in pulling a cart up a hill. There was no rest in it—it might conceivably be done if necessary but it gave no change except that of exhaustion to the brain and muscles and inevitably worked against the swift drafting and marching conclusive accomplishment of any sustained piece of work. Philip knew exactly the kind of job he wanted and believed less and less in the probability of getting it as the days went by. One morning he snatched at a straw—or a tail feather of Fortune—and hired himself out desperately to a chicken ranch some dozens of miles up state in the hope that if his hands were kept really busy at brainless labor, the rhythmic part of his being might begin to function again.

It proved to be a disastrous fortnight. He was established as nurse and serf to a roomful of incubators and brooders. He worked at night, for the newborn things, pink featherless scraps or feeble little tassels of yellow fluff, were horribly sensitive to changes of one degree in temperature and died on the slightest provocation. He played Juno, goddess of accouchements, he thought, to whole armies of oval, stupid-looking eggs. He slept heavily through most of the day and during his long night-watches had to develop the feverish vigi-

lance of a starving spider lest some eccentricity of the
perverse heating-apparatus slay thousands of his charges
at a breath. He took a savage pleasure in eating eggs
for breakfast—the joy of the South Sea Islander who
feasts on the baked persons of his private enemies. Despite all hindrances however—and especially the thirst
for sleep which, because of his sudden exchange of night
for day attacked him at any and all moments when he
was not actually in bed—he finished the opening chorus
and first fifty blank verse lines of his "Io," rang and
altered and burnished and reburnished them as a bell-
founder tests and tinkles a great young chime of bells,
and knew that they were the best work he had ever done
and that they had taken into themselves as a man drinks
wine every sparkle and thrust of the sudden new eloquent force that had hold of him like squeezing fingers.
And then came the slaughter of the innocents. He dozed
off between two and three of a placid morning and woke
up to find the room rather chillier than usual. The
heating-apparatus had died quietly in that hour, that
was all, and the incubators were full of holocaust and
dead little chickens. Philip faced the avenging wrath
of their owner with a heart naked with joy at release
from peepings and pinfeathers, got away as soon as he
could, sans wages or character, and turned up again at
Los Angeles like a lost bad penny. He took the beginnings of "Io" with him, and a distaste for cold chicken
that lasted him all his life.

It was wholly by chance that he finally got what he
wanted—Stafford Grant, a scientific farmer with a small
but intensively cultivated fruit and truck ranch, came

into town looking for a handy man to boss his handful
of Japanese laborers, ride a horse, run a Ford if necessary, and do it all for as little as he would give. Philip
liked the set of his mouth and his obvious enthusiasm
for his ranch and the country in general—like many of
the most fervent Westerners, he was an adopted son,
born and bred in Massachusetts. And Philip's college
and service record appealed to Grant as much as his
nominal price—he had gone to Massachusetts Agricultural himself and was one of the new type of business-
like small proprietors with a knack for machinery and
a knowledge of soil-analyses and government bulletins
before whom the goat-whiskered, slipshod farmer of
" Way Down East," who spurted tobacco-juice and unbearable dialect at the slightest provocation, had vanished like a misplaced caricature from a *Life* of the
seventies. They settled what terms were to be settled
that evening and eight months of steady, hard, high-
hearted work began.

It was in these months that Philip was able to group
and appraise the various disconnected and vagrant kinds
of life through which he had passed as a naturalist
groups and appraises the genera of a novel species, re-
lating each individual by some particular attribute of
cry or color or structure to the articulate whole. He
would be twenty-six in November, and he saw that considered by any sensible standards, his adventurings since
he left New Haven must be dismissed as the peripatetics
of an ironic, wandering dream, having no part or bear-
ing at all on what those who take correspondence courses
to strengthen the will call innocently, " The Business of

Life." He had seldom been sensible, however, and certainly never business-like, and he did not believe in the uselessness of those years.

They seemed to him an education of body and mind by everything from Aladdin-like riches to three days' thirst beside which the much talked about "University of Hard Knocks" appeared like a finishing school for wealthy sub-débutantes. He could imagine no better post-graduate work with essentials and biting preparation for experience on the emery-wheel of a world full of people, than that which he had had. His mind was one of those that are sure to begin in facile brilliance, a kind of false dawn of the intellect, but must come to any true growth late and after pains unless they are to exhaust themselves on a dozen little shiny victories of easy talent and easier money before the bodies that belong to them reach thirty. Instead of this, instead of scattering what gift he had like a basketful of half-ripe hothouse pears, he had been forced to conserve every seed and spore of it like a pirate's treasure, and generally against his will. It meant salvation, no less, for he had passed the stage of being only a clever young man. He would not make parlor conjuring tricks any more with words or paints—the soil in him, leathered with heat and cracked with sun, shook now to the thunder of spring rains, delayed and overwhelming—it waxed fat and fertile and was ready to put forth an astonishing harvest.

What luck he had had, what illimitable luck! A little twist in things and he might have left college to enter a school of design or an advertising agency, started turning out he-and-she short stories in five different safe flavors to be illustrated unread, or bounced about Greenwich Village in a batik smock and a red tam-o'-shanter, eating curious messes in stables and feeling shocking and persecuted and full of Art. Instead here he was, looking down from the saddle of a horse on two acres of peach-blossom—and " Io " was half finished and all the rest of it sure as a half spoken sentence somewhere in the back of his head. Reviewing the months of the army, he checked off another.

Item—Growth (he fumbled for phrases).

To see all things without shame or fear in the mind or sentimentality. To test by irony as one tests with burning acid for counterfeit coin, yet not to be swallowed up completely with irony and so merely stay preserved like a specimen abnormality in a jar full of alcohol. To live and die in the present, without regret or repentance for what, being done, is done. Not to worry after the manner of overfed housewives and physical culturists about any of the external appurtenances of life, rather alternating a feast and a fast than a dozen good nutritive meals of warm oatmeal. To treat sex, the best practical joke in life, with befitting humor. To create simply, hugely, nakedly and in the grand manner. Two quotations rather struck him as being in place—they were both from a masculine poet.

" When the gods for one deed asked me I ever
    gave them twain "

and

" When thou hearest the fool rejoicing, and he
   saith, ' It is over and past,
And the wrong was better than right and hate
   turns into love at the last,
And we strove for nothing at all, and the gods
   are fallen asleep,
For so good is the world a-growing that the evil
   good shall reap ! '
Then loosen thy sword in the scabbard, and settle
   thine helm on thine head,
For men betrayed are mighty, and great are the
   wrongfully dead ! "

He hummed the deliberately archaic lines over to
himself, hot with the large, plain words and the prance
of the meter. Then he saw that one of the Japanese was
creating uninstructed havoc with a sprayer, jumped off
and ran down to stop him. Philosophy, borrowed or
genuine, was over for the day.

And the days swept along like racing skaters over
thin ice. Philip woke at dawn and worked till sunset,
but it was not back-aching use of physical strength of
the kind that chloroforms the mind, it was rather work
that occupied and kept out of mischief his body and the
part of his consciousness that busied itself automatically
with such things as eating and dressing and talking
the weather or politics. The creative element in him
sat as aloof as an enchanter under his stuffed crocodile
and gazed into a crystal ball where there eddied through
fabulous darkness or visionary lights all the subtle and
illuminated shapes of the countries at the back of the
sky and under the secrecy of the sea. They materialized
like fiery spooks in the haunted rooms of a soul, they

took on crying flesh in words, they stood up like djinns in a desert, taller than stars.

He had one day, Sunday, completely free—a concession to his ridiculous wages—and he spent it from nine to six in his small neat room that smelled of brown soap and spring grass, putting down in a tideless surf of energy, as fast as his pencil would write, the colored tissues of the tapestry of "Io" that his mind had webbed in secret through the first six days of the week. He wrote from rough, illegible notes, made in bed under the spotlight of an electric torch when he should have been sleeping, but he could compare the actual composition of the poem itself to nothing but the chipping away and uncovering of a new bronze statue, limb by limb, from its mold. It was unique in his experience—the verse flowed with the released and effortless strength of an electric current—he did not have to alter one line in twenty, and when he did exactly the right correction was unhesitatingly supplied. One Tuesday evening he made fuller notes than usual—the lines began to take hands and run down the red-lined pages of his stenographer's note-book almost without volition—he no longer wrote, he existed in a breathless, burning center of force, as calm as the middle of a whirlwind, as bright and exquisite as a turning wheel of white, molten glass.

"Io," he whispered. "Io! Oh, Lord, Lord, Lord!"

Nothing was in the world but his scribbling hand and the little dancing and fighting dolls in his mind, that he had made, like God the creator, out of dirt and breath. He saw all the million eyes of Argus, the watch-

ful beast, shudder like jewels before a flame as Apollo
stood over him, the silver kingly bowstring tugged back
to his ear, the feather of the ravenous shaft like a gay
piece of silk against his curls. . . . Zeus mourned, the
earth was terrified at his trouble, in the lands of Hyper-
boreans strange gods with the eyes of sea-crabs hatched
before Chronos out of the cold gray egg of Time, crept
back to ruinous altars and prophesied to their abominable worshipers that Zeus would die. . . . The stiff
fingers scrambled on, the point of the pencil grew blunt
and soft . . .

Philip was aware, when the hypnosis of making
ceased, that there was a curious light at his window.
He got up, exhausted and cramped, and looked out into
a gray world of morning. He went through the long
day like a drunken man and resolved that he had better
not do *that* any more.

But the knifing joy of such hours, the joy that is
conception and giving birth and recognition all in one,
was his all Sunday and every Sunday till the poem was
done. He had the clean bodily delight in it that a dog
has in running down a fox and the spiritual effacement
and happy annihilation that comes with complete ob-
literation into the service of a cause or the words of
a prayer. Moreover, he was being used to his fullest
extent for the first time in his life, every power and
active particle in him strained on its highest overtone,
mind and body working to extreme capacity like the
engines of a liner butting through a January storm. He
had had an elaborate allegorical plan for " Io " at first
where the girl pursued by a god was the soul, perhaps,

or liberty, and Argus stood for "Amurricanism" and Apollo walked about as Box-Car Democracy. But as soon as he actually began to compose, he threw this piece of mechanism overboard and reduced its essential features to a few straight lines. An allegory remained when he had finished, an allegory for anybody who wanted an allegory, but the poem was not woodenly built around it and for its sake.

The last quarter was the hardest to do of all, and lasted through the beginning of June.

On the second Sunday in June, about three o'clock in the afternoon, Philip finished making a fair copy of the final forty lines—there were no typewriters on the ranch—got up and stretched with limitless content, then sat down again, dipped his pen in the soggy bottom of the inkbottle and signed his full name at the bottom of the sheet with a rotund flourish. Then he put the completed thing away in a drawer under a nest of collars and went out to a little grove of stunted live-oaks that bunched together like a ballet of crippled dancers at the top of an uncultivated hill.

The hill belonged to Grant. Next year, when there was money enough, he would bring it under the plow but now it was the same burnt, brown giant's muffin it had been since the Yosemite redwoods were three feet high, a wild, patient, mountainous, living thing with the sleepy heat of a big warm animal under the westing sun.

Philip couched himself against the knees of a live-oak and looked into the center of the sky, a blue shadow, a blue gauze that yielded before the sight like faint

smoke and shimmered away through infinities upon
infinities. The blue core of a flower that the eyes
roved into like bees and yet could not touch the utter
softness of its heart and gather its deep honey—the blue
mid-wave of a sea that the thought plunged at like a
white diver, like a falling knife of ivory, only to be lost
in depth beyond glinting and glooming depth, never to
return with the deeply-sunken pearls. Philip did not
think as he looked at it, he did not feel, though
he was very tired; he knew only that something was
past.

He had made, he was the mother who bears a child
and the father who begets it. He was the child itself,
a living nakedness, violent and sensitive, without sight,
without speech, without comprehension, with nothing
but the five blind mouths of the senses and somewhere,
hidden away in its pink ignorance like a drop of glittering rain, a soul. He had gone through the hourly desire
and the hourly despair—through the convulsion of love
and the destruction of bringing forth—now something
in the world had being that was as vague as foam and
lifeless as stones in a field before he touched it with
his hand—now a rushing spring, a wise image, a bursting seed. He was broken with a peace like the peace
Death brings as enchanted drink in the hushing cup of
the poppy, and yet, as he looked at the sky, it seemed
to him that, if he wished, he could take it and tear it
in two like a breadth of blue cloth.

After a while he turned his head on his arm and fell
asleep. He smiled in his sleep at the arrogance of the
dreams he had. When he woke the sky was gay as a

war-bonnet with the ochers and Indian-reds of sunset, and he walked down singing from the hill.

Nevertheless, there was something more to be done. He spent till early September in having the manuscript typed, revising it and making eighteen illustrations in black-and-white. These last gave him a good deal more trouble than the poem itself had, for he wanted to keep them Greek in spirit without either the complete imperturbability of the pithless and perfect figures of Flaxman or the flagrant undressed modernity of some of our prominent magazine illustrators who made the plains of windy Troy the theater for the combats of a host of collar-advertisements with property spears and without their clothes. As a result, those who admired the drawings did so because they were so flatly reminiscent of William Blake and those who disliked them called them lifeless imitations of Greek design. The two attitudes combined threw Philip into such a fever of annoyance that he wished he had never learned to draw—he was not old enough at the trade to realize that most healthy, expert criticism can always be depended on to give the artist one pure and Rousseauish joy—that of feeling himself completely misunderstood.

When the book was finally finished—looking pitifully neat and compressed like the body of a seven months' child in its new clean clothes of typescript—Philip sent it out into the world with the hesitations of a grandmother dispatching her favorite sheltered grandson to his first morning at public school. He registered it and insured it with the greatest care, and after trying to remember which publishers had rejected his first starveling book of verse, decided on a recent radical firm of the bustlingly progressive order devoted to free verse, popular detective stories and foreign novelists hitherto unheard of in any country whose bushy countenances peered out above titles made out of consonants in the advertisements of the firm like photographs of a new strange species of shrub. He enclosed twice as many stamps as were necessary for return, and in three weeks got back a battered parcel and a brisk uncivil note.

"We like the vim in your lines," said the reader chattily, "but 'Io' and her ilk are pretty well played out, don't you think? for anybody but college professors. Moreover, Tennysonian blank verse is hardly in our line. You have talent—use it on a fresh live subject—there are plenty of them in modern America if you will only look around you—and we would be glad to see more of your work, without the illustrations, however, which are quite impossible.
"Sincerely."

Philip swore.

He bundled "Io" up and sent her at once, in his ignorance, to a prominent successful bravo of a vanity-publisher who offered to bring her out in an ooze-leather edition-de-luxe if Philip would pay him a thousand dollars and expect no royalties on the first fifteen hundred copies. Philip rescued "Io" with difficulty and only by threatening legal measures. He put her away for the present in the bottom of his suitcase.

This was toward the end of November. Lucia and Philip had been corresponding regularly. Then her

letters stopped for two weeks altogether and a telegram
came instead.

" Your father seriously ill. Come home at once.
                                        " MOTHER."

Philip arrived at San Esteban after a day and a night
in which compunction and memories of Phil in his own
boyhood had played a continuous double Canfield that
never solved out inside his mind. He saw where often
he had mistaken the mere hardness and shelliness of
youth for strength and its bluster for logic—and while,
look back often as he might, he could not see on the
whole how he could have acted otherwise, he was bitten
always by the teeth of that small revolving wheel that
scores on us uselessly in times of finality how differently
if we had stopped here, or talked to somebody there, or
taken another road than the one that had fate on it,
all things in the world might be. And when Lucia met
him at the station and the first passion of their greeting
was over, as the car began to climb the white sloping
road under the arch of disheveled trees where he had
made battles once for hours at a time with eucalyptus-
nut-soldiers, all he knew under the sky for that instant
was that he was coming home.

Phil had passed the crisis of his pneumonia before
Philip came, but he was very weak and Philip did not
see him at all till some days later. When they met it
was under the aseptic supervision of nurses, Philip
viewed him lying on the bed, a wax image of himself
that spoke painfully as if any words at all belonged to

a foreign language. Even when Phil was well they never formally made up their dispute or directly alluded to it. Philip. with the hasty wish to settle things of the young, wanted to talk it all out and bury it, but whenever he tried to start Phil began to look delicate and wonder if it wasn't almost time for his tonic or his walk or his eggnog, and so the affair remained up in the air, and there desiccated in time like a raisin and blew away.

Phil had become the consciously model invalid as soon as he was sure of getting well and when convalescence flowed back into positive health he adopted a new and harmless pose—that of the exquisitely aging old beau with a sigh, a gold headed cane and perfect manners—that made things much easier for everybody concerned. He was barely fifty, but his hair showed feathers of white—the ruddiness and fever of living had gone out of him, he gave up tennis for golf and later won prizes for putting—his existence became more and more a conservation, a series of petty victories over digestion and modern errors in taste and common mispronunciation—he had not yet got to the point of writing letters to the newspapers signed "Old Playgoer" but he would come to it in time. Maiden ladies said he kept up wonderfully for his age.

Between Philip and himself there was endless mutual amusement, for Philip knew how to take his father now. They fenced with buttoned foils, careful never to hurt. Day by day Philip thought his father became more and more like a sedulous imitation of an essay by Charles Lamb. He recovered much affection for that essay—

it was so happy in its quaint and careful periods, so pleased with each aging, deliberate gesture of its own hands.

Stafford Grant wrote Philip twice, urging him to come back, the second time with the cautious offer of a partnership if Philip had money to invest. Philip answered noncommittally and let matters slide—it was a long time since he had seen Lucia except in snatches. Besides, "Io and the Gadfly," on Phil's advice, had gone to another publisher, a solid old conventional firm, and they had written with temperate enthusiasm—if Philip would make certain minor alterations they would accept the book.

All art is a fighting dream with sleep heavy as the sleep of a bear in the pauses of the contest. Till January Philip slept from the struggle of the last eight months. He knew that such peace and comfortableness were not permanent, so he enjoyed them while he had them without remorse. The Fates that played pool with him had run him into a pocket for a period, in a little while the balls would be racked up again and the game go on.

BOOK VIII

THE FEAR OF THE LORD

(1919-1920)

OLD AND NEW TESTAMENTS

DINNER for five at Steve Brackett's house in Chicago. Uncle Ashbel was an uncle whom Philip remembered only as a legendary perfect little boy who never fought, spilled food or asked for third helpings, and a real dimly whiskered form that fell out of the sky into San Esteban when Philip was eight and gave him a powerful methodical spanking for burying a box of its Perfectos in the garden with full military honors. He existed however, as unseen relatives do, an exemplary spot on the worn carpet of family conversation, and now, having contracted Bright's Disease under the skilled advice of a number of good physicians, he died after a long and most respectable illness in the decentest manner possible. Phil, though markedly courageous when he hears the news, does not brave draughty sleepers and February slush to attend the funeral, speaks wanly of his age once or twice as if it were a restraining moral principle, and delegates to Philip the task of representing the family in a black necktie and an expression of meek, sociable grief. This suits Philip well enough— Steve has written him about a reunion of the four of them. So Philip, after living through the choice horrors of the funeral—a little puff-ball of an undertaker with the manners of an obsequious Death, very much concerned that each relative shall both receive and put on a suitable pair of mournful gloves—the grave, a windy

329

hole in the ground that a new storm is already beginning to patch with pallid flurries of snow, so elemental,
so outdoors, so cruelly large and unheated a resting-
place for Uncle Ashbel, looking curiously crumpled in
his smooth frock-coat—the fast indecorous trot of the
returning procession of dingy hacks, like a flight of
lame old blackbirds—Philip gets over to the warmth of
the Blackstone as fast as possible and is there grabbed
hold of by both hands the minute he steps into the lobby
by a bronze-faced, rolling stranger with a limp and
the roaring welcome of an affectionate elephant, Steve,
two months back from France. Dick and Reggy blow
in together on the next train from New York and
the four go up to Steve's and talk for hours and
hours.

They have four large, hasty years, stuffed full of life
and running over as a sausage is stuffed with meat, to
spread out and digest together in a single evening; and
the talk, while it begins consecutively, soon loses all
order and proportion and goes back and forward and
sideways like a giant's game of hop-scotch between
France and England and war and Italy and America
and jail and the sea and ranching and what's the point
of the Bolsheviks? and thirst and love. Dick has a
cautious mustache, there are hawk-like puckers about
Reggy's eyes, Steve has lost his cherub's rotundity and
grown massive. Philip knows he must look as changed
and yet the same as they, but cannot imagine quite how.
They state facts—Philip is publishing his book, Reggy
has been engaged for three months and expects to be
married in April, Dick is going in for a Ph.D. and

teaching, Steve is starting at the bottom in wholesale drugs; ten years and he may be being restrained as a trust or giving new dormitories to Yale. They are all a bit diffident with each other at first—the other three especially so with Philip—but the initial tensions of unfamiliar politeness soon pass—they get rapidly acquainted again—they dig down through the earth and leaves silted over their friendship and by the middle of dinner they have found it and dragged it out whole, clear and solid as a carved block of lapis buried deep under ruin and years. That will not alter, that cannot burn or break, that is permanent, a fixed centrifugal force. A sense of wonder, a shudder of everlastingness, sure as sleep, wild and eloquent as the central thought of a single deathless mind that reclines a divine, calm substance in the hollow between the two candles of birth and death, comes over them all as they sit at the table. They will do this many times in their stroll between nothingness and nothingness and always go away fed, soul, body and thought. Or so they think in the impudence that Time finds stubborn as a curl to smooth out flat and spoil.

Exit first youth, however, like the corpse of a king in yellow armor, borne out with torches and slaves. They know it is gone, the light-headed, frantic, winged thing, the careless glamorous fool; sweet odors blow back from its last processional with the wizard keenness of spice thrown into a fire; the delicate body chars down to a cynic ash, wind eats it, it is utterly consumed. They see that it is so, that it must be so, and salute that imperial departure with reverence and satire and clear

eyes. War and peace, those two wise worms that teach
age to the soul, and for three of them through months
at a time the continual imminent presence of bodily
death, pressing down on them like a helmet, clothing
them like their skins, has taken away the rapt carelessness that is the stirrup and sanguine spur of youth's
first riding. College and the affairs and half-friends of
College lie behind them, a cave where they once played
Indians together, a tall toy-city, sparkling, distinct and
small. When they go back it will be as definite alumni,
to find the campus shrunk and its inheritors well-dressed,
unaccountable boys. Ahead is the fight of each for his
own hand, rough weather and the working years.

They all talk a good deal about John without conscious or throaty emotion. At the end of dinner they
drink to him and his luck, wherever he is, without any
need of a formal romantic toast. Throughout it is, as
has been said, a dinner for five.

Next day they play about Chicago bizarrely to make
some new memories—Dick and Reggie go back that
night to New York and their various affairs. Philip
stays on with Steve for two more days and then hurries
back to San Esteban before he has time to catch more
than a minor cold.

Philip got in unexpectedly on an afternoon of driving
rain, called up the house impatiently and could get no
answer. He thereupon hired the one town " taxi," an
ex-grocery-truck with compound arthritis of the ignition,
and was stranded by it at the foot of the long hill. He
slammed out his suitcases, paid the driver, started to

walk and in five minutes was wet through to the skin. Home was a long half-mile away and the rain fell as if it had never rained in the world before and the skies were exhaustlessly delighted with their brand-new accomplishment. As for the suitcases, they had turned to pig-iron as soon as he started to carry them. He slogged on desolately through the wet, a soggy spectacle with his hat-brim falling down over his eyes. All that came into his head as a marching tune was a pollyinanity some one had sent him once on a Christmas card to accompany a hand-painted book-marker—" It is not raining rain to me, 'Tis raining daffodils!" and he cursed the cheery sentiments hurriedly but effectively, his soaked mind with no room for anything but blind hearty lust for hot new food and fires. He dropped the suitcases at the second turn in the road, shook the cramp out of his fingers, picked them up again, and plugged on without looking ahead. There was suddenly a skittering noise behind him followed by the quack of a horn, he jumped like a shying horse and landed with both feet in a puddle, swearing. A little pink roadster slithered to a stop beside him. He looked at it with dumb hate.

" Well, what in—" he began.

Then he saw that Sylvia Persent had the steering-wheel and that she was shaking all over with laughter. She opened the door.

" Come in out of the rain, you poor imbecile," she chuckled, " and don't stand staring there as if you'd never seen me before in your life."

" I haven't," said Philip flatly, but he wedged himself

in with his suitcases and they started to shake hands and make greetings.

" But where—"

" But when did you—"

They began and stopped simultaneously, looked at each other, laughed.

" Yesterday," said Sylvia. " Mother's up at Aunt Anne's and I'm recuperating from a breakdown from overwork—or that's what they tell me. At least that's why they wouldn't let me stay over when the Division came home. But I'm the healthiest invalid you ever saw—I've learned to make cocoa for about a million men at a time and shoot craps and swear in French and wear flannel underclothes and—oh, Lord, it's pleasant to see you Phil for I'm crazy to talk and so are you and we've got weeks to tell it all—"

" Years," said Philip.

To analyze the alterations of character under stress is to pass a long strip of moving picture film slowly through your fingers. Between this picture and the next the changes are infinitesimal—between the first and last of the series they may be as wide as Asia. The war had not suddenly converted Sylvia from a débutante two years " out " to a Y. W. C. A. Joan of Arc—it had rather accentuated certain salient qualities of valor and humor and by substituting the friendly and rather impersonal adoration of some thousands of men at a time for the personal possessive amorousness of college seniors and rising young business men, had cured her of two things, scalp-hunting, from fraternity pins to proposals, and somewhat dubious adventures in speech, kisses and other intoxicants because of the young delight of never taking a dare and always going faster. She had ceased to be an adventurer in love—the standard set for her conduct by the men she worked with was inarticulately without conventions but it had certain bounds as inflexible as the mind of a Continental chaperone; she had seen girls overstep them, from ignorance or wilfulness and lose instantaneously and irrevocably not merely the respect of even the loose, which was much, but a certain indefinable almost religious worship, troubadouring, hardy, never clearly expressed and fragile, which she valued as fiercely and secretly as she did her own independence—the thing which made the French sing the "Madelon" song. She kept, if it may be put so without offense, through her various experiences a chastity not only of body but of intent— she did not deliver moral lectures but she stopped privates from getting drunk too often on cheap wine with the same ease and audacity with which she pillaged the sacred stores of the Y. M. C. A. when the regiment was down on its luck or behind in its pay. For the first time her personal comfort was her least concern, for the first time herself—her mental and physical selves, both naturally fine, both carefully trained to be as brilliantly selfish and lazy as possible—were being used every waking minute to the crest of their capacities. She could fake with fellow débutantes and lizards, but she could not fake with the regiment because the life and the issues in it were real, not painted, and the men who saw her in the canteen had the caustic precision of ruth-

less children in detesting affectation. Moreover, casually
spoken of, joked about, defied in a thousand ways, Death
stood over every man with whom she came in contact,
with the arrogance of a first-sergeant, ready to order
them off whenever the whistle blew.

She made mistakes, but she gave unsparingly and
unceasingly, and as a result she grew because she must.
She succeeded and, succeeding, had burnt out of her,
as an electric wire burns out unhealthy tissue, the smal-
ler febrile curiosities of sex. She even acquired a respect
for herself that was not based on the positive claims
of her hair and her white skin, a respect that was a
reflected image of the respect of those she gave to, but
an image strong as bronze. Her education by realities
was both subtler and briefer than Philip's, but she was
more fluid than he in many ways, and it was fully as
complete. When she came back to America it was not
with an idea of reforming the world by wearing ten-
dollar hats in a settlement or writing a book about herself and the war, but with a conception of service and
sanity through service that was unique to most of her
contemporaries, and thoughts on marriage that would
have shocked her elders as much by their modernity as
they saddened her friends by showing her reactionary
and old fashioned. She came up to San Esteban to rest
and think herself and her future out, met Philip and
was instantly more undecided than ever.

Love in the mist—love in the rain—Philip never
looks back at San Esteban this last time without seeing
it a place of tall torn trees and dripping fog—a phantom

bubble of a world gray-and-black with the clinging dyes of cold smoke and the wet shine of branches drooping with rain—a world like the top of a mountain covered with journeying clouds. Through the ash and twilight of this universe moves dreamy, wise Sylvia, a sparkling phantasm, a gilded shape, and Philip stumbles after her among wisps and apparitions like a man following the wings of a bright bird through a wood full of trolls.

Ever since their absurd reunion on the road, he has known what is the matter with him with the certainty of the fey. The proud angel has stooped from his sky and flung his lance. This love has not come, as his love for Milly did, with the butterfly gestures of a dancer and the swift soft hares of youth running wild in the blood—it is a melting of all he knows and feels and is like metal over a flame, to cast him anew when it has finished into an unknown thing or pour him out in bubbles of slag on the ground. Pain, fear and worship, delight and a strangled burning like thirst in fever—he goes up and down through them all like a chip on a seesaw. And Sylvia is so intensively unconscious, so stubbornly cool and boyish, that his sense of humor grows to the disproportions of a deformity and stops him again and again when he is most the fabulous egoist by merely showing him his own face in the distortions of its mirror that images most men and all lovers too stumpy or lean or pale.

They have gone down to the edge of the bay on an afternoon that is white and wraithy with fog. The water heaves in front of them like pools of heavy gray oil, causelessly unquiet, shut off fifty yards away by a pale fleece. A few gulls rock like rowboats on the long round waves, diving their necks down now and then for green victual and calling to each other in voices like lonesome women lost in a marsh.

"They sound like broken violins," says Philip poetically.

"They look terribly comfortable and matronly somehow, Phil. It's as if they were acquiring much dowager merit by swimming at all when it's so cold. Come on and skip stones—I can skip them farther than you can."

"You always could—you used to get unreasonably snobbish about it."

"I must have been a vile little child."

"You weren't. You never got scared."

"I did too. Remember when we sneaked off about five o'clock in the morning and swam over to that island in Beaver Lake?"

"Shades of Aunt Agatha, yes! You turned over and floated when we were square in the middle and told me firmly that you were absolutely certain we were both going to drown."

"I was quite decided about it. My arms and legs felt funny. But then you hit me in the eye."

"It was on the nose, as a matter of fact, cheerful liar. It worked though—you came after screaming and swimming like a fish, trying to sink me, so I made straight for the island and we both of us fought in the water like enraged seals as soon as it was shallow enough."

"I know it, and then made up, and I still was perfectly sure that I'd die if I swam back, so you did and got the rowboat and were very Perseus about rescuing me. Then your father came out and stubbed his bare foot on a rock and told us he'd like to drown us both like puppies."

" You wouldn't hardly speak to me for two days."

" I should say not—I got left out of the pack-trip to Pyramid on account of it. Worthless being ! "

" That was nice all the same, then, up there," says Sylvia, chinking two flat stones in her hand.

" Um. Sylvia, how long are you going to stay ? "

" You sound beautifully hospitable. Till mother comes back from Aunt Anne's. Another week, perhaps. It's heavenly of your mother to take me in like this. I was pretty tired. You ? "

" I'm not sure. Go back to Grant, possibly, I like the work—and with Uncle Ashbel's money and grandmother's—write anyway—anything so long as it isn't precious or precocious. Blow around like a kite in a wind till something cuts the string. This world, and another, Sylvia, and the game's up. But I'm pleased with the game."

" You oughtn't to be allowed to land in so many places that send you back to ' Messenger-boy, Square one,' " says Sylvia rebelliously. Then she adds, feeling sure of her own clarity, " I don't mean you—I mean me."

" I think—" answers Philip uncertainly. Then he stops, for he is looking at her face. Her eyes are as dubious as a confessor's, and yet somehow full of anxiety and delight. He takes one of her hands up angrily and shakes the stones out of it.

" Ouch ! " mourns Sylvia.

" I love you," says Philip. The whole melancholic scene of sea and sky trembles in front of him an instant as if clear water had passed over it. Within him he feels the stomachless agony of a man poising to dive into water he cannot see. Then he kisses Sylvia scufflingly over the ear.

She does not either burst into tears, slap him, or comment pertly—she is not at her first dance. Instead she turns up her face, rather expertly if he knew it, and this time they kiss elvishly and long, like passionate ghosts.

" I love you," says Philip again, with a feeling that the statement is of some importance.

" I love you," answers Sylvia. " I think I love you. Oh, Phil, Phil, maybe I just like you to kiss me. Stop kissing me ! I don't know ! "

They scramble up, facing each other, like tottery patients just come out from under a dull, sweet drug. Sylvia pushes him away from her with strong wrists.

" I *won't* give you anything unless I can give you everything ! " she gulps. " I *won't* let you kiss me unless I want you to marry me ! Oh, Phil, why did you spoil it? I hate it ! We were both so nice and just being ordinary and friends ! "

Philip, once more at grips with the inexplicable, is uselessly male.

" Of course you're going to marry me ! " he chatters. " For Heaven's sake—for God's sake—Sylvia, come here ! "

But she is running down the sand and sloppy rocks with no flippant wish to be overtaken and petted.

"Keep away from me!" she yaps savagely over her shoulder. "Keep away from me and let me think!"

Philip makes lumbering pursuit, calling dolefully, "Sylvia! Come back here! I won't touch you! Wait a minute! Oh, Sylvia! Oh, damn!"

She scuttles around a corner with the agility of a land-crab, the torn heel of Philip's shoe catches on an edge of rock, comes off and sends him sprawling. When he pulls himself to his feet, his hands full of sand, the gray patch of her dress and the yellow patch of her hair have melted into the gray coiling and uncoiling of the fog. A distressful fog, a procession of shapeless fluid beasts without color or sound, where Philip wanders like a peewit, crying, "Sylvia! Sylvia! Sylvia!" with a plaintive noise. He loses his way, gets blind angry, gets over it and returns to the house in time for tea, wildly hungry and soaked through like a sponge.

That night at dinner Sylvia has a devil. She behaves to Philip exactly as if he were twelve years old, mocks at him with cool lips and frank untroubled eyes and segregates herself from him with uncanny skill whenever he tries to cut her out from Phil and his mother and be heavily adoring with her alone. It is she who suggests bridge after dinner and pairs off Lucia and Philip against herself and Phil. The game goes on like an everlasting bad dream—Lucia detests cards and has an unteachable faculty for finessing nines and never leading out trumps. Philip is in the delicately explo-

sive condition of jarred nitroglycerin—he plays abomi-
nably and is pitilessly anatomatized at every error by
Sylvia's leaping tongue. They play for two hours—
Phil and Sylvia winning by some thousands of points
—and Sylvia goes to bed immediately after the last
rubber, flinging Philip a brisk, cousinly "Good night."
It leaves Philip in a pitiable condition—he reads the
paper aloud to Phil for another tortoise of an hour, taking sanguinary joy in the more luscious divorce-cases
and jumping like a cat whenever Aunt Agatha dozes off
and drops her crochet-hook. After the others' bedtime
he goes for another walk in the weeping fog. It is the
peregrination of a burnt shadow among wet, scoffing
shadows, but he walks the dizziness and wishes for annihilation out of his mind and comes back to some sleep
and broken dreams.

Now he knows, with the empty completeness of the
griddled, what alone is fit to run beside and before his
irony, strong hounds in a double leash, what alone can
master and form him and aim him like a snowball at
the heart of the divine, derisive shield. The knowledge
is never, apparently, to do him much good, but he is glad
of it without sarcasm nevertheless. He would rather
lose Sylvia wholeheartedly than win any other dice-game
with Atropos and her sisters, for he no longer needs the
smoked glass of other men's wisdom even to view his
own eclipse and he sees that the proud thing desired
and the haughtiness of the attempt is all. Moreover
when he thinks of Sylvia it is with such straight reverence as he has not had since the day he first saw the
gleaming incredible arch of a lunar rainbow step across

two night-soaked hills and take possession of the stars
and the sky. With all which, he could have given a
description of every one of her more important mental
and physical qualities and failings that an impersonal
jury of archangels would have thought exact—but he
knows that not one of her traits or tricks or manners,
not her courage nor her silver vanity, her sensitive folly
nor her headlong genius for comradeship, matters more
than the buttons on her dress beside the luminous diverse
changeling thing, herself. So with half of him in the
mood of " How could I ever deserve," and the other
tattered with the pure need of a starving baby, " She
must love me—I'll die if she doesn't—she must—she
must ! " he manages to get through the night and come
down to breakfast.

He had meant to make breakfast sensational, a grim
picking at bits of food, but he dozed off completely
about four o'clock and Lucia took pity on him and let
him sleep till ten. He was healthily engrossed in bacon
and eggs when Sylvia came down, looking rather tired
of being intrepid. They discussed tennis and the make-
up of the Davis Cup Team hardworkingly through the
meal and were very polite.

They went into the living-room, hardly looking at
each other, and Sylvia cushioned herself with a book in
front of the fire of eucalyptus wood that burnt in gusts
with a bright, aromatic flare. Philip stood at the
window, looking out at the shifting facelessness of
the mist. Neither spoke, the only sound was the snap
and spurt of the fire and Sylvia turning her pages a
little too fast.

Neither spoke, but in that interval something fell upon them both like a dazzling noose. It seemed as if a tree had grown up between them like a plant under the hands of an Indian juggler, a tree full of spice that blotted out with the shaken rustle of thousands of dim, long leaves, the ceiling, the room and hours. They were alone in this house of open boughs, in the windy heart of its green chambers where young morning, strange, naked and holy, walked like a haughty bird. They had never known each other before in their lives, and yet they were such spiritual kindred by wish and thought as two words in the talk of the same saint, such bodily friends as two brothers dead beside each other in the same battle. The branches of Ygdrasil, the tree whose roots are the reins of the world, moved over them gently. Both waited—there was no more desire or reason or fear—only dumbed expectancy, silent as the dark radiant cloth Night draws over the furnaces of sunset, expectancy of a drum, of a proclamation, that should take their two clay pictures and change them everlastingly as wind changes the light hesitating patterns of September frost.

Philip turned around from the window as if he were drawn on threads. He noticed, with a separate clarity that seemed no more part of himself than the floor, that Sylvia had stopped reading and that her face had the puzzled, astonished deference of a sensible person seeing the hands of a clock begin suddenly to move the wrong way. It took all the courage he had in his flesh to go over to her—and the steps were as stiff as if his knees were tied together and he were walking the end of a plank from a pirate ship. But he did, and somehow or other she got up on her feet to meet him. Then the room was quieter yet, except that two people were kissing each other in front of the fire.

THE FEAR OF THE LORD

Ten days later, Sylvia having gone into San Francisco for the day on business he could not help her with, Philip finished correcting the paged proofs of " Io and the Gadfly," found himself tobaccoless and decided to walk down to the village. He took along with him in his pocket a copy of " Piers Plowman " that he had read and re-read continually since he first picked it up on a second-hand-book counter some months before. He had discovered, with the infantile delight of the newly-engaged in finding small mutual points of similarity, that it, " Huckleberry Finn " and " A Shropshire Lad " were the three books that Sylvia had brought back from France.

" It was just like this," she explained. " When I was dog-tired or my feet hurt I read Mark Twain and forgot about it. Housman was for cold nights and hard mornings when I'd have sold the whole Allied cause for a hot water bottle that didn't leak and woolier blankets; and this thing for straight *cafard*, when I was sick of everything from uniforms to air-raids—it's so split between angry exaltation and rockbottom sense."

Philip found the description exact; the broken hand-gallop of the plain vehement alliterative lines stirred him as much of Chaucer never had, though Chaucer

was incomparably the finer artizan. The world that
Langland saw and smelt was a world so recklessly modern in many ways—a field full of folk and the seven
deadly sins; Meed, the moneyed and her servants, Wisdom and Wit, bribing judges and officers with the
mannered ease of corporation-counsel; the sheepish multitude starting out to seek Saint Truth and thinking
much better and more sensibly of it in the first half-
hour. It was a letterless world and a world poorer in
money, a world where the Church had actual power
over bodies and souls and however Cis, the cobbler,
might hate the idea of a hell full of flames and a har-
per's heaven, he never once thought of disbelieving in
them—but a world where the quiet essentials, love, hate,
labor, fear, prodigal pride and a twilight seeking for
faith, were much the same. Philip smiled and thought
of many paper-radicals when he read of Wastrel and
his dispute with Piers Plowman, who lived by his hands
like Adam his ancestor.

> " Then gan a wastrel rise in wrath and would have
>   fought with Piers,
> Threw down his glove, a Breton man, a braggart,
> Bade Piers go with his plough for a cursed starvel-
>   ing.
> " Wilt thou or wilt thou not, we will have our will
> Of thy flour and thy flesh, will take it when we
>   please.
> Ay and make merry with it for all thy grudging."
> Courteously the knight, as his manner was,
> Warned wastrels all and bade them do better.
> " I was not wont to work," says Wastrel, " and I
>   will not begin—"

" Hunger came in haste, took Wastrel by the
    mouth,
Wrung him by the belly, brought water to his eyes,
Beat both his boys. He near burst their ribs.
Had not Piers with a pease leaf prayed Hunger
    cease
They had like been in their graves."

Wastrel was still alive, fat and roaring, though now
he made eighty-five cents an hour of an eight-hour day
and would not work a whole week through for love or
unions.

Philip bought his cigarettes and started back home,
but the sky, gray and bulging all the morning, finally
decided on rain and a spatting shower drove him up on
the porch of St. John's Church. The door was open and
he sought stuffy shelter inside. He found a back pew
under a window that mottled his book with deep reds
and purples and settled himself to read, completely
alone.

He read how the pilgrims, true and false, came to
Piers, the poor Plowman, and how he only of the company knew the way to Saint Truth—how he plowed
his half-acre with knights and fine ladies to help him—
how they came by the road to Truth at last in spite of
Wastrel and Meed and the educated malice of Divinity.
And then followed the last great vision, as simple and
heart-breakingly sincere as a nursery rhyme, of how
Piers, the People's Christ, went down to hell and took
the damned souls out of it, and then, before the triumph
of Anti-Christ and the resuscitated kingdom of Greed
and Covetise, disappeared. But

"By Christ," quoth William Langland, "I will
    become a pilgrim
And walk as wide as the world lasteth
To seek Piers Plowman."

"By Christ," said Philip softly as he finished, his
heart still drumming with the verse, "I will become
a pilgrim, and walk as wide as the world lasteth to seek
arrogance and love."

He shut the book and looked around him. The gush-
ing of rain on glass and wood had ceased—outside the
world would be gallant with the scents of steaming
earth and washed new grass. Philip sniffed at the
dried air about him—it was sick and musty—the whole
church had the smell of clothes shut up in a closet that
have not been worn or used for a very long time. From
the altar with its limp cloth border that said "Holy!
Holy! Holy!" forever to emptiness, to the crisp black
hymnals bought two years ago and still stiff and rattling
and as good as new, God's official house drowsed in a
plushy solitude, a prim catalepsy, that belonged neither
to the queer drunkenness of living nor the queer sobriety
of death. "You wouldn't even come looking for a minor
virtue here," thought Philip, "unless you wanted it em-
balmed. And as for St. Truth—"

All over America there were churches, and all over
America, except at Christmas and Easter, the churches
held a sprinkling of women, a few bored men, two
church wardens to pass the plate, a minister, a choir
sometimes, a collection always. People turned to
Theosophy, to Spiritualism, to fortune-telling, to good-
luck charms, to books on cheering-up; they filled them-

selves with east wind of a dozen flavors in the search
for anything in which they could utterly believe. They
could not believe in the church. Restless, neurasthenic,
impotent, the old food without strength or savor, all
life chewed out of it, the new foods merely the old one
served up again, overheated and badly spiced, giving
spiritual indigestion to those who nibbled at them—
millions of men and women seeking like sick animals for
a salt-lick for some shape or vestige of St. Truth.
The church empty, the tavern shut, faith flat on its
back with the church, gone by with the tavern what was
left of two most large-hearted things, the liberal heat
and humor of mind that has made Mr. Pickwick an immortal and the mood of sacrificial libation and rejoicing
in every fruit and mystery of the earth that saw Bacchus
as young and a god. The world shuddering like a man
in a chill with the afterclap of the war, nothing better
to live or die for than the efficiency of graphs on a chart
and the success that is measured by a fat waistcoat
and incipient hardening of the arteries at forty—all
the machinery of success-books and uplift-pamphlets and
house-organs gearing and speeding up flesh and brain
to go through as many swift motions each minute of the
day as possible, without question as to their use or lack
of use. Exercise taken like a pill for the sake of greater
efficiency in office-hours—classes of sad fat business-men
throwing medicine balls at each other in the electrically-
lit cave of an indoor gymnasium. Love, the double
miracle of gay sex and gallant spirit; people hot-eared
with shame or sweaty with lust at the thought of the
first, discounting the second because they hadn't time

for such things, they had to telephone or attend a gin-
ger-up meeting of their sales-staff or go to the movies.
A field full of rotten grain, thought Philip fretfully,
turning these phrases like knives over and over in his
mind.

He thought of the Heaven of childhood, when tinsel
is as solid as steel in gods and toy swords, that kind,
small place somewhere on top of the sky. That Heaven
and all its saints had fallen to pieces when he first discovered cruelty that was both causeless and unpunished
—it had been replaced in a measure by living, in a
measure by the crude atheism of twenty that thinks it
wickedly fine to defy the lightnings that never descend.
Then had come Milly, and after the loss of her, much
irony, a working-doctrine of irony that healed as it
seared the mind with its freezing wit. Now even irony
would not answer completely any more, in face of Sylvia
and the vast unreasonableness of life.

Nevertheless Philip held on to his irony like a bar of
iron in the next few minutes. For it seemed to him
that he could see through the familiar husk of the
church in which he sat and the larger pod of the whole
spinning globe it clung to, and that pews and heavens
and earth were transient and infirm; cold gestures of
air that for an instant of self-deception had taken on
shapes less solid to the touch than snow. They tore
like the screens of a Japanese paper-house, they hung
in the air like the mirages of a mind at war with itself,
beyond them was nothing, and they had neither consist-
ency nor cause nor form.

He built towers and towns and forests out of them

craftily, and they shook back under his hands to vapor and rain. They dried up like a drop of water in the hot sun, they left nothing but a boundless emptiness as far as the eye could see. And in the middle of this thin huge emptiness he stood alone.

He tried to speak but the words stuck to his throat. "There must be something," he said desperately. "Beauty . . . Pride . . ."

He made a rose and saw that it blossomed, and a sword with a keen edge. When he took his fingers from the shapes they were dust that dissolved into finer and finer particles till he could not even see of what pigmy atoms the dust had been made.

"Love," he said, but the word was sucked into vacancy as a stream dries into sand. There were no echoes from the windy immensity in which he stood.

Then an emotion that was like nothing he had ever felt, like eyeless fear, like white reverence, like the confident homage of a courageous son, like the headlong defiance of swimming against strong sea, came into him as drink goes into the body and he denied the appearances around him for life or death.

He regarded the space into which he had been thrown like a broken ball, the space which had neither gods nor realities, the uncreated, undestroyed eternal formlessness that swims like a bottomless sea outside of life and all the delusions of the sun.

"There is something," he said steadily, "something better than my own sod. Something living as lightning and merciful as rain. Something neither to be adored as an image nor hated as a foe, but a thing to be followed like a banner through the bones and wrecked armor of all the faiths in the world. Something comradely and despised by prophets, something lordly that wears all beauty like a careless coat, something greater than myself for which I am ready to die forever, if it be necessary, but something that will not let the least senseless cell of me wholly die. I accept it, God or love or art, I accept it. And I am ready to search for it and serve it and glorify it through life and the fear of life forever and ever until I come to the eyes of Irony and the stupor of the end."

He ceased, and for a moment the nothingness about him was dull with all the nameless color of an eclipse. Then in front of him something formed that he had not made, that the nothingness hated. Out of vacantness, out of despairing fog there grew like a wraith of white magic the palm and five fingers of a hand. It shone there, pallid and vague, a luminous living flower, a girl's hand, Sylvia's hand. It seemed like a hand thrust between two gray curtains, a hand about to part them, for it moved. Philip shook; he knew that he had been heard. He was terribly joyous, terribly afraid . . .

His eyes opened on the stuffy aisle of the church. He was walking up the nave; blurred misty-colored pictures of saints and crowns fell at his feet as he walked, the bronze wings of the eagle that held up the Bible glittered startlingly for an instant in a sudden flick of sun. And as he came abreast of the pulpit, in the heart of the smell of warm varnish and prayerbooks, he saw some one kneeling at the communion rail, head in hands.

It was a woman with a twist of bright hair under her close hat and he was as sure that it was Sylvia as he was that he was seeing the impossible. For a moment and a jerk of unbearable pain he thought it was one of the fetches that went between old lovers, heralding death. Then he noticed the loose button on the belt and knew it was really she. He went up on tiptoe and knelt down beside her. He had no idea at all of, for what or to whom she was praying, but he inarticulately and alternately prayed and thanked for her all the powers outside of flesh that he believed in and did not believe. After a while he put his hand on her arm. She turned her face and he saw that her eyes were true. He closed his again for a moment and knew the respectable odors of the chancel sweeter than any airs ever filled with the rose, for he had just been taken out alive from under plain Death and the fear of the Lord.

"Sorry," she whispered, "I got back early. Then it rained, and I came in here."

"Don't do it again without telling me," he said with breaking relief that took itself out in devoted irritation. "I was there in the back and I saw you—and how was I to know you were real?"

She took his hand in hers under all the reproving stares of the holy things in the windows.

"Let's go out," she said. "The rain must be over and this place smells like an overheated front parlor. Let's go up to our hill."

He nodded and they went out by the side entrance. They stood on the steps for a moment looking at the clean sky driftingly patterned with blue patches and the scattered white wool of clouds.

" Nice," said Sylvia. Her lips were as cold as a mermaid's as he kissed them. The sound of a man's feet near them broke up the indecorous embrace.

He was a laboring man about fifty years old—one of the fishermen from the Portuguese colony by his look and dress. Philip remembered dimly having seen him somewhere once—but the memory was mixed with dreams and he had not spent much time in San Esteban in the last eight years.

The man turned his head and looked at them with calm gentle eyes. Then he smiled over white teeth.

" Good Luck! " he said cheerfully. They thanked him, Sylvia rather prettily, and he stopped for a moment considering them.

" You have been in there? " he said slowly, waving his hand toward the church. They assented.

" I—I—used to go there too," he announced. " There and—other places like that." He smiled as if at a great secret joke of his own. " Now I stay outdoors," he said. " It is better that way."

" It certainly is less stuffy," said Sylvia conversationally.

" Much." He stroked his beard. " And you can—find things more easily. People can find you, too, and that is an advantage in my trade."

" Fishing? " Philip asked.

He fairly grinned, the grin of a pleased boy.

" Sometimes," he said over his laughter. " But I was always a handy man with my tools as well."

He looked at them for a swift and aging instant as a carpenter looks at a couple of straight, proper chairs. They both put their hands on each other, they did not know why.

"Well, you are nice children, both of you!" he ended suddenly. "Good night!"

He swung his hand at them and went off down street, a tool-box under his arm.

"I like his condescension!" said Sylvia indignantly. "Nice children! From a village wop who probably beats his own whenever they get in his way! He talks like one of my ancestors!"

"Maybe he is," said Philip with wry amusement. "And on the whole, you know, Syl, I'm just as glad he regards us as good material."

For he had seen into the eyes of the stranger as he went whistling away, and the face was young as the sunrise, but the eyes were curiously gray and vivid like pieces of clean glass.

They went up to their house. It was on top of a hill and nothing was left of it but a weathered door-frame and a red lump of a broken chimney and around it the fields were as lush with long grass as if they had never been under the scythe.

"Whoever lived here, anyway, Phil?" said Sylvia, her arms about her knees as they sat together on a stone where the dining-room table had been and looked out through the gray rectangle of posts that framed like a picture the golden mists that settled like roosting birds in the valley.

"I'm not sure—I heard about them once. Pioneers, I think. They came all the way from New Hampshire in an ox-cart and stayed here and raised children here in the fifties and sixties. Then the old people died and the children moved away. They must have had quite a time—stubborn old men and women in check shirts and white beaver hats and ginghams and sunbonnets. I found a rusty derringer once in the blackberry bushes the first year I came back from school and was out exploring. And they had the woman's spinning wheel down on exhibition in the Palace window. She was old stock—said she couldn't abide store cloth."

"We're going to have quite a time for the next fifty years," said Sylvia.

"Aren't we? Aren't we? Even with flivvers and victrolas."

"With everything there is. With everything there will be. With you and me."

They were silent for a while, hands tight in each other's, looking at the clouds go by like the future, color of moon, color of midnight, blonde with lights, full of sun and thunder and rain. Philip bent over and tugged up a long stalk of grass by the roots. Fertile earth clung solidly to the fibers, heavy earth smelling good with first Spring and crumbling to pieces like brown cake.

"Fat soil," he mused. "With a little trouble anything in the world would grow here."

"Our house," said Sylvia possessively.

He laughed and quoted:

" Some shall sew the sacks for fear the wheat be
    spilt,
And ye wives that have wool work it fast.
Look forth your linen, labor ye hard on it.
See the needy and naked, take thought how *they*
    lie.
Throw clothes upon them. Truth would love that.
For I shall give the poor a living as long as I
    live,
For the Lord's love in Heaven unless the land
    fail."

" The land won't fail." Sylvia cut him off.

" Not this land. It never has since Portola's time.
It never will except for fools and gentlemen farmers."

" We aren't gentlemen farmers. We're intelligent,
modern, highly-educated—"

" We're the new pioneers. We're the sons and
daughters of Belial who knew not the Lord, in church
at least, and drank up his vintage-irony when he wasn't
looking. We're a portent and an astonishment and a
horror to all the rocking-chair people who ever shivered
over 'This Side of Paradise.' We're—golly, what does
it matter? ' Save sacred Love and sacred Art'—"

" ' Nothing is good for long.' "

" The two things I swore I'd never marry," said Sylvia
presently, " were a poet and a man who raised vegetables."

" I had moral ideas about ex-débutantes," Philip
confessed.

" What does it matter? "

" What *does* it matter? "

Sylvia took his hand and held it up against the sun.

"If you were a genuine letters-and-biography poet the light would shine through it tenuously," she complained indignantly.

"If you were the right kind of person to write poems about, *your* hands would look like crepe de chine."

"What's the matter with them? They're nice. I like my hands."

"I do too when cleaner," said Philip. They squabbled undignifiedly and made peace. He took her head in the hollow of his shoulder and they leaned back against a bush and saw with infinite charity and gentleness all the spaceless wastes of ragged sky and trampling hills.

"Oh, great, holy, blaspheming God!" whispered Philip suddenly. "It's good to be young. It's good to be young and in love."

Sylvia mocked him out of the Vision of Piers in a voice like falling silver leaves.

"'By Christ!' says a gentleman, 'he teacheth us
     the best,
But on this theme truly never was I taught;
'But lead me,' says he, 'and I will learn to plow.
I will help thee labor while my life lasteth.'"

"While *our* life," amended Philip, "for this is only the start of the first lesson."

He closed his eyes—Sylvia was very near. And then for the last meeting till breath should go out of his body, he had a daydream of the Fates. But this time they were neither terrible, nor august like aunts, nor particularly important. They were three little scuttling gray animals the size of ladybugs, and they ran about

in a busy timid stupor, caught between his hand and
Sylvia's hand. . . .

From the porch of a house in California, Philip
looks out at evening over his new fields. Sylvia is beside him, a warm, slumberous Sylvia. The poem that is
only rhymes in the head and scribbled paper will be a
book, the unborn child learn to walk under the little fig
trees that have not borne fruit yet, stretch its hands and
cry for the high purple bunches. Preachers will preach
and old men moralize and young men drink and
another thousand poets publish volumes of verse as the
earth goes round the sun. But Philip and Sylvia, wise
with a buried wisdom, will not greatly care. For they
know the whole ungodly round world was made for
them and their children, and they have forty-odd years
of cavalier life to spend, like the devil among the indo-
lent sons of God, going to and fro on this earth and
walking up and down in it.

THE END.